FORERUNNER

T.S. PEDRAMON

This book is dedicated to my wife, who believed in me since I started writing a novel in 2010. It has been a long journey to get here, though we're not done; that novel is still incomplete. I dedicate this to my children as well, whose desire for bedtime stories has drawn some fun tales out of me over the past decade-plus.

This book is also dedicated to all those who wish to adventure, who desire to do great and brave things. May you find ways to expand your horizons and stretch yourselves to make the world a better place.

Also, to musicians and people who love to swim and run. You're my people.

And babies. Babies are wonderful people.

Acknowledgements

Thanks to my wife, my children, and my sister, who played integral roles in the development of this book. They acted as sounding boards, helped brainstorm, and offered general support.

Further thanks to all who beta read for me. This book would not be as cool as it is without your feedback.

And special thanks to my Kickstarter backers, who contributed to the campaign in January 2024, prior to the book's release to the public at the end of February. This enabled me to buy full rights to the cover art, to use the design however necessary to help people connect to Colnuinard, the world of the Nightshade Unicorn.

*

The full list of Kickstarter backers follows, in chronological order of their pledges:

The Creative Fund by BackerKit

Walther Family

Elizabeth Paloma

Julianne Roan

Jaclyn Pingel Day

Alexandra

Justin Ferrell

Russell & Nancy Merrill

Eddie Bishop

Brittany Tilley

Arioch Morningstar

Francesco Tehrani

David DeHaan, Tyler DeHaan, Noah DeHaan

TSP the Elder

Alexander Groggett
Boeger Girls
Amanda
Rosalina Night
Vance Neudorf
Chanel Holm
Jake Allred
Marie Campbell
Justise Briones
LJF
Katie Blackwell
Katie C.
B. S. H. Garcia
Laura McCartney
Giselle Trejo
C. Nichot
Christine E. Schulze

CONTENTS

THE ISLEWILDS
MAINONNY
NORTH SEA
NORLORNA
YLONGA
GLOSENSTAT
KWI
WESLAN
GLOSEN TRIBAL LANDS
NYLORNA
KUTOT GULF
GLOSENWOOD
CYLGIANA
THE KETTLE ACCESS
ALERV
ANTILLIAN CHANNEL
EAST ARN
SOUTH SEA
D
BOLSNARD
ARN TRIBAL LANDS
BOIT
BOLS SEA
SOUTH
COLNUINARD
THE WORLD OF THE
NIGHTSHADE UNICORN

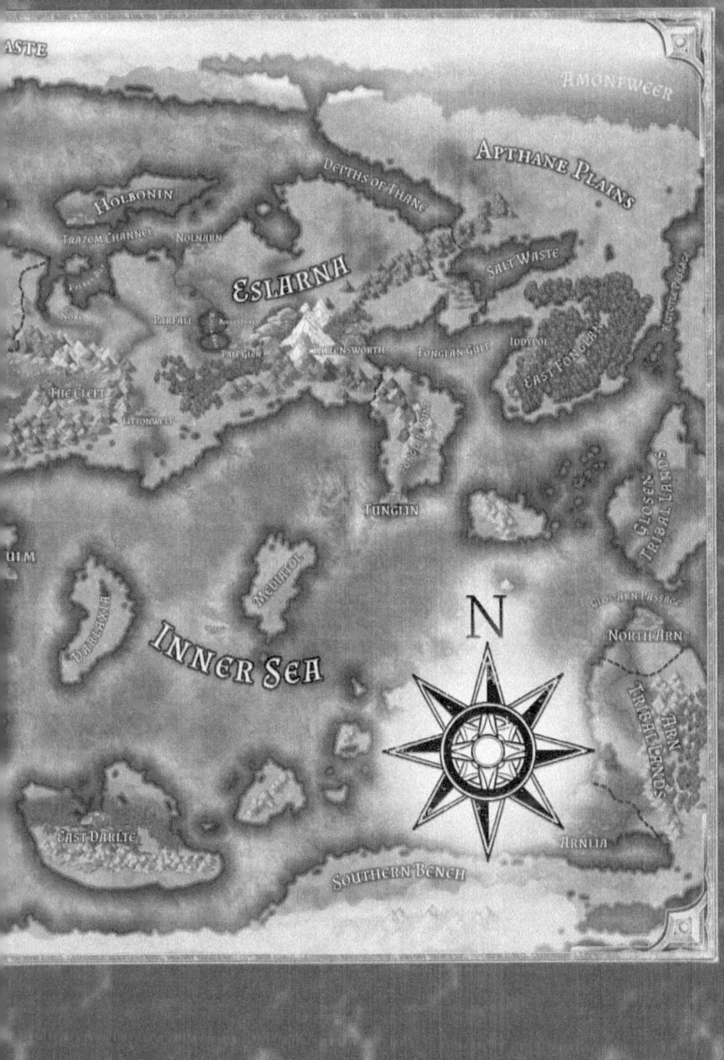
ASTE
AMONFWEER
APTHANE PLAINS
DEPTHS OF THANG
HOLBONIN
TRAZOM CHANNEL
NOLNARN
SALT WASTE
ESLARNA
NOK
PARFALL
FONGLIN GULF
IDDYPOL
PALE GLEN
LILLENSWORTH
EAST FONGLIN
FIE CLEFT
LITIONWELL
TUNGLIN
GLOSEN TRIBAL LANDS
ULM
MCDUROL
GLOS ARN PASSAGE
DARLAXIA
INNER SEA
NORTH ARN
N
ARN TRIBAL LANDS
EAST DARLTE
ARNLIA
SOUTHERN BENCH

Trazom Channel
Falren Bay
Norl
Parfa
Night River
The Cleft
Littonwelt

Colnuinard:
Eslarna
RN
The Disaffected
Tallens Road
Roula Seas
Roula Docks
Palf Glen
Tallensworth
N
South Sea

PROLOGUE: THE STORM BEGINS

Tylonus sat on a crate at the bow of the merchant ship *Armadillo*, gathering his thoughts while the morning sea air tousled his loose hair. He took in the open view of the wide expanse of sea and sky, appreciating the freshness of the spray, even if it was frigid.

Tylonus had departed from home with a rather simple goal but had caught word of better prices for his cargo if he would just accompany his goods to the next port. After an extended trading voyage, purchasing passage and cargo space on one ship and then another, he would finally soon set his face toward home. Now he was nearly done, he'd decided. He would be home in another month or two. Permanently.

The majority of the ship's crew was off shift at the moment, resting below. The morning's heavy work was mostly done already, the few who remained working to maintain the proper heading.

"Beware the Nightshade Unicorn!" one of the sailors bellowed in his face.

Tylonus flinched at the abruptness of the man's outburst, then rolled his eyes. "Please, not another sea story."

"No story here, turf man," the sailor said while he held his arms out in innocence.

"Must you use a derogatory, Pontil?" Tylonus said to the sailor. "Just because I'm not a member of the crew or a regular seagoer like you..."

Pontil wasn't a bad man in Tylonus's eyes, but he had shown himself to subscribe to various superstitions before, casting him in a dubious light as far as credibility was concerned.

"My apologies, thank you for reminding me, stonefooted Tylonus."

Pontil bowed in jest, raising an eyebrow to invite Tylonus to engage.

Tylonus breathed in deeply and then exhaled, consigning himself to a few minutes with the man. He hoped it would at least be entertaining.

"Very well, Pontil. I've been all over the Glosen and Nylornian coasts and the seas in between, but please, tell me about what definitely exists but I've never heard of from a credible source."

Pontil harrumphed.

"Vlon, you remember what I told you, right?" he said to another sailor. "Turf man here doesn't believe in the Nightshade Unicorn."

Vlon piped up, "Listen to him, dirt-walker. You don't know what you don't know."

Vlon returned to adjusting some rope attached to the sails—Tylonus still didn't know the difference between all the ship's ropes—casting a judging glance at Pontil for not helping.

Pontil didn't notice the older sailor's gaze and took Tylonus's unenthusiastic invitation to heart instead.

"The Nightshade Unicorn lives on an island–"

"Can't you call them the Nomord, instead of unicorns?" Tylonus interrupted.

"Why?" Pontil looked confused.

"Because that's what they're called," Tylonus explained slowly.

Pontil blinked and started again, unfazed.

"The Nightshade Unicorn lives on an island in the northern waters–"

"Yes, you've said as much before," Tylonus cut in again.

Pontil continued, "–in northern waters, like we are now."

"But I've been tracking our progress with the ship navigator," Tylonus interjected again. "We'll put into Malnonny within a week, to the northeast. You claim the island to be to the west, closer to Glosenstat or Ylonga. But we're quite some distance from that, and of course you'd say it's in the Islewilds because there are hundreds of small islands there. It's too easy to be vague about which one you're talking about."

Pontil spread his arms wide again, attempting to make a professional show of innocence despite the alcohol on his breath. At nine in the morning.

"I didn't pick the location. That's just where it is."

"And it's where we might end up, Pontil, if you don't help me with this rigging," Vlon said. "I don't like what the wind is doing this morning. It might get rough tonight. Captain especially wants to make sure we're all ship shape since our great hatch cover got smashed while we were loading. Until it's repaired, any bit of rain will be a nuisance."

"In a minute, man," Pontil deflected. He turned back to Tylonus again. "As I said, beware the Nightshade Unicorn. The dark beast was born of everything evil in the world, and he cannot wait to be free from his cursed isle to devour people and demolish cities."

Tylonus couldn't hold back a small grin at the ridiculousness of it.

"A Nomord, eating people? They're the most peaceable of creatures, and no bigger than horses. A Nomord would never resort to eating flesh, not if you call it Nightshade or even paint it black."

"I'm trying to warn you, turf man," Pontil insisted. "You need an iron charm to ward him off if you travel in these waters. You never know if you'll wash ashore in his domain."

"Ooh, maybe he's swimming toward us," Tylonus teased.

"Shrongelin forbid!" Pontil exclaimed, alarmed at the idea. "No, his hooves wouldn't be good for swimming very far, I think. Here, I have extra charms that I got in Dullsworthen. I had a friend what saw the dark beast once. He was first mate on his ship, and he swore they couldn't find the island again because their compasses didn't work."

Tylonus had expected Pontil to dive into some tale or other, and it seemed the sailor didn't disappoint. Tylonus smirked to himself while Pontil told more about his friend.

"Said they struck ashore looking for fresh water. Barely made it to the beachhead on account of a storm. Found the water, but the island was full of strange wildlife. Cast off quick as they could. But a great, dark unicorn stepped out of the woods, staring hate itself at them and at the water what prevented it from getting to them. They was at least a day's sail away, and the sky was overcast to boot when the compasses would work and they could get their bearings again. I can only say I's been lucky never to see the Nightmare Unicorn."

He gestured widely, attempting to convey the great bulk of an antagonistic animal chasing them.

Tylonus sighed at the sailor's ineloquence.

"Why don't you call them the Nomord?"

"Is the Nightshade really one of them?" Pontil mused to himself.

Tylonus thought the sailor's question might actually have merit, if the creature existed at all. "Unicorn" was just a slang word for the Nomord, after all.

Pontil shrugged it off. "Anyway, Rauling–that's my friend–and his crew could feel the Nightshade's influence. He was trying to make them ill, you see, every last man. Normal unicorns can heal, you know, but the Nightshade Unicorn's magic works backward. He unheals his victims before he eats them."

Tylonus indulged in another eyeroll. Pontil didn't notice.

"But Rauling and his men, they had charms. Those who didn't have charms got seasick."

"Could it be because they were at sea?" Tylonus asked rhetorically.

"No, they had their sea legs," Pontil refuted. "Here, I'll let you have multiple charms. Four marks each, and the big baddy stays at least five paces away."

The sailor held up a collection of ramshackle knick-knacks bound with twine and wire, offering them to Tylonus.

"Don't be preposterous," Tylonus replied. "I beware bad trades and defective product. I'll keep my marks to trade in Malnonny, then I'll head home. I came with my share of the cargo, I'll make my last trades, go home, and be done traveling."

He pulled his coat more snugly around himself against the northern chill.

"Rauling's not a dolt, stonefoot," Vlon said. "If he says he seen it, he seen it."

"I'm sure he did."

Tylonus turned away from the men and looked to the horizon, trying to enjoy the sunshine without engaging them. After a moment he stood.

"Beware the twisted isle!" Pontil warned again. "The Nightshade Unicorn wanders there and eats poor travelers who wander in. Just four marks..."

"Excuse me, I think I've had enough of this tale."

Tylonus stepped around the sailor and walked aft of the *Armadillo*, heading down to his berthing. He would rather spend his time drafting a letter to pass on to a cutter home as soon as they reached port. He had been trying to gather his thoughts for this before Pontil had other ideas. He heard the sailor start singing behind him, releasing a shanty from his throat that Tylonus had heard many times before.

Tylonus descended to his quarters shared with another passenger, a man from the university in Bolsnard. His cabin-mate was in their quarters, already occupying the small board that passed as a desk. The shipboard accommodations were tight and simple.

"Do you think you'll be long, Rubiro?" Tylonus asked.

"Oh, no," the academic said. "As a matter of fact, I'm all finished. I'll clear off now."

"Thank you. I need to write and clear my head. I've had enough talk of old fables up top. Nightmare Unicorns and all that."

"Ah, yes," the professor acknowledged. "You know, we cannot say for sure there isn't such a creature. In fact, the old stories my colleagues have dug up seem to mention something—mind you, they're not the easiest to translate—which may not have been a proper Nomord, but was some kind of magical beast."

"You, too?" Tylonus looked at the scholar in disappointment.

"Well, the stories have that in common, the beast. They speak of a great calamity that followed the appearance of a dark beast, and...most of them identify that beast as being *like* a Nomord."

Rubiro finished packing his papers away and stood.

"Yes. I'm sure they do." Tylonus replied, sitting at the desk and pulling some stationery from the satchel hanging on his bed.

Rack, he mentally corrected himself. *On ship, the bed is called a rack.*

"But the supposed time of calamity was thousands of years ago, and the stories don't actually say the dark beast was the calamity, right?" Tylonus asked.

"Well," Rubiro blinked, thinking. He cocked his head, "Some do, but there is disagreement between texts. At the very least, the dark beast appears before the calamity. And there are old battlefields that we—"

"Don't mention dragons again, please."

Rubiro was indignant. "I wasn't going to. Only that there are–um, that we have discovered battlefields where we have no historical record of a battle occurring. And the calamity that follows the dark beast is supposed to affect the whole world over. Indeed, we find intriguing artifacts..."

Tylonus ignored the man and put his attention on the letter he wrote, trying to focus as the winds outside, the winds Vlon had complained of, continued to play mischievously, and the *Armadillo* began to sway.

Tylonus awoke with a jolt, falling out of his rack. His sleep had been hard-won with the *Armadillo* rocking the way it did in this weather. Now he propped himself up on his elbows, shaking the sleep from his head.

"Tylonus, get up!" Rubiro shouted, carrying a pair of large scoops with handles.

Bailers, Tylonus thought.

"Captain says we need all hands to help. Take this."

The professor offered Tylonus one of the bailers with one hand. Blinking, he pulled it back and held it under his arm, then offered his now-empty hand.

"But we're not crew. I paid my passage," Tylonus protested.

He took Rubiro's hand and climbed to his feet.

"So did I, but this storm is something else. I personally fancy the idea of making it through and surviving the night."

Tylonus nodded, seeing the alarm in Rubiro's eyes.

"So do I."

Accepting the bailer, he followed him above decks and into a cacophony of shouts, thunder, whipping wind, and the constant roar of the heaviest rain Tylonus could remember seeing.

Men rushed about, hollering at each other to pull this rope or tighten that sail, and one of the sailors approached him and Rubiro.

"Go back below!" he shouted.

Tylonus held his bailer up, wondering where he might be of help.

"Below!" the sailor bellowed again, pointing at the gap in the great hatch cover in the center of the deck.

The large, rectangular hole would normally have been properly covered, but now its broken cover revealed a steep ladder leading down through its gaping hole.

"Go below, fill your bailer, hand it up, and receive another!"

As Tylonus understood the plan to keep excess water out of the ship, the sailor practically shoved him, making him nearly fall belowdecks as the ship's heaving continuously robbed him of his good footing.

"Aye-aye!" Tylonus responded, using the sailor terminology as the clearest way to indicate his immediate compliance.

He jumped down, using the side of the hole to steady himself as he fell the modest distance. He still slipped when he landed, but got up again. It was easier to see down here, where the air wasn't full of raindrops and the lanterns swinging from their hooks on the overhead didn't require a hood to keep water out.

Looking to one corner of the chamber, Tylonus saw water gathered, while a man rushed from a forward chamber and handed his bailer up above decks. Rubiro climbed down the ladder in the great hatch, catching up to Tylonus, then both of them started bailing water out of this chamber while men continued to rush past from the chambers below, closer to the bilge. Tylonus and Rubiro found themselves crowding each other as they tried to bail the same area independently.

"Stand here!" Tylonus said to the professor, pointing at the deck under his feet as he stood below the great hatch. "I'll hand to you, you hand up!"

Rubiro nodded, understanding the shortened phrasing. Tylonus ran to the corner and filled a bailer, brought it back to Rubiro, received an empty bailer, and repeated the process. A passenger named Clonnel, a smith from one of the Colnarn

Protectorate states, had been pressed into temporary service as well, receiving the bailers that Rubiro handed up to him.

Tylonus worked as fast as he could, but the rain was insistent on filling the ship with unwanted water. He slogged and fought against the downpour, keenly aware of not only the rain that fell directly through the hole in the hatch cover, but also water that spilled in from the main deck despite a small ridge that existed specifically to prevent that. The torrent threw enough water at the *Armadillo* that it sloshed over continuously.

Tylonus tired of the heavy work but pushed himself to continue. Then, with a great smashing crack, the deck under his feet jumped and yanked itself against the bouncing and rolling.

"What was that?" Rubiro shouted in the dim light.

"Aground, we've run aground!" voices shouted from above.

"Rocks! Rocks!" A lone voice screamed over the top of the din. "We hit rocks!"

"Let me see with my own eyes!" bellowed an authoritative voice that Tylonus recognized.

The captain jumped down the great hatch, landing beside Rubiro. He barely noticed the slippery deck as he rushed fore, into the bowels of his ship to assess the flooding for himself.

Tylonus felt the ship around him seem to hang at one corner, making the other side of the room rise and fall more dramatically, sending the water washing from one side to another. He chased after the water with his bailer, scooping what he could, and tried to hand it to his fellow traveler.

Rubiro was distracted, watching the sailors skit about abovedeck. The storm continued to rage, but the human activity hit a lull as all ears strained to hear what news came from below.

Tylonus heard a cry raise from the deck fore and below, first one voice and then others repeating it.

"Abandon ship!"

The captain came running back past Tylonus, waving his arms and directing activity.

"Follow procedure, abandon ship!"

This caused a new, intense flurry of movement as all hands shifted to a new plan. Men left their stations, untying or even cutting ropes, letting sails flap loosely in the gusts that buffeted the now-dying *Armadillo*.

"First mate! Passengers! To my cabin!"

Tylonus and Rubiro climbed the ladder to the top deck and went aft, passing through a door to the captain's cabin, following Clonnel.

Captain Yalnan and his wife, Thonalu, were waiting for them, bracing themselves on the captain's desk to stand against the ship's bucking. One more passenger entered behind the other three.

Yalnan spoke.

"The rain was a nuisance with our open great hatch, but it's worse than that now. Our hull is punctured and we're taking on water. You each have a space on our lifeboats, as you know. You can bring with you only what you can carry in one arm. One arm."

He held a finger up to accentuate his point.

"My sailors will help you board. Are there any questions?"

He paused for a moment, then continued.

"You'll all be going west toward Ylonga. I wish you the best." Yalnan stopped talking, staring at the passengers.

"Well, what are you waiting for?" Thonalu barked. "The captain spoke, now make it happen! You have two minutes to grab what you will from your cabins and get on the lifeboats. Go!" Her face was hard, unreadable.

"Yes, First Mate." Tylonus responded as he turned on his heel, nearly running out of the cabin. He assumed the other passengers followed, but didn't turn to look.

Sailors crossed in front of him and around him as he rushed to his cabin, quickly threw a few things into a bag, and made his way to the bow of the *Armadillo*.

"Well, it's about time you're here!" Vlon belted, hoarse from shouting in the wind.

"You ready?" Pontil asked, manipulating a rope on a pulley to lower the lifeboat to the water.

"Ready to survive, if we're so lucky!" Tylonus said.

"Then climb do—" Pontil started.

At that moment a thunderous boom sounded as lightning lit up the night and the mainmast snapped in two. It leapt forward and to the starboard, catching a sailor on the starboard bow as it tumbled into the sea.

"Umblan! Man overboard!" a nearby sailor called. "Man overb—"

"Abandon ship!" First Mate Thonalu screamed in his face, veins on her neck popping out. "He's gone! Follow procedure and save yourself!"

Tylonus moved to climb into his boat, watching Rubiro approach his lifeboat while its corresponding crew lowered the craft to the water line.

"Shrongelin save Umblan, but bless this day!" Captain Yalnan called to the sky with relief in his eyes.

"How can you say that?" Thonalu turned on her husband.

"As you said, Umblan is gone!" he shouted back. "Had we time, we would mourn. But I—"

"No!" Thonalu cut him off, anticipating what he was going to say. "I will not go!"

"It is meant to be," Yalnan insisted. "You will live, my Thonalu! Go!"

"What will life be without you?" she said back.

"Any life, whatever you want! Just go, and live!"

Yalnan moved forward, grabbed his wife in a bear hug, and carried her to the designated lifeboat. She fought against him, hammering his back with her fists and bellowing cries of protest.

"No!" Thonalu screamed. "Not without you! You were always why I live! Come with us! We'll make it stay afloat!"

"You well know there's no room!" Yalnan shouted back, delivering her to the two sailors loading themselves into the adjacent boat, and they wordlessly took her over the edge of the ship by force.

Tylonus tore his gaze from the spectacle and climbed the rope ladder down from the port bow and into his lifeboat.

Pontil and Vlon followed, then cast off from the hull, putting space between the lifeboat and the *Armadillo* as quickly as possible to avoid being dashed to pieces on the side of the larger craft. They squeezed themselves side by side, each manning one of the oars to maximize their driving force.

The next lifeboat cast off as soon as they could be certain to avoid collision, then the next, and so on. The storm appeared to wane in this moment, its rain calmer, and its chill winds still driving but no longer casting up waves that would have threatened to topple the ship they had just abandoned.

"Shrongelin bless us all," Tylonus said. "Maybe we will yet survive."

Tylonus landed the small craft on a cold beach, looking uphill at curious vegetation.

In the dark of night with the wind howling, seas raging, and the rain pelting them, they could barely see well enough to hazard a guess at which direction was west, let alone keep track of the other lifeboats. Now they were alone. The captain was most certainly dead, but Tylonus hoped the rest of the crew and passengers survived, somewhere.

They had taken turns rowing. The two sailors, strapping men of muscular bulk, had taken turns first. As dawn approached, the wind calmed and the sun gave them a stronger sense of direction. They had adjusted their course accordingly. As the morning progressed, they trusted Tylonus enough to take his turn rowing, judging direction by continuing to head away from the sun. Now, sun high overhead, they both slept, keeping each other warm under an oilcloth blanket.

"Vlon, Pontil," Tylonus said, "we're here. We're...somewhere."

He leaned over and shook them awake.

Pontil pried his eyes open sleepily.

"Shh," he hushed Tylonus. "We two rowed in the storm. Heavy work. Let us rest for now."

"Fine," Tylonus assented. "I'll just have a little look around."

He stepped out of the boat, freezing in his clothes. Yalnan had said he could bring only what he could carry under one arm, so he had grabbed trade documents that would be important when he got back to civilization. Right now, he wished he'd grabbed his coat.

The vegetation ahead of him was nearly as green as what he had seen farther south, but it was somehow...wrong. Misshapen. Walking up the beach, ahead of him was a solid line of pine trees, if he was to believe the signature needles growing on the branches. But the trunks and branches themselves were gnarled and grew at random angles, confusing him. Perhaps this was just a species he was not familiar with. Besides, the weather was fair now.

The sand underneath his feet moved the same under his weight as the sand at countless other beaches where he had landed for trade, but its color was a rusty brown with streaks of green and black. He picked some of it up in his hand to look at it more closely. As he did so, it seemed to change in hue to a more typical tan color. Despite this impression, when he looked back and forth between the sand on the ground and in his hand, he couldn't put his finger on the difference between the two. The texture seemed the same but something about it was off.

This place was patently odd.

Tylonus walked into the forest, observing all sorts of perversions of familiar things of nature. A deer looked at him as it walked toward him, which Tylonus had never known a deer to do. As it approached, it seemed to open its mouth hungrily, baring fangs. Alarmed, Tylonus drew his belt knife and held the blade toward the cervine, hunching his shoulders forward. It cocked its head.

Since when does a deer do that?, Tylonus thought.

It bolted without warning, vanishing through ferns and bushes.

Tylonus didn't want to be alone, but he appreciated the quiet moment away from Pontil's ideas. The sailor would have a fit at all this. Tylonus willed himself to breathe normally, but kept his knife in hand. Maybe he should go back to the boat and wait for both sailors to wake up. Vlon appeared to have a more level head than Pontil, even if he subscribed to the same superstitions.

He came across a large, downed tree, giving him a waist-high hurdle in his path. Tylonus placed his hand on an adjacent tree trunk for steadiness, then yanked his hand away with a yelp. Looking where he had supported himself, he saw a yellow-gray moss or lichen. Moss wasn't supposed to sting. He shook his hand, still feeling the burn.

They had been blown far off course. They must be in the Islewilds; this didn't look anything like Ylonga, if Tylonus judged by descriptions he had read. Ylonga was well known to provide good lumber, but this place was...alien.

He continued walking inland, hoping to see some sign of civilization, but saw none. The animals he saw and these plants that he walked past now were nothing he was familiar with, either. He pressed on, lowering his expectations as he went, hoping to find help, people, clean water, and something that he could feel safe eating.

He hadn't believed the sailors' stories, but now he wondered. This place looked as though the Creator had taken his plans for it and bumped a table on the way from the drafting board to the fabrication board, resulting in everything being mixed up and painted in a darker shade.

There were some things in the world that he couldn't explain, but they were at least consistent with each other. The Nomord did exist, and they had well-known magical abilities; they could heal and could make things grow. There were other commonly known creatures as well. Occasionally one might come across a jackalope and it would scurry away and find a burrow, jumping down a hole that would be impossibly small to fit its antlers, but down it went, fitting in somehow.

Then there were things that maybe existed, or maybe were true, like the belief that one could attract the Nomord by laying out certain herbs or fruits overnight. One could never really know whether that was effective. Sometimes they would show up and sometimes they wouldn't, but that seemed to be the case no matter what people did, let alone laying out specific fruits. One just couldn't know.

But any reasonable person would put no stock in these sailor stories of mermaids and dragons and griffons, let alone the ridiculous idea of the Nightshade Unicorn. Some stories of the Nightshade stretched even farther than Pontil's version, portraying him as a huge horned beast, some thirty hands tall at the shoulder, with sharp fangs, that demanded the blood of children.

According to the stories, the north wind would arise and resurrect the dark beast, which would kill anyone in its path. Tylonus placed no stock in these stories. But today... Perhaps today was a day to consider whether the impossible might be dangerous, even if it couldn't exist. This land did look...twisted, but now his curiosity pulled him along.

He walked several more minutes and the air grew distinguishably warmer. The sun shone pleasantly down. To Tylonus's relief, the plants looked more normal.

He came to a spring and jumped down to take a drink. He paused, wondering if the water might be poisonous. A deer walked up to the stream two dozen paces down from Tylonus and drank, assuaging his concerns about poison. He straightened up to look at it better, but it bolted when it saw him. No strange teeth or odd behavior from this one.

Tylonus bent again and drank from the spring, quenching his thirst. Deciding to let caution get the better of him, he straightened and turned to head back to the beach. He knew where water was, so they could live several days at least while they found edible food.

Tylonus paused as he heard splashing nearby. He looked to the source of the sound and saw larger hooves, as dark as coal. This beast was closer than the deer, and apparently not afraid at his presence.

A deep voice sounded that made Tylonus feel his teeth rattle. The first word was the most terrifying.

"Tylonus. Perhaps you think you have weathered storms, such as the one you just survived. The true storm is yet to come. Are you ready?"

Tylonus lifted his gaze from black hooves, up midnight-colored legs, and finally looked up into dark, serious eyes which were perched on either side of an equine forehead from which sprouted a single, lengthy horn. The horn seemed to hide in shadow despite the daylight. While certainly not gargantuan, as was the beast in Pontil's story, this creature the size of a large horse was far from anything to be trifled with.

Tylonus found himself struck with bone-deep terror. He sank into those pits of eyes as if he were struggling to escape quicksand, pulled under and gasping for breath, lost in a non-place, the sensation of a nightmare.

The Nightshade Unicorn stared back, boring into his soul, pulling him farther under. Not only did it stand before him in the flesh, but it knew his name.

The dark beast precedes the calamity.

Tylonus shouted a guttural, primal cry of fear.

PART I: THE CLEFT

Chapter 1

Allabva and Mellier

Allabva Roalke walked near her home in the Valley of the Five Moons in the afternoon. It was during one of those contested months when people had a hard time agreeing on whether it belonged to the cold season or the growing season. The truth was that the Valley of the Five Moons was solidly in the throes of springtime, when the Nomord migrated down from the Grand Mount through Pine Canyon and into the valley.

"Allabva, where are we going?" Allabva's younger brother, Mellier, asked.

"We're going up to the mouth of Pine Canyon to gather rosemary, and Mother and I both already told you that," Allabva recited.

"Do I have to come? I'm six now," he added, as if that had any bearing on him accompanying her up the trail.

"Yes, and Mother already told you that, too."

Allabva kept walking as she talked, glorying in the fresh air, so Mellier had to keep up if he wanted to continue pestering her.

"Just enjoy the springtime," she told him.

"Why do they like to go up to the Grand Mount, anyway?"

Apparently Mellier was thinking about the Nomord as well.

"I don't know. Nomord stuff, I guess."

"Do they go other places?"

"I don't know that, either, but I suppose so."

"Is it true the first unicorn of the season grants a wish?"

"What? Where did you hear that?"

"At Graystone Observance."

"A month ago? Alright, but who told it to you?" Allabva prodded.

"Just some other boys."

"Some other boys like...Jonder? Ultlan?"

"...Yes."

"Mellier," Allabva tried to say with patience, "Jonder and Ultlan have very active imaginations. You have to take everything they tell you with some level of incredulity."

"With what?"

"With a grain of salt. Just don't automatically believe everything they tell you."

"Why not? Where do I put the salt?"

Allabva sighed and replied, "Because they told you the first unicorn of the season grants a wish. Because at Blackstone Observance they told you the month was named after the Nightshade Unicorn, black like *his* heart. And don't call them unicorns. That's slang. They are the Nomord."

Mellier stopped, confused and mildly offended.

"What's wrong with that? The Nightshade Unicorn sounds awesome. I bet he made the red lightning the week after Whitestone!"

Allabva paused and shook her head. The red-sparked outline of a tear in the sky, accompanied by something like thunder, had appeared one day a few months before. She couldn't explain it, but neither could anybody else. It had been terrifying for a moment, but nothing had happened. Life went on, and people had long stopped talking about it. Mostly.

"I'll concede that we still have no idea what that was. It was pretty amazing, but it doesn't mean there's an evil Nomord out there."

She nodded again in their direction of travel.

"Come on."

She resumed walking up the trail and continued talking.

"One: You have to come with me because we need to gather rosemary. We need rosemary to grind it up and scatter it on the fields and orchards as soon as the shoots appear, in order to keep the bugs off. You come with me so we can bring back more than I can carry alone. I have my bags, you have yours."

Allabva glanced back to make sure Mellier was keeping her pace as well as following what she was telling him, then continued.

"Two: There is no Nightshade Unicorn. Nightshade Nomord. Whatever. That's an old story made up to scare children. I take it that it doesn't seem so scary to you. I'm glad; I don't think we should try to scare children. But that doesn't make it real. You've seen Nomord before, right? What are they like?"

"White. And they run and jump a lot."

"That's right. And?"

"And they have horns. Uh, one horn."

Allabva shook her head again in amusement.

"Yes, that's why people sometimes call them unicorns instead of horses. But what else? Never mind, I'll tell you: They're *all female*. But, of course, the *Nightshade Unicorn* is male, and *his* coat is black. It's just a reactionary story to say that there's something different. It doesn't exist."

"But unicorns aren't all exactly the same! I know because I've seen them!"

"How different do they get? Their hair is all white. They never get sick or old. They all act alike."

"Well, they have different colored eyes, and one time I saw one with yellow hair."

"No, you didn't. Different eyes, maybe. No yellow hair."

How much farther, now? Allabva wanted to arrive at the mouth of the canyon, gather their rosemary, and go home.

"Well, it was at least cream-colored."

"It must have been the light. Come on, let's get this over with."

"But why do *we* have to gather rosemary?"

Mellier didn't give up when he didn't want to.

"Because somebody has to. Mother has her chores, we have ours."

"Can't there be somebody else?"

"Well, there once was, but Father is still lost at sea."

"I don't remember him. What was he like?"

"You always ask that," Allabva breathed.

She couldn't resist telling him, regardless.

"Father...is great."

She tried to remember to use the present tense when talking about him, despite the years he'd been gone. She continued.

"He always made me laugh, and always helped me when he was able. I still love the little shoes he gave me when I was your age, even if they don't fit anymore. I didn't need them, but he said he simply had to buy them for me, and that he was forced to do so because I would look so lovely in them."

She couldn't hold her smile inside, allowing it to bleed out onto her face.

"When will he come back?" Mellier asked.

"You always ask that, too."

Allabva picked her way through the trail they walked, sighing and letting her smile fade.

"He'll be back when he'll be back. He'll return just as soon as he can, but the sea is dangerous, so we have to be prepared for him not to make it back...maybe ever."

Despite her sometimes-impatient tone with her brother, Allabva didn't mean to antagonize him. She loved the Nomord, too, although she felt that with her age—almost seventeen—she had a better idea than her brother of what the world contained.

She glanced back to check that Mellier was still following. She saw him stopped on the trail with a pout on his face.

"I wish I could remember him like you do," he said feebly.

"Hey, hey, it's alright," Allabva did her best to reassure him, walking back to put an arm around his shoulders. "Mother still believes Father will come home. That's good enough for me to think so, too. How about you?"

Mellier said nothing but looked to his older sister for a cue.

Allabva conscientiously maintained her composure. She crouched and faced him at arm's length.

"Don't worry about Father. Mother needs us to stay strong and help her with the crops and household chores. That's what I'll do. What do you say? You're the one who can grow up to be a man like Father is. How about you show Mother how big and strong you can be?"

"Well, alright," Mellier said. "Are we almost there? I bet I can gather more rosemary than you."

Allabva laughed, giving her brother a hug before standing and continuing up the trail.

"Almost."

Allabva had seen the seasons change through all eleven months, watched the Nomord come down through the canyons and graze in the copses and the meadows, observed how they played and teased every year. She, like many other residents of the Cleft (another name for the Valley of the Five Moons) had savored a few moments throughout her child-hood when a Nomord had come in close enough to touch, had been uplifted by hearing their laughter every summer and seeing the smile in their eyes. She had even had the honor of touching a unicorn in a gentle caress of friendship, and she could see the Touch in others who had received the same honor. None of them ever spoke of it, but once she had been touched, she had always been able to see it in others if she knew to look for it. She knew she wasn't alone in this.

Unlike most residents of the Cleft, she believed, Allabva had once conversed with one of the Nomord. It had been a simple conversation, appreciating the beauty of the valley, the seasons, and the sky overhead. Neither of the two had spoken of anything of import.

Allabva and Mellier arrived at the mouth of Pine Valley and began to collect rosemary, cutting it with the knife she brought and loading it in their bags.

"Allabva, look, a unicorn!"

"You mean Nomord."

"Uh-huh."

Mellier didn't bother to correct himself.

Allabva looked, genuinely interested in seeing one of the creatures. It stood some seventy paces away, looking directly at them.

"She sees us," Mellier said happily.

"Of course she sees us. We're not hiding."

"But she's looking at us."

"True, my little man, true."

Allabva smiled at him, then looked back at the Nomord, intrigued. It wasn't looking at them, it was staring at them. Allabva couldn't help but stare back. The Nomord tossed her head, shaking her mane. She opened her mouth and spoke.

"Allabva."

The Nomord stated the name simply and gently, the sound traveling up the trail clearly despite the distance. Her voice sounded clear and resonant, though lower than any human female. Many Nomord did, having throats much larger than humans. Allabva wasn't surprised that the beast could speak; they seemed to be able to use their mouths for speech the same way humans did, despite their distinct physiology. She was very surprised that it used her name, however.

The Nomord trotted forward, hooves hitting softly in the dirt of the trail. She came within five paces of brother and sister and it became clear that she was staring at Allabva, not at both of them.

"You are nearly ready. Or perhaps you are now ready."

Allabva was taken aback. What an odd thing for a flighty creature to say.

"Ready? For what?"

"Yeah, for what?" Mellier copied.

Allabva looked down at the rosemary she had gathered. She wasn't almost done with this task, and she doubted the creature was saying they were almost ready to go back home.

The Nomord blinked, then sniffed through her large nostrils. She tiptoed toward Allabva.

Mellier stepped toward the Nomord, who spared him a glance before disregarding his presence.

Allabva brought a hand up to greet the Nomord, which brought her face closer to Allabva and nuzzled her hand, and Allabva then ran her hand up the Nomord's face.

Mellier reached up and touched the Nomord's shoulder. She again glanced at him, then turned her attention back to Allabva.

"Well, today is Greenstone Observance..." Allabva trailed off, swallowing. "Um, it is my year for the Crossing, do you mean... It's this community gathering, and um, at Greenstone..."

She reached up tentatively with her hand to touch the Nomord's nose. The Nomord took half a step back and lowered her head to bring the point of her horn down toward Allabva, who reached up and touched the tip of the horn with her fingers. The creature then drew away slightly and brought her horn down to touch Allabva's forehead. Allabva's eyes widened as the Nomord lifted her head and looked at Allabva through one eye.

"What is this, an interview?" Allabva asked. "It feels as though you just saw through every part of me, cold and warm at the same time."

The Nomord tossed her head again and pranced, bouncing into the air as she danced from side to side. She whinnied and laughed, displaying the energy and playfulness the Nomord usually showed.

Allabva laughed, along with her brother Mellier.

"You're a really unpredictable Nomo-Nomo," she said to the creature, using the diminutive term reserved for affection or derision. She shook her head in wonderment at the animal's behavior.

The Nomord stopped dancing for a moment.

"I am Hronomon. I will come back. Prepare yourself."

Then Hronomon reached down to the bundle in Allabva's other hand, took a large bite of rosemary, and turned away, bucking and dancing before she prance-trotted off, shaking her head as she went.

Allabva noticed something more about the Nomord.

"That was no regular Nomo-Nomo," she said, wide-eyed.

Mellier agreed.

"I know. It was weird how it came right up to you and looked at you so carefully. That didn't seem like a silly joke, it seemed to be serious."

"Yes, but that's actually not what I meant," Allabva said. "That wasn't a she. Every Nomo-Nomo I've ever seen was female."

"Do you mean it was a boy unicorn?"

"Ye—no. It was a male Nomord. Can there be male Nomord?" Allabva wondered aloud. "And she...he...told me his name. Have you ever heard a Nomo-Nomo's name?"

"Like a boy horse?"

"No, like a boy Nomord."

Allabva rolled her eyes, then looked down at the slightly reduced bundle of rosemary in her arm.

"Come on. We have to fill our bags and get home. We don't want to take too long and miss the start of Greenstone Observance."

"You're hoping you get to dance with Delgan during the Observance."

Allabva opened her mouth, but nothing came out, and she turned red instead. Allabva had known Delgan since they were little, had seen him at the monthly Observances. When she had played with groups of children from the village, he was there. She had always liked him, but how did Mellier...

She spoke quickly as she tried to regain herself.

"Little brother, how can you have so much trouble with the concept of a boy Nomord, and then a moment later you show this much perception? Yes, I do hope to dance with Delgan during the Observance."

Allabva and Mellier resumed their chore, joking as they worked together to cut sprigs of rosemary and fill their bags. It may have been because of the singularity of their meeting with the odd Nomord, but on this occasion, they seemed to finish the task in record time.

Back home, Allabva and Mellier brought their bags of rosemary to their mother. Allabva opened the front door as its hinges gave their usual loud creak.

"You're back a little early. Did you find it closer to home than usual?"

Allabva set her bag down on the countertop in their modest kitchen.

"No, but we had an interesting experience that I think lifted our spirits a little, and that helped us finish faster."

"Allabva wants to dance with Delgan tonight!" Mellier declared as he dropped his bag on the floor and turned back around and went outside.

Allabva's eyes went wide, and she looked back and forth between her mother and younger brother, mouth agape.

Mother called after Mellier, "Get back here, young man. You need to wash up properly."

He came back inside to argue.

"I don't wanna wash up. I'm fine. We didn't get dirty at all out on the trail."

"Maybe not, but I can see on your face that you did a bit of sweating. I'll prepare you a bath and you can bathe before you get dressed in your clothes for tonight."

Mellier's eyebrows rose, seeing that his attempt to argue had backfired and made the situation even worse.

"No, it will be too cold!"

"I'm sure you'll survive somehow. Now, come have a little bite to eat while I go prepare the bath."

Mellier didn't have to be told twice to eat. He came to the table and sat down in front of his bread and cheese, digging in with gusto.

Mother looked at her daughter with a smile.

"I guess the cat's out of the bag," she said to Allabva. "Well, Delgan seems like a nice young man, so I don't fault you for liking him. I just hope he's good enough to deserve you. And thank you for this," she added as she gathered the bags of rosemary from the table and from the floor.

"Of course, Mother."

Allabva's felt her indignation to Mellier pacified.

"So, what miracle happened out there that brings you back early?"

"Id waff a unigone," Mellier spoke through a mouthful of food.

"Don't chew and talk at the same time, son. And don't say unicorn, it's slang. So, you saw one of the Nomord?"

Mother lifted one eyebrow and looked to Allabva for the answer, waiting for the details that made it a special occurrence.

"Yes," Allabva answered. "But this Nomord was not a regular Nomo-Nomo. First of all, it acted partly serious. It came up very close to me and even took a bite of the rosemary I was holding."

"An id tushed her fohead," Mellier interjected.

"Mellier. Don't talk with your mouth full," Mother scolded. "Go on, Allie."

"It's true. The Nomord looked at me straight in my eyes and then brought his head forward, and touched my forehead with the tip of his horn."

"His?" Mother didn't miss anything. "You misspeak."

"No," Allabva insisted. "It was a male. A male Nomord, not a mare like all the rest."

"Maybe it'th the Nightthade Unigone!"

"Mellier, what did Mother tell you?"

"Oh."

"No, it's not the Nightshade Unicorn," Allabva lectured her brother. "The Nightshade Unicorn is a fable. Stop listening to Jonder and Ultlan. They make stuff up and repeat old nonsense."

"It's alright for you to play with them," Mother stepped into her role before Allabva could usurp too much, "but you need to learn to separate truth from fiction. Your sister's right, though."

Mellier swallowed his mouthful.

"But it was a boy unicorn. All the rest are girls."

"Nomord," Mother and Allabva corrected him in unison.

Mother got up to leave the room.

"You two can figure it out. I'm getting that bath ready. Allabva, don't let him escape."

Allabva paused. It *was* the only male Nomord she had ever seen. Maybe there could be some truth to the fiction.

"But his coat was white, definitely not black," she tried to reason with Mellier, and herself. "White, just like all the

Nomo-Nomo we've ever seen or heard of. It's just weird that he was a he."

"No," Mellier contradicted again. "It was weird that he touched you with his horn, too."

"That is true also," she answered, folding her arms in thought. "Fine, but there's still no Nightshade Unicorn. Just a male Nomord that acted strangely, but wasn't spooky at all. I'm going to wash up. Don't go anywhere."

She closed the door to cut off his exit, creaky hinges acting as the alarm if he tried.

Chapter 2

Allabva and Brelin

As Allabva finished arranging her hair that evening, a knock sounded at the door, tapped in the familiar pattern that she was waiting to hear.

"Mother, I'm leaving," she called to the other room, where she could hear Mellier's protests against his preparations. "Brelin is here."

Allabva opened the door to see her friend standing on the doorstep.

"Alright," Mother replied.

"I want to go with Allabva and Brelin," Mellier said.

"You're not even dressed," Mother countered.

"I'm almost ready. They just need to wait."

"No, they won't wait. They have to get there early to rehearse the Greenstones' Dance for their Crossing."

Allabva rolled her eyes at her brother's antics, then smiled at Brelin.

"Are you ready?" Brelin asked.

"Let's go!"

They set off walking through the streets.

Allabva wore a dress made with green fabric on the shoulders and sides, and cream-and-purple accents on the sleeves, neckline, and down the front and back of the bodice and skirt. Her dark brown, curly hair was crowned with a wreath of leaves and blossoms of verbena and lavender to complete the set. Brelin was decked in white and gold, the gold sewn in geometric patterns on both bodice and skirt and providing a border around her sleeves. A matching headband held her straight sandy hair in place.

"No, but are you *ready*?" Brelin poked.

"For what, adulthood? Why not?"

"Mm. Different reasons."

Allabva rolled her eyes.

"I'm ready for tonight. I like dancing."

"Is that all?" Brelin said, sounding disappointed.

"Look, I know you're ready to start courting, but I'm just going to keep working the orchard with Mother."

"Do you mean you don't want to see Delgan?"

Allabva looked at Brelin sharply, smiling.

"Of course I want to see Delgan. I've always liked him."

"And? Now that you can take the next step?"

Allabva laughed.

"Then that's a possibility, but it's not like I'm going to go chasing him. He's a friend, and I'm happy with that. Why mess with it? Well, I mean, yes, I do really like him. I would like to explore that. But why rush it?"

The two of them strolled through the village, happily bantering about the young men they hoped to see at the Observance. They watched the sun lowering in the west as the shadows lengthened around them and their conversation came back to the here and now.

"I'm so glad it's not hot like it was earlier today," Allabva said.

"What do you mean? It wasn't hot."

"Oh," Allabva blinked, thinking. "I guess you're right. Well, I was hot because I had to walk up the canyon and gather rosemary, but I was still wearing what I put on this morning against the cold."

"I love your dress, though," Brelin complimented. "The piping looks very nice, especially with that green-and-purple combination. I know Delgan won't be able to stay away."

"Thank you, but it doesn't hold a candle to yours, Brel. The gold accents really bring out your hair. I wish I had hair like that. Alvern will love it, too."

Allabva punctuated this by poking Brelin in the ribs.

"Like mine? But my hair is so normal."

"Yes, nice and straight. It looks so lush."

"Allie," Brelin turned her head to deliver the line. "Allie, your hair is gorgeous."

"And so much trouble."

"It's gorgeous," Brelin insisted. "Almost exotic. The curls are dignified."

"And you just want to jump into things right away?" Allabva asked. "You don't thing that red crack in the sky a few months ago means anything?"

"So what if did mean something?" Brelin dismissed. "I can't do anything about that, and Alvern is still Alvern."

"If you say so, Brel," Allabva conceded to stem the current flow of the conversation, taking time to appreciate the beauty of the route they walked.

The houses and shops they passed on their way showed an aesthetic sensibility that reflected the town's status in the region. The Cleft lay somewhat isolated and protected from main industry, far enough away from the sea, its position above the confluence of the five creeks into the Night River making it irrelevant for shipping goods to other lands. All the same, it received visitors often enough that the residents of the Cleft were conscious of the world around them. Consequently, there was an air of caring about what their appearance presented to the world, without crowding out the local culture in favor of sameness.

Each building was either of brick or wood, material from mud and trees being readily available in the area, and often painted in pastel shades with the occasional deeper red or yellow hue, and roofed with thatch from the creek banks. Home fronts were generally kept clean, and signage announcing commercial enterprises in the town were reserved in appearance, giving an atmosphere of tranquil living but with no dearth of services available, should one need a shoe repaired or somewhere to buy a new coat.

The two young women arrived at the town square as the cool of the spring evening set in. The town hall was wood, painted a pastel blue with a wood shingle roof, seasoned to a dark brown in the elements. The front windows had white frames with blue shutters to match the wall, and the decorative eaves hung from the edge of the roof, also painted white.

They sought out Churloe Tunnigan, the Mistress of Ceremonies for the evening. They quickly found her surrounded by the other young men and women whose year it was for the Crossing at Greenstone Observance.

"Girls—pardon me, young ladies—I'm glad to see you could make it for the most important day this year, as far as you should be concerned. Place yourselves over there with your fellow Greenstones, behind the Tonalstga twins."

Allabva and Brelin joined the Tonalstgas in a double line at one corner of the green in front of the town hall, with the line extending along the side of the building, and stood with their feet apart, clasped hands resting in front of them. They could see some of the young men on the other end of the front of the building, with the line disappearing from view along the opposite side of the building. Mistress Tunnigan scurried back and forth, ensuring the young people found the correct places and remembered their parts in the evening's ceremonies.

With this year's prospective ceremonial graduates into adulthood taking up two corners on one side of the square, Mistress Tunnigan had a lectern set up in one corner across the green in front of the building. There was a small consort of musicians setting up their instruments in the remaining corner. The typical musical consort in the Cleft, often known locally as an orchestra, was made up of five to seven musicians with both stringed and wind instruments.

As those participating in the ceremony prepared, other helpers set up rows of tables and chairs on the cobblestones in front of the green, pulling them out of the town hall, which did not have enough space indoors for this evening's activities.

"Allie, look!" Brelin whispered with a furtive glance across the front of the town hall.

Allabva looked across the way and nearly blushed as she saw Delgan's eyes jerk away from her and back to Master Tunnigan, who was addressing the young men at the moment. Allabva quickly turned her own gaze back to Brelin.

"Brel, we're not supposed to be talking right now. Just look forward."

"Allie, look again. We're not standing in the right spots if you want to dance with you-know-who."

Allabva stole a glance over to the young men again. It was true. The dance they would perform for the town was choreographed so that it would pair each girl with a boy depending on her place in line. It wouldn't affect anything else in the ceremony nor after, but it apparently mattered to Brelin. Not that Allabva would mind dancing with Delgan, either. She rolled her eyes and smiled back to Brelin.

"That doesn't matter. It's just a ceremony, and you wind up with whomever you line up across from."

"Yes, but that doesn't mean we can't try to make it a bit nicer, does it?"

"Shh."

Allabva talked out of the corner of her mouth, looking forward and hoping her face didn't give away her eagerness.

"No," she admitted.

"That's what I thought," Brelin said through a conspiratorial grin. "Don't worry, Brel's got you."

"What do you mean?"

"Young ladies, don't talk," Mistress Tunnigan said as she returned to address the double line of young women. "Show the town that you can be grownup and practice some self-discipline, please. Do you understand?"

All the young women nodded in reply.

"Very well. I will be back again before we start." Mistress Tunnigan walked to her lectern and flipped through some note cards, then went to go talk to the consort leader.

Brelin didn't stop. "I mean I've got your back, Allie. Don't worry about it."

"What—"

"Psst! Aulbwin!"

Allabva closed her eyes shut hard, trying to convince herself this wasn't happening.

"No, leave the Tonalstgas out of this!" she whispered sharply but almost inaudibly.

Brelin ignored her. Some people just didn't want help, but she would provide it, anyway.

"Aulbwin! Yalrou!"

Aulbwin turned her head slightly.

"Leave us alone."

"Just trade us places," Brelin said. "Quick, while she's not looking."

"I said leave us alone."

Aulbwin apparently didn't want Brelin's mischievous nonsense, either.

"Come on—" Brelin stopped abruptly as Mistress Tunnigan finished her conversation with the consort leader and walked back to face the group of girls.

"Girls." She spoke flatly, a serious tone conveying the weight of the matter in her opinion. "You're still girls until after this. Then you'll be women—when this is over. Until then, be on your best behavior. Show us all that you're ready for this important step. You are our future, after all." She took a deep breath to punctuate her message, then turned around to walk back to her lectern.

As soon as Mistress Tunnigan's back was turned, Brelin leaned forward toward the Tonalstga sisters.

"Come on. It doesn't matter to you, but it does to us. Just swap us places. I'll give you half my shortbread at dinner."

Yalrou turned her head. "All of it."

"Three quarters."

The price was right. Yalrou stepped to the side and back, opening her spot for Allabva. At the same time, Aulbwin looked at her sister with surprise, then followed suit. Brelin shot Allabva a satisfied grin as she stepped forward into her new spot, and Allabva, flustered, now fully blushing, sheepishly stepped forward into hers. All was done in a moment.

Mistress Tunnigan arrived at her lectern and turned, facing at an angle toward the crowd with a few stragglers now taking their seats. She shot a last look at her husband standing next to the orchestra, who gave a signal accounting that the boys were ready. She looked back at the girls but appeared not to notice the last-minute swap. Then she looked to the audience.

CHAPTER 3

GREENSTONE OBSERVANCE

"Families, tradesmen, and Council, welcome to this year's Greenstone Observance," Mistress Tunnigan began. "We also welcome any visitors to our humble valley with open arms. Our program tonight, following our tradition, includes a special dance performed by our young men and women who have reached the age of majority. That means they are adults now and are prepared to formally join our local community. Following that, we will hear an address from one of our Council members, and then of course, dinner will be served and the dance will be opened to all."

She took a breath and smiled at the crowd.

"We'd like to thank the Council and everyone involved in the planning, and our local orchestra for providing the music for the dancing."

She paused a moment to allow give way to applause.

"Before we begin with the presentation of this year's youth, Blacksmith Ntoffel will now provide the opening Expressions. Master Ntoffel."

Master Ntoffel, sporting a deep red formal coat and silver hair, came forward to the lectern as Mistress Tunnigan took a few steps back. He raised his arms out wide, and, looking at the audience, sang a prayer.

> Let us remember these times, let us remember the chill
> Of the air of the night, and the warmth of goodwill,
> Let us recall in our minds, those to us who've been kind,
> Let us all emulate, before it's too late,
> Those acts that resound, the charity found,
> To spite not, as Nomord, to speak only kind words,
> In our haven of green, of winters not lean,
> We will share the stream, the water's bright gleam,
> We must always care, to help everywhere
> We will treasure the moments of peace.

As the blacksmith brought his arms down, the orchestra began playing the introduction of an upbeat tune and Mistress Tunnigan stepped forward again.

"Thank you, Master Ntoffel. Ladies and gentlemen, please welcome this year's Greenstones. No doubt their parents are proud—some relieved, some sad, but all proud—to see their little ones grown up tonight."

Allabva and Brelin, along with the other Greenstones on both sides of the town hall, brought their feet together and stood with erect posture, poised to file out onto the green. Allabva, forgetting the stress she had experienced from Brelin's meddling while basking in the beauty of Master Ntoffel's poetry, breathed a deep sigh of satisfaction and looked for her mother's face among the small crowd. Finding it and observing a twinkle in her mother's eyes, Allabva also caught Mellier's gaze, which carried less significance in his boyish face, though it was just as friendly.

The music picked up after the introduction, and on cue the Greenstones danced out onto the green in step with the beat. Fears now distant, Allabva followed the girl in front of her and soon found herself across from Delgan Dlorovin. They smiled at each other as they danced, not only because they were supposed to as part of the occasion, nor simply because of the enjoyable atmosphere. Allabva had her own reasons to back up her smile.

After all, most of the young ladies in the Cleft considered Delgan good looking. He certainly wasn't the worst dancer, either. Or the worst company. They had grown up in this town, and she always enjoyed time spent around him.

"Somebody paid attention during our rehearsals to prepare for tonight," Allabva complimented him as they danced together.

Delgan demurred.

"Of course, I paid attention. Isn't that the most basic thing you can do when you're in a class?"

"Some people's attention levels would argue otherwise," Allabva joked. "But, yes, though I mean that you really got the steps down confidently and solidly."

"Well, thank you. Takes one to know one," he shot back, grinning at his childish-insult-turned-compliment.

"So, what's next for you?" she asked. "Are you going to take over your father's farm like a lot of the boys here?"

Allabva remembered something.

"Oh, wait," she said, "I forgot that your older brother is already farming half the land. So what about you?"

"I was thinking of taking up smithing."

Delgan twirled Allabva once and then continued.

"Actually, I already talked to Master Ntoffel, and he said he could use an apprentice. What's next for you?"

Allabva opened her mouth to reply, but just then her position and the direction she faced gave her a view down the street and beyond the town to a nearby hillside, where she saw in the distance a stately Nomord. It looked like any other Nomord, but she knew it was Hronomon. His stance and focus made it obvious this was no Nomo-Nomo, but a Nomord with a specific purpose. Allabva missed a step in the dance and almost tripped.

"I'm sorry," Delgan said. "I didn't mean to ask anything intrusive. I hope it's alright—"

"No, it's fine," Allabva tried to reassure him. "I thought I saw something weird."

She could still see Hronomon on the hillside, but she pretended he wasn't there, not looking directly at him. She tried to talk it away.

"Just a Nomo-Nomo standing there and staring into space."

Delgan glanced over his shoulder. Hronomon was now prancing off.

"Oh, I see."

The music they danced to signaled for all the girls to divide from all the boys. It turned out that Brelin may have done her meddling not solely for Allabva's benefit. As Allabva turned around, she saw Brelin with a huge smile on her face.

"Oh," Allabva said to Brelin, "I see you caught yourself an Alvern," using the young man's name as if he were a fish Brelin had hooked.

"Yes, I did," Brelin replied with enthusiasm. "What are you trying to say about it?"

"Nothing, Brel. I think... I think that was genius."

Allabva shook her head in wonderment at her friend's forthright manner at spending a bit of time with Alvern.

"How is it going with Delgan? Anything official yet?" Brelin teased.

Allabva scoffed in disbelief and embarrassment.

"No way."

"Do you mean to be ungrateful? Do you not like this toy I gift wrapped for you?"

"Toy? Gift wrapped? He's a person! He's not mine."

"Yet."

"Hey. You can't just yank strings—"

"But I did, and now you're dancing with him. Take advantage. Make him yours by the end of the night."

"I can't just make him mine—"

"Sure, you can. Don't you like him? Don't you want to get married?"

"Well," Allabva stammered, "Of course I want to get married, to somebody, sometime. But you can't force things. Sometimes they're not meant to be, and you could force something that could turn out not to be a good thing after all."

"Whatever, Allie. Your loss. Alvern's going to be mine by the end of this dance."

Allabva nearly broke her composure with a laugh at that moment. The music rescued her, signaling for the girls and the boys to pair off again, and the two friends split apart from each other.

Allabva came back together with Delgan, her cheeks still red and her ears burning from the haphazard manner of Brelin's courtship intentions. She picked up the conversation again with Delgan to shake it off.

"To answer your question, I'll continue helping my mother in our orchard. With my father still gone, she needs my help. When the time comes to start a family—um, with somebody—we can probably build another small house next to the orchard. But who knows anything that far ahead, without knowing who my husband will be?"

"Makes sense, make sense," Delgan nodded his head. "Well, I guess this year is the time to start thinking about that, isn't it? I mean—you could, if you wanted to. I mean, you probably wouldn't have any trouble finding one. A...a husband, I mean. If you wanted to."

He almost sounded as awkward as Allabva felt.

Allabva couldn't help smiling. Was he complimenting her on purpose? Maybe Brelin was right. Delgan undeniably was right, that this was the year to start thinking about that. Was there anything wrong with Brelin wanting to jump right in on purpose? Technically, no...

"Thank you," Allabva managed to say. "You probably wouldn't have any more trouble than I would, finding one."

Allabva appreciated his coat for a moment, a black piece with silver and gold embroidery washing down from the shoulders and across the back and chest.

"A wife, I mean," she added belatedly, blinking, her eyes wide. "Especially with this coat. Where did you get that? Tailor Gundralsen doesn't do embroidery like that, does he?"

"No, I don't believe so. This came from the port downriver. But Tailor Gundralsen did alter it for me." Delgan hesitated a moment as if unsure of himself.

"It's a nice coat," Allabva repeated to cover the awkward pause. "I like it. You look dignified, and that matches this dance very appropriately."

"Thank you." Another moment's hesitation. "After the dance, would you like to come dine with us, with my family?"

There it was. That's why he had hesitated.

"Thanks for the invitation," Allabva replied. "I'd love to. Just let me check with my mother first."

The Greenstones' Dance continued, young men and women weaving in and out in reels and lines. It was longer than the average dance, paying homage to the significance of this occasion in their lives. Eventually it ended with the young men and young women filing out in double files on opposite sides of the green, the young women passing behind mistress Tunnigan and the young men passing behind the orchestra. As they left the green, they scattered to reunite with their families. Mistress Tunnigan stood at her lectern, allowing most of the bustle to diminish before continuing with the ceremonies.

Allabva spoke briefly with her mother, who encouraged her to join Delgan's family.

"We'll be here. Just don't forget about us," Mother said.

"I won't forget!" Allabva promised as she left to join Delgan's family at their table. On the way there, she felt again that she was being watched. She looked off into the hills at the side of the valley and spied Hronomon once more, seeming to stare at her. Trying to ignore him, she quickly looked away and found her way to the Dlorovins' table. She shared pleasantries with his parents and sat down next to Delgan as Mistress Tunnigan introduced the head of the farmers' guild to deliver the evening's speech.

The guild leader stood behind the lectern and addressed the crowd with a soothing, slightly gravelly voice.

"Good evening, everybody. I am Tunralger Faetlan. I don't know why they're letting an old man like me out in public, but for some odd reason, they're even going so far as to put me in front to talk to you all tonight."

Gentle laughter from the townspeople acknowledged his self-deprecating humor.

"I'd like to join Mistress Tunnigan and welcome any visitors we happen to have here with us today. I'm glad you're with us, but I question your judgment when you come willingly to such a backward place as our little town. Well, now that you're here, I suppose I'd better let you in on some traditions we hold around here. You younger children, listen up, just in case your parents forgot to tell you all this."

"Oh, dear," Delgan said under his breath. "Get comfortable. We'll be here a while."

Allabva rolled her eyes and smiled at him.

"He always gives the same speech every year, but I'm not worried about it. I'm with good company," she said.

Master Faetlan continued.

"We live in the Valley of the Five Moons, though if not even I can remember the reason for the name, I'm sure that nobody can remember with certainty why it's called that. We all have our individual theories. Some say it's the five creeks that flow into the valley from the various canyons roundabout, pooling together into the Night River at the bottom of the valley, and flowing slowly out toward the southern sea. But anyone who lives here also knows from childhood, scampering around the valley, that there are dozens of smaller streams that join those five creeks, and some of those streams are not that much smaller than the creeks. Where exactly is the distinction between a creek and a stream? Why not say four creeks, or six? Eight?"

"It's the grains," Delgan forecasted to Allabva with wide his eyes as he predicted the next line.

The old farmer droned on, "Some here will tell you that our valley gets its name from the five grains that we grow in the lower lands of the valley, but to be honest, we can never agree on which five grains those are. There is wheat, of course, and rice. Maize. Then it starts to get murky with chia, quinoa, and amaranth. Those, we all grow in significant amounts, but we argue whether they are all actually grains. Then there are the lesser crops of barley, oats, rye, and others, so I personally believe that the grains can't be the valley's namesake unless things were different, generations ago."

"No, wait, it's the summer months!" Delgan whispered to Allabva with exaggerated expression.

Allabva chuckled but maintained her gaze toward the speaker.

Faetlan continued, "Some say it's the five months of productive growing season. Others argue it's the five months of cold when we can't properly grow much. But these two factions argue about which five out of the eleven months of the year really count in one season or the other."

Allabva took a turn, looking at Delgan and imitating the style with which he delivered his insertions to the speech.

"No, wait, it's divine edict!" she whispered.

The speech followed in kind. They had heard it several times before and learned it well.

"Every now and then, you'll even hear that the Valley of the Five Moons was given its name by the Shrongelin himself, named for his five fingers holding his great sword that he dragged behind himself one day, digging the Cleft out of the stone. I personally give little credence to the Shrongelin being so large that his sword could carve the valley, and to the idea that he named it, seeing as he lived four thousand years ago. I still think it's worth mentioning because I want to invoke the sentiment of old traditions."

"Almost as old as he is," Delgan panned.

"You'd think we don't have enough people here in the Cleft to get all political like this, but we do, all the same. In the end, the rationale behind the name is long lost in time. Many say that it doesn't really matter. The fact is that we are here, this is our home, and we have our traditions, like Greenstone Observance."

"Shh," Allabva warned Delgan. "I like this next part."

"Now, I'd like to take a moment to appreciate the symbolism of what we witnessed here a few minutes ago, our youth celebrating a time when they are leaving their childhood behind, but keeping with them everything they learned along the way. As their adulthood commences, they will choose their paths and find their way, hopefully not only to see how they can contribute to the community, but also to find their own happiness and contentment as the season changes. And, I know some of you think it's still winter, but I say now it's spring."

He paused, giving a good-natured glare at the crowd to dare anyone to disagree that it was spring.

"As I said, as the season changes, so change the seasons in our lives. Some might think it more appropriate if our youth graduated from childhood at the dawn of summer, as spring is more analogous to childhood than winter is. And I don't disagree with that. Right now, as spring is setting in, now is when we plant. And I wish well to all my fellow farmers. May you plough, plant, cultivate, and harvest a bumper crop this season. May you listen to the wisdom of the ages and all the farmers who have gone before you to achieve success."

"Can't forget the downriver big city lawyer joke," Delgan interjected.

Master Faetlan obliviously complied.

"Of course, I'll be here ready and willing to help out in any way I can, as long as you sign my disclaimer and an all-inclusive waiver of liability in case your crop doesn't perform as hoped."

The old man laughed at his own joke while Allabva laughed at Delgan's manner of announcing it. The speech wasn't so boring when she had his remarks to lighten her mood.

"So, to get to my point: As I was saying, I think it is fitting to hold this Observance in the spring, because these young adults are now in their metaphorical planting season. What they do during this time will have a great and lasting impact on the rest of their lives, in ways we can't expect and they can't even imagine at this time, no matter how clever they may be. Greenstones, thank you for the lovely presentation. It was executed immaculately, and I wish you all the best in your endeavors. You have Crossed. Now have a good planting season!"

The old farmer was interrupted by shouts all around, and fervent applause.

Delgan turned to Allabva again and said, "They're all happy because he's finally done!"

When the commotion died down, he finished his remarks very simply.

"Greenstones, I think it sounds like everybody else supports you as well. Now is it just me, or does that food smell delicious? Let's eat!"

CHAPTER 4

DINNER WITH DLOROVINS

Volunteers from among the townsfolk carried out platters heaped with pheasant and turkey, cabbage, beets, perch, and trout, and many dishes dressed in onion, garlic, and carrots, with rolls and biscuits on the side. All of this, they set in front of the people to allow them to serve themselves.

Later, that would be followed by sweet potatoes, both in pies and out, accompanied by milk cakes and flan flavored with secret homemade recipes.

Allabva had listened to the speech as well as she could, but she was distracted the entire time, nervous to be sitting with the Dlorovins but glad to be sitting with Delgan.

Once the food was placed before them, Delgan reached for the serving plate nearest him and sat poised with the large fork, ready to spear some meat.

"Allabva, do you want pheasant, or turkey? Or both? And can I get you some gravy?"

"Oh, thank you. You know you can call me Allie. Um, turkey, please. And yes, that would be nice."

Delgan knew his manners well. That scored him some points in her book.

Allabva didn't want to appear useless. She grabbed the next tray over.

"Perch or trout? And would you like some lemon sauce?"

"Breaded perch, please, and not too much if you don't mind," he replied. "I've never been one to love fish much, and perch has a milder flavor. So, I'll take it breaded, and with lemon sauce. It's good enough that way."

"You know what, I'm not the biggest fish eater, either," Allabva admitted.

So, she thought, *if we wound up married, probably neither one of us would drive the other one crazy with the smell of fish, or a high appetite for it.*

Perhaps she should start keeping a tally as Delgan scored even more points.

"Oh, is that because your father drowned at sea?" Mistress Dlorovin asked. "I could see that having some influence on your tastes."

"Um, no," Allabva replied. "At least, not mostly. I know I already didn't like it before he left on his last voyage. And we don't know that he drowned, only that he hasn't come back."

Leave it to the future mother-in-law to unabashedly say the awkward, insensitive things, she thought. Then, *Not 'future' mother-in-law!,* she corrected herself. *'Potential' mother-in-law.*

Allabva and Delgan weren't even officially courting, after all. Yet.

She surprised herself with these thoughts. Brelin's behavior must have had more of an effect on her than she expected. Not that it would be a bad thing, necessarily...

"Mother," Delgan rescued Allabva from her reverie, "you know they're still hoping for him to come back. Her mother isn't out to look for a new husband."

There he goes again, more points.

Delgan's father stormed into the conversation, addressing Allabva first. "Mistress Roalke, allow me the pleasure of being the first to address you as such. Congratulations on your Crossing. Delgan, can you pass me that plate? Janfla, I know you'd prefer the pheasant," he said to his wife.

Allabva was glad for Master Dlorovin's interference as well.

He steered the conversation to something more germane.

"Now, young Mistress Roalke, what is next on your plate, proverbially speaking? Opening a tailor shop, a bakery, anything specific?"

Allabva mentally thanked him for not asking about any prospects of courtship. She wouldn't know what to say. She repeated what she had told Delgan earlier, during the Greenstones' Dance.

"Nothing specific that would require any change. We still have the orchard, and my mother still needs help, so the plan is to stick around and grow the best fruit we can."

"A noble pursuit," Master Dlorovin assessed. "Noble work that needs somebody to do it, nothing more, nothing less can you ask for in life. Why, we have Delgan here about to start an apprenticeship with Blacksmith Ntoffel as soon as we get our wheat and maize planted for the season. I'd say the same thing about that work. Noble, necessary, and honest sweat."

"And a lot of sweat, at that," Delgan inhaled and then puffed his cheeks out as he slowly exhaled through a small hole in his lips.

"No truer words, right?" his father agreed. "But that's what you want, right?"

Master Dlorovin turned back to Allabva.

"Delgan's always wanted to make things with his hands. He enjoyed doing crafts when he was young, and he's been fascinated with the smith's forge ever since we gave him one of those iron puzzles when he was little."

"Thank you, Father. I think that's enough about me. Allabva, are you alright?" Delgan turned the attention back to her with the question, his fork halfway between the plate and his mouth.

She was caught staring off into the distance again. Hronomon. Again. Staring at her, staring into her soul from what must have been half a league away. He wasn't going to leave her alone, apparently.

"Indeed." She came back to herself. "Just that silly Nomo-Nomo again, I could have sworn he—uh, she—she was staring at me again."

The whole family turned to look and saw Hronomon roll in the dirt, then get up and start bouncing down the hillside while cocking his head from side to side.

"I know what's going on," Delgan said. "She's looking at your dress, wondering why she's never seen such a perfect color combination before."

Somehow, Allabva didn't love the compliment right now, even though she was glad to know he thought so. It was a little too much attention, too fast. She didn't hold it against him, though.

Master Dlorovin came to the rescue again.

"Some fanciful joke she must think she's making, that Nomord. Stare at somebody trying to eat dinner at Greenstone Observance and try to make that person look like a fool. Well, she's too late. We already know you're perfectly sane."

"Thank you, I'm sure that's it," Allabva squeezed out.

She was relieved at least that Delgan's family didn't think her odd in the head. Even Delgan's father was winning more points for him. She tried to shrug it off and turned back to the table and Delgan's family.

Moving the conversation away from the odd Nomord, she said, "Did the Council provide all the meat and vegetables? I think only the desserts were potluck, right?"

They ate and conversed about additional boring topics, Allabva feeling more comfortable in the mundane, until Mistress Tunnigan stood up again to announce that the dessert table was open, and the dancing green would now be open to all. The small consort of musicians struck up a lively local tune to get people on their feet. Allabva agreed to join Delgan in a dance and quickly found herself lost in the joy of the familiar steps.

Their small talk was interrupted by Brelin romping through with Alvern Swiskopfel.

"Watch out!" Brelin shouted and Allabva dodged out of the way, pulling herself closer to Delgan.

The faster moving couple vanished again into the dancing crowd, laughter trailing behind them. Brel certainly wasn't wasting any time putting her plans in motion. Allabva couldn't help but shake her head, Delgan mirroring her rueful smile back to her.

"It's kind of surreal, don't you think?" she heard herself saying.

"What's that?" Delgan asked.

"Well, Del, here we are. Adulthood, by all accounts. But I don't feel any different than I did yesterday. At least, not physically or mentally. I'm not any taller or stronger. I don't think I learned any great truths about the world since yesterday."

"But now we're empowered to make our own big decisions." Del finished it for her.

"Exactly. Look at Brel and Alvern. They look like they're jumping in with two feet."

"I don't know that that's necessarily a bad thing."

"Oh, of course not. It's just that she's so ready to be so…"

"Committed?" Delgan was reading her mind.

"Exactly, again. Now, I just don't know if I'm there yet with this adulthood thing."

"I hear what you mean, Allie. I'm not sure I'll be the best blacksmith around. But I guess I am committed to it; it's definitely my first choice. I'm glad I'm free to pursue that. But I don't feel confident I'll always love the weight of the work."

"Oh, don't worry, Delgan. I've never known you to back down from a difficult task. You'll be fine."

"Whatever you say."

"No, seriously. You'll grow those big blacksmith muscles, and the work won't feel so heavy all the time, I think. You've done fine helping on your parents' farm, haven't you?"

"Well, I guess so. We'll see. And you? Do you feel unsure about helping on your parents' orchard?"

Delgan just kept hitting it right, aside from that one moment at dinner when he almost insinuated that she could be so beautiful that a Nomo-Nomo couldn't stop looking at her. At least he had directed that comment at the dress, not at her. And now, he called it her parents' orchard, not just her mother's. Allabva appreciated that.

"No, of course not. I just don't feel like it's a big adult decision, that's all. It's the obvious thing to do right now, and it doesn't require any drastic change. We've been letting a third of our land grow wild because we can't keep up with it. We've been trying to find the time to bring it back into production, but it hasn't happened yet. She needs me. So...here I stay."

"Makes sense. And did you have any thoughts about..."

Suddenly, the conversation, though still amicable, thickened.

"Well, about Brelin?" he finished.

"Brel?" Allabva laughed. "Brel's going to do what Brel's going to do, and I'm going to be her friend, anyway."

"No," Delgan said, intention hanging in the air, "I mean, what do you think about...about seeing me again? Perhaps next week, you could come over for dinner?"

His punch line was soft. That was good. Ease into it.

"Oh," Allabva stammered, wishing for more time.

Why didn't I catch on to his meaning?

"I'd have to—"

"Allie!"

Brel came bounding back, hooking her arm in Allabva's, and pulled her insistently.

"Come here for a minute. I'll bring her back, Delly!"

"What are you doing?"

Allabva asked for an explanation but allowed herself to get pulled along, turning and giving a surprised wave to Delgan.

"Where are we going?" Under her breath she added, "And how did you get such perfect timing?"

Brelin laughed out loud. "Allie, you *have* to try the cream punch the Faetlans brought. It simply cannot wait. Also, because I've been watching you, and I'm here to make sure you don't make a big mistake."

"What big mistake?"

"Delly-kins just asked you over, right?"

"Yes."

"And you were going to say yes, weren't you? Here you go."

Brelin served two glasses of the cream punch and handed one to Allabva.

"You'd better say yes."

"I was about to say that I'd have to check with my mother, because she might need me."

"You like him, right?"

"Yes. I want to go, but if Mother needs me—"

"No. This is important, Allie-poos. Tell the Delly-kins 'yes,' and your mother will understand. If she doesn't, just send her to *me*."

Allabva couldn't help but laugh at Brelin's antics and odd nicknames.

"Alright, um, Brelly-welly. But what if I'm needed? I don't want to lead him on."

"Allabva Roalke. Have a little faith and tell him yes. Now take that glass of punch and share the rest with your Delly-kins. He'll like that."

"Sharing the glass? But we're not—"

"Shh, Alla-Roal," Brelin interrupted her as she led Allabva back toward Delgan, who had taken a moment to try some miniature milk cakes.

She spoke conspiratorially, "If things go right, soon enough you'll want to kiss him, so you might as well share a glass of punch. It won't kill you. Now say yes."

She raised her voice to a more audible level.

"Here she is, Del."

Brelin gave Allabva a gentle push toward Delgan, who now held a mini cake in each hand, and was offering one to Allabva.

"Hi," Allabva stalled awkwardly, "um, let's go for a little walk."

"Sure thing." Delgan stepped aside to let her lead the way. "Here, have a milk cake."

Allabva accepted the small pastry and led away from the festivities, walking through the town's main thoroughfare. They wouldn't go far, she decided, but this way they could talk with some amount of privacy, fairly safe from interruption by Brelin or by anybody else. Once they were far enough away, Allabva broached the subject Delgan was probably waiting for.

"Delgan, I like you."

"Alright, I think I like where this is going."

"No, seriously I do. But I don't like leaving people high and dry, so when Brel grabbed me and whisked me off, I was about to say that I would need to talk with my mother and make sure she would be alright without me that evening. But apparently Brel thinks that if I told you that, it wouldn't be fair to keep you waiting for an answer."

"I see. And what are your thoughts about Brel's thoughts?"

Delgan's expression was... Hopeful?

"Wait, what am I doing?" Allabva stopped herself abruptly. "Have some cream punch."

Delgan looked at it and his eyebrows rose slightly.

"It looks like you already drank some of it."

She didn't want to bear the suspense any longer. She rushed into this now, releasing the immediate tension.

"Yes, I'll come to dinner. I'd love to. Maybe I just need to be more confident and let Mother handle things on her own. She's quite capable, so why not? Now have some punch."

Delgan's eyebrows soared high in the sky as his mouth cracked into a large grin and he brought the glass to his lips.

"If you say so, boss."

He drank while maintaining his smile.

"Should I bring anything?"

Allabva still didn't want to appear useless. Especially not to Delgan.

"Strawberry!" he exclaimed, surprised.

"Like, a strawberry? I don't think we have any right now. It's too early."

"No, the cream punch. It's strawberry, and it tastes so fresh. How did they make this before the strawberries are out this season?"

Allabva had completely forgotten about the cream punch, feeling the strength of her inner turmoil instead.

"Oh, yeah. It does taste rather fresh, doesn't it? Let me have some more of that."

She snatched the glass away from Delgan as if to make sure he wouldn't finish off the punch by himself, and took a large swig. If anything, it seemed to taste even fresher after she accepted his invitation to dinner.

"Where does that put us?" Delgan asked. "Is it just dinner, or is it... Well, I'm assuming Brel and Alvern will probably be an official item by the end of the evening."

He smiled knowingly.

"I'd say it's just dinner *so far*," Allabva said. "We'll see where this goes."

"Sounds good to me, and I'd say it sounds like you have a sensible head on your shoulders. I'd even say I like where this is going so far myself."

"So do I," Allabva breathed redundantly.

It felt nice to open up a little more. Then she surprised herself.

"But to be frank, I feel like next week is a little too far away. I don't want to put upon you and your folks unfairly. Let me check with Mother, and maybe you want to come over on the weekend? We could cook and, I don't know…"

"Cooking sounds nice," Delgan replied. "Let me know what your mother says, and—"

Allabva took his hand and led him back to the Observance. Then, letting it sink in that she was beginning a courtship, she let his hand go and proffered him the glass of cream punch.

"Come on. We already talked to your folks; come make some small talk with Mother and Mellier."

"Sure thing," Delgan said.

They made their way back to the square and found Allabva's mother at the edge of the green, laughing with delight as Mellier danced in a manner that almost nobody except a child his age would, his movements committed, betraying excess energy and comically ridiculous.

"Mother, did you try the cream punch?"

"Of course," Mother replied. "I've been coming to these since before you were born. What makes you think I wouldn't know exactly where the best food and drinks are going to be?"

"Good point," Allabva conceded.

"I really liked your Greenstones' Dance. It was well organized, and you looked so lovely and happy dancing."

"Thank you, Mother." Allabva had had enough praise for one evening.

"And I see you brought your dance partner. Hello, Delgan."

"Hello, Mistress Roalke. I really like the cream punch, too, but I think my favorite dish tonight was the garlic and rosemary pheasant."

Mother looked at Delgan appraisingly with an eyebrow cocked, then at Allabva.

"You told him. You told him, right?"

Allabva shook her head, but her mother wasn't convinced.

"No, I know you told him."

"Told me what?" Delgan tried to puzzle out the exchange between Allabva and her mother.

"That's my recipe," Mother answered.

"You made that?" Delgan sounded impressed.

"Well, no, not exactly. Tonight's dinner was a cooperative effort. All the pheasant was prepared the same way, but they cycle through recipes throughout the town every year. This year was my recipe. I didn't personally cook the pheasant here tonight, but I directed its preparation."

Delgan was still impressed.

"Well, it was incredible."

"Alright, don't push it too hard," Mother waved him off.

This seemed to be going well enough in Allabva's eyes, but then she saw that blasted Nomord again, this time on a different hillside, staring across the distance and straight into her.

No.

She recovered faster this time. She was having a good time, and perhaps setting a courtship in motion that could last her entire life. She would not let some ominous, feather-brained Nomo-Nomo mess up this evening for her. Maybe Brel *was* right to jump in.

"Hey, Del, how about tomorrow?"

She tore her eyes away from the horned equine and gave Delgan her most engaging smile. Then, before he could react:

"Mother, I'd like to invite the young and esteemed Master Dlorovin to dinner tomorrow."

"Tomorrow?" Mother asked. "But there will be work to be done, and you'll be tired after this late evening. Do you think you'll be done in time?"

"Absolutely." Allabva held her mother's gaze firmly, her expression committing to do whatever it would take.

"I'll help cook," Delgan bargained, "and I'll bring my xylophone and play for you."

Allabva was taken aback. This was even more than she was hoping for. "You don't have to play for us."

"I want to," he affirmed.

"Very well," Mother said. "Delgan, we'd be honored to have you, but you don't have to cook for us, either."

"Why wouldn't I cook? I think it sounds like fun. And I thank you for the invitation."

"You know what?" Allabva intoned abruptly, her immediate mission having been accomplished. "Let's dance a bit more."

"Alright," Delgan agreed.

He walked her onto the green, where he again showed his competence in motion. Allabva could do worse than Delgan Dlorovin.

They continued dancing together, lively and slower tunes alike, Allabva occasionally making eye contact with Brelin and receiving overly encouraging gestures and facial expressions, until Mistress Tunnigan took the podium a final time for the evening and thanked everyone for attending and wishing all a good night.

Chapter 5

Dinner with Delgan

The next day, Allabva's mother reminded her that there were still chores to do around the house apart from the gardening and the orchard. Allabva eagerly helped however she could, and even Mellier was amenable to doing a little more than normal because of the prospect of a special visit. It didn't matter to him that the visitor wouldn't be his guest.

Allabva could hardly contain herself, waiting all day, but as their chores turned into cooking toward the end of the day, dinner time did eventually come with the guest, announced by a rap at the door. For once Allabva eagerly awaited a knock at the door other than Brelin's signature tapping.

When the knock came, Delgan stood there with a hand in one pocket, the other hand holding a small bag on a strap, and his xylophone clinging to his back by means of a shoulder sling that crossed from one side of his neck to the other side of his lower torso.

"Come in, Delly-kins!" Mellier nearly shouted.

Allabva jumped, turning around to give her brother a shocked look. She managed to keep her voice level, though.

"Where did you hear that?"

"I heard you and Brelin talking."

"Is that so? Well, his name is Delgan."

She didn't give Mellier time to respond, preferring to move things along and hope that Delgan could forget about this.

"Hi. Yes, please come in."

Delgan stepped inside, looking around himself as he entered.

"This is nice. I like the decorations you have on the walls."

He pointed at a landscape painting hanging on one wall, depicting the valley as seen from up on the Grand Mount, then at some dried flowers arranged in a fan on another wall.

Allabva didn't know what to do with herself now.

"Hi," she repeated meekly. "I was thinking of making some cheese scones. We have a block of cheddar and some parmesan, and Mother has a great recipe. And I was thinking we could also do some dessert with preserves. Maybe. If there's time."

Hopefully he wouldn't walk right back out again, bored at her poor conversation.

"Awesome," he replied, grinning her confidence back into her. "Let's do it. Can I put my xylophone down here, next to the couch?"

"Seems as good a place as any," she said, her smile finding its way back onto her face. "Come on into the kitchen. Mother, Delgan is here."

"Hello, there," Mother replied. "Delgan, would you like to handle the muscle work? Take this cheese and grate it—the whole thing. Allie, why don't you mix the dry ingredients? Mellier!" she called into the sitting room, "leave the instrument alone."

"Aw. How did you know?" he called back.

Allabva turned around in the doorway to the kitchen to see Mellier resting the xylophone back against the couch.

"A mother knows. Here, Allabva, measure out the flour, sugar, and the salt first. Mellier, come in here and crack some eggs."

As they set about baking, Mother started chopping carrots and splitting open pea pods. The entire time as they cooked, Allabva couldn't believe that Delgan was there, in her house, doing basic chores with her, and that he appeared to be having as much fun as she herself was, just because he was there. When the scones went into the oven, Mother shooed the two of them from the kitchen, encouraging Delgan to show Allabva his xylophone. Mellier followed them, also eager to see.

Delgan walked over next to the couch and grabbed his bundle that was leaning against the arm.

The instrument had two rows of dark brown wooden bars fastened to a metal frame and held in place by large pins. The construction was unornamented, except for a craftsman's sign stamped into the side of the frame to the left of the keyboard.

Allabva watched in surprise as he lifted it while unfolding the stand that sat underneath it with practiced hands.

"I didn't know you could do that. How does it fold up and unfold so easily?"

"Well," Delgan replied, "it's built to be easy in order to be practical for quick use."

"I wanna see how it works," Mellier said.

He leaned in to have a look at the hinges where the legs of the stand folded out from underneath the xylophone. After a brief inspection he sat back on his feet and looked up at the instrument itself.

"How many bells does it have up there?"

Delgan readily played the part of the show-and-tell presenter.

"They're not bells. This is a xylophone. That means these keys—these wood bars—are made of wood. Bells are made of metal, typically either brass or steel."

"Whoa."

Mellier seemed impressed at odd things sometimes.

"So, how do you play it? Where are your sticks?" Allabva asked.

"They're right here, but these are called mallets."

Delgan withdrew from his bag a pair of forearm length wooden dowels with tight balls of yarn on one end of each.

"You hold them kind of like this, where your thumb and first finger hold this part of the mallet. The mallet is a lever, and your fingers here are the fulcrum. Your other fingers control the movement up and down, along with your wrist."

Both of his hands were facing with their palms toward the floor, his hands about the width of a serving platter apart from each other, and the tips with the yarn wound around them coming close together to form a triangle in front of him.

"Then you move them up and down however you need to so you can get a good sound out."

His hands bounced the mallets up and down on one key, playing a note many times per second and making the pure pitch ring through the modest house.

Allabva's mouth dropped open.

"That looks fun! Can I try?"

"No, play something for us first," Mellier objected.

"What do you want me to play?" Delgan asked.

"'Five in the Morning, Five at Night,'" he requested.

"I don't think I know that one. How about 'Snow on the Mount?'"

"Ooh, yes, please," Allabva agreed.

"Alright."

Delgan extracted from his bag a second pair of mallets and held them in his hands as well, these poking out from in between his second and third fingers, so he now held four mallets in total. Then he started to play the instrument, mallets moving slowly at first across the keyboard and in sync with each other to create chords. He also often struck some notes repeatedly in quick succession, sustaining a point in the phrase as if the song were sung and a word were being held longer.

The contours of the melody rose and fell, as did the intensity with which he played, breathing new life into a song well known in the Cleft. It depicted their nearby summit being covered in snow by a large, menacing storm, then faded away peacefully into melting spring streams. He ended with a decrescendo and ritardando on a single low note as his mallets gently slowed to a stop.

Allabva was enchanted. "That was beautiful. What else do you know?"

"I want to hear 'Five in the Morning, Five at Night,'" Mellier repeated himself.

Delgan and Allabva laughed.

"How about this one?" Delgan said as a spun one mallet in his fingers.

He jumped right into playing the music that had accompanied the Greenstones' Dance the night before, easily executing its lively rhythm and recreating the impression of several instruments with all the keys he had on his xylophone. He didn't use his second pair of mallets as much on this tune, only occasionally to highlight a chord.

"When did you learn that?" Allabva asked while he played.

"Over the last few weeks, while we were all practicing the dance." Delgan spoke haltingly, revealing the fact that this piece took some concentration.

"Well, obviously, not literally while we were out there practicing the dance. I mean that after our rehearsals, I went home and pecked it out, figuring it out bit by bit."

"It sounds great. Come here, Mellier," Allabva said. "I'll show you a few steps."

She grabbed her brother's hands and led him through some of the Greenstones' Dance. He cooperated begrudgingly, clearly enjoying the music itself, but appearing shy when it came to dancing. As he moved about, however, he seemed to get more into it.

After several minutes, as the music came to a close with an improvised ending, Delgan added a brilliant flourish to the final cadence. Allabva and Mellier clapped, and Mother leaned in from the kitchen doorway to show her appreciation as well.

"Alright, now show me how," Allabva prompted, moving closer to Delgan.

He stowed his second pair of mallets and offered her the first pair for her to hold, stepping aside so she could stand in front of the instrument. She took hold of the mallets and tried to imitate his stance and grip. It didn't seem to be quite right.

"One second," Delgan said.

He leaned down underneath the xylophone to mess with the stand that it rested on. He lowered it a few inches so that it matched Allabva's height better. Then he stood next to her and reached around with both arms to adjust her grip and position over the instrument. Allabva couldn't help but notice that he smelled nice.

"Good," he said, "now play this note here, letting the mallet bounce off the key."

She hit it once.

"Bingo. Now do it again and again, on a repeated steady beat with both hands."

Allabva slowly tapped out a beat, alternating which hand and mallet she was using to strike the key.

"Now don't go wandering around. Stay in the middle part of the key. Do you hear how it doesn't ring as loud when you strike next to the end?"

"Yeah."

"And let the mallet bounce a little more like it wants to. They make some mallets with softer yarn and others with harder yarn. These mallet heads are the right hardness for this instrument. They want to bounce a certain amount, so let them."

Allabva was enjoying this time, doing something with Delgan not because it was necessary, but because it was fun. She tried to find the sweet spot he was guiding her to, and as she did so she could hear the note ring with a less muffled tone that resonated longer.

"There you go, good work."

"I want to do it," Mellier proclaimed.

Allabva tried to delay Mellier just a little. "Here, you can have a turn, but go get the little stool from the kitchen to stand on so Delgan doesn't have to change the height again. I'm not sure the stand goes low enough for you, anyway."

"It doesn't," Delgan confirmed. "A stool is a good idea."

While Mellier went to retrieve the stool, Delgan coached Allabva through a simple tune. Allabva could hear her mother blessedly running interference for her, asking Mellier to grab her this ingredient or that kitchen implement to delay him to give them more time without him.

By the time Mellier returned with the stool, Allabva had succeeded in playing "Night River at Morning" passably well, if she would say so herself. It was only a four bar tune, but it was still fun to play.

Mellier got up on his stool and snatched the mallets from Allabva's hands. He didn't need to wait around for any coaching. He just jumped right in and started hitting keys.

"Easy there, Mellier," Delgan intercepted. "You don't want to hit it as hard as you can. It's possible to damage the keys and wear out the mallets too fast. Don't lift the mallets any higher than right here."

He held his hand about a foot over the keyboard.

"And truly, you probably only need to raise them about half that high most of the time."

"Why?"

"Because that will help you control how hard you are hitting the keys. Music isn't all about playing as loud as you can. It's about playing as loud as it makes sense to. If you want to play a really pleasant song, then some notes will be softer than others."

Allabva stood back and happily watched this clever young man teach. He wasn't afraid of hard work. He understood people in a way that promised a steady life, and he was charming with both visage and manner, and now he revealed a talent that could soothe and excite. Brelin was sounding more and more right. No need to rush still, but Allabva felt like she was on the right path with him. The key would be to not mess it up, she told herself.

Delgan decided to let Mellier have the reins at the instrument and came over to talk to Allabva. At that moment, Mother poked her head around.

"Can you two help with setting the table?"

They placed dishes and food on the table in the front combined room, where one end was the dining room and the other was the sitting room. Once the table was ready, they all sat to eat a humble but beautiful spread of sauteed peas and carrots, the cheese scones they had made together, and some rewarmed pheasant and turkey left over from Greenstone Observance the night before.

"I hope you don't mind a little bit of leftovers," Mother said to Delgan.

"Of course not, ma'am. I grew up on a farm after all. It happens all the time. And if the leftovers in question are last night's pheasant, there's nothing at all to question."

"Good to know you're down-to-earth folk, like we are here."

Dinner was as tasty as it was aromatic. As they finished, Allabva's mother disappeared into the kitchen with a smile.

"One moment, I'll be right back," she said.

She reappeared quickly, carrying a tray of some sort of flat dessert cut into squares.

"Here we go. I hope you like this."

"What is that?" Mellier said excitedly.

Allabva was incredulous. "Mother, when did you make that?"

"It's blackberry-raspberry jam shortbread bars. I made them yesterday when you were gathering rosemary. I didn't plan specifically when I would pull them out, but we didn't need them last night and tonight we have a guest, so here we are."

"Yay!" Mellier weighed in.

"Watch out," Allabva warned Delgan. "You thought the pheasant was good? My mother appears to be out to shatter your preconceptions."

"I'm all for it. Shatter away," he smiled.

"Young Master Dlorovin, here you go," Mother said, handing him a small plate with a square portion on it. "There's the cream over there. I would highly recommend it with a bit of that on top."

She served Allabva and Mellier next, then herself.

As dessert disappeared, Delgan spoke.

"Mistress Roalke, this has been wonderful. Thank you for letting me come over and get in yours and Allabva's way this evening, making you trip over me in the kitchen and all that. Now if you don't mind—and I know already that Allabva doesn't mind, unless something changed since yesterday—I'd like to invite her to dinner next week, and afford her the opportunity to get in our way at my home."

"Of course. Anything to get her out of my house," Mother joked. "The good-for-nothing child—uh, woman—is always taking care of my problems for me. I can't feel any sense of accomplishment for solving anything myself. Take her away so I can live my own life for an evening, for once."

Her eyes twinkled with mirth.

"Mother, you do so much," Allabva retorted. "Surprise dessert that you baked just because? All I did was gather sprigs of an herb."

"And dance beautifully last night."

"And you touched a unicorn!" Mellier spilled. "Well, we both touched it, but it touched you with its horn!"

"Mel Roalke," Mother said with a flat tone that told him he'd stepped where he shouldn't have. "I think that's something for Allabva to talk about if she wishes to. Let her tell whom she chooses."

Allabva's heart sank. She hadn't wanted to talk about the strange, male Nomord with anyone besides Mother, at least not yet.

"Whoa," Delgan let out as his eyebrows lifted into his forehead, looking at Allabva. "Really? What was it—uh, I mean, never mind. Your mother is right, it's your call."

Awkward pause.

"Mm," Delgan salvaged, "Mellier, how about we see if we can figure out how to play 'Five in the Morning, Five at Night' on my xylophone?"

Mellier forgot instantly about the talk of the previous day's close encounter as surely as everyone else had neglected to correct him on his use of slang this time. He jumped down from his chair and already had a pair of mallets in hand when Delgan arrived next to him. The two started noodling and pecking at the keys on the instrument with the mallets, searching for the notes to play the popular song.

"Mother, how about I help you clear the table?" Allabva suggested, looking for an excuse to be alone with her mother and talk for a few minutes.

They gathered dishes from the table and carried them into the kitchen for washing. Once there, Allabva spoke softly so her words wouldn't carry into the next room.

"I didn't get a chance to talk to you about what happened yesterday. I wanted to. It was a unique experience."

"I imagine it must be, if it was a male Nomord," Mother said.

"I know it must be hard to believe," Allabva started to say,

"Not if you say it, love. I know you don't use idle words, and I knew you wouldn't say it unless you were sure. Go ahead and I'll hear you out."

Allabva was relieved to receive this much trust.

"He came up and spoke my name. It was the first thing he said to me. He just knew my name without asking it. Then he walked up, slowly, staring into my soul. He came close enough, then I reached up—I still thought it was a regular, female Nomord—and touched him on the face. He brought his face down and touched my forehead with his horn."

Allabva paused.

"He stared into me and I felt as if I knew that he could see everything, understand me fully. But there was more to it."

Mother listened with rapt attention.

Allabva took a breath and continued. "He told me his name was Hronomon."

"I've never heard of any Nomo-Nomo to say whether she had a name at all," Mother remarked. "Did he seem lucid?"

"Absolutely. He did some bounding and prancing like we're used to seeing the Nomord do, but I feel like it was more to fill our expectations. He didn't seem to be composed fully of lightheartedness. Then, he told me I was ready, or almost ready, but he didn't say for what."

"For wh—oh. Well, it does make one wonder," Mother said.

"He said one more thing that I remember. He said he would come back."

"Come back? Come back for what? When?"

Mother stopped and blinked.

"Come back at all?" she reflected further. "Never have I heard of any of the Nomord promising to do anything in the future. They all seem to live in a cloud of the present. What do you think? When do you think he'll come back?"

"He kind of already did."

"What's this 'kind of?'" Mother looked at Allabva intently and raised one eyebrow.

"I saw him during the Greenstone Observance yesterday. He was up on the hillside outside of town."

"Does he look different from other Nomord? Different colored hair?"

"No, he has the same white coat and single horn as all the others, but I knew it was him because I could feel him staring at me. When he touched my forehead with his horn in the Canyon, I felt... seen. Comprehended and considered. During the Observance, I felt the same thing, although not as strong."

"What do you make of it, then?" Mother prompted. "You're the one being sought out. You felt that kind of mental probing. What do you think, or even feel that it means?"

Allabva hesitated.

"I don't know. I was kind of hoping you might have some idea."

Mother waited for Allabva to go on to propose some reasoning herself.

"He said I was ready, but he didn't say what for. I wondered if he meant for adulthood, which kind of made sense because yesterday was my Greenstone. Speaking of that, I hadn't considered whether or not I was particularly ready for my Crossing. I was just taking it in stride. But then Brelin added another dimension to it, talking about being ready to take on marriage, and I hadn't really been thinking about that, either. But with Hronomon and Brelin both combined, now I find myself thinking about it and wondering. And I do really like

Delgan, but I don't know if I'm ready to decide anything like that...and it would be too fast right now..."

Allabva stopped to breathe after what she had just rushed through.

"There's no need to rush it, dear," Mother comforted. "Whether it's time for you to take a step like that, you'll know either way, and I support you either way."

It felt reassuring to hear that.

Mother kept going, "Besides, what does some magical beast know? This is your life. So what if he can see into your heart or soul, even if it is true? That doesn't mean he can decide these things for you. You just live as your conscience directs."

"Thanks, Mother. I appreciate it."

"Now what do you say we rescue that boy from your younger brother and say good night to him?"

Mother led the way back into the front combo room, where Delgan and Mellier were playing "Five in the Morning, Five at Night" at octaves from each other on the xylophone. Mellier actually had an expression of concentration on his face as he played, which amazed Allabva because he never seemed to focus on anything for long.

"Alright, little man, it's time for you to get ready for bed," Mother said to Mellier.

While Mellier protested, Allabva spoke to Delgan.

"I guess it's time for us to say good night as well."

"Very well. I'll see you next week as we talked about before?"

"Yes. I'll be there. Don't eat without me."

Delgan laughed.

"Don't worry. My mother would never dream of allowing such a breach of protocol to happen under her roof. Oh! I'll *make* you come over."

"Oh, really?" Allabva asked coyly. "How do you think you're going to make me?"

Delgan was fiddling with his jacket that he had just put on in preparation to go outside, opening the first button again. Then he reached around his neck and pulled on a chain, revealing a necklace he had under his shirt.

"What's that for? You think you're gonna put some kind of chain on me and pull me along?"

"No, silly girl. Woman. Whatever." Delgan smiled. "I'm going to use your own honesty to force you to come."

As he pulled the chain over his head, the end came into view, revealing a small, silvery flute a few inches long, hanging on a loop on the chain. The chain had another ring as well, similar to a keyring.

"What's this? More musical instruments?" Allabva asked.

"Just one more, but this used to belong to my grandmother. She used to play this when she watched the sheep."

Delgan offered the flute to Allabva, and she took it in her hands, turning it around and looking it over. It had some engravings on the back. A few wavy lines, a couple of triangles, a small circle.

"Is this the Valley of the Five Moons?"

"Bingo," Delgan replied.

"And what's this other ring for?"

Delgan looked sheepish.

"Apparently, when I was little, I used to get lost. Like, it was my favorite pastime. My parents hung a bell from that loop."

"Where's the bell now?"

"Well, my second favorite pastime was taking things apart, so that bell is long lost."

Allabva couldn't help but laugh at this.

"So, you often lost yourself, and you permanently lost the bell, but your parents still let you keep your grandmother's flute?"

"Yes. I was obsessed with this flute. I never let it out of my sight. There was no way I would lose it."

"Alright, sounds good."

Allabva looked momentarily to the side, wondering when her brother was going to interrupt this conversation, but blessedly it seemed her mother had corralled him upstairs to let her talk to Delgan in peace.

"And you're going to entrust it to me?" she asked.

"Let's call it a trial period. You hold on to it for me for a few days, then bring it back to me when you come over for dinner. How does that sound? I think it sounds like a plan."

Allabva smiled.

"I guess it does sound like a plan. That is, as long as you don't have any great hopes from me. I don't know how to play it."

Delgan's eye twinkled, making Allabva wonder what else he could be up to.

"That's all right, you don't have to. In fact, that's the best part because it literally plays itself."

"What do you mean?"

"Exactly what I said," Delgan replied, his grin reaching from ear to ear. "You see, one time while my grandmother was tending the sheep, she had some trouble with wolves. She managed to beat the wolves off and save the sheep but then they attacked her instead."

Allabva couldn't see how this was supposed to be a good thing, but Delgan continued.

"She got bitten and scratched pretty badly. She wasn't able to protect herself, but then one of the Nomord came by and fought off the wolves. It healed her and then took it a step further: she blessed this little flute. Since that day, this flute will play itself, will play my grandmother's favorite tune that she always used to play on it—the Nomord must have heard her—if you hold it and say, 'beware the wolves.'"

Allabva looked at the small flute she held in her hand, then back at Delgan.

"Go ahead," he encouraged. "'Beware the wolves.'"

Allabva held the little flute tenderly now, appreciating the simple form before uttering it.

"Beware the wolves."

A beautiful, sweet tune emanated from the small silver bar. Allabva was amazed, first at the flute itself, then back at Delgan.

"I can't keep this for you," she said. "It's a family heirloom. What if I lose it?" She had placed it around her neck but now took it off, offering it back to Delgan.

"I'm sure you won't lose it, and it's just a few days until you come to dinner. Bring it back when you come."

"Well, I—well, alright!"

Allabva threw herself forward to give Delgan a hug. He received her and hugged her as well.

This felt nice. She could stay here a while.

"All right, so I'll see—wait, how do we get it to stop?" Allabva stepped back, noting that the flute was still playing his grandmother's tune.

"You can either wait for it to finish the tune, or you just say the same thing again, 'beware the wolves.'"

"Got it."

She held it in her hand again and repeated, "Beware the wolves."

Beaming, she looked up into Delgan's eyes while he opened the door and stepped halfway out.

"Can you show me how to play it properly? Just a bit?"

Allabva held the flute out to him, but Delgan hesitated.

"All the way out," Mother called from upstairs. "It's chilly out there, so close the door."

The two complied, stepping outside and shut the door. Taking the flute, Delgan went through the motions.

"It's easy to play different notes. Just blow in the top here and use your fingers to cover the holes like this. For some notes you have to cover half—"

A thundering boom shattered the night as a glowing, jagged crimson line split the night sky, as it had once before. Allabva and Delgan both jumped, flinching at the sudden noise and light. The red line cast sparks, vibrating and making the stars appear to oscillate. It held for the space of several breaths, the two Greenstones staring up at it, before it dissipated into nothingness.

"Wow," was all Allabva could say.

"Another one," Delgan marveled. "It makes me wonder again what caused the first one."

The front door burst open behind them, revealing Mellier, now in his pajamas.

"Did you see that?" he shouted.

Mother appeared as well, still in her day clothes.

"Was that the same as last time? I only saw it through the window. Was it as big this time?"

"Yes," Allabva said. "It reached across the whole sky."

They all stood for a moment, waiting to see if anything else would happen. Finally, Mother broke the silence.

"And here we are, standing with the door open. Mellier, come inside. You have to get in bed."

"Awww. Why?"

"Because you need more sleep than your sister. Allie, don't take too long, yes?"

Mother took Mellier's hand and pulled him inside, closing the door behind them.

Allabva found herself alone with Delgan again. She blushed as he awkwardly handed the flute to her for the second time.

"So, uh, yeah, that's how you play it," he said.

"Thank you. I'll bring it when I come to dinner, I promise."

She took the flute, then thought of the inexplicable sign they had just seen in the sky.

"Delgan?"

"Yes, Allie?"

"Be careful out there. You never know when some Nightshade Unicorn might turn out to be real," she said, patting him on the chest.

He raised an eyebrow.

"The Nightshade? What makes you bring that up?"

"It's just something my brother said yesterday, and this weird lightning had me thinking."

"Oh. Well, I guess we should say goodnight," he grinned at her.

That smile, Allabva thought.

"I guess so."

"Um. What would Brelin say?" Delgan mused. "Goodnight, Allie-poos?"

"Ahh!" she said playfully. "Goodnight, already. Walk safely."

She shoved him away, opening the door and going inside. She turned around and closed it quickly, but smiled while she did it.

Life went on. But she kept thinking about that red rift. What did it mean? Where did it come from? Was it bad, or just a different kind of lightning?

How could she top Delgan's loaner gift when she went to see him, if she kept thinking about the sky cracking open? She needed a clear mind...

Allabva had the red lightning on her mind while she went about getting herself ready for bed. Planning her work for the next day was impossible. She fell into a fitful sleep, happy about Delgan but troubled about the strange sign, the flute hanging by its chain around her neck and tucked inside her nightgown.

Part II: The Road to Palf Glen

Chapter 6

Visitation

An insistent, scraping knock at the front door awakened Allabva in the wee hours. Blinking sleep away, she arose and pulled her robe about her against the spring air.

Allabva woke her mother on the way, not wanting to face an unknown visitor alone in the dark. Mother lit a lantern, and they both walked down the stairs to the front door.

Allabva tried to look through the front window to one side of the door, but all she saw at this hour was shadow. Mother set the lantern on the table so it would cast its light in the doorway when they opened the door, then stepped protectively between the door and Allabva. Allabva moved to position herself where she could look out the open door without blocking the lantern light, allowing the light to fall on the visitor to reveal his or her face immediately when the door cracked open.

Mother opened the door wide enough for a beam from the lantern to shine out and illuminate whoever had been knocking. As the door opened, they could see that it was not human.

Hronomon stood there, front hoof raised, ready to knock again.

"Yes?" Mother demanded. "What brings a Nomo-Nomo to our door at this hour?"

Allabva recognized the Nomord, unsure how she knew although his face looked like any other Nomord face to her eyes. Mother must have thought she was talking to a mostly witless beast.

"Mother," she intercepted, "this is Hronomon, the Nomord who visited us in Pine Canyon."

"I suspected as much, but I don't see what that changes at the moment," Mother gently retorted. "What is he doing here right now?"

"I don't—"

"Good Faethlen Roalke," the beast spoke. "I am here to see your daughter on an urgent matter. The Shrongelin needs her assistance. The *world* is in need and only the Shrongelin can provide. He requires Allabva's help to fulfill his mission."

"What?" Allabva asked in disbelief.

She was struck at the implausibility of his statement. He certainly hadn't beat around the bush before making it.

"How am I supposed—"

"How in the world do you expect her to do whatever it is the Shrongelin needs to do?" Mother interrupted. "She's just a girl, despite having reached her majority. She's young, and human at that. What is it that you or the Shrongelin would ask of her?"

"There is a great evil awakening to the north, as has happened many times before. The Shrongelin has held it at bay since it was imprisoned long ago. Now it squirms and threatens to break its bonds, as has also happened before, now long forgotten by your kind. The Shrongelin has protected this world, enduring ages of attacks from the imprisoned evil.

Now he grows weary. At the same time, that evil comes near to overflowing its bounds."

Allabva stood, staring at Hronomon. *This* was what he wanted to talk about? Was this real?

"What do you mean, overflow its bounds?" Allabva asked.

"Perhaps you saw the sky split open last night?" Hronomon said.

Allabva shared a look with Mother, then both nodded, faces pale.

"And a few months ago," Mother said. "What does that have to do with this?"

"Those are cracks in the prison. More will come in the next months. We must prepare, be ready to stop it. When the evil bursts its prison, all the world will feel it."

If those were only cracks, what happens when it breaks? Allabva thought.

"In what way will we feel it?" Mother asked.

Hronomon ignored the question and continued, "He must imprison the evil once again, but this requires power that no Nomord can wield alone. I know that other humans would see your daughter as a common enough young woman. By your people's measures, she is healthy but unremarkable."

Allabva wondered whether she was supposed to feel slighted by that comment. Hronomon did not wait for her to object.

"I am Hronomon. I am the Forerunner. I can see her heart. In her kindness, in her desire for harmony, she is uncommon. The Shrongelin needs one such as her in order to tap the power that can contain the evil known as Sacalai."

"So, you're saying it has to be my daughter?" Mother asked. "You can't go scrape the paint off some other poor soul's door at dark-thirty in the morning? Why did you come now, when she's barely an adult? Can't you find somebody older? Maybe a big, powerful man."

Hronomon paused, then said, "No. And no. It didn't necessarily have to be Allabva Roalke. She was not chosen by birthright or other arbitrary means of selecting a champion. It could have been somebody else.

"However, I am tasked with finding a Companion for the Shrongelin. I am tasked with finding somebody who is kind and selfless, capable and ready. As it happens, I felt her pulling me here three weeks ago—I mean to impress upon you the rarity of one fitting the need so perfectly—and I came to investigate. I find her qualified.

"It is clear now that we can delay no longer. Those cracks in the prison came earlier than we expected. Sacalai is pushing hard. Allabva, you are ready enough. It is good that you arrived at your majority before I came. As you begin to look at the world differently, you probably had some experiences in the last two days that have helped round out your character to be the ideal companion to assist the Shrongelin to stand against Sacalai."

Reflecting on her brief encounter with Hronomon in Pine Canyon, Allabva could still feel that internal glance at his heart and mind. She knew she could trust his word and intent. She knew that if he, with his immortal knowledge, declared that this must be so, then she would go with him.

"What do I need to do?" Allabva spoke at the same time that Mother said, "Would this be dangerous to her?"

"You must come with me at once, Allabva. We must journey to meet the Shrongelin, then you will travel with him. Yes, madam, there will surely be danger."

"Why doesn't this Shrongelin come to find my daughter himself?"

Mother still appeared to be more concerned with Allabva's safety than anything else.

"If you were anyone or anything else," Mother told him, "I'd have closed this door on you as soon as I'd opened it. The only reason I've spoken to you this long is because I've never known a Nomord to have a shred of maliciousness. Frankly, I've never seen a male Nomord, either, but your race does you credit either way. Why doesn't the Shrongelin come here himself?"

Allabva's mouth hung open at her mother's boldness, the ease with which she spoke out against the Shrongelin, no matter how slightly. Their traditions held him to be a great, benevolent being.

"Please pardon my lack of complete explanation," Hronomon replied. "I will not take the time to explain fully now. I do not know what you know, or think you know, about the Shrongelin. Many human lifetimes have passed since any of you knew him. A story is changed in the retelling, as it surely has been through your generations. Whatever—"

"What's your version, then?" Mother interrupted.

Hronomon seemed unperturbed.

"Whatever you think about the Shrongelin, this is what you must know now: that he has been protecting the world for thousands of years, that he needs Allabva's help to overcome this challenge, and that because of Sacalai's influence already permeating the world, he cannot approach Allabva until the appropriate time and place, or all would be lost. Were he to approach her prematurely, they would both be soft targets to Sacalai, easily enough disposed of. Now, we truly must depart now, before the sun is up. The fewer eyes to see me here, the better."

He turned, evidently expecting Allabva to follow.

Allabva opened her mouth "But—"

"Wait just a minute," Mother said flatly to Hronomon. "This is absolutely preposterous. You show up here with no advance notice, expecting her to traipse all over the continent just because you and your friend think she's special? You show up, telling a mother that she has to sacrifice her daughter to some perilous mission, intimating that she may never return to the bosom and embrace she knew first of all?"

Tears welled up in her eyes as she gave the unannounced visitor her mind.

"That this mother is to simply stoically carry on as if her only daughter weren't about to disappear into the night with some silly Nomo-Nomo on a word and a prayer because *the Shrongelin* supposedly needs her? Her, and only her?"

Mother's face changed from mourning to indignation.

"No! I will go instead! It matters not if I return. I place full confidence in my Allabva to do what's right with the orchard, and probably do a better job than I could myself at raising her brother in my absence. I will give myself to the Shrongelin and we will *destroy* this, this 'Sock-eye' that you say threatens the world! My daughter will stay here, stay sa—"

Mother's voice cracked with emotion.

"My sweetheart will stay safe! You can go let this Sacalai eat you alive, for all I care, but Allabva will live a good life! She will raise apples, cherries, peaches...she will raise her brother...she will raise her own children. She has a beau! Might become a proper suitor. He's a very nice young man. He could be her husband one day and they could raise their own children!" Mother shouted angrily at the intelligent beast in the doorway. "Can't you let her live her own life? Take me instead. Please."

Mother Roalke's shouts gave way to pitiful sobs as she resisted the inevitable.

Allabva swallowed, struck by the emotion of her mother's delivery. Then she spoke, reaching out to and embracing her mother.

"Mother, I have to go. Hronomon says he can see me for who I am. I don't know if he's aware, but the glance goes both ways, though perhaps far weaker in my direction. I can see him. I know we can trust his honesty. I can see that he intrinsically desires the good and well-being of all."

"But why you?" Mother asked rhetorically. "My baby. We already lost your father, as far as we know. And now you?"

The Nomord stood silently by as the heartfelt exchange took place in front of him.

"Mother, I know how selfless you are. You have worked so hard to care for Mellier and me. You have knitted blankets for others' babies. Just this week, you gave your time to coordinate the best roast pheasant Greenstone Observance ever saw. Now you offer yourself in my place. You love and you sacrifice; it's who you are. All that Hronomon is asking is that you let me go and...be your daughter."

Allabva leaned in to give her mother a tight hug.

"I wish I could shout from the rooftops to let the world know how great you are. Instead, I will do the only thing I can: I will go, and be the woman you raised me to be, Mother. And I may not have the power to keep this, but I promise I'll return. I will come back, and if anyone tells me they think I did anything special, I will tell them they owe it to you. You have given me all that I am. Now...I must go and do what I can."

Hronomon spoke up.

"Dear, kind madam. Your firstborn is grown. I congratulate you. Please accept my apologies for what I must ask. Your daughter's youth is another aspect of her qualification for the task. The road will not be easy. We cannot allow ourselves the risk of injury that comes as your kind ages. It would too easily slow you down."

He turned his head slightly, not needing to turn around completely to look over his shoulder because of the side-set eyes on his equine face.

"If it helps, Mother," Allabva said, "maybe you can touch him and see what I saw."

Mother looked at Hronomon sideways. Allabva thought that normally her mother would have no problem touching a Nomord, but under the circumstances she appeared to prefer to stay far away from him. But she gave in.

"Fine," Mother said. "May I?"

Hronomon nodded, using the human expression.

Mother approached, reaching her hand up to touch his nose. As she did, Hronomon leaned down to touch her forehead with the tip of his horn.

Mother's eyes widened when he made contact, then she blinked quickly several times and her eyes teared up. Allabva recognized the expression; she had learned that she could trust Hronomon's words.

"We need to go," Hronomon said. "There is no telling where Sacalai may have influence. This valley has good people, but we must depart unobserved, regardless."

Mother protested the hastiness.

"This is impossible. She needs to get dressed. She needs provisions for the road. Can you give her half an hour? What about her friends? Can anyone accompany her?"

"Nobody else, just her," the Nomord said gravely. "We must maintain the utmost secrecy until she is bonded. But very well. Half an hour."

Allabva and her mother began a mad scramble about the house, gathering clothing, food, and personal tools they thought would be useful. Despite Hronomon's indication that first he, and then the Shrongelin, would protect Allabva personally, Mother insisted she carry a knife. Most of the time they spent packing was used to determine which items would be the most useful and weigh the least. In the end, Allabva carried a bag over her shoulder that included two changes of socks and inner clothing, one set of outer clothes, and other sundry supplies. Her food included some cheese, dried meats, hard bread, and a waterskin. She covered herself with a cloak that would be wearisome during the day, but which she certainly needed at this hour, as much as she would during the nights to come on her journey.

All kitted out, Allabva stood, prepared to depart.

"Mother, go back to bed and get some sleep. Mellier will be awake before you know it, and you will need all your strength."

"Look at you. That's why Hronomon came for you instead of anyone else. Always looking out for others. Don't worry about me, my girl. The hard part will be telling Mellier where you've gone. Of course, I can't tell him what's really going on, but I don't want to lie to him, either. Take care of yourself."

A realization hit Allabva.

"Mother. I won't show up for dinner with the Dlorovins. I can't even tell him I'm not showing up."

"I see. Well, I'll tell Delgan something for you. We can't have him waiting for you if you're not going to show up."

"Thank you. Can you be sure to tell him that I really did want to come? That I was looking forward to it, and I was very excited? And maybe I'll catch him next...sometime?"

"Oh, deary. I'll tell him something. I'll make sure he knows you really care. Now go, or this here unicorn is liable to blow a blood vessel."

Mother and Allabva looked to Hronomon to gauge his reaction to her use of the slang term for his species. He simply stared back.

"Come, young one," he spoke at last. "Now we must hurry. Madam, I bid you leave. I depart in peace, and I hope to come in peace again. Farewell, and best fortune for you during the days to come. May this calamity miss your village."

"Come, Allabva," Hronomon prompted. "You must give your quickest sustainable pace. I cannot carry you there; the Construct demands that you must travel on your own feet."

Hronomon turned around and led Allabva away from the only home she had ever known, not knowing when she may ever return. Allabva followed, her heart in turmoil. The sudden turn of events tore her up inside, crashing into her in a moment when she had been a newly minted young woman looking forward to life. She had hoped that would be a life with somebody as nice as Delgan Dlorovin to spend it with. Now, she unexpectedly became a wayfarer, not knowing where she was going or what she was supposed to do when she arrived.

And Delgan. She didn't want Delgan to be sad. She didn't want him to be upset. But she wanted him to need her, so then, because she was going to be absent, that required her to want him to be sad and upset that she wasn't there. Hopefully, she could return soon.

The girl and beast walked briskly into the night long before it gave way to dawn.

CHAPTER 7

THE TRAIL

Allabva walked in silence for some time, pondering on the life she had just left behind. She knew not when or if she would be able to return to her home. She kept this silence, not only because of how much she had to think about, but also because she assumed that her traveling companion would oppose conversation. It would probably risk revealing them to anyone outside of their line of sight.

Allabva wanted to play with Mellier again, chasing each other through the orchard. She wished she could hear what Delgan thought of her dress that Brelin had complemented, and longed to stay behind and help Mother concoct new variations of recipes. They could harvest fruit in the summer and fall to sell in town to the merchants who would take it downriver. She desired for one more shopping trip with Brelin, ogling the thread and fabric most recently brought to town by the merchants.

All that was a thing of the past. Now she walked in silence with a male Nomord who promised to take her to the mythical Shrongelin. Hronomon seemed very stern and serious. If he, being previously unknown to her, had a connection to the Shrongelin, whom she had heard of before, how much more somber would the Shrongelin be? What other impossibilities would she find to exist?

Allabva looked about her as she walked, letting Hronomon direct their route. She had no fear of the dark, but now she had a heightening apprehension about the unknown. Why was it so important that they leave in secrecy, under the cover of darkness? The Cleft was full of good people. Who could there be in this area that would wish her harm?

According to Hronomon, the Shrongelin needed somebody like her to defeat something nefarious. Evidently, this fight had a magical aspect to it, or Hronomon would have been searching for a fearsome warrior instead of Allabva. What kind of magic were they up against, and what magic did the Shrongelin bring to the table? How would that involve her? And if the evil adversary had magic, could this evil be watching Allabva right now?

She found herself trying to peer into every dark space under a tree or behind the bushes they passed on their way. She pulled her cloak about her and put the hood over her head, trying to appear nondescript.

When they left Allabva's home, Hronomon walked side by side with her, but quickly placed himself about two body lengths ahead of her. Allabva wasn't sure if he was trying to maintain an advance lookout in front or if he was expecting her to stay by his side, setting a pace that she would not be able to keep up with. As it was, Allabva was walking as fast as she thought she could go and still be able to walk all day. She suspected that Hronomon was hoping she would catch up to him so he could start walking even faster.

They left the Cleft heading east, heading toward the pass leading out of the Valley of the Five Moons. Early in their journey, they crossed Pine Creek and spent some time traveling parallel to Ash Creek. Ash Canyon was farther from home and from the town than Pine Canyon was, and it was a couple of hours before they entered the mouth of Ash Canyon. Once they were in the canyon, they started to gradually climb. The trail wound among many examples of the canyon's namesake, and as the grade continued upwards, Allabva was afforded an occasional peek back into the valley.

As she looked behind her, she could see where Oak Creek met with Ash Creek, and the two carried on toward the west. She could also see a few lights in the now-distant village; there were a few people waking up now, though it was still dark. She blinked and tried to hold this image in her mind, mentally carrying her home with her and trying to imagine where her house could be found when seen from this distance and angle.

As the first light in the east brightened the sky, Hronomon stopped, turned his head to look at Allabva, and waited for her to catch up. When she did, he started walking again, albeit more slowly.

"You're doing well enough so far, I believe. My aim is to go as fast as you can bear. You will need to let me know if the pace that I set is too much. I know you humans don't perceive pace and distance quite the same as the Nomord do. We are in a hurry."

"Where are we going to meet the Shrongelin?" Allabva asked.

"I hesitate to say at this time, even to you. I know the makeup of your heart, not the strength of your mind. It could be that you unintentionally give away details to agents of the enemy. We are going to the same place where the Shrongelin's Companions have met the him before, though this is knowledge not to be found among the human family. Even our adversary does not know it. It is hidden from her mind, and

I would have us be sure not to tell her now. Once I know you better and can gauge the safety of information in your possession, perhaps then I can tell you where we are heading."

"Fair enough," Allabva assessed. "I suppose you slowed for me to catch up. We can maintain our previous pace."

She sped back up to the pace he set through the valley floor, and he matched it. As she did, she reflected on what Hronomon had told her.

"What is this evil?" Allabva asked. "You just said 'she.' What are we up against?"

He gave her a long, sideways look.

"I am sometimes astounded at what you humans forget. I am also sometimes quite dismayed at what I have forgotten."

He added the second part with a resigned tone.

"What have you forgotten?"

"All will be revealed in due time. To be completely honest, I am not aware of everything I have forgotten. I do not know where all my knowledge gaps are. The Shrongelin has forgotten some things, too. Hopefully, together, our knowledge is complete."

"The Shrongelin can forget?"

"Yes. He has forgotten, just as I have forgotten, but he has now recalled some things and forgotten others."

"How do you know this?" Allabva furrowed her brow, intrigued. "How do you know that he has forgotten things?"

"That is the way this cycle goes."

"What cycle?"

Hronomon sighed heavily.

"Sacalai. Gha-Nomord and Ta-Nomord. Hronomon. Shrongelin. Companion. All of it."

"What are...what are Gha-Nomord and Ta-Nomord?"

"I am Gha-Nomord. I expect I'm the first Gha-Nomord you have met. We don't travel among humans as the Ta-Nomord do."

"I don't understand," Allabva confessed.

"Male and female. You have only known Ta-Nomord in your lifetime. You sometimes call them Nomo-Nomo."

"Oh."

So there were other Gha-Nomord.

Or as Mellier would have called them, boy unicorns, Allabva mused, already wishing she were still back home.

"Hronomon, you mentioned your name in between the Nomord and the Shrongelin's. What is the connection? Aren't you Nomord?"

"Yes, I am Nomord, just like your so-called Nomo-Nomo, and just like the Shrongelin."

Allabva stopped walking, astounded at the pronouncement.

"The Shrongelin is Nomord?"

She blinked, shook off her astonishment, and started walking again.

"You humans don't teach your children anything, do you?" Hronomon shot. "Of course the Shrongelin is Nomord."

"Oh. I had no way of knowing that. It's not my fault I'm not immortal, you know."

Allabva thought his manner was a little brusque. Didn't he know she was a product of her culture, which had forgotten such things generations ago? She considered how different things must seem to Hronomon's perspective and knowledge, albeit spotty, from his long life.

"You know what it's like to forget. But why did you forget things?"

"Humans," he said dismissively. "Sorry, Allabva. Pardon my frustration, but I'm trying to tell you. It's all part of this cycle. I guess I can't blame you, but I am disappointed that your kind does not remember these things and pass them from parent to child. I will try to catch you up. From the beginning, then."

He breathed deeply before continuing.

"Sacalai is evil, was too powerful, and had to be stopped, contained. To do so, we founded and built a prison for her. This prison required the strongest magic of the Nomord. I hope that I do not insult your intelligence, but I assume you know that the Ta-Nomord can heal wounds?"

"Yes," Allabva confirmed. "At least, I've heard. I've never seen it happen myself."

"Very well. That is a magic exclusive to the Ta-Nomord. We Gha-Nomord have our own magic. Significant among our abilities is the strengthening of mortals. To strengthen a mortal, we must forge a bond with that mortal, which also grants us added strength. Most of us can bond up to three at a time. This bond fades on its own if not continuously renewed, like your orchards would if unattended. This bond also affords limited influence upon the physical and mental aspects of individuals or the world around us, either to invite or to block."

Hronomon paused to allow Allabva to ask questions before going on. She stayed silent.

"Sacalai was wreaking havoc on the world. Her magic was too powerful. She had followers that waged war on her behalf. We could not stop her, unless we could magnify the scale of the Gha-Nomord and the Ta-Nomord influence on the world. To this end, we confederated, all Gha-Nomord lending a portion of our strength to one Nomord, who then forged a special bond with a single human. This Nomord, the Guardian, the Shrongelin, with the power we gave him, forged a bond far stronger than any Nomord had been able to before."

"Does the Shrongelin's single bond also...strengthen?" Allabva asked.

"Yes, but there is more. The Ta-Nomord also combined their strength. Unlike with the Gha-Nomord, the Ta-Nomord did not give up any of their strength by sharing it with one of their own. By combining together, they were able to increase their total power. They gave that surplus to one, without diminishing themselves. The Mhosorem, the female counterpart of the Shrongelin, was also set in place.

"This confederation of the Nomord, Sacalai did not expect, and it was her undoing. The Shrongelin, with his bond and the willing spirit of his Companion assisting, was able to build a prison for Sacalai. A physical aspect locks her away from the sight of the world, in a secluded place where life doesn't come near enough to her to be corrupted by her influence. A spiritual aspect contains her magic and influence in her immediate vicinity. Or, so we thought."

Allabva thought to realize that she needed to sustain her body in order to continue walking as long as Hronomon wanted to. She took out a morsel worth a few bites and gestured to Hronomon to continue talking.

"The prison, though forged with all the might we could muster, fades over time, dozens of human generations. It is now at this time, cracking and bleeding. She is yet mostly contained, unable to leave her prison, and impotent to exert any influence on the physical world outside. But her influence leeches into the ground and the wind, causing greater discontent in humans and in nature."

"How bad is it?" Allabva said.

"At this point, some might still try to explain it away. I take it that you were unaware of things shifting, hidden away in your hamlet in the valley. But things are changing. More violence, greed, and lust leaking into the world. And it is accelerating. The Shrongelin believes we have just enough time to catch up and head her off, re-imprisoning her before she can wreak havoc in the world. If we fail, if we are late, or if he can only perform a patchwork renovation on the shield, or prison, the world will be doomed to tear itself apart while Sacalai laughs."

"What is your role in this cycle to save the world? And the Ta-Nomord?"

"Strictly speaking, the Shrongelin does not save the world. He put the prison in place, but Sacalai's influence was already loose in the world. It would still have torn itself apart. The shield has two sides to its spiritual aspect, an inside and an outside. All the Gha-Nomord are inside the shield, locked inside with Sacalai. The world, along with you humans? You sit at the boundary, trapped underneath the edge of the shield, making it hypothetically possible to slip in either direction. The Ta-Nomord are locked outside the shield, standing in diametric opposition to Sacalai's corruption and influence.

"It is the Ta-Nomord who continuously save the world, day in and day out. Their influence tugs and pulls at the world and at the hearts of mankind, maintaining a balance so that it were as if Sacalai did not exist. I? I am the Forerunner. Human life is far too short for the same Companion to last from one cycle to the next. I help the Shrongelin to find and prepare his Companion to re-imprison Sacalai."

"I see."

Allabva wasn't sure she completely saw it, but she felt that she got the gist of it. She tried repeating it back to Hronomon.

"So the prison breaks from time to time and it has to be rebuilt, which requires a new Companion in order for the Shrongelin's magic to be strong enough."

"That is correct," Hronomon replied, but Allabva felt like there was a detail she was missing, and he was intentionally not explaining it.

As the sun broke over the trail ahead while they continued to head east and uphill, Hronomon seemed to take on a more cautious air again.

"When we leave the canyon, we will have our selection of side roads and deer trails across the land."

He spoke in a softer voice.

"We can appear unconnected, I as one of the Ta-Nomord, when we are on the plains as well, as long as we don't get too near to other people. However, while we are still inside the canyon, we are restricted to this one road. We must be alert and ready at all times to jump into the brush on either side of the road. As we walk, always keep an eye open for hiding places, and constantly decide where you will duck into hiding and arrive within five paces."

He looked at her shorter legs.

"Perhaps three paces."

"Got it," Allabva replied.

She contemplated her physical limitations compared to this much larger, magical creature. He must have felt frustrated to be constrained on this journey to what she was able to do. She told herself that she would not be a liability, that she would keep up and complete this mission. She *would*.

He spoke again.

"As the morning continues to dawn, let us hold silence until we are out of the canyon and can see longer distances ahead and behind."

Allabva nodded, determining that she could be more easily hidden than Hronomon could with his bright white coat. The two walked on in silence again.

Hiking continuously upward, Allabva felt the desire for a staff to lean on. In the early light she saw a branch with the proper amount of straight length for a staff before it split into smaller branches, fallen from a tree beside the trail. She leaned over and picked it up, then walked upright again while she broke the twigs off. It still had some extra length above, being longer than she needed it to be. It was a little too thick to give it a clean break over her knee. She would use her knife to cut the excess off when she got a chance.

Chapter 8

Ta-Nomord

At what Allabva thought was probably around nine-thirty in the morning, she thought she caught a glimpse of light and movement on the trail ahead. As she thought of facing the day, she started to feel the sleep she had missed, especially since her shortened time in bed had been poor because of the rift in the sky.

"Hronomon, did you see?" she whispered.

Hronomon apparently had seen. He was already scrambling between a pair of large bushes on the south side of the trail. Allabva had forgotten to keep her eyes out for immediate hiding places, but she scrambled into the brush behind Hronomon. They both hunkered down to wait for the other traveler to pass.

Allabva looked back downhill and saw their own tracks coming up the trail and disappearing into the brush at the side.

"Hronomon, our tracks," Allabva barely mouthed the words, pointing at the disturbed earth they had left.

Hronomon looked at her and then shook his head, as if to say, *There's nothing we can do about it now.*

Allabva waited and practiced keeping her breath still and silent. Shortly, they heard the approaching party's footsteps on the ground. The newcomer rounded a corner and Allabva could see her in full view. It was a Nomord.

Unsure of what to do, Allabva looked to Hronomon to see his response.

Upon seeing the Ta-Nomord coming down the trail, Hronomon immediately stood up and stepped out of the bushes.

"Come on, Allabva. It's fine."

When Allabva stepped out onto the road, the other Nomord held her head back in surprise, then moved her head from side to side to inspect Allabva through one eye, then the other.

"Why were you surprised when I came out?" Allabva asked the Ta-Nomord.

"Because she can't see me," Hronomon replied mournfully.

"Why not?" Allabva perplexed. "You're right there, as plain as a hippopotamus in the desert."

The Ta-Nomord came sniffing at Allabva.

Hronomon answered the question. "She and I are on opposite sides of the shield. I am on the inside, and this beautiful creature here is locked on the outside, repelled away from Sacalai's influence and helping to balance the world away from it as well. As a consequence, her mind is not fully in this world. And...she cannot see me."

His voice belied more than a serious sentiment. Was it loss?

"Do you...do you know her?" Allabva asked.

"Yes," Hronomon answered, his eyes distant. "It's hard to remember. She and I used to play together when I was a foal. She..."

"What's her name?"

"I cannot remember. Duty calls, and I must let go." His expression darkened and hardened.

"Not from here, you smell from down in the valley," the Ta-Nomord said to Allabva.

Allabva's eyes glistened with empathetic tears.

"That is so tragic. You are separated, Ta-Nomord and Gha-Nomord, by your duty, by your service to...us."

"What's sad? You have dried apples!" said the Ta-Nomord, still oblivious to Hronomon's presence.

"Give her some dried apples," directed Hronomon.

"What? I need all my food for the journey."

She started to open the bag anyway.

"Buy me time. Give her some, but slowly."

"You want some apples?" Allabva invited, complying.

The Ta-Nomord danced in anticipation. Allabva wondered at the prolonged attention the creature gave her, longer than she had seen a Ta-Nomord focus before.

Allabva dug out a single slice and held it out in her hand, opened flat.

"Tell her about your home," Hronomon prompted, again without explanation.

"What's your name? Do you know what? I grew this at home. I grew up on an orchard and my mother cultivates apples, and peaches, and cherries, and other wonderful fruit. We also keep a vegetable garden."

"More about your family."

Allabva pulled out another two dried apple slices. "My mother raised me, and now is raising my younger brother, Mellier. He can be mischievous sometimes, but mostly he's just curious. I guess I can't blame him for that."

The mare nipped an apple slice off of Allabva's palm.

"That's sufficient," Hronomon informed her. "Don't give her any more of your food."

"Well, it was nice meeting you. I think I need to be going now." Allabva returned one slice to her bag.

The Ta-Nomord was already trotting down the trail, now resuming the flightiness for which her kind was known.

"What was that about?" Allabva quizzed Hronomon.

"A favor to you."

"What favor?"

"As Gha-Nomord, I can bear some modest amount of influence on minds. I was implanting an idea, nothing more. If it is something that would please her, and I believe it is, then she will take this idea and carry it out, never suspecting where it came from."

"What idea?"

"She, a Ta-Nomord, is able to bear direct influence on the solids in the physical world. If I am correct about our visitor, she will now go seek out the home and family you just spoke of, and bring them a very successful growing season."

"Is that really true? A good year for the orchard, just like that?" Allabva asked.

"Again, if it is something that she would already be inclined—"

"Thank you!" Allabva threw herself on Hronomon's neck, giving him a tight hug.

Then, standing straight again, she remembered that they were supposed to be silent until they knew they had more space.

"Sorry," she whispered.

Hronomon simply nodded understanding, gestured up the trail with his head, and resumed walking as if nothing had happened. Allabva continued walking as well, keeping pace beside Hronomon.

As the pair marched on, Allabva snacked on the provisions she had brought. As the day warmed up, she first lowered her hood, and then doffed her cloak entirely when it became too uncomfortable. Now she carried it draped over her shoulder, opposite hand hooked on the hood to keep the cloak from falling. She also drank water as she felt necessary, removing the stopper to drink, putting the bag to her lips, pulling it away again and replacing the cap, all without breaking stride on the trail. It was unavoidable, but in the late morning her waterskin was empty.

"I'm going to need to refill my waterskin," she informed Hronomon, whispering.

"Very well. But as we travel, you should try to find a way to make the need less frequent. We cannot stop so often."

Lower down in the canyon, closer to the valley, refilling her water would have been easy to accomplish. Here, closer to where the canyon would open up and give way to grasslands, the trail no longer ran alongside the creek. In fact, there wasn't much creek yet at this height, since rainwater runoff did not gather in a central stream until further downhill, far to the backs of Allabva and Hronomon.

Eventually, they found a small stream with a quiet trickle of a waterfall. Allabva filled her skin.

"Drink it all right now, and refill your bag," Hronomon instructed.

"But I'm not that thirsty right now."

"You will be later. Perhaps you should even drink and refill twice before we go on. It will reduce the number of stops we must make. Also, as we leave the canyon, we may not find so convenient a stream and standing water is not as safe for you to drink."

Allabva saw the wisdom in this and drank all from the waterskin, refilling it again twice. Once she had filled it the third time, she capped it and they continued walking again.

Finally, as the sun stood high overhead, Allabva and Hronomon crested the canyon entrance and looked out over the high prairie, broken behind them by Ash Canyon and others, but smooth and unending ahead.

"Now we can see for miles ahead and we can see that nobody is approaching," Hronomon observed, his voice normal rather than whispering. "Did you have any questions to continue your history lesson?"

"Not right now," Allabva breathed. "I always loved the hills in the valley, but the prairie view is also breathtaking when it is fresh."

"It is all the same: monotonous. Don't misunderstand me, it looks delicious."

That wasn't the word Allabva would have used to describe the view.

Hronomon continued.

"This prairie has quite the variety of grasses. I will have no lack of food while we cross it. But once you have seen a patch of it, you may as well have seen the entire landscape."

Allabva nodded.

"It's true. This patch doesn't look any different from that patch, but I love the vastness of it. My father used to describe the plains as an ocean of waving grass with the occasional island of trees, underneath the sky so large you almost feel nervous you're about to fall up into it. He'd seen the plains of Weslan Fields, but I suppose this might also be like that."

"They're quite different from my perspective," Hromon replied. "Those grasses are juicier than these."

Allabva laughed, replying, "He used to take crops down-river to Nylorna, and he'd come back with stories about how the bay looked when he stood on the docks. I wonder if looking out on the prairie might be similar to that."

Wordlessly, the young woman and her equine escort continued to walk. Midday surrendered to afternoon while they watched hawks and falcons hover and circle overhead in search of prey. At one point, Allabva saw a mass of cloven hoofprints imprinted across the path, betraying the passage of the plains bison.

Allabva felt more of the weight of her sleepiness, exhaustion beginning to call to her. Her feet felt heavier, but while she still had strength she wondered how long her reserves would last.

Her spirits were lifted at one point when she gleefully pointed out a fae-bird flitting by in front of them, its multicolored crest reminiscent of a wreath of flowers encircling its head and neck. The yellow plumage flashed to black and back as it popped in and out of its veil of invisibility. Allabva watched it flee in the distance and wondered if its nest was already laden with shimmering bluebonnets. Fae-bird nests, when one could find them, yielded flowers that took decades to wilt. But it was probably too early in the season for that.

Though it was still chilly, being springtime, Allabva didn't feel the cold due to the effort of walking so far. On the contrary, she did feel the sun's effect on her face. She draped the cloak loosely back over herself, using the hood to block the sun. At least she wouldn't have to keep the cloak on very long, since the sun was now slowly falling to their rear and her hair would serve to protect her neck.

Her biggest concern then, was her feet. Hronomon began to notice her gait had changed slightly.

"You humans. Your socks and your boots. It's overly complicated. Why can't you just have hooves like a sensible creature?"

"Was that a joke? From a somber Gha-Nomord?" Allabva poked.

Hronomon didn't respond to the questions, but his eyes held a hint of mirth. Allabva was gratified that he was letting his guard down a little. It was relieving to see that he had a little room for joy despite the burden he carried.

"What do you need to do so you can keep walking? I hope you realize I am no horse. I will not carry you, nor does our mission allow that possibility."

"Let me just change my socks."

Allabva cast her eyes about and found a low rock. She seated herself and pulled her boots off.

"I should give you some credit, even though you're soft footed. Among your hoofless kind, your ability to continue walking is at least halfway decent."

"Oh. Well, thank you. When I'm not working on the orchard, I'm hiking or jogging through the canyons. I think I'm used to covering ground."

She took her socks off and examined her feet. Mostly good, with a little bit of rubbing. She just needed dry socks and she'd be good as new.

"Perhaps I shouldn't be too surprised, though. You are young, after all, your body working quite well still, not so aged as your mother."

"You think my mother is old?" Allabva said, pulling her dry socks on.

"She is older than you."

"But that doesn't mean she should be called old. Haven't you seen other humans?"

"Of course, I have."

"Don't you think some of them looked far older than she does?"

"I suppose so. I'm not very much used to thinking about how to tell humans apart from each other."

Allabva shook her head in amusement.

"My mother is older than I am, but she's not old yet. I'm not even sure she qualifies as middle-aged."

Allabva finished pulling her boots back on and stood, holding her old socks in her hand to let the sweat on them dry so they could be used again when her new socks were no longer fresh. She resumed walking and Hronomon continued by her side.

Something Hronomon had said hung in the back of Allabva's mind. Since it wasn't going away, she gave it voice.

"I'm fine walking, but why did you say specifically that our mission 'doesn't allow the possibility' of you carrying me? Is that just some way to prevent me from even asking to be carried?"

"No," Hronomon answered.

"I see you're back to your somber self. You didn't answer my question, by the way."

"You are correct," Hronomon said, inhaling and exhaling deeply. "I warned you and your mother that this journey would not be easy. While there is no requirement that it be difficult, per se, you must travel under your own power to meet the Shrongelin."

"Does that figure into part of the magic somehow?"

"You are beginning to catch on, I see. It does, indeed. The Shrongelin needs to form a bond with a human. This human must be of pure intent and desire—I spoke of your kindness as being a requirement—but you must also not be directly aided by magic prior to forging this bond. Furthermore, you have to come to it willingly, giving your own efforts. If I were to carry you, it would stunt the potency of the bond, and neither you nor the Shrongelin would be as mighty as you could be otherwise."

"I see. And what's this talking about me being mighty? I will be changed by the bond?"

"You will not be altered in mind, spirit, or appearance. You will, however, gain in physical strength, endurance, and stamina beyond the capacity of any natural human once the bond is active. Additionally, you will be able to tap into the Gha-Nomord magic of influence upon minds. Hopefully, it will be enough."

"If I'm supposed to gain such great strength, does that mean that once I meet the Shrongelin and we forge the bond, that I will be safe? That the danger in this journey lasts until then?"

"Far from it. When you forge that bond, you and he will become a beacon, bringing targeted attacks. You will be protected for a time, as the bonding will temporarily strengthen the Construct and the prison. You will also be very capable of defending yourselves against those attacks once the extra effect of the bonding fades, but while you wield that strength, Sacalai and her forces will be able to seek you out and will attempt to head you off at every opportunity to prevent you from fulfilling your mission. You will need to hide the bond."

"How do we do that?"

"I can only say that the Shrongelin will know. I have never been in that role. Not only does our mission require that I not bond you on our journey to meet the Shrongelin, but the nature of that bond is different."

"So, you can't even bond somebody else to gain the benefit of that strength on our journey?"

"No, I cannot. It is beyond me, perhaps for the better. The bond is not commonly performed since the days of the Sacalai cycle began. Perhaps if I were to forge a bond, it could be detected somehow. As things are, the only thing that may mark us as a priority target for the enemy is the fact that Nomord and human are traveling together."

"Why did you forget how to bond? I thought that was in the nature of the Gha-Nomord."

"It is. I forgot that when I became Hronomon, the Forerunner."

"When you became Hronomon," Allabva repeated his phrase, pondering. "You were not always Hronomon?"

"No. I became Hronomon when the Shrongelin became Shrongelin."

"That's what I had understood. So you mean when Sacalai was imprisoned, the Shrongelin...became Shrongelin, and you became Hronomon in order to imprison her. The Gha-Nomord take turns being Hronomon?"

"Not exactly. The Shrongelin became Shrongelin once Sacalai was last re-imprisoned, and I became Hronomon at that time as well."

"I thought that was what I said," Allabva puzzled.

Hronomon looked at her and blinked with impatience. "I became Hronomon when the Shrongelin stopped being Hronomon. I stepped into an empty role."

"What? He was you?"

"No. It is a cycle, which I said before. Sacalai grows restless and must be re-imprisoned. The Shrongelin, who has been maintaining the prison all this time, bonds a Companion and the two forge the shield anew. While the Shrongelin maintains the inner shield, bearing the brunt of Sacalai's evil, Hronomon maintains the outer shield, keeping the world away from the prison. Hronomon also aids the Shrongelin to find the best Companion to ensure the prison is rebuilt at its highest integrity."

"But what do you mean that the Shrongelin stopped being Hronomon? Wasn't he always the Shrongelin? Isn't that..." she hesitated. "...his name?"

"It is a cycle," Hronomon repeated. "Forging the prison anew requires all the Shrongelin can give. His magic is spent in the making and he is left with none remaining. Hronomon becomes the new Shrongelin and maintains the shield. Another Gha-Nomord steps forward and becomes the new Hronomon. The Shrongelin is Guardian, as I am the Forerunner. That is sufficient naming for both of us."

"What happens to me when the Shrongelin's magic is spent?" Allabva wondered aloud.

"The bond fades. You go back to being a normal human."

"So if we survive, it is possible that I could go back home?" Allabva asked hopefully.

"Yes, it is possible. I cannot say how feasible or how much you will desire it at that time, but it is a possibility."

This lifted Allabva's spirits. She stood up straighter and it felt easier to keep pace with Hronomon, now that she had a specifically articulated prospect of returning home again.

"How long does it take for, you know, for the old Shrongelin to regain his magic after he renews Sacalai's prison?" Allabva asked tentatively.

Hronomon let the question hang in the air, walking in silence, taking in the endless waves of grass. At length he answered.

"He does not."

Allabva blinked, processing this, considering the implications. "So that's why there has to be a new Shrongelin."

Hronomon gave no response.

"And a new Hronomon, too," Allabva mulled.

She felt that he was still withholding something.

"Does it...does losing all his magic kill the Shrongelin?"

"No, though it might as well. He survives the resealing, though his magic is spent in the process. He becomes a husk, no longer a true Nomord."

"Oh."

This dampened Allabva's spirits. She walked in silence, snacking on her provisions as she needed and hoping that Hronomon wasn't forced to dwell on the subject because of her questions. It seemed to be most likely the best thing at the moment for her to just walk in silence.

The afternoon waned on and Allabva's water ran low again. Thinking of needing to refill her waterskin made her wonder if they might find a well. "Are there any towns along this road? We took a fork back in midmorning at that stand of trees, and I'm not familiar with this route. Will we find a well somewhere?"

"Perhaps. A well, or some other water, we will find."

His mood seemed less serious now, perhaps lightened by the fact that they had covered some good ground today.

"Have you not traveled this road before?"

"No, but I have seen both ends of it. I took this road to avoid meeting other travelers. You'll see that it is not well maintained because it is not heavily used. So far, we have successfully not met other travelers on this route."

"So you don't know where water is."

"No, I do not. But I know how you humans are, so I would be surprised not to find some viable water source."

That seemed to make sense to Allabva.

"But how soon would that be?"

She hoped it would not be too long before they encountered some.

Hronomon shook his mane in what Allabva guessed was his equivalent of a shrug.

Allabva silently walked along beside him. The dryness in her throat made talking unpleasant, anyway.

Chapter 9

Cold Sleep

Eventually night came and Allabva's fatigue peaked with the disappearing of the sun. They had found a well not long after their conversation, where Allabva had filled and emptied her waterskin twice, then filled it again the third time.

Allabva's feet felt almost numb from the leagues she had walked this day, and her eyelids heavy from being awake since the early hours back home. Hronomon insisted that they continue pressing forward until they found a copse of trees. There, they could hide their presence from anybody else, if others traveled along this road at night.

Allabva curled up at the foot of one of the trees, holding her cloak around herself, trying to use it as a blanket.

"Do the Gha-Nomord sleep?"

"Yes, but we do not need as much of it as you do. I will sleep, but expect me to rouse you again before light."

"But there's nobody here to hide our departure from."

"There are leagues to cover before we reach the Shrongelin."

"How long will it take?"

"At your pace today, I think it will take us eight or nine days. Today, then seven or eight more."

"If my feet hold up."

Allabva realized she should keep a close watch on the well-being of her feet while she was on the road. She sat up, removing her boots. Before taking off her socks, she opened her bag and put away the socks she had taken off in the afternoon and aired out since then. Then she pulled out her next fresh pair of socks, using them to replace the socks she had been wearing. She tied the pair which she had just removed outside her bag to air out. Finally, she put her boots back on to keep as much warmth as she could during the night. Then she lay back down and pulled her cloak overheard, leaving only a gap for air.

In this position she spent the night, trying to use her arm as a pillow and shivering in the cold. Three or four times she woke up, closing the air hole in her cloak in order to retain the warmth of her breath, opening it again only when the staleness of the air overwhelmed her.

When Hronomon woke Allabva, she was both sorely still in need of more sleep, and relieved that it was time to stop the frustrating effort of trying to get sleep under these conditions. They set off again After Allabva kicked a hole in the dirt with the toe of her boot, took care of her morning business while Hronomon stood on the opposite side of the copse, and covered it up again. Allabva continued suffering with the sleepiness in her eyes for a time after they started walking, so she didn't feel inclined to speak in the beginning.

As the sky began to fill with light over the horizon ahead of them, Allabva woke up more, and her mind became more active.

"Is there any way we could invert our traveling schedule?" she asked Hronomon.

"Invert in what way?"

"The hours."

"You want to travel at night?"

"Yes. Really, I want to sleep during the day. It's too cold at night. My sleep was very poor and I am carrying over some of yesterday's fatigue into today."

Hronomon's horse-like eyes appeared contemplative. "It may be for the best. The danger with traveling at night is that we will constantly be coming upon that which we do not so easily see. But if you need to travel at night in order to keep your pace, then that may be what we need to do. But if we begin a new schedule this afternoon, I do not think we can afford that much of a delay."

"Perhaps we can start it with naps? Maybe we can do just a few hours this afternoon, and then continue on our way."

"Very well," Hronomon responded. "This afternoon, you can sleep in the warmth."

"Thank you."

"In the meantime, I think we should spread apart from each other. There is danger in being recognized as traveling together, human and Nomord. Keep walking this pace along this road. I will wander as the Ta-Nomord do, but although I may not always be within sight, I will keep myself near enough."

"Alright," Allabva breathed.

Walking by herself might get lonely.

As Hronomon turned to prance off into the grass to their left, Allabva thought she would really like a certain young man's company along this walk. With that thought she remembered the flute Delgan had given her, still hanging around her neck. She had forgotten to leave it with her mother to return to him!

She pulled it out of her shirt now and removed the chain from around her neck. As she walked on still, she looked to her left and saw Hronomon trotting through the tall grass, meandering toward a lone tree as if to investigate it. Allabva looked back at the flute in her hands, turning it over again to inspect all sides. It had an empty bore from the bottom up to a stopper in the top. The stopper had a hole through which one breathed, and immediately below the stopper on the front was a vent with a wedge at the bottom. Below the vent there were tone holes that she practiced covering with her fingers. Then, admiring the silver sheen, she looked at the back and traced the engraved lines with one finger.

"I *will* make it back to this place," she voiced aloud.

Deciding that she didn't need Hronomon's permission to make gentle noises while ostensibly traveling alone, Allabva held the flute up and spoke willfully, though Delgan hadn't said that her tone of voice was important.

"Beware the wolves."

The same sweet tune rolled forth out of the little flute, and Allabva listened to it closely. It was both pure and haunting, and the music made her feel like it spoke of days past and yet looked with hope to the future.

Allabva cast a glance over toward Hronomon. She thought he had lifted his head sharply a moment after the music began, but he was too far away in the tall grass for her to see clearly if he was looking at her. At least he wasn't standing still, so if he did disapprove, it must not have been a very great issue.

Allabva had an idea. Maybe this expedition need not seem so monotonous, nor lonely. Perhaps she could feel as if Delgan were there with her. She placed her walking stick under one armpit to free up both of her hands.

"Beware of the wolves," she spoke again, and repeated it as soon as the music had started.

Holding the memory of the first note in her mind, she brought the flute to her lips and blew. It didn't match the pitch she held in her mind. She put her fingers down to cover all the tone holes, then tried it again. She lifted fingers until she found the same pitch as the one that started Delgan's grandmother's song.

Once she had the first note, she held the flute firmly in her hand again and spoke the phrase to activate the song once more. As it began, she quickly stopped it, then brought the flute to her mouth and found the second pitch.

In this manner Allabva passed the morning, and as she learned additional notes, she had to start from the top playing the song to ensure she could remember everything she learned.

Not all notes were equally easy to find. She quickly discovered that there were not enough tone holes on the flute to produce the different pitches that appeared in the song. She had to find combinations involving leaving a higher hole open, or half covered, while covering lower holes along the body of the flute.

It worked to some extent. Allabva found that the music, the last tune she'd heard at home, helped her feel closer to her family and everyone else in the Cleft despite the distance. She thanked Delgan for that. At one point she was reminded how she was standing him up for their dinner engagement, which made her lament the journey she had begun, feeling resentment toward Hronomon. She mentally corrected herself; Hronomon wasn't at fault, nor was the Shrongelin. It was Sacalai's doing that made it necessary.

Having disturbed her own practice flow, Allabva put the flute away under her shirt and pulled out some of the food she had brought with her. As she did so, she looked at the collection she had brought and did a tally in her mind of what she had consumed the previous day, then divided her remaining supplies by that amount in her mind. This ought to last about five more days. It was unfortunate that she would need to find food somewhere on the way, but that was the reality.

Allabva was finishing her meal on the go for now and putting the rest of her food away in her bag when Hronomon trotted up.

"You walk faster when you're playing that whistle. Good work."

"Thank you." Allabva guessed it was because it lifted her spirits. She hadn't noticed she was walking any faster.

Hronomon didn't seem to be in the mood for chit chat. "We're nearing a couple of towns. It is more likely now that you'll meet travelers on the way. If they raise conversation, I suggest you tell them you're from Palf Glen. Your family farms rye. That's generic enough in this region that nobody should question it, and it's far enough away that they will be less likely to think you may know somebody they know."

"Wouldn't that be lying?"

"Yes, is that an issue for you?"

His question was matter-of-fact and didn't sound accusatory in any way.

"I'm not used to telling falsehoods. I just like to be who I am."

"And I commend you for that. But you're going up against Sacalai, the greatest evil this world has known. Any measure taken to guarantee success would be justified. It would be no great crime to protect yourself."

Allabva didn't expect this interpretation of morality from one of the Nomord.

"I agree that there's nothing wrong with protecting myself. I'm not sure that means it's alright to suppose I can take the reins on what's right and wrong. Or to suppose that even you can take the reins."

"I see. I'll romp along closer to you while we are near settlements if there's a higher risk you may come under danger."

Hronomon paused talking for a moment while falling into step beside Allabva, then elaborated.

"I have to admit that although it may prove inconvenient, I like the way you think. Do not assume that what I tell you is always the right thing. I promise not to guide you astray intentionally, and I like to think that I have a fair handle on right and wrong at my age, but you should still run everything through your own moral checks."

Allabva wasn't sure how to reply to what sounded like a compliment of character coming from an immortal magical beast.

"Then I promise to continue to speak frankly."

"Good. Don't stop. Who knows, but we may need your perspective. Play that flute some more and keep the pace up while you walk."

"Wait," Allabva said, sensing that Hronomon was about to meander off again, "if the Ta-Nomord couldn't see you, then why were you able to see her?"

"I am not entirely sure. Perhaps you should ask the Shrongelin when you meet him. Apparently, that aspect of the shield goes one way only. Perhaps there are other aspects that go the other way, of which I am unaware."

"Some more things you have forgotten?"

"I'm afraid so. Like the bond," he added.

"Yes, you told me about the bond. You forgot how."

"Yes. That is something the world must hope that the Shrongelin has remembered. It is something that he had to forget also when he was Hronomon."

"I guess I can see that," Allabva conceded. "How does it feel to know about something, and know that you have forgotten it yourself?"

"It feels...awry. But awry is not a new feeling to the Nomord. It has been part of our existence ever since we founded Sacalai's prison. We had to change the nature of our existence to put that shield in place. Nothing has been fully right since then."

Hronomon's voice sounded forlorn, missing something significant.

"When we rebuild her prison, are we really fixing things?"

"As much as can be hoped," Hronomon replied weakly.

"Is it possible that the Shrongelin won't remember how to perform the bond?"

"It is always possible. So far, every Shrongelin has remembered it."

"And if he doesn't?"

"Ruin reigns. Sacalai will break free from her prison and rule the world with armies and terror."

"But people would fight against her. The Nomord would fight against her, right?"

She paused, thinking.

"But *can* the Nomord fight if the Ta-Nomord cannot even see the Gha-Nomord? Can you work together if you're invisible to them?"

"Of course some people will fight against her, but others will be bent by the influence that she wields over their minds. The Nomord will fight against Sacalai and her followers to the last beast among us."

"And what about the Gha-Nomord and Ta-Nomord?"

"When the prison falls, as it eventually will, we Gha-Nomord will no longer be locked inside the outer shield, and the Ta-Nomord will not be trapped on the outside. The Ta-Nomord will regain full faculty of their minds, ready and capable to join the fight."

"That's good news," Allabva said.

Hronomon nodded and said, "We will be able to commune once more, but we would gladly give that up again in order to reconstruct the prison. But our power is already dedicated to the Shrongelin and Hronomon. If the Shrongelin forgets the bond when he must create it, that does not break the Construct. Instead, it simply leaves him powerless to re-found the prison. Unable to fight mightily enough to even survive to that point, perhaps."

"But you say that every Shrongelin so far has remembered," Allabva stated as fact, waiting for Hronomon to confirm.

"Yes. Otherwise, you would not have been able to grow up in peace as you did. The world would already be in chaos ages ago."

"How long ago did Sacalai take power? How many Shrongelins have there been?"

"That... I do not remember."

Hronomon did not offer anything else.

"Can we really win this?"

"Of course, young one. We have re-imprisoned Sacalai successfully every time so far, haven't we?"

Allabva found this encouraging to think about.

"So, it's like a recipe."

"A recipe?"

"Oh. I guess the Nomord don't cook, do you? When we make bread, we have a recipe. A set of instructions. If you do it wrong, the bread turns out flat, or too salty, or something else. As long as you follow the instructions correctly, you'll get good bread."

"Then yes, it is like a recipe. As long as we follow the pattern set in the Construct, we will successfully re imprison Sacalai and the world will be safe until the cycle repeats."

This was comforting.

"Alright, so I just need to hurry along and meet the Shrongelin first, and we'll go from there?"

"That is correct. Now, if you'll excuse me, I must stop walking alongside you when we may encounter people. Play your flute and walk fast."

"Wait," Allabva said again, thinking of Mellier's fascination with stories. "You exist, which I hadn't supposed before. What about the Nightshade Unicorn? Does he...does he serve Sacalai?"

Hronomon snorted in derision.

"I have heard of these tales. The Nightshade Unicorn is a concept, an idea. There is no Nightshade beast to fear. Excuse me."

Saying nothing more, Hronomon meandered off into the tall grass on the south side of the road.

As Allabva watched him go, she wondered about the accuracy of saying that remaking the prison meant the world would be safe, if there was still a certainty that Sacalai would return again. It seemed to her that they would never be settled unless Sacalai were finished off.

According to Hronomon, each cycle used up one of the Nomord. How long would it be until they were all gone? If the Ta-Nomord couldn't see the Gha-Nomord, she didn't think there could be any new Nomord created to take the place of the long line of Shrongelins. Eventually, there wouldn't be any Gha-Nomord who still had magic left to step into the roles of Hronomon and Shrongelin. Did this mean that Sacalai would inevitably win the final day?

Troubled, Allabva tried putting the flute to her lips again to learn its haunting song. She found she was still distracted by the desire to puzzle out some better way through the eternal crisis with Sacalai. She listened to music instead, activating the enchanted flute's ability to play itself, listening to the tune time after time.

Allabva almost tripped over her own boots when she was pulled out of her reverie by a group of people coming slowly her way. She should have seen them when they were still farther away.

"Beware the wolves," she muttered, holding the flute in front of her and stopping the music.

Then she immediately brought it to her mouth and tried to play its song manually, placing her fingers over the holes the best she could remember after her study this morning. Hopefully, the other people were far enough away that they wouldn't notice it wasn't Allabva playing the flute at first. She'd rather avoid any questions that might lead conversation toward any single-horned equine creatures.

She walked with some trepidation and put the flute away to greet the party as they neared. On second view, it was easy to tell now that the party was traveling in the same direction as Allabva, but she was walking faster and thus would overtake them soon. She looked all around for Hronomon and spotted him in the distance to the south, watching her. She hoped he was close enough in case there turned out to be trouble.

She continued forward. She saw that they appeared to be a family: a man, woman, and two boys who appeared close in age to each other, and both a little older than Mellier. One of them dragged a small two-wheeled cart behind him with one hand. The boys noticed her walking up behind the family, one of them commenting to the other and pointing back.

"Hello," Allabva said, waving.

There was no sense in losing her manners just because she was trying to stop the end of the civilized world.

The mother and father turned to look, then waved back.

"Hello," the mother replied. "Where are you headed?"

"Heading east, toward Palf Glen."

"Business or pleasure?" the father said.

"Business," Allabva replied. "I'm not entirely sure if I'll end up near Palf Glen, or if I'll wind up heading beyond it."

This was true. She didn't know where her destination was, and she wasn't certain how long Hronomon thought it would take her to walk to Palf Glen.

"Are you traveling all alone, a young woman on the road?" The mother asked.

"No. My escort is much faster than I am, though, and he likes to step off the trail. He veered off, going toward the south a while ago. I'm sure he can't be too far. He actually may have gotten ahead of me."

Allabva could see genuine concern in their faces relax a little when they heard that she had somebody, at least, ostensibly watching over her. She didn't slacken her pace during this conversation.

"And where are you going?" she returned the question, curious as well.

"Parfall," the mother answered. "It's a lot closer than Palf Glen. We're coming home from my sister's wedding in Littonwelt, half a day southwest of here."

"Congratulations to her," Allabva said with a smile. "Was it a good reception?"

"Fiewren was involved," the father pointed at the mother, "so it was complicated."

"Banduchy, stop it," the woman laughed, hitting him on the arm. "Honestly, what am I supposed to do with you? Soon enough, the boys will pick up making this kind of remark from you?"

She looked at Allabva again, who was now walking backward to continue the conversation, having passed by them.

"Yes, it was very lovely, if I do say so myself."

"It's true, it was indeed lovely," Banduchy conceded. "There was so much food, we had to take some with us. It was lucky that Amarkal insisted on bringing his little cart to carry travel supplies. But it was complicated," he laughed as he blocked another blow.

"Are you in such a hurry?" Fiewren asked as the gap between them and Allabva widened.

"I suppose I kind of am."

"Safe travels, then. Have a nice day!"

"You as well!" The conversation ended at an elevated volume, then Allabva turned around to walk forward, and pressed on. She pulled the flute out from under her shirt and kept playing.

CHAPTER 10

IN THE COOL SHADE

When she felt the heat of the day beating down on the back of her neck, Allabva was struck with sleepiness. The truncated sleep of her last night at home was followed by the cold, interrupted dreams of last night, and it was taking its toll. As if on cue, Hronomon showed up again, stepping out of the tall grass and onto the trail.

"Hronomon, I think it's my sleep time," Allabva drawled. "I'm certainly feeling the need for it."

"Yes, I thought it was probably about that time. Let's find you a safe spot."

Hronomon led her off the trail and, in the middle of tall grasses, he lay and rolled to flatten the patch. Nobody could see it from the road, and there would be no reason to go looking for it. Allabva stretched out, using her bag as a pillow. She set the walking stick aside and wrapped herself in her cloak, similar to last night's accommodations. She was asleep before she realized it.

Allabva was awoken by the sound of human voices talking and a gentle nudge at her shoulder. The sun was gone in the west, though its light still shone in the sky.

"Good evening," Fiewren smiled down at her.

"How..." Allabva managed to say, quickly sitting up and trying to blink the sleep away.

She grabbed her bag and stick, standing.

"We followed a Nomord here!" One of the young boys supplied eagerly.

Allabva looked back, mouth agape.

"It didn't say anything," Fiewren explained. "It wandered up and looked at us curiously. It kept wandering off and then back to the road until it left the road only a little and waited for us to follow. Bit by bit, it brought us here. Apparently, it found you and was concerned for you. Are you alright?"

Allabva blinked again, then squinted at Fiewren. She wondered about Hronomon's motives if he had brought them here.

"I guess so. Was there anything else noticeable about this Nomord that led you to me?"

"No, that's about it. Odd behavior, I'd say."

"Are you sure you're alright?" Banduchy said. "Why were you sleeping during the day? Are you ill?"

"No, I'm not ill. It's just that I set out traveling light. Turns out I wasn't prepared for the chill of the night, so I decided to keep myself warm at night by walking, and that way the sun can warm me while I sleep."

She didn't mention that it was also supposed to decrease the likelihood of encountering strangers on the road.

"Alright. I can respect that. I'm sorry we woke you, but it seemed the correct thing because of how that Nomord brought us here."

"That is fine. I needed to get up sometime, didn't I? Waking me up now will probably help me swap day for night a little faster. Anyway, I suppose I'll be going on my way."

Allabva placed her bag over her head and shoulder and held her walking stick in one hand.

"Wait," Fiewren said. "We were going to camp soon for the night. Won't you join us around a warm fire and wedding leftovers?"

"I need to hit the road."

"Please, I insist. Banduchy told you there was too much food; some of it will spoil before we reach home."

Allabva *was* hungry. If she shared some of their food, then her trail provisions would last her that much longer. If Hronomon objected to this, then he could make himself known to her to let her know. They seemed like good people, and after finding her asleep and helpless, all they did was wake her up and offer to share their food with her.

"Very well. I'm in, as long as it doesn't take too much time away from my journey."

"You really do want to hit the road, don't you? What's your name?" Fiewren awaited an answer with kind eyes, too kind to lie to.

"Allabva." She was under no obligation to provide that much, let alone any more. She still felt bad holding back.

"Well, come on. Let's find a good spot for a fire. We can't do it here in the middle of this grass. This spot is too dry despite the spring rains. We'll move out onto the road and find a spot from there."

Allabva joined them in their walk back to the road. They continued east for a few minutes before finding a spot that appeared to have been used for campfires before, as it was cleared of vegetation in a ring surrounding what looked to be a pile of ash. There were even a couple of large rocks to the side of it, ready to be reused as stools.

The other boy, not Amarkal, was currently dragging the cart behind him. He pulled it into the circle and set down the handle of the cart, lowering it slowly while at the same time catching anything that threatened to fall off the cart as he tipped it down.

Banduchy reached the cart and unloaded a leather case, from which he extracted a hatchet.

"We knew we would camp on our way to Littonwelt and back, but Amarkal's cart does make it easier to carry supplies. I was going to bring this hatchet anyway, but I didn't anticipate bringing back so much food. Amarkal, Ambinos, go and find some wood, will you?"

The two boys didn't have to be told twice to go forage if it was going to produce a campfire. As they wandered off to find some trees that may have dropped limbs, Banduchy took a few more items from the leather case and started roughing up some tree bark to use as kindling.

"I hope you like the spread," Fiewren told Allabva, proceeding to remove several small bundles from the cart, unwrapping them and placing some sausages and cheese in a frying pan. "It's not as fresh as it was at the reception, of course, but some of it should liven up with a bit of heat."

"Sounds good to me," Allabva smiled. "The only supplies I brought with me were selected because they'll last several days on the road, not because they were delicious to begin with. I'm sure wedding fare will be different, no matter what you brought."

"It's the least we can do for a lone traveler."

Fiewren blinked and looked at Allabva.

"One second. You said you weren't alone. Where is your companion? You were napping alone, just like you were walking alone."

Allabva opened her mouth to say she wasn't certain where her companion was, but Fiewren didn't give her a chance to speak.

"You know what? You never mind that. I won't pry into that. If you're giving us a line you prepared beforehand in order to make people think you're not defenseless, I will let you hold to your story. If it's true, then I'm not going to make any judgments about your escort just because he likes to stay out of sight of strangers. Just, do please be careful on the road. You never know who you'll meet with."

"I—thank you." Allabva felt validated that these were good people that she had fallen in with.

"I will, naturally, invite you to camp with us, and to travel with us as far as our routes coincide. You'll be safer with us than you would alone, or even with only a solitary escort."

"I'll second that," Banduchy added. "If you need anyone to travel with, here we are."

"I appreciate the offer, and I'll remember you for it," Allabva said. "But I'm guessing your boys won't travel as quickly as I need to, especially if they're pulling that cart. I have a little brother not too much younger than they are, so I know how it is."

"Yeah," Banduchy commiserated. "They get distracted and stop to look at a beetle or a rock they say is interesting even though it's a normal, boring rock. They decide they're tired one moment, even though the next moment you mention something they want to do and suddenly they found their energy again. They decide they're too hot to go as fast as you're going, even if you're the one pulling the cart and they just had water. Need I go on?"

"Yes, that's pretty much my brother to a tee," Allabva laughed out loud.

"No, come back," one of the boys whined as they approached the fire ring. "Mama, Amarkal took my stick."

"No, I didn't," Amarkal rebutted. "I picked it up."

"But I saw it first, and I already wanted to pick it up when you saw it."

Fiewren rolled her eyes.

"Banduchy, I was going to chide you for speaking negatively about them in front of Allabva, but I think they just exposed themselves. Ambinos, does it really matter? It's just a stick. Aren't we going to burn it, anyway?"

"Well, but I want to burn it. And I want to cook with it first. I want to whittle the point down and roast sausages over the fire with it."

"No, I want to," Amarkal butted in.

"I was talking to your brother."

As Fiewren handled the disagreement, Allabva felt a smile tugging at one side of her mouth. This was familiar. Good people had sides of themselves that they would rather not put on display in front of the world, but it was part of being human. People tried to figure the world out throughout their lives, and the way she saw this family playing it out reminded her that she was on a journey to ensure that life like this could keep happening. People learned. People grew. Allabva promised herself that this would continue.

A stick, of all things!

"Thank you, Amarkal, and thank you, Ambinos," Allabva butted in.

"For what?" Amarkal said.

"You reminded me that I have my own stick sitting in my lap. It's not a fire stick, but you reminded me that I wanted to whittle it down, too."

She looked at her walking stick, with its extra length beyond a marked bend in the wood, pulling her knife out of her bag. She continued her pitch to the boys.

"I'll tell you what, Ambinos. Would you like this piece? It traveled a day and a half to be united with you. I'll cut my walking stick here—" she notched the stick at the point where it bent, "—and you can have the rest for your fire stick. Then, do you think your brother can keep the stick he's holding right now?"

"Alright," Ambinos said, somewhat begrudgingly. Amarkal said nothing, but appeared placated.

Allabva used her knife to divide the stick where it bent, leaving her with a relatively straight staff to walk with. She handed the remainder to the boy, and he set to whittling one end of it to a fine point so he could stab sausages and other morsels with it.

By the time Banduchy had a fire going, Fiewren had sliced food into the frying pan and promptly set about heating it up as a pan fry. While she did that, Banduchy produced some different types of bread.

"Here we have some garlic-Littonish bread. The Littonish cheese was aged two years, then grated just before sprinkling on top of the dough. And some thyme-sage-rosemary sourdough. Some oregano-basil knots. We'll combine that one with a bit of smoked salmon."

Allabva was taken aback. "This meal sounds and smells too good. What can I do for you for your kindness?"

"Nothing," Fiewren refused flatly. "I already told you, some of this wouldn't even make it home with us before going bad. What can you do for us? Just enjoy it and stay safe out there."

Extracting the promise from Ambinos and Amarkal to stop sword fighting during dinner for the rest of their journey, Fiewren unpacked dessert for all five of them. They enjoyed their honey cakes with butter while the family got sleepy in the darkening evening.

"What music were you playing earlier?" Amarkal caught Allabva off guard with his sudden question.

"What?"

"What music was it? I didn't hear it clearly because you were far away. It sounded like a flute."

"Oh, you mean what I was playing on the road? I don't know what the song is called. I heard it from a friend."

"But where is your flute?"

"It's right here." Allabva grabbed the chain and pulled the flute out from its hiding place.

"Can you play for us?"

"Ammie, you can't just ask her to put on a performance for us," Fiewren corrected him.

"No, it's alright. If it will make him happy, then I'll be glad to. You've been kind to me. Although I must admit, I only started trying to figure out how to play this tune this morning. I'm not any good."

Allabva felt self-conscious, but she thought perhaps it might help his mother by getting him in the mood for bed.

"Yay!" Amarkal reveled.

Allabva put the flute to her lips, set her hands over the tone holes to produce the first note, and did her best not to disappoint. Her playing was halting because she did not immediately remember all the fingerings in order in the tune, but she thought she was still able to produce an overall pleasant sound.

"Mama, you know this song,"Ambinos said.

Allabva's eyebrows rose with delight, and she stopped playing. "You do? Do you know what it's called? I have only ever heard it on this flute."

Fiewren smiled ruefully at Ambinos.

"Yes, I do. It's called 'In the Cool Shade of the Mount.' I'll tell you what, boys. I'll sing it for you once, and then it's time for bed. Allabva, I'll reiterate that you're welcome to travel with us, although I'll admit we can't easily solve your problem of the chill at night because we don't have a spare bedroll for you to use. It's up to you."

Banduchy was untying the family's bedrolls from the cart while Fiewren cleaned up after dinner.

"Well, boys, will I have your cooperation?"

"Yes, Mother," Amarkal and Ambinos said.

Fiewren took some deep breaths, stretching her shoulders, then inhaled one more time and started to sing. Banduchy stopped what he was doing to listen. Apparently, Fiewren was known for being a good singer. Allabva prepared herself to capture the words and whole experience in memory, listening attentively as Fiewren sang "In the Cool Shade of the Mount":

> In the cool shade of the mount,
> My love came to call in the morning, (to me)
> And I knew not when he'd return,
> So I held him forever that day.

Take me there, through the ash and pine,
Take me there, to the desert or sea,
Wherever you go, do not leave me here,
I will not be parted from thee.

O'er the deepest, bluest sea,
My love went to sail in the morning, set free,
And I stayed all alone in the shade,
Wishing I could share his embrace.

Take me there, through the ash and pine,
Take me there, to the desert or sea,
Wherever you go, do not leave me here,
I will not be parted from thee.

In the darkest, fiercest war,
My love was affrighted to leave me, (weeping)
And I feared he might cease to be,
And could never come back home to me.

Take me there, through the ash and pine,
Take me there, to the desert or sea,
Wherever you go, do not leave me here,
I will not be parted from thee.

In the cool shade of the mount,
My love came to call in the morning, (to me)
I had known not if he'd return,
So I held him forever that day.

> In the cool shade of the mount,
> My love came to call in the morning, (to me)
> And I knew not when he'd return,
> So I held him forever that day.

Stillness lay over the campsite when Fiewren stopped singing. A twig snapped at the edge of the ring, pulling Allabva out of her trance. She looked up to see Hronomon standing opposite her, behind Banduchy and Fiewren. "

That's the Nomo-Nomo that led us to you!" Amarkal proclaimed. "I can tell by the tufts at her ears."

"Honey," his mother addressed him, "Nomo-Nomo is the term we use for the Nomord when they are behaving in a silly manner that we don't understand. The proper term is Nomord. This one just showed up, not doing anything silly."

Hronomon didn't speak. He shook his head and his mane, then bobbed his head twice. Finally, he backed away from the ring and calmly walked in the direction of the road, disappearing in the shadows beyond the reach of the campfire's light. Allabva took this as a signal.

"I think it's time I head out and resume my journey. Thank you so much for this dinner, and for sharing your warm fire with me. It was all beautiful. I must be going."

"Not so fast," Fiewren contradicted. "Take some more leftovers with you. Eat these first, since you mentioned that your trail food should last a little longer."

She grabbed a few bundles and handed them to Allabva, helping her open her bag to put them in while she used her hands to put the flute away and also to pick up her walking staff.

Banduchy had been watching Hronomon vanish in the darkness with a thoughtful face.

"Allabva, I'm not trying to pry, but if you have any connection to the Nomord then you need to be careful on the road these days."

"Why is that? I don't see the connection."

Why would she need to be more careful if she had a connection with the Nomord?

"Well, everything gets political, doesn't it? If you mention loud enough that you like apples, somewhere there's somebody who will ask you why you hate strawberries. Anyway, there are people who dislike the Nomord."

"Why would anybody dislike the Nomord? They're always happy and they never hurt anybody."

Banduchy continued the thought, "And it's not uncommon to see one, and they have the ability to heal, and sometimes if one decides to sleep in your fields then your crop turns out well, to see enough of them you can probably expect good weather, can't you?"

"Yes, but those all sound like reasons to like them."

Allabva liked the Nomord for all those reasons, and because they appeared to have such a gentle disposition.

"Correct. But when do they do these things? When do they act benevolently toward people? When do they do us these special favors?"

Banduchy spread his hands wide to invite Allabva to give a definitive answer to his questions. He appeared almost menacing because at the moment he happened to bring up this topic of conversation, he held the hatchet in his hand, being in the middle of cleaning up.

Allabva thought only for a moment, frowning. They weren't difficult questions to answer in a certain fashion.

"When they want to?" she intoned as a question, thinking it obvious enough. "There's never any rhyme or reason to it. It appears to occur by happenstance."

"Right you are. But have you ever really thought to wonder why it's like that?"

His eyes were wide and his voice was soft, as if he were speaking ill of his mother while she was asleep in the same room.

"Well—" Allabva started.

"Bandy, please don't tell me that you're into this line of thinking," Fiewren interrupted. He didn't look at her, continuing to speak to Allabva.

"There are those who ask these questions. We call the Nomord 'Nomo-Nomo' when they are silly, but we consider them simply to be silly and fickle creatures most of the time. There are those who think they are unkind, perhaps even malicious."

"Why would anybody believe the Nomord are malicious?" Allabva asked, incredulous.

"They think the creatures *like* to know that we suffer. That they help us from time to time just to show us what they *can* do, so we feel the difference more when they hold back."

"Bandy..."

"Don't worry, Fiewren. I don't buy in. I still love seeing the Nomord. But Allabva, you need to watch out for these Disaffected. I've heard of them even gathering together and wishing they could kill some of the Nomord. If they think you might have some connection to the Nomord, they might not take too kindly to you."

"Bandy, I love you, but this is all nonsense. I want you to be careful about what ideas you put in the boys' heads. Boys, don't stop getting ready for bed."

"Agreed, Fie. I'll stop. Just be careful, Allabva. Be safe." Banduchy resumed putting things away for the night.

Allabva wondered how much Banduchy or his family had inferred about Hronomon and her from him having led them to her. There was nothing to be done about it though, apart from hope that they were as good people as they seemed to be.

"Thank you, Fiewren, Banduchy, Ambinos, and Amarkal. I will remember all of you. I will be careful."

Allabva stepped away from the firelight, mentally reviewing the words to the song. "In the Cool Shade of the Mount," she now knew it to be. The formerly nameless tune became even more significant in her mind, now that it was attached to a story that was so heavy and uplifting at the same time.

She herself had left her mother and brother, people she loved, not knowing when she'd return. Facing danger in a large, cold world. And she thought of Brel and Delgan, too. Their presence in the last couple of days before she disappeared into the night felt like it cemented their presence in her mind. She hoped this mission could all go away, that she could go back to her quiet life. That her worries could be as quaint as hoping to have somebody to "hold forever" someday. Maybe that could be Delgan?

Chapter 11

Resume March

Allabva resumed her eastward journey once she was back on the road. Hronomon joined her shortly after.

"It sounds like you enjoyed your dinner."

"Oh yes, I most certainly did."

She smiled at Hronomon, feeling rested and well fed. Apart from the parting admonition to beware the Disaffected, it had been quite a positive encounter.

"Good. I'm glad."

His voice was flat, however.

"You led them to me, didn't you?"

"That, I did."

"Why? Aren't you suspicious of every unknown factor potentially trying to frustrate our progress?"

"I am."

He stopped talking and a chorus of nighttime insects that had been singing the entire time took over Allabva's hearing, gently punctuated by the tap of her walking staff on the packed earth at her feet. She wasn't satisfied with Hronomon's terse reply.

"Then why did you do it?"

"A few reasons."

But he offered none, only walking. Allabva determined that she would get him to open up more before the end of their journey together.

"Like what?"

"You need your food to last you longer. I followed them for a time and they seem to be good people, so I thought it likely they might share with you. You need human interaction. They provided that. Most importantly, they were other people, which meant you are not alone. I could keep my distance from you and yet you were protected by the presence of others."

"I guess you could tell they were good people the same way you said you were drawn to me?"

"No. I no longer have that gift. That comes to the Hronomon as part of the Construct, and only functions until a Companion has been identified. All Nomord have a weaker version of that sight—I still have that—but it requires touch. No, I was not completely certain they were safe, but it seemed most likely because they had healthy children."

Allabva cocked her head. "Because they had healthy children?"

"Yes, healthy and generally happy. I have observed that adults who have children who are well cared for tend to do exactly that, they care for their children. They find themselves less interested in wishing to do harm to others. It's not perfect across the board, but I've found it to be a helpful guideline."

"And if you were wrong this time?"

"I can easily overpower a family of four. I watched them carefully the entire time."

"Then how did they make me any safer than just having you around?"

"I already told you that. They provided a visible deterrent to trouble. I need to stay out of sight. I could stop most trouble, but it's more likely to start if you look like you're alone to begin with."

"Oh."

"Keep your pace up. Maybe you shouldn't play the flute in the dark. You need to watch your step. Also, you hazard coming upon other travelers who would hear you well ahead of time."

"But the road is rather flat and the crickets are rather loud. I think I'll be fine. Can't you scout ahead as well, since you prefer that I not appear to be traveling with you?"

Hronomon sighed, a half-neigh sound that Allabva found interesting. She had never heard any Nomo-Nomo sigh before.

"Very well. Play if you like, as long as it helps you keep your pace up. I thought it would be a good idea for you to spend some time with other humans and to share their food, but you should remember that we are on a mission with a critical deadline. Do not slow down."

Hronomon broke into a trot and Allabva watched him grow farther ahead of her.

Rather than pulling Delgan's flute out immediately, Allabva reviewed the lyrics she had heard Fiewren sing. She had already thought the tune was beautiful before, but now she decided that the entire song was even more so than she had realized. Thus, Allabva walked forward briskly, singing to herself and repeating every part of the song to make sure she would never forget it.

When her voice had grown hoarse from singing, she drank from her waterskin, then tucked her staff under her arm and pulled out Delgan's flute. Trying to stave off the creepy sensation of walking alone in the chill of the night, she played softly to herself. First, she played "In the Cool Shade of the Mount," then she decided to distract herself more strongly again by attempting to figure out the notes for other songs.

She tried "Five in the Morning, Five at Night." It was a child's song and had a rather simple tune. After noodling with different fingerings in time with the rhythm at the start of the tune, Allabva was able to find a combination that seemed to work to produce the correct intervals. She was happy with herself for having been able to discover the method to play this song, but she bored quickly of the repetitive motif.

Next she tried playing the Greenstones' Dance. She attempted the opening of the tune several times, experimenting with different fingerings and searching for the intervals between the notes that would make the tune sound right. Unfortunately, she wasn't able to produce it. She had no reference to get started, as she had used with the flute's enchanted tune. After some time filled with nothing but repeated failed attempts, she gave up.

Allabva walked, her staff tapping the ground in time with her step, trying not to think of what ills may await her in the dark. She knew Hronomon was out there in the night, but knowing that he was there was not as comforting as having him right by her side. She tried not to think of the Disaffected, whom Banduchy had claimed would wish her harm if they discovered she had any connection to one of the Nomord.

Tap, tap, tap, went her staff.

Crickets replied with their unending song.

"How long is this journey?" she asked herself.

The crickets again answered in the same chirps as before.

"What is Sacalai like?"

Tap, tap, tap, chirp, chirp, chirp.

Allabva decided she could not continue all night like this. She pulled out the flute again.

"Beware the wolves."

The flute sang in its high-pitched tones as if it were played by a human, intoning obligingly its sweet song, communicating both a haunting sorrow and an indomitable optimism. The second sentiment only had half its intended effect on Allabva's heart right now, but she tried to open up and be swallowed in the intimated embrace, to bask in the warmth of the desired conclusion.

"Will you be there, Delgan?" she spoke aloud to the night.

Tap, tap, tap.

"Will you hold me like the song's love held her?"

Tap, tap, tap.

"I'm on a dangerous quest now. Will you forgive me for not showing up for dinner—"

She thought for a moment, having to dedicate her mind to calculating what day it was. She had lost track, having been whisked from her home by the Gha-Nomord who called himself Hronomon. Was it after midnight now?

She finished her calculation.

"—tomorrow night?"

Tap, tap, tap, chirp, chirp, chirp.

The flute finished its song, playing only the verse, the chorus, and the verse again. Allabva swallowed hard.

"Beware the wolves."

The flute started over.

Tap, tap, tap.

"What kind of dangers will this journey really bring me?"

Thieves? Wild animals? Starvation? Sacalai? What kind of danger was she?

Chirp, chirp, chirp.

Allabva lowered her voice.

"What dangers will tonight bring me?"

Winter fever? Frostbite?

Tap, tap, tap.

"Mother, Mellier, will you still be safe? Will the orchard be heavy with fruit when I come home?"

Chirp, chirp, chirp.

Needing to break the mood, Allabva sang along with the flute's melody, choosing to review the chorus and the final verse, trying to internalize them to the fullest. She modified the lyrics, seeing fit to adapt them to her situation.

> Take me there, through the ash and pine,
> Take me there, to the desert or sea,
> Wherever I go, I'll not leave you there,
> I will not be parted from thee.

> In the cool shade of the mount,
> My love came to call in the morning, (to me)
> And I know not when I'll return,
> I will hold you forever that day.

Tap, tap, tap, sniffle.

Allabva caught herself tearing up, confronted by the reality of vast uncertainty greeting her in every moment since she left home. She wiped the tears from her eyes with her sleeve, then restarted the flute to play as comforting background music.

"Beware the wolves."

Allabva rummaged in her bag and pulled out her gloves, keeping her fingers warm. The frosty night seemed colder than it should have been.

Allabva saw Hronomon approaching from ahead. She stopped the music and returned the flute to its hiding place inside her blouse.

"Allabva," he addressed her flatly.

"Yes?"

"What did that man talk to you about after I showed myself outside the ring and then waited for you on the road?"

"He said there were people that he called the Disaffected. He said they wouldn't like it if they knew I had any connection to one of the Nomord. Why do you ask?"

"Because it's too cold."

"What does the weather have to do with the Disaffected? Will they blame you for the weather?"

"Perhaps indirectly. All the same, I blame them likewise, indirectly."

Allabva waited for an explanation, looking at Hronomon as if he were crazy. Hronomon snorted, then supplied his explanation.

"Sacalai has too much influence in this world. She should not have so much yet. The fact that these Disaffected are known to exist belies a stronger grip on men's hearts than Sacalai should have yet. This means we are likely under a greater urgency than the Shrongelin or I had realized."

"What does this have to do with the weather?"

"Your race is so forgetful," Hronomon accused. "Human lives are so short that you do not remember the most basic things about my kind."

Allabva confronted him. This wasn't fair.

"That's not my individual fault. I've learned what I can, haven't I? The Ta-Nomord can heal, the Gha-Nomord can confer strength, but it requires a bond... And I've been trying to learn more from you. You need to open—"

"You know that the Ta-Nomord can encourage plant growth," Hronomon interrupted, giving in to answer her question about the weather. "The Gha-Nomord cannot do that directly, cannot directly influence plant life or crop growth. We can help in a way, because we can influence the elements. It is not absolute, and it is rather localized. In the days before the Construct, we could band together with the Ta-Nomord and achieve great positive effects to benefit both human and Nomord. We cannot combine to achieve those effects because of the Construct, but I should have been able to keep you warm at night. At least, warmer than tonight."

Allabva was struck.

"You can influence the weather?"

"Yes, to a limited degree, but so can Sacalai. If she can cast her influence into the world and keep the night this cold against my will, then the hazard presented by the Disaffected is greater than I anticipated. You must travel faster."

"I'm not sure I can do that. You told me to set a sustainable pace, and I am."

"Then exceed your sustainable pace. We must meet the Shrongelin with the greatest haste. I will continue to watch the road ahead."

Hronomon trotted forward, swallowed up again in the blackness and chill of the night. Watching him go, Allabva stumbled and then caught herself. Her false step was caused by unevenness in the road. She hadn't noticed it while focusing on the music, especially under the cover of darkness, but the landscape was starting to change. Now there were more trees, more frequently spotting the plain. Likewise, the plain itself was giving way to gently rolling hills.

Now distracted from her premonitions of doom by wanting to take in the interesting view despite the obscurity of night, Allabva started to feel hungry again. She fed on her provisions as she walked and wondered how she was supposed to go faster than her sustainable pace. By definition, she wouldn't be able to keep it up. Regardless, munching on wedding leftovers, she mentally took note of her speed and length of gait whenever she was traveling slightly downhill, then tried to maintain it when the road was level or went uphill.

She continued this the best she could through the night, nearly reaching a constant jog on the downhill and level patches and allowing herself to slow to a quick walk during any amount of climb. She listened to the flute's music on and off, while wondering to herself what sort of creature this Sacalai was, that the Nomord should fear her so. Allabva thought she was doing well to maintain an accelerated pace, but was apprehensive that she would need to sleep sooner. She was also concerned that her fatigue from tonight would still follow her after she slept. Nevertheless, she pressed on, not seeing Hronomon again for a good stretch.

Then it began to rain.

Part III: En Route

Chapter 12

Tripped

Jogging, holding her staff off the ground with one hand and keeping her bag steady with the other, Allabva pressed on through the night. Every time Hronomon showed up, he seemed to bring bad news, making her plight and the world's fate sound ever darker. If that were going to keep happening, then she would will herself reach her goal sooner, before everything could get too bad. She would wear herself to the bone in doing so, but if that was what it took, then so be it.

She had grown up believing that the Shrongelin was either the Creator of the world, or that he had some close connection with the Creator. Now she was told by one of the Nomord that the Shrongelin was just another Nomord. The Nomord were immortal, unless that was also a lie or misconception that her poor, wretched, short-lived class of beings called humans had misinformed her about...

The Nomord were immortal, as far as she knew, a species made up entirely of benign individuals, but that still meant the Shrongelin was far less powerful than she had supposed.

So, the Shrongelin was Nomord. And he had a partner called Hronomon, but apparently both of these were titles, meaning something along the lines of guardian and forerunner. Did they even have proper names? And if these were titles, and all that Hronomon was using to speak of himself and of the Shrongelin, was Sacalai a title as well? What was it supposed to mean?

And now this Sacalai had apparently surprised Hronomon with her ability to influence the weather while she was still in prison. What else could Hronomon be unaware of, or be wrong about?

No, Allabva reassessed. The situation didn't get worse only when Hronomon showed up to give more news. It seemed to be getting worse right now as she simply thought about it.

"Did it have to be me?" she panted. "Why couldn't he have found somebody closer to where I'm going?"

She jogged on, trying to strike a careful balance between lifting her knees to lengthen her stride, and conserving energy by not going too fast.

She was glad to be moving quickly; it kept her warm. With the weather being much colder than it should be, her fingers would have been freezing without the exercise to make her heart pump. But the rain, although not heavy, was starting to make the dirt of the road into mud, which she was then kicking up onto her boots and her cloak as she jogged.

"Doesn't curly hair exempt me from having to travel in the rain?" Allabva asked the night.

It didn't reply.

"I could be courting now. I like this guy. I want to be back home," she complained.

Normally this pace would make her feel more alive, allowing her to cover ground somewhat quickly and yet not tire excessively. But tonight, with the threat of Sacalai's influence over her, she did not feel free to enjoy the sensation.

"Who ever heard of a male Nomord, anyway? And he's coherent! Not like all the other Nomord. It's weird, right? He actually talks intelligently."

She now knew it wasn't, but rather it was tragic that the others didn't have their wits about them.

Allabva focused on keeping her footfalls and breathing steady. She tried to stop complaining and focus on putting one foot in front of the other to keep herself moving forward. She eyed the road in the dark, watching its contours to avoid stumbling and falling to the ground. She couldn't help herself.

"I bet Hronomon's not so cold. I bet he's not getting mud in his mane right now. I bet—"

Suddenly Allabva fell hard on the road, saved from scrapes by the long sleeves and gloves that the cold weather had forced her to wear. Thinking she had tripped on a rock that she had failed to see because of the darkness, she came up to her hands and knees, planning to gather her bag and staff and rise to her feet. Instead, she felt a pull at her foot and discovered a rope wrapped around her ankle.

Her confusion turned to fear when a shape formed from the darkness to her right and rammed into her, forcing her back down. This was followed quickly by a hand covering her mouth before she had a chance to shout for Hronomon.

"Tunbloth, come grab her staff," a voice whispered behind her.

A man's arms held her in place as she tried to struggle out of a grown man's grasp.

Another shadow emerged from the grass on the north side of the road, running to assist the first. The second man snatched the staff from her hands before she found a way to land any blows with it.

"Give me a gag," the same voice whispered behind her. The second man produced two strips of cloth, shoving one strip as a bundle into her mouth after forcing it open, then using the other strip to tie it in place.

"How much do you think she has on her?" the second man wondered.

"I don't know but it's probably a fair amount. Traveling alone at night. Wearing a nice enough cloak. She probably has some urgent business that she came ready to pay for somewhere."

The man named Tunbloth grabbed Allabva's bag and opened it, rummaging through.

"There's no purse here. Only food. A knife. Socks? Alright, little lady, where do you keep your scrip? Halmon, let's search her. Thoroughly."

Money had not been high on Allabva's list of concerns when she madly dashed about with her mother to pack for this journey, but she carried some.

"Mmffm," she tried to communicate. She pointedly eyed her belt near her left hip, intentionally giving them the money they sought in hopes they would leave her alone afterwards.

"Too easy," Halmon said.

Tunbloth undid Allabva's belt and pulled both ends away from her body, revealing her small coin purse tied to the inside. Removing it, he opened it to inspect the contents. He frowned.

"That's it? That's all you have? This can't buy us anything but a few nights in a cheap inn."

"Come on," Halmon goaded. "You've got to have more. Where is it?"

Allabva's eyes were wide this entire time, genuinely fearing what the pair may do to her and wondering how far away

Hronomon was. How soon would he hear this and come back? She shook her head furiously, crying. "Mmffhhm-mm!"

Putting one leg underneath her, she sat on it and then tried to stand. She was halfway up when they shoved her back to the ground.

"You're staying there," Halmon directed. "If you cooperate, we won't hurt you. I think. Do you understand?"

Allabva nodded, trying to appear meek.

"Good. Look, I have your knife and your staff. I have the capacity to hurt you. Tunbloth here will ungag you for a moment and will ask you a question or two. You won't shout, or we will hurt you. Do you follow?"

Allabva nodded again.

"No tricks now. I'm ready for you."

Halmon appeared as though he would not hesitate to make good on his threats.

Tunbloth worked to remove the gag.

"Halmon, you've got to work on your knots. This one's a mess."

Halmon didn't wait before beginning the interrogation.

"What's your name?"

"Allabva."

Despite the security ramifications of telling them her real name, she still didn't feel good about lying.

"Allabva, eh? No last name? Very well, you can keep some secrets. Now, where are you headed?"

"East for now. Toward Palf Glen." Allabva felt apprehensive about telling them that much.

"Toward. Not *to*?" This man was dangerous. "Why are you heading there?"

Allabva said nothing, only staring back.

"I see," Halmon pursed his lips. "And where are you coming from?"

Allabva stared back, still.

Halmon took a moment to look at Allabva's clothing and bag. "I'd say this comes from roundabouts of the Cleft, wouldn't you, Tunbloth?"

"I wouldn't know," Tunbloth replied, "but it doesn't look too shabby. Why don't we just take those things and be on our way?"

"Because."

Halmon glared at Allabva intently, scrutinizing her. Allabva squirmed, wondering what the man was thinking.

"...Because why?" Tunbloth asked.

Halmon took a deep breath.

"Did you not hear her before we pulled the rope taut?"

"Of course. That's how we knew she was coming."

"No, you dolt. Didn't you hear *what* was saying?"

Allabva's blood ran chill. What had she said?

"Uh, maybe?" Tunbloth said.

"It was something about an intelligent unicorn," Halmon accused.

He leaned in close to Allabva.

"Are you as alone out here as you appear to be?"

"No," Allabva answered, showing the whites in her eyes.

It was the truth, but she didn't think Halmon fully believed it.

He squinted at her.

"And yet we find you, looking very much alone, hurrying so quickly through the night that you're not using your walking stick. I could see you had to steady your bag because of your pace. But then again, how does one such as you come to be on the road, this far from the Cleft, or any other settlement to the west, for that matter?"

"I'm not alone. I have a companion up ahead. He'll probably come back here any moment. He could take the two of you easily."

"Is it the unicorn?" Halmon asked, unknowingly hitting upon the truth. "No, I don't think so. I don't believe you're actually conspiring with the beasts. You're not so special that they would entrust you with anything. But somehow I think you're trying to do something for them."

"We're the ones who aren't alone," Tunbloth said. "We have the two of us, and three others in the brush back there."

He pointed behind himself with one thumb.

"You see, we're on watch, the two of us," Halmon picked back up. "We've been on watch for some time. If your friend—unicorn or not—had come through here, we would have seen him. We were here for two hours, freezing our fingers off for our mates because it's our shift, and you're the first thing to come by on two feet."

"Some dumb unicorn came through, but that was it," Tunbloth agreed. "No travel companion of yours."

Allabva resisted the urge to correct the vagrant and his use of the slang term.

"Go ahead, spit it out." Halmon taunted. "Tell him the correct term is *Nomord*." He spat the word out with derisive inflection.

These must be Disaffected, Allabva thought.

What were the odds that she would fall among some Disaffected mere hours after Banduchy had warned her?

"Well..." Allabva let it hang.

"Let's tie her up," Halmon directed.

"*Unicorns*," Tunbloth dripped the word in Allabva's face, then set about putting her gag back in place. "When you behave as selfishly as they do, when you're as sadistic as they are, you hardly even deserve an appropriate descriptive word like that. They are unicorns, and cannot lay claim to any term that's supposed to sound more dignified. Not with the way they treat us humans. 'Unicorn' is more than they deserve."

Halmon Took Allabva's hands behind her back and tied her wrists together.

"On your feet. We're going for a little walk first, then we'll hobble you around the ankles. Come on. Tunbloth, you go on ahead, so she knows where she's walking. Little girl, no games now."

Allabva followed Tunbloth off the road, Halmon following her with her knife. She wished she could fight against them or run free, but she was too in touch with reality to try. With her weight and strength disadvantage, there was no way she could hope to overpower two grown men in a struggle. They had the knife and staff also, so there was absolutely no hope of her hitting them quickly and running while they were down. Allabva didn't think she could premeditatedly use her knife against people anyway, no matter how nefarious their behavior. She might use it in the heat of the moment if she found herself defending.

Finally, making a break for it and running would be useless as well. She was tired from hours of walking and jogging, so she didn't have any energy left in her for a sprint. Tired as she was already, her only hope in running would be to lose them quickly, then rest while hidden until they gave up. Without any chance of success to escape, she walked with them and hoped to keep her life.

They soon came to a small depression in the ground where there were two horses tied to a tree near a wagon. The wagon contained two men asleep in their bedrolls, with another man asleep in his bedroll on the ground.

Halmon took Allabva by the arm and led her to the wagon, where he tied her hands to one of the wheels. Tunbloth went from man to man, waking them without raising any loud noise.

"What?" a new voice said, "Tunbloth, why did you wake me up? It's still the middle of the night. And it's cold. Least you could do was build the fire back up."

Halmon answered him.

"Nillan, I have somebody to accompany us on our way to the encampment, but we need to put some distance between ourselves and this place quickly."

"Somebody how?" Nillan demanded.

"Some diversion. Little girl won't tell me where she's going or where she's from. We took her money, and we figure we shouldn't leave her here after she's seen us, so we should take her with us, at least for now. Besides, before we stopped her I heard her saying something about talking to a unicorn. Might be something the Wise will want to know."

"You think they'll let you talk directly to the Wise?" Nillan yawned. Then he turned to the other man next to him in the wagon, whom Tunbloth was still shaking awake.

"Qurast, how many times does he have to tell you? Get up. Strike camp."

Qurast sat up begrudgingly.

"But Nolder was the one who tied up the horses. Get him first, then come get me."

He tried to lie back down but a sharp pain in his leg caused by Nillan's knuckle prompted him to get up.

"I said get up. We might as well be awake. Don't tell me you were getting good sleep with this cold and rain. At least the rain is starting to let up, but Halmon's right about one thing—we need to put some leagues behind us."

As Qurast climbed out of his bedroll and the wagon, Tunbloth roused Nolder.

The men rushed around, gathering their things and attempting to destroy any evidence they had stopped there. Once they decided they were prepared, Halmon and Nillan untied Allabva from the wagon wheel, bound her feet together, then lifted her into the wagon and lay her there like a log. Qurast sat in the driver's seat, the horses tied in front of him, and led the wagon back onto the road.

Once on the road, Qurast asked where they were going.

"Same as always," Nillan answered. "We just have some cargo to take with us."

He cast a dirty look at Allabva. "Why are we taking somebody with us? Is she trying to join, too?"

"No, and don't worry about it," Halmon said. "Just drive."

Allabva looked up from her vantage point in the bed of the wagon. Qurast sat on the front with Nolder, and Halmon, Nillan, and Tunbloth rode with her, each of them sitting at a different point and supporting his back with the outer board of the wagon bed. She lay in the middle of the bed, surrounded by their bedrolls and miscellaneous other items, including her bag and walking stick. She looked from one man to another as they held their conversation.

Nillan looked to Halmon for more explanation, which he gave. "We stopped her for her money, but she didn't have much. Also, she said some odd things. Mentioned a unicorn. Didn't you, hornling?"

That was a new word for Allabva. She supposed it sounded like he was insulting her with it, connecting her to the Nomord.

"She said she wasn't alone, but she sure looked like it. I want to get some more questions answered. If we can't, somebody at the encampment should be able to. She might be nobody, or she might be something. One way to find out."

"You woke us up for this?" Nillan blinked, then continued with forced patience in his voice. "I take that back. Yes, once you robbed her, you had to take her. But you could have just let her pass, couldn't you? I was having one of my favorite dreams in which I get to keep my fingers because it's not so cold. Right now, I'm considering getting back in my bedroll and riding on warm and cozy."

"There was more to it, I'll tell you later," Halmon insisted.

Nillan rolled his eyes, then rode on in silence.

Allabva needed to make a decision. She didn't know where Hronomon was. He must come back for her. Was he any good at reading tracks to follow them? She had no idea. The only thing to do there was to wait and see if the Nomord showed up.

She obviously couldn't escape from among the middle of them, bound and gagged as she was. But they had left her cloak on her and the bed rolls around her provided some small amount of insulation. Since she couldn't do anything to improve her present situation, she decided to maximize her capability within it. Regardless of the cold, after the running she had done and not knowing what was in her near future, she needed rest. With this in mind, she deliberately put everything out of mind and fell asleep.

Chapter 13

Disaffected

Allabva woke up several hours later after a chilled and fitful sleep, still lying in the wagon. She had a pain in her hip and shoulder and her neck was sore, but at least she had slept. She felt certain that she would be better off for it than she would be without it. She wished she could take her gloves off and blow on her fingers to warm them up, but found that her hands were still tied behind her.

She was woken by the sun in her eyes. Blinking and squinting, she worried for a moment that perhaps Delgan's flute had been taken from her. She twitched, and the motion moved the metal rod under her blouse, the cold object announcing its continued presence. Good. At least she still had that.

Allabva could see that she was still accompanied by three of the men in the wagon bed, and the other two men sat on the driver's bench. Not bothering to determine if everyone was still in the same place around her, she turned over to give her sore shoulder and hip a rest and to get the sun out of her eyes. Seeing that her situation was unchanged from the night before, she willed herself to fall back asleep, the rocking of the wagon working against her.

A few hours later, Allabva woke again, this time feeling markedly improved in her being. Now both sides ached equally, but it was a dull ache that she could live with. She yawned through the gag she still held in her mouth and blinked to bring herself more fully into the waking world.

Looking around inside and outside of the wagon while still lying on the bed floor, she took stock of her situation. Blessedly, she had slept. It felt as though the cold must have let off when the rain did, or the sleep would not have counted for anything as far as rest went. She thanked her young legs for being able to forgive her so quickly for the jogging last night. The sun was now high, giving its light on the innocent and malevolent in close quarters.

Allabva noted the current location of each man. They had rotated themselves. Tunbloth now drove, Halmon riding beside him. Nillan, Nolder, and Qurast rode in the bed. Nolder and Qurast were asleep.

Nillan raised a finger to his lips. "Shh, don't wake my babies, little girl."

She watched him, wondering what his move would be.

"Hal says your name is Allabva. He also suspects that you're from the Cleft."

Nillan looked her over again.

"I would agree with that, assuming that you're wearing your own clothes from your hometown."

Allabva waited in silence.

"Little girl named Allabva, I am Nillan Protfund, and you are our prisoner."

Allabva wondered if Nillan would seem as dangerous as Halmon had the night before. It appeared that he carried some clout, as the other men seemed to defer to him. So far, he didn't seem as menacing as the other man had when brandishing her own knife at her the night before.

"Of course!" Nillan acted as if he were coming to his senses. "Where are my manners?"

He reached behind her head and tugged on the strip of cloth coming out of the knot at the back of her neck. The strip came untied and Nillan pulled it away, then he pulled the wad from her mouth.

Allabva worked her jaw and tongue, trying to lick the away the memory of the wad of cloth that had resided in her mouth for so many hours. It was a relief to be able to swallow normally again. While she got herself back to normalcy, Nillan continued speaking.

"I'm curious about some of the same ideas my friend had when he found you last night. For example, where were you going in such a hurry?"

Allabva merely gazed at him, wishing for a way out.

"Don't be afraid. You won't offend me. I just want to know for, let's say, personal reasons."

Allabva found the will to speak.

"Where are you taking me?"

"Nah-ah, little girl," Nillan rebuffed. "I asked you first."

"I'd be more inclined to speak after having some water," Allabva bargained.

"Of course, child," Nillan condescended.

He grabbed her waterskin from where it lay next to her, uncapping it to offer her a drink.

"I'm not a child."

"What?"

Nillan turned his interest from the waterskin back to Allabva.

"I'm not a child. I have reached my majority."

"Of course you have, child. The Cleft is so quaint, isn't it?"

Allabva knew that Nillan was insulting her, but she didn't quite catch the point of his remarks.

"Here's your water," he continued indifferently.

He plopped it in front of her face.

Still tied up, she had to wriggle somewhat to position her mouth at the spout, remove the stopper with her teeth, then she had to lower her face as much as she could to the floor while she drank.

"Lovely," Nillan said, and flashed a cold, patronizing grin at her. "I'll ask you again: where were you going and why?"

Allabva sighed. She would get nowhere by refusing to answer this basic question, and they would get nowhere by receiving an honest answer.

"Eastward toward Palf Glen, but I don't know why. I already told Halmon where I was going last night."

Had she just told Nillan more information than she had given to Halmon and Tunbloth?

"Going east, we but you don't know why. Well, we are going east and we do know why, although we're not on the same road we found you on."

Their conversation started to wake up the sleeping men. Allabva blinked and waited.

"We are going to the encampment of the Disaffected," he supplied simply.

There went that word again.

"What does it mean to be Disaffected?" she inquired.

"Wouldn't you like to know?" Nillan asked, narrowing his eyes. "But I'm asking the questions. My mate Halmon here says he heard you talking about a male unicorn. One you talked to."

She decided the less she said to him, the better.

"Ah, so that's how it is," he said softly. Dangerously. "You want to know about us, despite us knowing so little about you. And clearly coordinating with the monsters."

He lifted his voice to be heard by everybody.

"Hardly fair, am I right, Halmon?"

Nillan didn't wait for an answer.

"Never mind. This is public information. The Disaffected are those who understand the truth of our unicorn tormentors."

Allabva raised an eyebrow at the surprising description.

"Tormentors?"

"Tormentors indeed, little girl," Nillan scorned. "You think the unicorns are our friends? You think that—what did she say, Halmon?—you think that 'Ron man' is your friend?"

Halmon apparently hadn't heard Hronomon's name clearly. Allabva didn't blame him.

"I don't know any 'Ron man,'" Allabva said defensively. "And I have only ever heard of the Nomord doing nice things for people. They heal people, for one."

"Everybody wants to bring that up. Let's get into it."

Nillan wore an expression of hate, an unexpected emotion to come out of talking of healing.

"Everybody goes straight there. Yes, the beasts heal people sometimes, or so I'm told. Gentlemen, what are some pernicious pleasant parables you've heard about the unicorns? Tunbloth, what's your favorite?"

The driver turned his head.

"Crops."

Halmon also replied, "Grave markers."

"Ah yes," Nillan said sarcastically. "I have heard reports, reliable reports, that the monsters sometimes increase crop yields. I have even heard a few tales where one of the freaks stood by the graveside of a recently deceased loved one for days, continuing to call out to her living husband. And he is supposed to feel honored, of course."

"I would think that increasing a crop—" Allabva began.

"You would, wouldn't you?" Nillan cut in. "Yes, increased crop yields would be a good thing. If you could count on it."

"I understand that a consistent increase would be helpful, but—"

"But, exactly," he accused harshly. "They aren't consistent. Any help they provide is evanescent. Tunbloth, where did you come from?"

"A failed farm," Tunbloth said. "It's mostly dust now. A unicorn helped us one year, then that was it. It was our last good crop, ever. After that year we had too much rain and a fungus took over the fields. Then we had a hot year, and the fungus dried up, leaving toxic soil that our seed won't grow in."

"Halmon?" Nillan prompted.

"I'd rather not right now," Halmon declined. "You go ahead."

Nillan took the liberty to do so.

"A unicorn stood at his mother's grave. For ten days it returned to the same spot—"

"Eleven," Halmon corrected, despite himself.

"For eleven days it returned to the same spot every day and stood next to the grave marker. As I mentioned earlier, it called to Halmon's father every day, not allowing him to let go of his wife's memory and move on, extending his grief for no reason at all."

"It changed him permanently," Halmon informed Allab-va.

"And what about you?" she asked Nillan. "Did a Nomord refuse to give you a ride on her back?"

"Do NOT trivialize this," Nillan admonished Allabva.

Halmon didn't want to let it go.

"I just told you that my father was never the same after one of those unicorns trampled on his heart while he was mourning my late mother, and you turn around and make a joke. I don't know why we ungagged you."

Allabva took the criticism readily, despite the current situation.

"I apologize, sir. If you suffered some great ill, it is not my intent to make light of your experience. I am noticing a pattern, though—"

"And I'm noticing that you're stuck in this old way of thinking, that the unicorns are infallible and can't be questioned."

Nillan's face was hard with intensity.

"Now you listen to me. I came to realize that the unicorns aren't the knights in shining armor that so many people think them to be, and I'm merely trying to educate you as well. Some of us have personal experiences that expose the monsters for what they really are. Not all of us do. Take Nolder here."

He gestured at the man, still sleeping.

"He's never had any personal experiences with one of them. He's just a good listener and came to understand because of what other people shared with him."

"Then what did happen to you?"

Allabva asked the question with no malice in her voice, her tone honestly inviting information that she lacked.

Nillan sat chewing his cheek, looking at Allabva and seeming to consider whether she was worthy of hearing his account. At length, he decided to let her in.

"I was married. We'd been married seven months. We had promised ourselves to each other when we were very young, and I could never see anybody but her. We always played together, joked together, and as we grew up, we planned our life together. We finally got old enough to have a proper wedding, and we got married as soon as we could gather enough to buy our home to live in together. Then she fell ill. We hardly had time to establish our household a few months before she became sick. One of the beasts visited us one night, and I was eager—"

His voice cracked, betraying emotion.

"I was just as eager as any other beguiled fool to help my wife up from her deathbed to come outside and meet the horned horse. She got up with my help, with great difficulty and intense pain, and came outside for the first time in three weeks. The beast was no farther away than the span of a large, dead tree that we had in front of our home. It looked straight at us—at her. It *spoke* to us. It asked how we were, and we told it that my wife was very ill. And then...it didn't move. We tried to come to it, but it shied away. My wife was in pain just to be out there, unsuccessfully trying to garner favor from this animal. We had to give up and take her back inside to her bed."

"Well," Allabva tried to connect, "they can heal, but they don't always—"

"The next day, the dead tree had blossoms on it! My wife died within the week after, and this stupid beast healed the tree. That's sadistic! That cruel...cruel..."

Nillan's face contorted with anger, lacking a sufficiently weighty word to describe what he felt. He breathed heavily as he searched for the best way to express himself.

"No. People think unicorns are gentle, kind creatures. I reject that. They should not live on this earth, do you hear me? If we can find a way, they need to be eradicated, period."

Allabva stared at the man, trying to think of the proper response to this tirade.

"I'm so sorry for your loss," she finally uttered.

"So sorry for your loss," Nillan mocked nasally. "That doesn't bring her back, does it? That doesn't punish the imbecile beast for holding out on us with a tiny help that she could have easily provided, does it? That doesn't save other people from this same kind of torment when the unicorns lead them to believe they're going to help, but then slap them in the face with something that can only be read as an insult."

Allabva stayed silent.

"This is Disaffected."

Nillan gestured to himself as if offering himself as a display sample.

"That is Disaffected. They are Disaffected."

He pointed to Tunbloth, then the rest of his party.

"We will do whatever we can to break other people out of the blindness that we were in ourselves. A better word might be Disillusioned, not Disaffected."

Allabva hoped to help them raise their opinion of the Nomord.

"I don't know if we can properly judge them for what they don't do."

Nillan wasn't going to give up his stubbornness so easily.

"If they have it in their power to do it and any reasonable, intelligent being can see it needs doing, we can absolutely judge them for what they choose not to do."

"Do we even know how intelligent the Nomord are? Their actions often appear non sequitur," she tried.

"They can talk, can't they? They understand what's going on, but they care about it less than cats do. Cats tend to be indifferent to human suffering."

"I'm not so sure—"

"They say you can own a dog, but you can feed a cat. A cat doesn't care about loyalty. A unicorn actively cultivates a sense of intelligent connection just enough to be able to trample on your expectations when it hurts the most."

Allabva didn't reply.

"We're going to the camp of the Disaffected. We will join ourselves with them there to build a new society. You're hiding information about yourself, so you're coming along, and we'll find out whatever we need to, no matter how trivial your business may be. Especially if you say weird things to yourself in the night about male unicorns talking intelligently."

Nillan stared at her intently.

Allabva swallowed, troubled by his determination to be a pain to her. She leaned back hard and felt the flute rock against her collar.

"What's that?" Nillan asked.

Allabva felt the chill of anxiety rise inside her at the question. She didn't respond.

"Halm, Tun, didn't you get her valuables?" Nillan said.

"Of course. Got her money right here."

Tunbloth smiled and held up the coin purse with two fingers.

"I didn't say money. That's only part of it," Nillan said as he leaned across the space between himself and Allabva, reaching for her neck. "There's a chain here."

Allabva's mouth fell open with the fear of loss.

"No, it's nothing. It's only sentimental."

She tried to writhe away so he couldn't reach it, but he only followed and there was nowhere she could go.

"Sit still, girl," he ordered, pulling the chain around so he could undo the clasp, removing it from around her neck.

"This doesn't look like nothing. Maybe this is only brass inside, but it's at least silver plated."

He smiled a dirty grin as he inspected Delgan's flute, betraying glee at having performed the small theft. Nillan pulled the front of his jacket away, depositing the flute and chain in an inside pocket.

Allabva rode along in the rumbling wagon, saying nothing and trying to hold back tears of anger, indignation, and sadness. The Disaffected spoke of being led along to believe there would be help when none would come. Didn't they see the hypocrisy in treating her they way they were, if they wanted to make the world a better place?

Along the lines of of absent Nomord, where was Hronomon right now? Was he giving up on her because she got captured? Was he finding a new Companion for the Shrongelin now? Was he leaving her to her fate, or should she trust him to come and rescue her?

Chapter 14

Bound

Allabva awoke from an unplanned nap in the afternoon, having been lulled to sleep by the warmth of the sun on her cloak and face. The morning's conversation had accomplished nothing in her favor, and had ended in her losing Delgan's flute. She sucked in the saliva from the corner of her mouth, proving the depth of her sleep, and opened her eyes.

Her joints complained again of her position, and she felt the desire to sit up despite her bonds, but at least she felt truly rested now. She took a refreshing breath and looked around.

"We need to water the horses," Nolder said. "Everybody, take a few."

Each man started getting down from the wagon and looking for a secluded spot to do his business.

"Wait a minute," Nillan said. "The little girl needs to take a break, too, unless we want the wagon soiled. Go ahead and take your breaks, then come back here quickly. We'll all need to be on guard while we let her take her break."

Allabva was glad that at least her basic physical needs were remembered in the moment, though it sounded like Nillan wasn't going to give her a chance to do anything more than that.

Nolder had stopped the wagon at the edge of a stream, with the front wheels in the water. The horses were afforded the opportunity to drink the water passing by at their hooves. The men had to climb off the back of the wagon in order to keep their feet dry, and they quickly disappeared into the trees around the trail behind the wagon.

Nillan stayed put in the wagon with Allabva.

"Don't worry, sweetheart, you're not going anywhere. We'll still get a full accounting out of you."

After a few minutes, a couple of the men had returned and Nillan appointed one of them to keep watch over Allabva, then he excused himself for a few moments' privacy. When all five men had returned, they untied Allabva's bonds and stood by while she climbed down from the wagon. Feeling rather self-conscious, she looked for a secluded spot and found a small dip between a group of trees. The men stayed outside the trees until she emerged again, then escorted her back to the wagon without delay.

Allabva inspected her surroundings during the whole ordeal. The landscape was markedly hillier now and she could see tall mountains in the distance to the east. It was also dotted with frequent trees of different types that were new to her eyes, unfamiliar to the Cleft. Most notably, to her dismay, there did not appear to be any significant feature of the area that the prospective Disaffected men had missed which might have given her the opportunity to make a run for it.

Through all the proceedings, from the moment they gave Allabva the use of her hands and legs until they returned her captive again to the wagon, Nillan kept a close eye on her actions. Halmon seemed rather observant as well. If she was going to attempt any kind of escape, she would need to find a way to get past their observation. She noticed that some of the others didn't seem as keen on making sure she was always prevented any opportunity for mischief.

Qurast, who looked closer to her own age, appeared in particular to need to be told specifically everything he needed to do to hold his part of the team's security over her. Nillan had to tell him where to stand, what direction he had to look, and specifically what to do if he saw her do anything outside of what she was supposed to be doing. Tunbloth appeared somewhat inattentive as well, but Qurast seemed less interested in treating her the same way as Nillan and Halmon thought she should be treated.

When Allabva was back in the wagon, Nillan had Tunbloth tie her feet again, watching to make sure it was done tight. They were about to tie her hands again when she protested and attempted to appeal to their sense of logic.

"I need to eat," she said. "I haven't eaten since before you gentlemen abducted me last night. I haven't had any water since this morning, either. Please let me eat and drink. I'll need my hands free for that unless you want to give me every bite, one by one."

Tunbloth nodded.

"That makes sense. I saw some food in your bag, didn't I?"

He seemed to be about to reach for the bag when Nillan interrupted.

"Wait a minute. You think we're going to give you your hands back, just like that? There's no telling what you'll do. And what do you have in your bag, anyway? Tunbloth, don't give her the bag."

"But I do need to eat," she pressed. "I'm hungry. I haven't given you trouble this far, have I? Just let me have my food so I can eat and my waterskin so I can drink water."

"No, I don't think we will."

Nillan seemed to consider that for a moment.

"I'll tell you what. We'll give you food, but not the whole travel bag. You tell Tunbloth here what it is you need from the bag and he'll hand it to you, one item at a time. If you want something else, you give back the first thing. You're not getting the bag so you can pull something out of a hidden compartment. We'll let you use your hands while you eat, but as soon as you're done, they'll be tied up again. Or we can just tie them back up again right now. What'll it be?"

Allabva sighed.

"Let me have some water first, please. I'm parched."

Tunbloth passed her the waterskin, which she uncapped and drank from before recapping and returning it to him.

"Now, can I get one of those hard rolls?"

Allabva did her best to enjoy the bread, then some cheese, and then some water again, each one at a time, as Nillan had mandated. This could get very tedious very quickly. When she had finished eating, true to Nillan's word, they rebound her hands behind her back as the wagon rumbled along eastward.

Allabva rode along, trying to be as comfortable as she could with her hands tied behind her back and sitting on the floor of the wagon. At least she could sit up and wasn't forced to lie down the entire time. This provided a view of the passing hills. After a time, even the hills began to appear monotonous as the sun crept downward behind the wagon's rear.

Allabva kept wondering where Hronomon was during this time. He had promised her mother that he would protect her, but she hadn't seen him since before she was abducted in the middle of the night. He was supposed to be scouting the road ahead, but he had missed the pair of Disaffected hiding on either side of the road.

Apparently the Nomord, although they had some magic and were immortal, didn't possess supernatural sight or hearing. Or smell. If he had somehow determined to abandon her and find a new Companion for the Shrongelin, she had no way of knowing it, but it would mean that she was on her own with these bandits. Realizing that there was no way to know if she was on her own, she knew that she had to find her own means of escape. She started planning.

They didn't take any more stops in the evening before deciding to bed down for the night. Allabva guessed that they had made a stop or two while she was asleep. When Nillan did call a stop for the night, they left the road and parked the horses and wagon away, where they wouldn't be seen by any travelers coming in either direction.

They followed the same procedures as they had that afternoon for everyone to relieve themselves and still keep Allabva under close guard. Same as before, she was able to find a small amount of privacy for a few minutes before they re-tied her bonds.

"Where is she supposed to sleep?" Qurast asked afterwards. "I'm not giving her my bedroll; my sleep is too important to me."

"You don't need quality sleep at your age," Halmon rebuffed. "You could sleep on a pile of rocks and you might feel a little tired afterwards, but you'd still come away with way too much energy in the morning."

Tunbloth laughed.

"Don't you know it, Halmon? At your age, you could sleep in a king's bed and have the best sleep in years, and still come out of bed grumpy. Nolder, too."

"She's not taking anybody's bedroll," Nillan directed. "She's got her cloak. She can wad the hood up for a pillow if she wants. We'll just leave her tied up in the wagon."

And, so it was. This time, as Halmon, Tunbloth, and Nolder bedded down, it was Qurast who was assigned to tie her up. He was more gentle about it than Tunbloth had been. It was clear that Tunbloth didn't care about her well-being. It didn't appear that he cared about much at all. Qurast perhaps identified a little with her because they were close together in age.

"Not too tight, is it?"

He had lengths of rope which he tied around her wrists at one end and one of the wheels of the wagon at the other end, and he did the same with her ankles.

"If you're honestly asking my opinion, I don't want the bonds at all," Allabva said.

"Good point."

Qurast was tightening the knot connecting the rope that bound her hands behind her back to the wagon wheel.

"But the boss says you have to be tied up, so here we are."

"Who says he's the boss?"

"He does. He found us, brought us together."

"How did he find you? And what for?"

"He came through my town talking about how the Nomord aren't really what they seem, how they don't actually want to help humanity or make the world a better place. Made sense to me, so I talked to him some more."

"But why is he the boss?" Allabva repeated.

Qurast moved to tie her ankles to the wagon as well.

"He's organized, and he has plans. I didn't just follow him because what he said about the unicorns made sense. I followed him because he promised that he can make my life better than it was."

"Has he done that?" Allabva questioned.

Qurast frowned. "Not exactly. Not yet. But I know he will. When we get to the Disaffected encampment, we'll be able to contribute to making a difference in the world and get people to stop expecting that these unicorns will do nice things."

"Why did you leave home?" Allabva pressed.

"Well," Qurast answered slowly, "in order to make it to the encampment, we kind of needed some supplies."

"And?"

"And, well, let's say that some of them may have been illegitimately obtained."

"So you stole, just like Halmon and Tunbloth wanted to rob me last night?"

As unsavory as Qurast's account was, it was consistent with what she had observed from the crew so far.

"What did you steal?" she asked him.

"No, I didn't steal anything. I mean, I did pick the lock on the gate so these other guys could take the horses and wagon." He didn't look like he was proud of it. "It just seemed like it was necessary so we could hit the road and get to where we can contribute."

"So now you'd be on the lam even if your friends hadn't kidnapped me. That doesn't sound like an improvement on your life," Allabva assessed.

"Not yet, I guess. But I think we'll get there. Now, uhh..."

Qurast looked uncomfortable.

"I have to gag you now."

Allabva consigned herself to more time being bound. She didn't love sleeping with a gag in her mouth, but it still seemed wisest to cooperate with her captors. She didn't struggle while he finished his task and left her helpless on the floor of the wagon.

Nillan had been posting the horses at a tree and providing them feed. He came over now, somewhat haggard after the extended day. After wordlessly inspecting the knots the younger man had tied to restrain Allabva, he spoke.

"Qurast, now that we have our guest all situated for the night," he gestured toward Allabva, "we should split up our watch. I'll stay here and watch camp. You go to the road and raise the alarm if we need to jump and scramble. Don't fall asleep. I'll come get you when it's time for us to change over with Halmon and Tunbloth."

Complying, Qurast disappeared in the twilight, walking back to the road. Allabva stayed awake, not feeling drowsy after the long day of travel because she had taken multiple naps in the time since they had nabbed her the night before. She tried to explore whether there could be any chance of escaping from her bonds. She twisted and pulled as much as she could, but Qurast's knots held firm despite being more comfortable against her skin than those tied by Tunbloth.

Allabva wondered if she might be able to gain any favor with the young bandit in order to take advantage of a moment when he might be distracted, or if it may even be possible to turn him around and convince him to help her on purpose.

But if she managed to break herself out, then what? If Hronomon had abandoned her, then she should simply go home. But no, she had already considered this halfway, hadn't she? She had no way of knowing if she had been abandoned. Perhaps, then, if she managed to break free, she should find her way to Palf Glen, since that was ostensibly her destination, more or less. Hronomon, if he had lost her, might look for her there.

Eventually her mind started to drift back to home. Mother would have told Delgan already that Allabva wouldn't be there tomorrow night, but that didn't stop Allabva from feeling like she was going to let him down anyway. The way she had disappeared in the night with no explanation to the young man probably left him confused.

Maybe he would feel disaffected as well, but toward her rather than toward the Nomord. That would make her quite sad, she thought. At least if she could break away with all her belongings and make it home, she could...

No. She had lost Delgan's flute and couldn't give it back to him unless she caught a moment of inattention from Nillan.

And Brelin. What would she think about Allabva right now? Was she even thinking about her, or was she too busy with Alvern to even notice she was gone?

No, that thought didn't give Brelin enough credit. She was a good friend and must be scandalized that she wasn't included. What would Mother have told her? What explanation would she give?

These thoughts tumbled around in her head for a good while, mentally wearing her out until she fell asleep with tears in her eyes.

In the morning, Allabva was awakened by the jolt of the wagon as it began moving. Alarmed, she opened her eyes wide. She had been tied to the wheel. If it rolled it would pull her out of the wagon and onto the ground. Disoriented, not realizing the rope had been disconnected from the wagon wheel, she kicked hard and accidentally propelled herself across the bed of the wagon.

She landed in Nolder's gut, who replied with a grunt and a shove back toward where Allabva had launched herself from. Same as yesterday morning, Halmon and Tunbloth sat on the driver's bench, and Nolder, Nillan, and Qurast rode in the bed.

"Why don't you watch it?" Nolder said.

"Mm-ffrhm," Allabva apologized. This was her first interaction with him, and she wasn't sure how he was going to behave.

"Oh, come here," he said patiently. "I'll take that gag off."

Once he had, Allabva was able to speak again.

"I'm so sorry, sir. I thought I was still tied to the wheel, and I would've been thrown to the ground by the rope. I needed to break free of that, even if I broke my hands doing it. I can live with broken hands, but if that wheel had yanked me off the wagon, I'm not sure I would survive."

"We're not so daft, little runaway," Nillan spoke up. "We untied the other end of the rope before we set off."

"Thank you for that," she said, put off by Nillan's usual manner.

She tried not to show it.

"Don't mind him," Nolder reassured her. "We're all tired after sleeping outside night after night. He's just a bit cranky."

"Cranky, maybe," Nillan rebuffed. "Maybe I'm just tired of having to be so patient with everybody while they try to catch up."

Nolder raised an eyebrow at him. "Catch up to where?"

"Maybe I just need a brisk morning walk," Nillan said.

With that, he raised himself from the bed of the wagon and rolled sideways off the back, hitting the ground at a steady stride to keep pace with the wagon.

"Maybe you need a brisk dip in a cold lake," Nolder said with a smirk.

The wagon rolled along.

Soon Allabva's stomach growled, and she felt another bodily need.

"Master, umm—"

She wasn't sure how to address Nolder.

"Lawgrin. Nolder Lawgrin," he stated. "Oh, and don't talk back to Nillan. Only I get the privilege of talking to him like that. He may run the show, but age hath its privileges."

He smiled smugly.

"Master Lawgrin. Do you think you can help me? I'm rather hungry," she said, half twisting around to show him her bound hands. "I could use a hand to eat—my own hand—if I had the freedom to do so."

She smiled sheepishly.

Nolder glanced at Nillan before glancing to Qurast.

"Qurast, can you help her out of those? Miss Allabva, here's your bag. I'll follow the same pattern as before. You tell me what you need, and you'll get it, one thing at a time."

"Before we get into breakfast, I think I need to, umm, find a private spot," Allabva admitted.

Nolder gave her a half smile.

"I don't think we can do that quite yet. We just set off to start the day and everybody else already relieved himself. Nillan, and everybody else, wants to make headway to get to the encampment sooner rather than later. Stopping again so soon wouldn't go over very well. But meanwhile, eat. What can I get you?"

He opened the bag and started rummaging.

Qurast scooted over next to Allabva to untie her hands. This would be an uncomfortable breakfast and time thereafter until she could get the party of Disaffected to stop for a break. She ate anyway, making the best she could of her circumstances. The men had refilled her waterskin from a stream before leaving their campsite, so she had water to drink as well. At least they were keeping her alive.

Chapter 15

By the Roula Seas

The men retied Allabva's bonds after she had eaten her fill. She had been hoping they would relax a little and not require that anymore, but she supposed that she couldn't keep her hopes up when she was among kidnappers. They left her ungagged, however. She settled back in and tried to endure the discomfort of needing to relieve herself. Eventually, that was resolved when they made another stop in mid-morning.

As the day wore on into late morning, they crested a small rise and Allabva saw an expanse of water ahead of her split by a narrow sliver of land down the middle.

"What's that?" she wondered aloud. "Is that the sea?"

"Can't be," Qurast answered. "We're at too high elevation for the sea to be here. It must be a lake."

"You're both right, in a way," Nolder said. "Those are the Roula Seas. They are lakes, truth be told, but the old name sticks. Palf Glen is on the other side of the South Roula Sea. We'll stay on this road and go right between the two seas—er, lakes—and we'll keep going until we come out on the other side. This is the Tallens Road and goes straight on to Tallensworth. If we passed the seas and took the north fork at the docks, we would eventually wind up in Nolnarn, on the north sea."

"Might there be traffic on the road, then, if it's the main road to run between Tallensworth and Nolnarn?" Allabva asked.

"Fair chance," Nolder considered. "I mean, most traffic coming up the Tallens Road and trying to get to Nolnarn would probably leave the road and board a boat at Roula Docks, on the southeastern shore of the North Roula Sea. Still, there are plenty of people who don't like to travel by boat, or who don't have money for the passage by water. So yes, I think it's likely enough we'll meet some traffic coming the other way."

Nolder looked at Allabva, frowning, then to Nillan. "You know we'll have to untie her, right?"

Nillan had been studying something in his lap, but looked up as he was addressed.

"Yes, I know it," he said, sounding annoyed. "And, little girl, do you realize that you might gain your freedom if you answered our questions? I won't guarantee it. Your answers might require us to hold on to you until we reach the encampment, or you might go free. But guess what? Not answering our questions does guarantee that we take you all the way to the encampment."

Allabva kept her mouth shut. While Nolder and Qurast may be worth talking to, Nillan was trouble.

As they descended into the depression forming a shallow valley surrounding the lakes, a neck of land maintained itself above the surface of the water on either side. It slowly narrowed from what Allabva supposed to be a league wide at the start of where it was flanked by the seas on either side, to the width of several carts as it continued forward.

Allabva and her Disaffected escort detail saw fewer trees as they left the higher ground. When they were in line with the shore of the North Roula Sea so that if Allabva looked directly to her left to see the line between land and water, she thought there must be some way to use this geography to escape if they were traveling the other direction. As it was, as the neck of land narrowed, she knew her prospects of escape at this time narrowed even more so.

"Ho, driver," Nillan commanded abruptly.

Halmon put a hand on Tunbloth's shoulder, who pulled the reins to stop the horses.

"Get out," Nillan said to Allabva.

"What?"

"I said, get out of the wagon. Qurast, untie her. Little prisoner, you're going to walk. There's nowhere to go but forward and backward, and we can see you. Don't run, or we'll make you pay for it later at first opportunity. You wanted to be untied; why stop there? Stop free loading off my horses, and get out of the wagon. Oh, and make sure you keep up. You fall behind, you'll pay. You make us keep a close eye on you and tell you to speed up, you'll pay. Keep pace. I won't tell you again for free." Nillan's menacing tone confirmed to Allabva that she was right not to tell him anything.

Qurast untied her and Allabva started walking behind the wagon. She quickly noticed that the wagon was going faster than was natural for her to walk. Every few steps, she had to extend her stride and take a bouncing step or two to keep up. This would have been fine, except for knowing that she would soon sweat, and her cloak would become as uncomfortable as she had known it would when she left home. Unfortunately, she didn't see any way around it, so onward she went.

Step, step, step, jog-jog. Step, step.

This annoyed her, but when she thought about it a little bit, it was a lot better than constantly jogging on.

"A little cruel, don't you think?" Nolder said to Nillan.

"Cruel how?" Nillan replied. "She likes running. She was born for it. See? She's running all by herself just for the fun of it."

He laughed at his own joke and at Allabva's expense at the same time.

Halmon piped in, "I concur! Nobody made her run when we found her. She told us she wasn't alone, but that was a lie. If she had an escort, then where is he? It's been nearly a day and a half and nobody's showing up." He laughed as well, and Nillan laughed louder than before.

"I don't know..." Qurast said.

"Look, ask her yourself," Nillan said. "Ask her if she minds jogging a bit for her health." He grinned sickeningly, and then met Allabva's eyes, showing a warning in his.

Qurast shrugged, not seeing Nillan's menacing gaze aimed at Allabva. "All right. Allabva, do you mind jogging?"

Allabva was smart enough to realize that she did not possess freedom of speech when she was among these men. She shook her head to indicate that she didn't mind, realizing full well that that was the prescribed response, regardless of whether she truly minded or not.

The wagon rumbled on and the men ignored Allabva, talking among themselves. Traveling this neck of land, Allabva watched it narrowing while they came closer to what amounted to a causeway crossing between the lakes. She wondered if Hronomon was still out there, but for some reason could not approach the Disaffected men and their cart. Who knew with these Nomord? It seemed there were so many things about them she had never imagined, because humankind had forgotten everything throughout the centuries.

Was he unable to come close to horses? Or, could it be that he was lying to Mother about protecting her? She didn't believe he had been lying, especially since she felt she could see his character, so she found it perplexing that he hadn't shown up to free her from her captors.

Allabva knew Hronomon wanted to avoid the two of them being seen together. Any obvious cooperation between human and Nomord would somehow be a signal to Sacalai that they were on this mission. If he was following the Disaffected, he must be keeping himself hidden on purpose.

This thought made Allabva realize something else that she found unsettling. If Hronomon had been following along from the shadows as she accompanied Nillan and his group, then when they ventured between the Roula Seas, the open surface of the water would deprive Hronomon of any means of staying hidden.

With his thought, she turned and glanced behind her, uphill at the closest trees, now quite some distance away. She thought she caught a glimpse of white, fleetingly exposed from behind some foliage. Could that be him? Could that be Hronomon?

Allabva searched her mind for any excuse she could use that might get the party not to cross between the two lakes. She didn't want to go because then Hronomon would be exposed to the risk of discovery, not only of traveling with her but also of being a male Nomord. Not wanting to be exposed or found out... That was what she needed.

"Is it wise for us to take this road?" Allabva raised her voice so the men in the wagon could hear her.

Nillan cocked his head and raised both eyebrows.

"Did she really—?"

"What do you mean?" Nolder asked.

"Well, I—" Allabva stalled, unsure. She glanced to Qurast. "I thought, since…"

"You want to tell me about my business?" Nillan started.

Realization dawned on Qurast's face.

"No, she's right."

"Right about what?"

"We shouldn't travel this road. We…our wagon and horses are problematic," Qurast let out.

"Problematic," Nillan echoed, turning his displeasure from Allabva to the younger man. "Problematic? First off, nobody is following us, clear from Littonwelt to here. That would be completely unreasonable. Second, you told her that? Just how much did you tell her?"

"Not enough for me to know that you started from Littonwelt," Allabva called out. "You just told me that yourself."

Nillan looked frustrated. "Watch it, girl. And Qurast, whose side are you on, anyway?"

"She's right, Nill," Nolder coaxed. "You're probably right, too. I bet nobody is still following us, but we don't know that for sure. And even if nobody is following us, there's the slim possibility that we'll meet somebody who knows these horses and may wonder how we came to have them. It's better to go around. We'll go around the South Roula Sea. It's not that much longer, and it gives us the chance to change our route on the way if we need to."

Nillan was red in the face, but he had recognized the wisdom in going around.

"Driver, you heard. Turn about. We'll take the Palf Road." He turned his attention back to Allabva. He didn't look happy. "Little girl, you can stay out of my wagon for a good, long while."

"Whatever you say, boss," Halmon said. Halmon and Tunbloth pulled the reins to get the horses to turn gently to the right first, then in a wider arc to the left in order to turn around.

The group had to backtrack for nearly an hour in order to come to the Palf Road, then turned left toward the south. After another hour, they stopped for a break and a change in drivers, taking their normal security to ensure Allabva didn't run off.

They resumed travel, and they soon found themselves once again close to the southern lake on its gently sloping shore, on clear terrain that was exposed from the water's edge, up some distance from the road to a border of trees. They didn't stop for lunch, but ate in the wagon while traveling. Each driver had a turn away from the reins to have his lunch. They did not give Allabva her bag, nor the opportunity to request anything from it while she continued to walk behind.

Instead, holding an apple toward the rear of the wagon as if to hand it to Allabva, Nillan said, "Here, free food!"

Then he tossed it to backward over his head as he faced her, launching the apple over the front of the wagon and far ahead of the horses. It hit the ground where the earth was hard packed, bouncing and rolling. By luck, one of the horses kicked it rather than trampling it, and the apple rolled down toward the water.

Allabva chased after it to pick it up, but then she had to climb back uphill because the contours of the lakeshore made the road snake over a rise at that point. Wishing she hadn't had to expend extra energy to retrieve it, Allabva ate the now heavily bruised apple.

While she ate she marveled at how destroyed he must have been inside to be so cruel. Were there actually people like this? Was it some traumatic event, or was he born this way, and only hiding behind the Disaffected rallying cry against the Nomord as an excuse? Did he treat all women like this after losing his wife?

As the road hugged the lakeshore, Allabva found herself step-step jogging behind the wagon again to keep up. As this continued, she gradually allowed more distance to build between herself and the wagon before she jogged to catch up again. She kept a careful eye on Nillan's mood to make sure she wouldn't run afoul. The more distracted he appeared, the more distance she allowed to build, so that she was not spending the entire time halfway between a walk and a jog.

Once the distance was far enough that she felt she didn't mind the alternating pace, she held that consistent and continued to travel in longer intervals of jogging and walking. She asked for her waterskin, which Qurast tossed to her without consulting Nillan, then she drank water as she needed. She was able to refill it in moments when they were close enough to the lakeshore that she could take the liberty to deviate from the road down to the water and scoop it up.

By mid-afternoon, Allabva had long ago removed her cloak in her discomfort and tossed it over one shoulder. As she jog-walked in the warmer weather, she was glad for the convenience that the wagon was carrying her bag and her staff for her, neither of which she needed at the moment, barring for food. She was also unhappy that it held them because it meant that if she did try to run off, she would have to sacrifice them to do so. Not to mention her knife, but more significantly, Delgan's flute.

She tried to make the best of the situation. She couldn't do anything to ensure her freedom at the moment, and as she began to tire, she couldn't stop to rest. But she could try to enjoy the view. The sight of the water to her left kept her glancing over the South Roula Sea, and she had the pleasure of watching seagulls and other birds. Occasionally she saw a fish disturb the surface of the water.

She could also watch the mountains looming on the horizon. How far away were they? She couldn't tell for sure, but she wished she could share the view with Brelin. The mountains also made her think of the tune Fiewren had sung over their campfire.

Allabva wished she could hear Delgan's flute play its sweet tune like she did two days before, or make her poor attempt to play the tune herself. She took little comfort in knowing where the flute was; Nillan still must possess the instrument, because he hadn't had any opportunity to sell it since yesterday. She dared not ask for it back, afraid that she might reveal that it had some connection to the Nomord. Besides, there was no chance that Nillan would return it to her, anyway. If she wanted it back, she would have to bargain a deal for which she had no leverage to trade, or she would have to find the seemingly nonexistent chink in his armor of vigilance over her.

She started to sing to herself, reminding herself of the words to "In the Cool Shade of the Mount." Then she immediately stopped herself, afraid that she might give away any information about the flute. Breathing heavily, more out of anger than shortness of breath from exercise, she fumed at how she felt boxed in. Tearing up yet again since being caught up with these Disaffected, she trotted along in silence, now upset that she was losing even the mood for the song.

Chapter 16

Lost Knife

That night they stopped in the shade of an aspen grove well away from the road.

Nillan posted Nolder as watch on the road so the crew could indulge in a campfire. As soon as Tunbloth finished his dinner, Nillan sent him to take Nolder's place while the rest of the group ate. During the afternoon, he had carefully gone through Allabva's bag while she watched from behind the wagon.

He had handed her knife to Qurast with a sarcastic declaration of "Happy birthday," but after laying everything out and confiscating a block of his favorite variety of cheese, he was satisfied that there was nothing she could use as a weapon or as a means of escape.

Now by the campfire, they handed Allabva her bag and waterskin, and she ate some wedding leftovers. Bless Fiewren for that. And Banduchy, too, for that matter. He had warned her about the Disaffected. She had no idea at the time that she would cross paths with them so soon afterwards.

Qurast burst into her mental space as she was putting her remaining food back in the bag, chewing on her last bite of dinner.

"Hey, where's that new knife?" he asked nobody in particular, checking his pockets and turning about as if to discover it lying on the ground next to him.

"What, that new knife that I ordered to be shipped all the way from the Cleft, just for your birthday?" Nillan feigned being upset. "That was special. I had it planned for months!"

"I had it right here, I thought. It was sheathed, and it was sitting in this pocket."

Qurast groped at the front of his trousers at the hip, then his jacket as well.

"How could you be so clumsy?" Halmon scolded him. "That knife wasn't too shabby, after all. And now you've gone and lost it. I bet you dropped it on the road three hours back."

Tunbloth joined in the sport of mocking their youngest member.

"You need to pay more attention to what you do with your things. And you need to value better what your wise leader has the vision to give you as a gift."

Tunbloth, Halmon, and Nillan All laughed for sport at Qurast's expense. Then Nillan got serious.

"Search the girl. Girl, give me your bag now."

Allabva handed it over without protest.

"Tunbloth, Halmon, make sure she doesn't have it in her clothing."

"My pleasure," Halmon seethed, picking up on Nillan's tone.

Halmon and Tunbloth rose and came forward to Allabva while she had flashbacks to the night before last, when those same two men had stopped her on the road.

"Cloak," Halmon held out his hand.

"And boots," Tunbloth grinned and waited.

Allabva removed her cloak and boots, handing them to the two men with fear in her heart. Halmon searched the cloak for anything hard and Tunbloth quickly checked the boots.

"You're probably right, Halmon," Qurast said. "I likely wasn't careful enough with the knife, and dropped it on the road."

"Nothing here."

Halmon tossed the cloak to the side, landing it in the fire.

Allabva gasped and reached forward and snatched it immediately, checking it for burns. There were black marks, but she couldn't tell without washing it if they were singes or soot.

"Nor here," Tunbloth said, tossing the boots far behind himself in different directions. "I guess we'll have to examine your clothing a little more...intimately. Coat, please."

He gestured for her to hand it over.

"You know how to say 'please.' I'm impressed," she said sarcastically.

He took another step closer and Allabva felt her breath catch.

Nillan laughed, watching the scene as if appreciating some spectacle.

Qurast interjected, trying to pull Tunbloth away, "In fact, I think I must have dropped it when I climbed into the wagon after our last break. It must be back there on the road."

Tunbloth ignored him, coming closer to Allabva.

Not knowing what else to do, she removed her coat and handed it to him.

He crumpled it in a manner that would quickly reveal if it had anything inside, then tossed it far behind Allabva. Both Tunbloth and Halmon took another step closer.

"You must have it hidden under another layer," Halmon said, leering.

"No!" Allabva protested.

She didn't have any more layers that she could remove without beginning to bare herself in front of them.

"That's enough!" Qurast shouted, showing more boldness than he normally did in the group.

He moved to place himself in between Allabva and the two men who were searching her for the knife.

"I said I'm certain I left it on the trail. Now leave her alone. We got her valuables from her, and we're taking her to the encampment so she can be properly questioned. I don't see how bothering her more about the knife is supposed to help free people's minds from the deceit of the unicorns."

"Fine, fine." Tunbloth backed off sullenly. "Quit overreacting. It was just a bit of sport."

"I don't call it sport when somebody suffers unnecessarily," Qurast rebuffed.

"Know your place, boy," Halmon counseled, giving Qurast a sidelong glance. "Be careful when you choose to interrupt me in what I'm doing." But, he also backed off from Qurast's stare, returning to his seat.

"Alright, you've had your fun, boys," Nillan said. "It's time to head to bed. Halmon, it's your turn to get a full night's sleep, you already know. Nolder's already on post and it's time that I should join him. Let's tie the girl back up and fix her in the wagon. For our two-man watch, have one visit camp frequently to make sure she's still tied up. Tunbloth and Qurast, we'll wake you for your turn on watch in a few hours, so bed down now and get some rest."

The crew did as he said. The two younger men helped tie Allabva up and put her in the wagon, repeating their method of tying her wrists behind her and attaching that rope to the wheel spokes. To Allabva's chagrin, they didn't forget the gag. Then they lay down in their bedrolls.

Despite being tied up as she was, Allabva was barely aware of the others bedding down, because she herself was already falling asleep, drained by the exercise of jogging on and off throughout most of the day. Lulled by the wind in the aspens, she drifted off to dreams of being torn from her home again and again.

Chapter 17

Unexpected Friend

Allabva felt some gentle prodding on her shoulder and opened her eyes under the starlight. The shadow standing over her was Qurast, holding a finger to his lips to signal her to stay silent. She could not have truly yelled out even if she had wanted to because of the gag in her mouth, but since Qurast had stood up in favor of her virtue in the campfire light, she felt inclined to listen to what he might have to say, anyway.

"Everyone is still asleep," Qurast whispered softly. "You'll need to go back to sleep as well. Tunbloth is on watch out at the road right now. I told him I was going to come back to check on you, just like Nillan said. I have something for you, but you cannot speak of this to anybody. Do you understand?"

Allabva nodded.

"Alright. Can you keep this hidden?" He held up her knife. "I never lost it."

She nodded again.

"I don't think it's right that we abducted you. I'm trying to free people from the illusion cast by the unicorns. I never set out to kidnap anybody. So, I'm giving you your knife back.

Please, please, do not attempt to escape tonight. Try tomorrow night, instead. Can you do that? Good. But this may be my only chance to pass this to you unobserved. And then you can escape tomorrow night, when it's my turn to get a full night's sleep. That way, nobody will accuse me of cutting you loose. I'm going to put this in your boot now, all right?"

Allabva nodded, recognizing the danger she could cause him if she didn't execute her escape with care.

"Alright."

Qurast pushed the sheathed knife into Allabva's boot, lodging it so it would not fall out.

"Now go back to sleep. This never happened."

He silently departed into the darkness. Allabva listened for a time to the sounds of the night and fell back asleep to a chorus of frogs from the lake.

The next morning was uneventful. Allabva continued to wonder if Hronomon would show up to help her, and continued to look for some opportunity to escape. She could have bolted a few times, but she knew that would not have helped her. These highwaymen would easily run her down and capture her again. She had to make sure that they couldn't do that whenever she tried to secure her freedom.

She wished her mother were here. Mother would give these Disaffected a piece of her mind and they would agree to let her go inside of ten minutes. Of course, Allabva would like to see Mellier as well, but she had her doubts as to how successfully he could annoy them into allowing her to go free.

When the crew set out and resumed their easterly travel along the Palf Road, they untied her as they had the day before, but today they allowed her to ride in the wagon. She was glad for that. She felt that sometimes one needed to move, and sometimes one needed to rest. Yesterday she did plenty of moving, so today she could bear to rest a little.

On this day, they encountered a man and a woman coming from the other direction. Nillan warned Allabva to keep her mouth shut or she would cause problems not only for herself but also for this couple. She dutifully kept silent, not offering any correction when Tunbloth volunteered that he could tell the other people that she was his sister.

As it happened, they merely shared a simple greeting and continued on. The men seemed to tense up before meeting with the couple, and then to breathe a little more easily again once the encounter was over. In contrast, Allabva felt disappointed that nothing had happened. Just about any possible change would have to be an improvement on her current situation.

The day passed, and the mountains loomed larger. The group of Disaffected was willing to talk to her, though they limited how much they would share along certain topics.

They told her that continuing along the Palf Road would eventually take them to Palf Glen, but their plan was to take a side road that would return them to bypass Palf Glen and return to the Tallens Road. Then they would then follow it east until nearing the encampment they sought. The planned turn toward the north before Palf Glen, and then east along the larger road, would take the mountains that she saw ahead of them and put them to their right.

Allabva sometimes rode in the wagon and sometimes got out for a fast-paced walk-jog. On this day, she spent more time resting than on rapid foot travel. She was still recovering from the day before. At one point, she found herself sitting in the wagon when she heard a shout of anger from Nolder, who was taking his shift with Qurast to drive the horses in the afternoon. She looked up and saw the unmistakable white coat of a Nomord in the distance, peeking out from among some trees.

"Cursed, foul horse!" Nolder shouted. "Go away!"

It was staring at Allabva. She sensed as surely as she could see the white equine body that he was watching her. It was Hronomon. Allabva felt excitement racing inside her, which she kept hidden. She was just a normal girl, she told herself. That was just some silly Nomo-Nomo. She had to wear the disguise to hide the truth from the Disaffected.

That didn't mean she couldn't take advantage of the opportunity to ask some questions.

"What is the issue that the Disaffected see with the Nomord?" Allabva asked him. "I understand that you each have your reasons for why you don't like the Nomord, but why do you think the world would be better without them?"

"Because human adoration of the Nomord is based on lies. Don't you think the world would be better with fewer lies in it?" Nolder spoke plainly, not roughly.

"I never thought of it that way," Allabva replied. "But people do genuinely receive help from them."

"We've been over this, little girl," Nillan jumped in. "Occasional teasings of assistance from beings with the capacity to help much more. All it does is make us believe that they are helpful and kind, whereas if you look at the pattern of them leaving us to our own wiles, then you see a very different story."

"How do the Disaffected propose to make the world a better place? What would you do about the Nomord?" she pondered aloud.

"Education, first off," Nolder offered. "A widespread campaign to get people to start thinking about it the right way."

"No disrespect intended," Allabva prodded, "but why would you consider your view to be the right view?"

"Because it is. Because it's obvious." Nillan interjected.

"Because it is according to our experience." Nolder spoke more sagely. "We have observed a pattern, and we believe other people are simply overlooking it, or in some cases, willfully choosing to ignore it and brushing it under the rug. If we can get people to start seeing the unicorns for what they are, people will feel more inclined to face and try to fix their problems themselves."

"That's what I've observed people do, trying to fix their problems themselves." Allabva replied. "I don't think anybody I know has relied on the Nomord even though they knew they could be helpful. I've known a couple of people who were blessed by the Nomord, but before and after that, they never hoped to rely on the Nomord's help."

"Isn't that just good for you?" Nillan voiced, dripping with sarcasm. "People in the Cleft must be sooo holy."

Nolder looked at Allabva and then at Nillan.

"You're both right," he said. "I have also seen people, although very aware of what the Nomord potentially could do for them, still only rely on themselves. But I've seen other people who owned fertile farmland let most of it lie fallow, wishing the unicorns would come and do all the work for them. The first type of people needs no correction, and will do just fine in life even if they never receive any help. The second group of people needs to be guided out of their indolence. *That* will make the world a better place."

"What if it's not even on purpose?" Allabva said tentatively.

"What's that supposed to mean?" Nolder asked. "Of course, the beasts do things on purpose."

"Alright, but what if their inconsistency isn't on purpose? What if their minds just don't work the same way as ours?" Allabva tried.

"Do you think you know something we don't, little girl?" Nillan shot back bitterly. "You believe that all your years of wisdom entitle you to tell us what to think?"

Allabva was a little taken aback. Maybe she should be more careful. She certainly didn't want to let them know that she did, in fact, know something they did not about the Nomord's minds.

"Of course not, sir," she intoned more meekly. "I just mean, what about how cats stare at the wall, or dogs howl in the night? We don't understand exactly why they do that, but it apparently makes sense to them."

"So you mean it's because they're stupid," Nillan put words in her mouth. "A cat stares at the wall because it's dumb, and dogs howl just because they feel like it. There's no rhyme or reason to it. So you're saying the freaks are just stupid."

"Well, I—"

"There is an obvious problem with your theory, Allabva," Nolder said more gently. "Unicorns can speak. They're obviously not as simple creatures as dogs and cats are. They are wise enough to speak, they have magic they can wield to help people, and yet more often than not, they withhold it. This speaks to me of malicious intent. They actually want to watch us suffer."

"I'm afraid I still don't see it that way." Allabva had received an explanation from Hronomon that seemed to be plausible, and she preferred to believe that. "So, what else would you do to convert people to your point of view?"

"Oh, there's more we can do than simple education," Nillan spoke as if he knew something that might change the world. "There are ways to counter them directly. Unicorns aren't the only source of magic."

His words sent a chill down Allabva's spine. Somehow she didn't think he was referring to jackalopes or fae-birds, but something more powerful.

"Where—what magic are you thinking of?"

"Nope. We're not talking about that. For all I know, you're in league with the animals. You can find out along with the rest of the world when those of us who are more Enlightened are prepared to take action."

Nillan turned to face forward to the road, intentionally exiting the conversation.

Allabva felt an ominous pall settled over her. She tried to dispel it as the wagon rumbled forward, silently reminding herself now that she *had* seen Hronomon, telling herself that he was coming to help. And yet, after this discussion, she felt she should stick to her plan to escape, pointedly not waiting for the Nomord's help.

The sky seemed to reflect her mood as heavy clouds appeared in the east, to the north of the looming mountain.

"Might rain," Halmon observed. "Probably coming in from the Fonglan Gulf. Tallensworth likely received a dumping this morning."

"What mountain is that?" Allabva asked. "It's taller than the clouds."

"That's Tallen Mountain," Nolder answered. "See the two peaks? The southern peak is the Bay Peak, since it lies a little further east and closer to the Gulf. The northern peak, the higher of the two, is much higher, reaching up to where you can feel the air is thinner."

"What's the taller peak called?" Allabva said.

"It sits bald without trees," Nolder continued, "and is often called Aspen Summit. But anyone who's ever seen a very old map knows that's a shortening of the original. Its real name is the Summit Above the Aspens."

"You dusty old man," Nillan accused. "Nobody cares enough to know that."

"Thank you for sharing," Allabva told Nolder. It sounded like he had spent some time in libraries. His manner when he spoke, except when he was speaking ill of the Nomord, made Allabva feel almost as if she had another ally apart from Qurast.

Nolder continued, now talking mostly to himself. "We were looking to pass through Palf Glen tomorrow, mid-morning, but if it rains on us very much, that'll slow us down. This road by the lake will get muddy and make the horses work harder. Mid-morning can turn into late afternoon if we don't push forward steadily enough."

The traveling party continued to make their way along the shore of the South Roula Sea, the wagon bumping along over the still-dry road. At dusk they pulled off of the road and traveled a few hundred paces south, away from the lake before setting camp.

"Enjoy the fire tonight, boys," Nillan suggested. "We likely won't find dry lumber tomorrow."

Allabva was given access to her bag, her captors now evidently supposing that they had rendered her harmless. She ate well, intending to cut herself free tonight with the knife Qurast had returned to her. She may need to maintain a high pace for some time to ensure she stayed free of them, so she ate her fill with this in mind.

As they tied her down in the same fashion as before, she hoped the knife in her boot wouldn't be too far to reach. She wriggled a little as she settled in, testing the amount of play they were giving her hands. Qurast caught her eye as he tightened the knot, looking back and forth between her hands and boots. Apparently thinking the same thing, he gave the rope a tug as if to test its strength and the sureness of the knots. It reassured Allabva that there was enough length there. But the tug was hard, causing pain in her wrists.

She released a short exclamation, causing Tunbloth to smirk. "Is it tight enough?"

"Just enough," Allabva grunted.

Qurast gave her a nod. "Good."

Then he turned away, preparing his bedroll underneath the wagon. Halmon and Nillan were also setting theirs under the wagon, with Qurast in the middle. Their two-man watch rotation occupied a total of four of the five throughout the night, affording the remaining man the opportunity for a full night's sleep. With tonight being Qurast's turn to sleep undisturbed, the other two on sleep shift bedded down on either side so they could more easily be woken and have their bedrolls replaced by the two men serving on the first watch shift.

Allabva listened to the three men below her doze off and snore, while the two remaining men stalked silently off into the darkness to watch for anybody who may catch their trail and approach from the road.

Her fingers itched to reach for her boot and extract her knife. She resisted, forming and clarifying a plan in her head. Allabva would *not* leave without Delgan's flute. She was certain that Nillan still had it in his inner coat pocket. She determined to pilfer it from him when it was his turn to sleep. He was on second watch shift, so that meant she had to snatch it during the first shift and be gone.

She hadn't spent today running behind the wagon, but instead she had been allowed her choice of riding or going on foot. She had walked a fair amount because she found herself getting restless if she sat still too long. Despite her mild fatigue, she mentally held onto consciousness.

But she was tired. Every day was a long day. Perhaps she could allow herself some rest—not sleep, of course—to be ready for what could become hours of jogging to stay out of reach of the five Disaffected. She just needed to make sure that she waited long enough so Nillan would be fully asleep when she went to retrieve the instrument.

Wishing she could commiserate with Mother, tease Mellier, joke with Brelin, and take Delgan's hands and apologize for allowing his grandmother's flute out of her sight for even a moment, Allabva waited.

Chapter 18

Run

Allabva took in breath sharply as she was prodded awake. The rain had arrived, but it was light. With her cloak covering her body and head, it hadn't woken her.

A large shadow stood over her. She started, worried that this shadow may wish her harm, that it may suspect something, now that she harbored a hidden knife in her boot. It leaned in and Allabva prepared to defend herself with what little freedom of movement she had.

"Allabva," Nolder whispered, "don't you think you'd best be going?"

Allabva's eyes widened in confused relief.

"Shh," he warned. "I just came to make sure everything was secure, now, didn't I? Now I'm going back to stand post with Halmon. He may want to take a turn to come check as well in a while, but it won't be too long before we both come to wake up the next watch. I recommend you be gone before then."

Head spinning in sleepiness, Allabva tried to grasp the whole situation. "But my flute."

"Ah. Almost forgot. By any chance, is your birthday coming up?" He pulled the flute from his pocket, holding it up to gleam in the starlight. "Here you go." He gave her a kind smile as he reached over to her bag, pulled it closer to himself, and slid the flute inside.

Allabva was still confused. Nolder and Qurast were part of the party who had grabbed her on the road and carried her unwillingly for a few days toward a camp of anti-sympathetic people, and yet they were helping her escape? On purpose?

"Don't waste any time." Nolder said. "Go on and get far away from here. With any luck, Halmon and the next watch will be lazy and won't check to look for you. We're only two days from a new moon, and it's overcast as well. The darkness may help you. But you've got to use your legs and get out of here."

Allabva stared in puzzlement at the man. Why was he helping? There was something she hadn't seen before...

"You were Touched," she said in amazement. "You have the Touch of the Nom—then why are you with the Disaffected? Nillan said you didn't have any personal experience with them. How can you..."

The thought of having communed with one of the innocent and joyful Ta-Nomord, and then having turned against them, was a notion so confusing to Allabva that she lost the power of speech.

Nolder looked back at her, an untold, heavy sadness showing momentarily on his face.

"Another time, perhaps. Just go quickly and silently."

Saying no more, he slunk off in the rain.

Grabbing hold of what had just happened, heartbeat quickening, Allabva bent her back and knees backward as far as she could, bringing her feet up toward her back. She couldn't quite reach the top of her boot, but she was able to grab the heel. Pulling on this, she might normally expect the boot to come off, but having her ankles bound made that impossible.

Wriggling, she forced the sheathed knife to fall out of the top of her boot, which placed it farther from her hands. A small wave of panic washed through her. What if she couldn't reach it, and they discovered her in the morning, in possession of the purportedly lost knife? No, she had to make this work. She moved her legs back and forth to inch the knife up toward her reach. That did it. Awash with relief, she wrapped her fingers around the handle.

Finally with the knife in her grasp, Allabva unsheathed it and began to saw at the rope that held her hands bound to the wheel of the wagon. She tried to avoid shaking the wagon, which was a factor that slowed her work. But she had to complete this urgently. She was able to lift her shoulders and bend her elbows, creating some slack in the rope, which she then grabbed with one hand while she sawed at it through the slackened loop with the other hand holding the knife.

Presently, Allabva had severed the rope holding her hands to the wagon. She bent her torso and curved her back to bring her the knife to bear on the rope around her ankles. She quickly realized this was rather awkward and focused instead on carefully cutting the rope around her wrists. After several minutes she was able to sit up and use both hands to untie her ankles.

One of the men underneath the wagon snorted and stirred. Allabva froze, terrified that she would be caught mid-escape. If that happened, she would bound more tightly, watched more closely, and afforded no second chance to get away. She listened intently, waiting to hear steady breathing against the background of chirping crickets. The steady breathing resumed again after several seconds, and Allabva returned to her task.

Within thirty more seconds, the knot at her ankles was undone, and she slipped free. For a moment she wondered if she should take the rope with her. It may show poorly for Qurast if the rest of the Disaffected saw the rope cut, showing that she'd had a knife. But the rope was still tied to the wagon, so she would have to untie or cut it.

But she couldn't risk shaking the wagon more. Besides, it was a hopeless dilemma; if she was gone, whether the rope was cut or loosened, it would probably look bad for somebody.

She grabbed her bag and walking staff, which had been placed at the back of the driver's bench, and climbed down as quietly as she could, wincing at every creak and crack the wood made as she shifted her weight across it. Allabva reached the ground with one toe first, then lowered all her weight onto the softening soil.

The rain continued dripping down, giving her a chill and making her glad that she was about to be on the move so that she wouldn't feel the cold except in her extremities. Allabva started to back away from the wagon, orienting herself in the night. She saw the horses off to her left, where they had been tied to a tree. Imagining a map in her head and remembering that they had come from the road in a certain direction, she decided which way must be east. Palf Glen was that way. She would have to go north a little way to come back to the road in order to find her way to the town, but for now she just needed to get away from Nillan's camp. She would go east and stay off the road for a couple of hours at least.

Just before turning her back on the wagon and horses, Allabva saw two eyes peering at her from under the middle of the wagon. They stayed silent. Qurast knew she was free, then. She gave him a nod of thanks, hoping he was able to see the gesture in the dark.

She turned and walked away, intentionally heading south first until she was out of sight. This didn't require her to go very far due to the overcast sky and the falling rain. Then, without doubling back, she turned her course east and walked as fast as she could. In the dark and with the soil turning to mud, she was very glad to have her trusty walking stick to stabilize her step.

She traveled east and began to pick her way through a landscape of intermittent trees and grass. No sooner had she traveled fifty paces in her new eastward direction than she heard shouts from the direction of the camp.

"Oh, no," Allabva muttered to herself. "Didn't I have at least a few more minutes? Maybe somebody else woke up."

Now it was time to start moving for real. She began to jog, moving as quickly as she dared, with the ground becoming more and more slippery with the rain. Allabva struggled just to see in the scant light. She used the tip of her staff to probe the ground ahead of her, but barely gave it time to touch the soil before she lifted it again to find her next step.

She tried to find comfort in the knowledge that the party had no dogs, but being honest with herself, she didn't feel very comforted. The situation would obviously have been much worse if they had dogs to track her and chase her down. Dogs would make it nearly certain that the Disaffected would find her in the dark. However, no matter how likely it was, if they found her, the outcome would be the same: she would be recaptured, and a second escape would be impossible.

That idea made Allabva wonder how good they would be at tracking her steps. Her trail surely wouldn't be hard to track if they outlasted the rain and into daylight, but that was several hours away.

Glad that she had first headed south, she considered doubling back now in order to leave an untraceable tangle of footprints.

She quickly discarded the thought. If they wanted to follow her, they had three options. The slowest of these would be to hitch up the horses and pull the wagon through this mess of interspersed trees. Entirely infeasible, they wouldn't do it.

The second option for the Disaffected would be to travel on foot, the same as she now did. She doubted that would help them. While Allabva knew she wasn't the fastest runner around, she also knew from the summertime Skystone Observance races they ran in the Cleft, that introducing stamina as a factor pushed the odds closer to her favor. Adding the fact that she spent many of her days back home romping through the canyons in the Cleft, she knew that her pace wouldn't be too shabby over a long distance.

Perhaps Qurast or Tunbloth, the youngest two of the five men, could probably overtake her if they tried. And Qurast wouldn't try, would he? But the other three? She would be surprised. Would the crew split themselves up and have every man travel at his own pace in order to catch her? Probably not.

And then, rather obviously, the third and fastest way they might try to follow her would be on horseback. This would also divide the crew because there were only two horses, so only two men would come and bring her back. Additionally, if they pressed after her in haste over the uneven ground at night, they would risk leaving their horses lame and lose use of the wagon, unable to pull it anymore. But setting the risk aside, if they could identify and follow her tracks, this would pose a very real threat to Allabva's newfound freedom.

First, they would have to find her. She was intent on making sure that it wasn't going to be easy for them.

Allabva found her sojourn with the five Disaffected gentlemen book-ended at beginning and end by the action of running through the rain at night. She was confident that this time there would be no bandits waiting across the path with a rope to trip her. The perks of traveling off the road seemed paltry and modest, especially since the rain was picking up, gradually increasing in intensity.

I suppose Hronomon isn't anywhere nearby, or I would have nicer weather right now, Allabva thought.

Despite all the factors that would make it difficult for the party to apprehend her once more, Allabva still worried. If Hronomon was still around, then she still had a mission as important as the world itself. If she still had her mission to be the Companion to the Shrongelin, then she still needed to travel with the utmost haste. Most significantly, she could not afford to be recaptured.

So Allabva ran on, ran haltingly, lopsidedly, and tiringly. Eventually, and after a considerable amount of work, she crested a rise that she would have guessed to be a hundred paces high. The vantage point gave her a view over the lake, but she didn't spare it a glance as she worked to descend on the other side of the hill as quickly as she could. Here, the ground was somewhat rocky. She held her staff in her left hand as she descended, using it to catch her weight to prevent her from going too fast down the steep slope.

At the bottom of the hill a stream wandered northward, across her current path and down toward the lake before the ground began to gently rise again. Allabva didn't have any time for the stream to slow her down. She approached it without slowing but as she was about to jump over it, she stepped on a patch of soil that proved to be too soft. It slipped over a rock that it covered, causing Allabva to slip. She threw her hands out as she fell into the stream despite trying to catch herself with her other foot.

Her landing was wet, soaking through her clothes in an instant, but that wasn't her worst immediate concern.

Allabva arose from the water, hobbling unevenly due to a sudden pain in her right foot and ankle. Now leaning on her staff more than ever, she climbed out of the stream and onto the east bank. Taking interrupted, halting steps, she climbed out of the cut in the earth surrounding the stream.

It was time to head to the road. Her injured ankle would not allow her to continue traveling on the uneven ground away from the road. Now half-hopping and using her staff as a crutch, Allabva wandered northward through the sparse woods.

It took her much longer than she expected. Either the road or her path through the night had deviated significantly from a due east direction. As she followed the slope of the land downward, she caught an occasional glimpse of the water's surface. Eventually, the trees gave way completely and she found herself looking at the road.

Nervously looking left and right, As Allabva came back to the Palf Road overlooking the calm waters of the lake, she turned to put the lake on her left. She had hardly hobbled thirty paces when Hronomon stepped out of the brush on the south side of the road, looking as stately as he had the first time she had seen him, back in Pine Canyon.

Chapter 19

Found Again

Allabva spent a good ten seconds utterly dumbfounded, doing nothing but staring at the stark white creature before her.

Hronomon lowered his head, looking at her, waiting. He lifted his head again and approached her.

Allabva began to shout at him accusingly, "Where were y—"

She stopped herself. He owed her an explanation. She would give him the chance to deliver it.

Forcing herself to steady her voice, she tried again, voice flat.

"I'm glad you're back, Hronomon the Forerunner. Shall we continue and catch up on the way?"

"Yes, we will continue forward. You have done well for yourself."

"I thought I should keep heading toward Palf Glen, but I still don't know where we are going in the end."

"We continue east," he said as he turned to face away from her along the road.

"I may need some help here," Allabva winced as she began to trot again. "I took a fall."

Hronomon matched Allabva's pace.

"What help do you need? I still cannot carry you. Can you keep this pace? It seems somewhat fast, especially considering an injury."

"I honestly do not know," she replied. "But I have to put some distance between me and... some people I met on the road."

She wasn't sure how to talk about them. They violated her freedom, holding her captive for days, and would have done so for much longer if they could have.

"I need to have a head start. They mentioned getting to Palf Glen by mid-morning before it started to rain. If that's still where we're going, then I'd like to be there by dawn."

"It is not our destination. It is true that we are currently headed toward Palf Glen, but we are to deviate from that course, traveling to the south of the town to avoid interaction. Our destination lies beyond."

Allabva couldn't believe the surrealness of the scene. She had been kidnapped, held for days, wondering where the Nomord had been. Now, she had escaped without his help, he showed up, and they acted as though nothing happened. She wanted that explanation.

"All right," Allabva panted. "On we press. You must have some questions, but I have some questions of my own."

"Perhaps you have more questions than I do," Hronomon said. "I've been watching your progress, so I believe I am aware of what you have been through these past few days, with small gaps."

Allabva was dumbfounded once more. She trotted along, limping to favor her right ankle. After some twenty paces, she came back to herself.

"You knew what was going on? Why—"

She struggled, grappling with her emotions and confusion.

"Why didn't you help out? You let me get kidnapped? You let me continue in bondage for three days, and didn't intervene?"

Hronomon watched her out of one eye but didn't respond immediately.

"Please help me understand," Allabva pleaded, trying to hold tears back. "You promised my mother you would protect me. And now I learn that you've been skulking in the background instead this whole time?"

Hronomon blinked, lowered his head, raised it again, and shook his mane. "I did not immediately know that you had been abducted. I was scouting ahead of you to try to be ready if we encountered anybody on the road. I doubled back and found you gone. I was able to follow the trail left by your abductors. It was easy to see the disturbed mud on the road where they grabbed you. By the time I found you, you were surrounded by five men. I could easily overpower five men. They would have been no danger to you from the moment I engaged them."

"Then why didn't you?"

"It would have left evidence of my interference in human affairs, something you do not see from the Ta-Nomord, is that correct? In your world, among the mankind of today, all you know is the Nomo-Nomo, the very definition of innocent to a fault. That would have changed if I had attacked."

"Oh."

Amazement at the mental image shone on Allabva's face.

"If I had fought solely to free you, I would have left five witnesses, not only of a Nomord carrying out violence, but more dangerously, a Nomord fighting to protect a particular human. It would have marked us both as targets for Sacalai's followers to hunt down in concerted effort. Also, I believe I was able to have some amount of influence on them and that is why they eventually dropped their guard enough for you to escape."

"I think those were Sacalai's followers," Allabva worked to piece together the puzzle. "And I'm sure you could take them on, easily. Why didn't they harm me?"

Hronomon considered her with an appraising eye. "She has others. Her influence goes beyond the human domain. We must not underestimate her. You say you believe these were Sacalai's followers?"

"Well, yes. They call themselves Disaffected. They're on their way to an encampment, where there are more of them. Their whole thing is that they don't like the Nomord," Allabva huffed as she jogged. "I think I'm going to need some help with this ankle," she probed again.

"Let me know what you need."

The two trotted along in silence for a long moment and Allabva noticed that the rain had stopped falling completely.

"I'll think about it."

But she still had pressing questions to sort out the last few days from his viewpoint.

"If you can protect me, but then you can't because there will be witnesses, then how are you supposed to be able to protect me?"

Hronomon regarded her for a moment before replying.

"I would not necessarily have to leave witnesses. Besides, I was sometimes close enough that I overheard them saying they wanted you to answer questions. They may not have harmed you just for that. Also, Sacalai's influence bears more heavily on some than on others. Perhaps these were not yet so far gone."

A killer Nomord? Allabva was surprised at the thought.

"Does that even work? Are the Nomord capable of killing?"

"The Ta-Nomord are not. In their present condition, they lack the mental capacity to commit violence of any kind. We Gha-Nomord are capable, though it takes an emotional toll. Also, we could never bear to do it except as a necessity to protect."

"Alright," Allabva allowed.

Something about his absence still bothered her.

"Why didn't you come and help me escape when most of them were asleep? There were moments when nobody was watching me. I only didn't leave yet because I didn't have my knife to cut the bonds."

Hronomon breathed a deep sigh before speaking.

"This carries an answer that is a little more complicated. When I found you again, although you were in captivity, you were on the road going east, carried by their wagon. It afforded you the opportunity to rest more and travel faster than you could have accomplished by yourself."

"If it was fine that I rode in the wagon, then why can't you carry me now?"

"A valid question, but it shows your ignorance of the Construct."

"Go ahead, I'm ready to be filled in."

Allabva grunted at a sudden pain in her ankle and made a mental note not to step on it like that.

"And you deserve to be filled in," Hronomon validated. "You have shown yourself to be extremely resilient and resourceful in the face of adversity."

"I would feel more resourceful if I hadn't twisted my ankle," Allabva half joked.

"The Compact requires a human who can come under her own power and willingness to bond with the Shrongelin. If you rode on my back, it would cheapen the contract, devaluing and directly weakening the power that it holds. If you bonded with the Shrongelin after that, it would make it all but impossible to overcome Sacalai. When you were abducted, your journey was not your own, not aligned with your accepted mission. You were being forced on a different spiritual path."

"Spiritual path?"

"During this time, your purpose was regaining your freedom, not journeying, whether willing or unwilling, to meet the Shrongelin."

"But I was still going the correct direction," Allabva puzzled.

"That was convenient, but irrelevant to your intent or anybody else's."

"If that doesn't matter, then what?"

"Then you could hypothetically be carried the whole way," Hronomon answered.

This didn't make a bit of sense to Allabva.

"So, it was a good thing?"

"As long as they carried you in the right direction and remained intent on keeping you alive for questioning, then I believe it was, overall, a helpful event. You traveled faster, and you were able to rest. It surely cut time off our journey."

"You followed along the entire way?" Allabva asked.

"Yes. If they had threatened your life or posed a threat of causing you serious injury, then I would have charged in.

There would not have been any witnesses left among them. But I didn't want to cause them any harm, either."

"So that was you that I saw when we almost traveled along the Tallens Road between the Roula Seas?"

"Yes." Hronomon confirmed.

"At that point, on that neck of land stretching out into the seas, I got the Disaffected talking about how there was nowhere for them to hide if they were pursued, because I knew that they were on the run. I got them to turn around and travel the Palf Road instead. I'm glad it helped."

Allabva tried to exult over the positive results, but her appreciation was conceptual, the emotion washed out with fatigue. Then she wondered what the alternative would have produced.

"What would you have done if we'd kept going? There would have been nowhere for you to tag along and stay out of sight."

"I had thought that, if necessary, I would stay far enough away that I would be indistinguishable from one of the Ta-Nomord. I would try to act the part as well. Perhaps I could pull it off, but it undoubtedly would have been a spectacle for them or any other travelers wondering at one of the Nomo-Nomo taking such a singular path. No matter how much I would wind and vary, or romp and roll in the water, it would have attracted notice, which raises the risk of suspicion."

"So you did mean it," Allabva panted as she jogged, still limping. "They weren't just idle words."

"I meant what? I never speak idle words."

"You promised my mother that you would protect me."

"Of course. And I had every intention of doing so. I failed, obviously."

"But I'm safe now." The chill in the air was disappearing along with the rain.

"Regardless, I failed to protect you from being abducted." Hronomon drooped his head until his single horn angled parallel above the ground. "I thought the road was empty, and I strayed too far ahead. For that error I am ashamed. But once I found you again, I followed along, ready to jump into the pack of men in whatever moment. But since they never drew a blade on you, it was less likely that they could do significant harm to you before I could arrive."

Allabva didn't understand everything.

"But if you were so close as you describe, then why didn't you reveal yourself to me until I came out on the road? It was quite some time and some distance after I left Nillan's camp."

"It is essential that I avoid us being perceived as connected in any way. You needed to get far enough away from them. Because of the Construct, there is little I can do to physically help you. It is impossible for me to directly speed you on your way without compromising the effectiveness of your future bond with the Shrongelin. If I had approached you and then those men had caught up with you, you could be recaptured. Of course I do not want this to happen, but if you had, what would the result be? You would once again be carried in the correct direction, and able to rest more than when you are alone."

Allabva was working very hard to avoid tears because of the pain in her ankle and the exertion with which she currently traveled. Hronomon's last remark sounded as if he didn't care about her at all. It was a bad combination.

"It almost sounds as if it would have been better if I had not escaped."

"Nonsense. You needed to be rid of them sooner or later. Now you are, and we are closer to our destination."

Allabva wondered how soon it would be safe to stop running and start walking, or if she needed to leave the road again in order to avoid being found by the crew. Just then, she realized that the rain had stopped and there was a cool but not chilly breeze slowly drying her outer layer of clothing. She remembered that Hronomon had said the Gha-Nomord could influence the weather.

"Why was it raining when I left their camp, and for so long after? If you were trying to help, why didn't you make it easier for me? Or is this rain also from Sacalai, like the last one was? Can't you suppress it at all?"

Hronomon nodded.

"Actually, this rain was mine. I did not suppose that I could help you significantly with a clear sky, but that I could hinder them with the rain and the mud. The rain hindered visibility, serving to hide you and your tracks as you fled them. The mud is currently making it more difficult for their wagon and slows down their rate of travel. I was summoning the rain, not trying to suppress it. I did not anticipate that it might lead to you being injured."

"Well, it did, but I would rather be limping with a bad ankle than still be tied up in their wagon and wondering what they're going to do with me in the end." Allabva would have shivered if she hadn't been sweating from exertion. "Speaking of this ankle, I really think I need to get some help. It keeps feeling worse and worse."

Hronomon glanced down but continued moving alongside Allabva. "Do what you can to keep pressing on, but do not be so stoic as to hide any pain or other problems from me.

Your feet are important. Why do you think I grow stones for feet myself?"

He pranced for a few steps, lifting his legs high and then striking his hooves on the ground hard, which may have sounded impressive if he were marching on stone. Was that a...joke? Nomord humor? Allabva didn't quite feel it.

"The pain is quite bad. How far away is Palf Glen? They must have a physician. Do you have any secret Gha-Nomord abilities that you didn't tell me about? I mean, I know it's the Ta-Nomord that have the power to heal. Do you have any...female...summoning power? Or would that count as assisting me too much in my journey to go meet the Shrongelin? Like, time out in a Pinerball match, disqualified, two minutes in the penalty box?"

Could a horse look confused? A certain Nomord certainly did at this moment.

"I'm afraid I don't have any ability to heal, to summon a healer, or sniff one out to help you."

"So you said I shouldn't be stoic and hide any pain from you?"

"That is correct. Is there something you need to tell me?"

Allabva groaned. "It's my ankle, just like I already told you. I need to get some help with this. How far is our destination?"

Hronomon seemed to consider and weigh in his mind for several moments. "You handled your captivity quite well. They didn't perform any torture, but now I do not believe that you would give in to such treatment, anyway. You will meet the Shrongelin atop the Summit Above the Aspens. It is a special place, hallowed by the Construct which instituted the Shrongelin cycle. It is protected from Sacalai's permanent memory, blotted out each time she is imprisoned. As soon as the enemy knows that is where we are headed, we will face great adversity trying to stop us, trying to stop you from reaching it."

Allabva considered the mountain with dread in her heart. "I don't think I can make it up that mountain in any reasonable amount of time on this ankle."

Hronomon opened his mouth and answered Allabva's previous question. "Palf Glen, at your current pace, is still perhaps half a day's journey from here."

"Half a day?" Allabva's heart sank, encumbered with worry. There was no way she could walk another twelve hours with this pain.

"Half a day's journey is half the distance you would travel on a normal traveling day," Hronomon clarified.

That helped. A little. Four to six hours was certainly better than twelve, but it would still be very difficult.

Allabva jogged and hobbled on through the night, Hronomon at her side. She was reassured now that the Nomord was back with her, but she was still impelled forward by fear at the prospect of the Disaffected retaking her.

Part IV: Palf Glen and Beyond

Chapter 20

Respite

Allabva and Hronomon began to see the town of Palf Glen in the pale light of the early dawn. The South Roula Sea now lay at their backs. A mist rose over the town as the previous night's rain evaporated.

"I must not go into the town with you," Hronomon said. "You will need to find a physician on your own. Do you have any money to pay with?"

"No," Allabva responded, "but maybe I can perform some service for the doctor in exchange, or maybe I will rely on charity here. At any rate, I have to try to get some help. I cannot keep going."

"Be on the southern road out of town not later than sundown," Hronomon instructed. "Head toward the foothills to the south. I will meet you on that road and then we will head east toward the mountain. Healed or not, you must come, or I will risk public attention to come get you. Sacalai would surely receive word quickly. It would not identify you, but it would identify me and mark me as Hronomon."

Allabva raised her brows. This was very serious. "I will be there by noon, then."

"That would be fortuitous. Then we could take a brief rest before continuing." Hronomon turned off the road and disappeared into the bushes and trees.

Allabva continued forward into Palf Glen, leaning heavily on her staff. She wandered a little through the town, trying to appreciate the sights of tiled and thatched roofs despite the pain in her ankle. This town had more variety in the building materials than Allabva saw in the Cleft. She saw wood and brick houses as she had back home, but here there were buildings of stone, and some of them showed plaster. The colors were different, too. While the Cleft favored lighter shades, Palf Glen generally leaned toward darker tones of brown or maroon, with the occasional beige or tan providing relief.

Allabva saw simple signs over shops indicating the nature of business carried out there, and she smelled bread baking and eggs frying as the town woke up and prepared itself for the day. She wondered how she was supposed to guess in which part of the town she was supposed to be able to find a doctor as she came to street intersections, choosing to follow one or another without any real rhyme or reason.

She came to a sign over a dark green door set in a gray stone wall which reflected the local expectation of common literacy. It straightforwardly said 'PHYSICIAN' and then underneath it, the name Brolfith Noteh. As it was very early still, rather than knocking and possibly waking anybody up, Allabva instead placed herself on a bench positioned conveniently outside the door.

She supposed she was safe enough where she was. Having never been to Palf Glen, nobody would recognize her, although perhaps they could identify her clothing as coming from the Cleft. The brigands who beset her on the road days ago were planning to bypass the town. Allabva was not currently with Hronomon, and carrying nothing that would tie her to him or his mission for her.

Allabva settled in, drinking from her waterskin and opening her bag to fish out some food. She was nearly out. She ate half of what remained and returned the rest. As she put the food away, her fingers found Delgan's flute. Taking it out, she redid the clasp of the chain around her neck and tucked the flute back under her shirt.

Allabva sat back to watch the morning take hold of the houses and shops on this street. She listened to muffled voices from indistinct locations and the chirping of birds in a tree growing next to a well fifty paces off.

The sun broke over the rooftops down the street. It shone so brightly after her exhausting run through the overcast night, forcing her eyelids closed despite herself. She tried squinting, but it wasn't enough. Her shut eyelids glowed red in her vision, and she covered her face with the hood of her cloak. She brought her knees up to support her arm with her hand holding the hood in just the right position. The birdsong and human voices sounded far away. They grew muffled. Eyes closed and accidentally tucked in, Allabva fell asleep.

"You can't stay there."

Allabva jumped, not recognizing the voice. It spoke again.

"You can't stay there. Move along. We take patients here." It sounded like a woman's voice, and a tad impatient.

Allabva opened her eyes, lowering her hood to the back of her neck. She blinked in the sunlight. It was still early morning; she had slept no longer than half an hour.

"Sorry," she croaked. "I didn't mean to fall asleep. It's just that the sun was so bright, so I covered my eyes…"

"You don't look like you're from here," the voice said. "Roula quarter? Somebody cart you in from the docks?"

"No," Allabva said, confused.

"No, I suppose not. That's half a day's trip. Nobody would have let you ride looking like that, not on horseback, not in coach. So where do you–you know what, it doesn't matter. You can't stay here."

Allabva tried to look up at the woman, but the sun was just over the woman's shoulder, dazzling Allabva's eyes. She looked down at herself instead, taking in the mud on her boots and clothing. She couldn't see her hair, but it must have been a mess as well.

Allabva gathered her wits and pushed the cloudiness from her mind. "I came here hoping to be a patient."

As the woman shifted, Allabva squinted up at her and could see her face. She was frowning, looking at Allabva as if wondering what to think. Her arms were folded across her chest, and she slouched slightly to the rear in the air as she considered.

"Alright, maybe it does matter. Where did you come from?"

Allabva wanted to tell her, but hesitated to do so. "From west of here. I would rather not say more. But I had to travel through the night, disregarding rain and cold. I slipped in the mud and fell. I need some help with my ankle."

The woman inspected Allabva, lips pursed, reconsidering whether she needed to shoo her away.

"Please. My journey isn't over and I'm traveling on foot, and it's very important, and if I could just get a proper wrapping, I'll be on my way, but I—"

"Come in, girl," the woman interrupted. "I can help you. Doctor Brolfith Noteh, at your service. Just come inside before anybody sees you. I understand you've seen a hard trip, but passersby may make uninformed judgments about me if they see you sitting here so dirty." Noteh stepped out of Allabva's way and held the door open, gesturing her inside.

Allabva stood shakily and supported herself against the wall and the door frame as she made her way into the building. Doctor Noteh followed Allabva inside, taking her cloak and then her coat to set them on a rack near the door.

"All right, let's make this pretty quick. I haven't had my breakfast yet. Which ankle is it?"

"My right ankle."

"Well, go on. Take off your boot and let me see it."

Allabva removed her right boot and then the sock as well. The ankle was red and swollen.

"My goodness, girly. You really do need help. Before I wrap it I want to put some golroot ointment on it to lower the swelling and speed up healing. I don't suppose I can convince you to rest and elevate your leg for the next several days?" Doctor Noteh stood and began looking in small clay pots on a shelf against the wall, lifting lids and peering inside.

"I wish I could, but I really need to get going again as soon as I can," Allabva replied.

"Hmm," Noteh said to herself, "I'm out of golroot ointment. No problem, I'll mix some more. What was your name?" She turned to Allabva and waited for a response.

"Allabva."

"Well, Allabva, just stay there and relax a few minutes. I need to go mix up the ointment to make a poultice. If you're bored, there's some reading material on the table next to you. Maybe not the highest quality, but I stock my shop mostly with reading material from my son's leftovers. It's what he likes to read." Doctor Noteh exited the room into what Allabva supposed must be the rest of the house, with her medical shop in the front where Allabva was.

Allabva looked next to her, where a few books sat on the table. While one appeared to be a history, the others were more like pamphlets with simplified woodcut drawings stamped in them to tell a story. She picked one up, evidently a horror story, the title *Nightshade Unicorn and the Sailors of the Roula Seas* spanning its cover. She flipped through its pages and saw images of a great black beast jumping aboard ships—who knew how far away the land was that it was jumping from—and skewering their crews. Disgusted with the depictions of blood, Allabva set it back down.

Doctor Noteh walked back in earlier than Allabva would have expected. "It looks like we're out of golroot powder. This will probably take a little longer, then. If you're so tired, go ahead and kick back right where you are, relax awhile while you wait. I'll have to go to the herbalist and get some more. Might as well take off your other boot and sock while you're at it. Let me see your other foot before we assume it's just fine. We'll set you on your way with two good feet, if at all possible."

Allabva removed her left boot and sock and Doctor Noteh looked over her foot, examining the several red spots.

"Not too bad, honestly. It looks like you've had plenty of chafing, though. We'll hit both your feet with that same ointment. Leave it in place for just a few hours, then change your socks. I'll give you a small pot of it so you can use it again tomorrow. You only need it once per day. Reapply the brace that I'm going to give you. I'll show you how to re-wrap it yourself."

"Thank you," Allabva said. "I was worried I wasn't going to be able to find a physician, and then I was worried that you wouldn't have time or be able to help me."

"Of course, I would help you, Allabva. You need help, right? That's what I do."

"But I'm afraid I don't have any money. It was stolen on the road."

"Well, that explains a lot, then." Noteh looked at Allabva appreciatively. "You must be tuckered out from running from the bandits. Sometimes you just can't believe people. But you're in luck here. Unless there's some significant cost associated with ingredient or device, I always help first and ask for payment afterwards, if it can be provided."

"Thank you," Allabva said again.

"Don't mention it. On second thought, let's not have you wait right here. We'll have people coming in and out of here all day, so let's move you to a back room. Please follow me; you can leave your boots off, and your socks as well." Doctor Noteh moved to exit through the back of the room, pausing for Allabva to stand with her things in her arms and follow her back. "I'm sorry," Noteh caught herself. "Can you walk a few paces alright, or do you need help?"

She approached, but Allabva waved her off. Allabva stood and followed the woman into a hallway where she could see a kitchen at the back. They stopped in front of a door to their left and Noteh open the door. Inside was a room showing a bed, a simple desk, and a chair.

"Welcome to our humble guest room," Noteh said. "I use it for patients, too. It comes in handy. Anyway, just sit tight. I'm still getting my morning started, so I can't rush off to the herbalist right now. I let my husband know to leave you alone so you can get some rest while you wait. It's the only thing to do for it."

"Thank you again," Allabva said. It was starting to feel redundant.

"Lie down," the doctor said, all business. "I know you're not going to elevate your ankle later, so do it now. You can use this pillow." Doctor Noteh grabbed the pillow from the bed and turned it sideways so that Allabva's foot would be higher from the surface of the bed as she rested it on the pillow. Then the matron turned and walked out, closing the door behind her.

Allabva found herself alone in a stranger's house, but grateful for it. Hronomon had said *by sundown*, so she still had all day to traverse the town after she left here. She hoped that would be soon. No matter how tired she was, Allabva knew that the urgency of her mission dictated a sustained pace. She couldn't remember if Hronomon had stipulated that there would be a fixed deadline or if it was simply a worsening situation and they had to be there as fast as they could. Either way, she figured she had gotten ahead of schedule because of her abduction, so her mad rush through the night to get to Palf Glen would add slightly to that. If Hronomon said to meet him at the end of the day and she really needed a tiny bit of rest and recovery, then she would take it.

Her stomach grumbled. The snack she had allowed herself while sitting on the bench out front had not been enough. She opened her bag and removed the last bit of food, a morsel of hard bread. She finished it off unceremoniously, washing it down with the rest of her water. Allabva didn't know where she would get her next meal and that worried her, but she didn't think it was something she could solve at the moment. She remembered the well she saw down the street, so she knew she could fill her waterskin whenever she left Doctor Noteh's practice.

As Allabva lay down on the bed, she wished Brelin were here to say something funny and help her stop thinking about her depleted provisions. Or her tangled mess of hair. Brelin said some wacky stuff and made up some ridiculous nicknames, but somehow it always made Allabva laugh and feel a little better. If Brelin were here right now, she might even observe that Hronomon's name sounded a bit like "honeymoon" and joke that Allabva was on such a trip with him now.

You know he'll be good to you, Brelin might say. *The proper protector.*

You mean if he's even around, Allabva could respond. *Some honeymoon: He left me high and dry for three or four days!*

Then she could feign indignation and disbelief and get a rise out of Brelin in return. Thinking of returning the favor, Allabva hoped that someday she could come back and do something for this kind physician who took her in off her doorstep and gave her a bed to rest in. She must have jogged eight leagues last night. Now she needed to rest.

CHAPTER 21

ALONE IN A
CROWD

Allabva woke, hearing muted voices in the hallway. She stretched, her muscles sore from the previous night's exertion. She was parched and also needed to relieve herself. Looking out the window, she noted the slanting sunlight, so she hadn't slept long at all. Wait. No, the sunlight was going the wrong direction and would now soon recede and give way to dusk. She had slept too long. Why hadn't Doctor Noteh woken her?

She jumped up, taking care not to bump or stand too heavily on her right foot, and grabbed her bag and staff. Where was her coat? Her cloak? Noteh had taken them in the entry. Her boots were here, along with... Where were her socks? She couldn't wait for the woman to return, but must be on her way, treated ankle or no. At the very least, she had rested some.

Allabva sat on the edge of the bed and opened her bag. She reached in for a pair of dry socks, but found no socks at all, nor underclothes. Carefully, she pulled on her boots, having to go without socks for the moment. She would have to talk to these voices in the hallway and ask some questions.

Allabva opened the door and stepped into the hallway. She could hear the voices to her left at the other end of the hall.

She turned right and walked into the waiting room at the front of the house. There was a man sitting there in one of the chairs, dressed in worker's clothes and holding a white cloth over one of his forearms. Allabva decided he must be another patient and not relevant to her, in all likelihood. Ignoring him, she looked at the coat rack standing empty in the corner... Empty. Where was her cloak? What about her coat, as well?

Thinking that her answers must be at the other end of the hall, Allabva turned and walked the other way. As she neared the other end, she saw that it opened to the kitchen, where a young woman similar in age to herself stood, stirring a pot over a fire. A man was there as well, chopping carrots and potatoes.

"Um, excuse me," Allabva said to both of them, "I'm looking for the doctor; do you know—"

The girl stepped away from her pot and walked to a flight of stairs that opened up next to the back of the kitchen. "Mother, she's up!" she called up the stairs. She returned to her the pot, resuming her post and stirring the liquid inside. Then she looked up at Allabva.

"What was your name? Was it Alaina?" She asked Allabva, appearing to show genuine interest. "Mother said you must have walked pretty far."

"It's Allabva," she answered, feeling a certain strangeness in the situation, standing in a physician's family kitchen, far from home, in the first building she had walked into in seven days. "And I guess I did walk kind of far. Did a little bit of jogging, too. What's your name?"

She could hardly think of anything but getting back on the road as soon as possible, but she didn't want to seem rude. Besides, under other circumstances, it would have been likely that she would take the time to befriend this girl.

"Zlana. Is it because you just like being outside?"

"N—" Allabva tried to answer.

"I love the outdoors and hiking. Whenever Father can take me, I like to go camping. There's this great campsite we go to just outside of town. It has a creek running right beside it and it's in the middle of the woods, but our campsite has a nice little clearing with perfect, lush grass. Of course, at some times of year you have to watch out for the flies. They can be so annoying."

Zlana's energy was infectious and Allabva was starting to smile, despite the persistent feeling of having been thoroughly drained. Then the creaking of stairs alerted her of somebody descending from the upper story. Doctor Noteh appeared, starting to give her daughter an earful.

"Zlana, stop talking the poor girl's ears—Miss Allabva, may I ask what you are doing with your boots on? I thought you came here to take care of your feet!"

Allabva grinned and blushed. "I did, but—"

"Boots off now, talk later. Extended suffering is not allowed under Master Noteh's roof." She nodded at the man chopping vegetables.

Allabva laughed awkwardly at the matron's manner of insisting to take care of her, then cast her eyes about for a seat.

"Not in here; let's get you back to the guest room," Doctor Noteh directed.

Once there, Allabva sat on the bed and doffed her boots, feeling them chafe on her raw skin.

Doctor Noteh stepped past the door to the guest room and leaned into the sitting room, saying, "Master Rheane, I'll be with you in a few minutes. Show me the bad ankle," Noteh said, joining Allabva, producing a jar of ointment, and dipping her fingers into a goo inside it.

Allabva produced her bad foot and the doctor took it, beginning to rub the ointment on.

"I'll goop you up pretty well right now, then wrap it with a brace that will hold your ankle more rigid. I hope your boot isn't too snug, but it's got to be done. The golroot will make it itch a bit. I'm sorry for that, but that's just how it works. Other foot."

Allabva raised her left foot for inspection and treatment but held her right foot suspended in the air, bare except for the medical cream. Doctor Noteh began to rub more of the cream into the red spots.

"Take care of your feet on the road. Not just on the road, really. The feet and the teeth are much more important than many people realize. You lose those or they become unusable, and your overall health will begin to deteriorate."

"Um, alright." Allabva wasn't sure exactly how to respond to this.

"So, tomorrow morning, you need to reapply. And with fresh, dry socks, do you understand? You're trying to heal, not invite infection."

Allabva blinked, worry returning. She had gotten caught up in the procedure of having her feet treated by the doctor.

"Where are my socks? And other clothes?"

"Oh, yes. Right." Noteh nodded, holding a finger up as she remembered. "We washed them for you. They were quite dirty. I'll get Zlana to bring them. We had them up to dry in the sunlight; it got a little warmer today than it has been recently."

Allabva shook her head, at a loss for words. "Thank you again. You're doing way too much for me. I appreciate it, but please forgive me as I depart expeditiously."

"Do you mind telling me where you're going in such a hurry, or what you're running from?" Noteh stood up from where she had been kneeling to examine Allabva's feet, opened the door to peek out, and called to the back of the house, "Zlana, can you bring her things?"

Noteh looked at Allabva expectantly and Allabva balked.

"It's fine, you can tell me. Whatever you're running from, I can help, or I can find somebody who can help. Nobody should have to do a mad sprint through the night like that."

Allabva waited several seconds before opening her mouth again. "I don't think I can tell you. It wouldn't be safe for you or for me."

"Wouldn't be safe for me? Why's that? Just who exactly did you tangle with? If you spent the day here, am I still safe just because I know nothing?" The doctor looked confused and more deeply concerned than before.

"I didn't tangle with anybody," Allabva said. "Not yet, at least. But technically, you should be safe either way."

"You were running from somebody, but won't tell me who," Noteh said. "Does this have anything to do with the Disaffected? Are you one of the Disaffected?"

"No," Allabva reassured her. "Kind of quite the opposite."

"And somehow this puts you in danger?" Noteh said incredulously.

A knock at the door announced the arrival of Allabva's clothing items. The doctor opened the door for her daughter, who came in with Allabva's coat, cloak, socks tucked together, and neatly folded underclothes. Zlana passed Allabva the underclothes as well as the socks. Then she hung the cloak on a hook next to the door and turned back around, holding Allabva's coat, ready to help her don it when the moment arrived.

"Zlana, we need to talk about Allabva's situation here," the doctor said. "Do you think you can give us the room alone?"

"Of course, mother. Let me know whenever you're done. I want to talk to her, too."

Doctor Noteh nodded and Zlana left the room, closing the door behind herself.

"Where were we?" the doctor asked herself. "Ah yes, watch how I wrap your foot." Noteh placed a brace alongside Allabva's right ankle and wrapped the ankle and foot in a bandage to hold the brace secure, covering the areas where she had placed ointment with the bandage.

"You have more ointment on your right foot than your left, so I covered the ointment with the bandage on your right foot. It's fine if your sock comes in direct contact with a small amount of ointment like you have on your left foot. Do you think you can remember how to wrap this?" Noteh asked Allabva, who nodded readily.

Allabva set the underclothes and socks on top of her bag sitting on the bed, then she took one pair of socks to put them on her feet, covering the bandage on her right foot.

As Allabva pulled her socks on, Doctor Noteh continued talking to her. "Please trust me when I say I only want to help. I can keep a secret for you if necessary, but I don't want you to have to run from anybody. You saw my daughter, close to your own age, I assume. I would hate for her to have to run scared from anything, so let me help you."

Allabva pulled her boots on, moving more slowly and carefully with the right foot. "Thank you, Madam doctor. I believe in your sincerity, and I thank you for opening up your shop and your home to me. I don't believe there is anything you or anybody else could do for this particular situation. I don't mean to offend, but I must go. I have already been here too long. Oh—do you have any facilities here to…"

"Of course," Noteh said. "Out the back door. I'll hold Zlana off so you can make it a quick trip. You must really need to make a visit after your long sleep. Come on, you can leave your things for a moment." She opened the door and preceded Allabva into the kitchen, sending Zlana to fetch some ingredient from the cellar. Allabva relieved herself and returned to the guest room, the doctor following behind her.

As Allabva placed her spare socks and underclothes in her bag, she wished she had a chance to change into the fresh underclothes right now. But dusk was fast approaching and it would take her time to get to the southern road out of town to meet Hronomon.

"Just do me one favor, will you?" Noteh asked. "Come by here again someday and reassure me that you're alright. Or send me a post. You know my name and where to find me. This is Malmar Street, in case you forgot."

"I will. Tell Zlana that I would have loved to talk to her about camping."

"You're not going to say goodbye?" Noteh asked. "No," Allabva answered. "I have to meet somebody—a friend—at dusk." Allabva lifted her bag, aware of its light heft. She had no food remaining. This family was very kind and Allabva felt sure that they would give her food if she asked for any. But she did not want to impose any further on their kindness, nor did she feel she could afford another moment staying in one place. Grabbing her staff and opening the door to the room, she stepped into the hallway and moved toward the sitting room at the front.

"Have it your way," the kind doctor conceded. "I wish you the best on your way. Please stay safe, Allabva. Now, Master Rheane..."

Allabva stepped past the man waiting in the sitting room. Doctor Noteh 's use of Allabva's name as she departed felt personal and endearing, conveying real concern for her well-being. Shrongelin bless this family.

Hmm, Allabva wondered, *where does that expression come from, and is it based in any valid power that can come from it?*

She stepped out into the street, now resuming her journey in earnest after being waylaid and potentially misdirected in her direction of travel for several days. The fact that the luck of the draw had made it so she continued in the correct direction did not belay her feelings of helplessness while she was within the power of the group of Disaffected. Allabva continued to need to limp to favor her right ankle, but in these first few steps she could already feel the benefit of the brace and the ointment. She made a quick stop at the well down the street, refilling her waterskin. She also drank a good fill of water on the spot, having kept her thirst to herself after awakening.

Leaving the well's bucket to fall back into the water at the bottom, Allabva stood from her seated position at the well and looked to the dropping sun in the west. Then she picked her way through the streets at a brisk walk, placing the sun behind her and on her right until she found the south road out of town. She wished she could stay here awhile, not only to enjoy the company of Doctor Noteh's family, but to get to know the town and appreciate the architecture in it.

As she walked the streets of Palf Glen, heading toward the southeast, she heard the sounds of the evening, of parents calling their children in for dinner, of shops closing for the day, and tradesmen heading home. Some of the tradesmen led a horse or donkey pulling a cart or wagon, returning home empty or full, as the case may be, after selling or purchasing today's load. Perhaps she was influenced by her recent experience, but with the sound of hooves and wheels on the ground, she couldn't help but think she was being followed by somebody who kept staying just a little too far behind for her to be able to turn and see.

Chapter 22

Already Acquainted

Allabva set the last of the houses and shops to her back as she exited Palf Glen, the sun just now dropping below the horizon. The shadows of dusk were setting in, and visibility became less easy than it had while she navigated the town's streets. When she was fifty paces clear of the last remnants of the settlement, she saw Hronomon at an upcoming bend in the road, peeking around a large bush at her and waiting for her to catch up. Then he backed up and disappeared from view.

"Makes sense," Allabva said to herself. "He needs to wait until I am out of view of the town." She increased her pace, reminding herself before he could that she needed to be atop the mountain as soon as possible.

As she neared the bush that Hronomon had peeked out of, Allabva realized she still heard the sound of hooves and wheels. The sound didn't seem to diminish as she gained more distance from the town.

This peddler or tradesman behind me must be going somewhere outside of town, she thought. Perhaps it was a farmer returning to his fields in the countryside. That might make some pleasant conversation on the road, but first she should check in with Hronomon as soon as she rounded the curve.

Allabva spared a glance back to the farmer, wondering if it would be a lone traveler or a family. As she looked back, her blood ran chill. It was no farmer following her, but Nillan's crew of Disaffected.

Allabva yelped. In a moment's panic, she began to run forward toward Hronomon. Then, realizing that he probably would still not want to be seen helping her, she ran into the brush at her side instead.

"Hurry up, worthless driver! She saw us!" Allabva heard Nillan's voice shout. "Move over. I don't know why I still let you drive."

It had been Qurast and Nolder that Allabva saw on the driver's bench before she ran.

Once Allabva felt she was far enough from the road to make it infeasible, if not impossible, for the wagon to follow, she turned back toward the settlement of Palf Glen.

They won't take me in the town. I need public places, she told herself. She was nearly doing a full sprint, or as close to one as she could with her ankle in its current condition.

"Stop! Stop the horses!" Nillan nearly screamed. "Come on, Tunbloth, Halmon. Tunbloth, you're probably fastest. Go head her off and don't let her get into town!"

Allabva tried swinging wider, away from the road, dodging behind shrubs and trees that she hoped would block their sight of her. As she did so, running as she was, she had a slow realization that she was losing her sense of direction. She put the sound of Nillan's voice directly to one side of her, looked straight ahead, and determined to continue in that direction.

Deep down, Allabva knew that it was ultimately futile. Tunbloth couldn't be so much faster than she was, so as to catch her immediately, but his chase meant that there was no way she could be sure to get past him and back into Palf Glen.

She would not surrender easily, though. She turned again, now at an oblique angle, not trying to head back into town, but just trying to lose the nefarious party in the wilderness. At least this time she knew Hronomon would follow her and find her.

But as she ran, she began to tire. She slowed from a sprint to a more sustainable jog. She continued as well as she could, feeling the pain in her ankle surge again. After several minutes, impending dread rose in her throat as she heard hoofbeats behind her. They had unhitched the horses to catch up to her.

Knowing there was no way to outrun them now, Allabva ducked into a cluster of bushes, pushing through the foliage to deposit herself deeper and hide in the darkest crevice she could find.

Soon the hoofbeats drew near. She listened to hooves and voices.

"Do you still see her footprints?"

"It's getting darker, Nillan. It's hard to see anymore." Halmon's voice.

"The trail goes this way, then this rocky patch makes it indistinct..."

"Wait, you can see this imprint here, pointed that way."

"And then somewhere between there and over here, the trail stops."

Allabva stilled her breath. They were close enough now that she worried they might hear her ragged breathing. She willed her heart to slow down as it demanded more oxygen. It didn't listen. The desperation for free and rapid breathing nearly made her burst as she waited for the men to give up and move along.

A soft thump announced that one of the men had dismounted, and soft footfalls on the earth followed him as he carefully examined the area for additional signs of Allabva's passing through. They paused next to the spot where she had dived into the bushes.

"Do you see this?" Halmon said.

"See what?" Nillan sneered. "There's no footprint there on the stone."

"No, better. There are leaves on the stone."

"I give up. What's so special—oh. So she went through there." Allabva heard a horse walk around the thicket, then return to where Halmon stood. "There are no tracks out, no fallen leaves. Maybe she left more carefully, or maybe she's still inside."

Allabva's vision clouded with tears as the realization that she'd been found set in. It wasn't supposed to go like this. She had made a quick stop to find medical help; that was all Palf Glen was supposed to be. But then her sleep, while very necessary, had given these cursed men the opportunity to catch up with her. She was supposed to reconnoiter with Hronomon now, not find herself ensnared with these malcontents.

No, part of herself wanted to correct. She wasn't even supposed to be this far from home at all. She should be tending her mother's orchard, joking and gossiping with Brelin, inviting Delgan over again... Allabva took a deep breath. *Don't feel sorry for yourself. Just do the best you can right now.*

"Little girl?" Nillan called condescendingly. "You can come out now. We know you're in there."

He dismounted as well.

Weren't they going to go around Palf Glen?

"We followed you into town, little girl," Nillan said. "You were obviously hiding things from us. We want to know your secrets."

Why did they think she was important? They didn't appear to know anything about Hronomon.

"I want my new flute back."

Do the best that I can do in this situation. She tried to make them go away by mental command.

"We'll come in there and get you out if that's how you want to play it."

Go away.

"We don't want to come in, you don't want us to come in, but we will, and we'll be more upset if we have to."

Just do the best I can...the best...

"I'm going to count to ten. One..."

Allabva considered waiting them out, waiting until they tried to follow her in. Maybe it was just dark enough now that if she made a run for it when they came in... No. They could wait a few more minutes and their friends would catch up with them. They would easily surround the thicket and it would be impossible to escape. Full darkness would not arrive fast enough.

"Five..."

Make the best of it.

"You win, I'm coming out," she finally answered him. Allabva crawled forward and worked her way out of the thicket, staff in hand. As soon as she had exited and risen to her feet, Nillan yanked her stick away and shoved her backward, making her fall down.

"You're not done with us," Nillan gloated, looking down at her. "Nolder and Qurast may have been too yellow-bellied to want to go through Palf Glen, but I won them over. We're too far from home and the charge against us is too minor for anyone out here to have heard of us. So when we came to town, we followed your footsteps right in. Get up and walk," he commanded.

Allabva stood and Halmon grabbed her arms, forcing them behind her back and tying a cord around her wrists. Halmon and Nillan both mounted their horses again, Halmon still holding the other end of the cord binding Allabva's hands.

"Now, keep up," Halmon said. He and Nillan prodded the horses into motion.

Nillan continued talking. "Sure, you beat us to town by a few hours, perhaps. But we saw your tracks on the road and…you were limping."

His voice rose in glee at the thought of her misfortune.

Allabva felt a chill run up her spine. If they had seen her tracks, had they seen Hronomon's tracks alongside hers as well? She didn't dare let on that she had any cause for concern.

"So we asked around town for doctors," Nillan resumed. "They only have a couple of them, since it's not a large city. We went to the closest one and watched. It really wasn't hard to find you. The ease of it makes me want to try again at questioning you myself."

He tilted his head, gloating and looking at their surroundings before continuing.

"You're really not that clever, as it turns out. I have to admit, I wouldn't know all the questions that need asking. I'll leave that for the encampment. They say the leadership there has certain powers of persuasion, something taken from the unicorns that they should never have had in the first place."

That sounded concerning.

"What do you mean taken from the uni—from the Nomord? They can heal and make things grow. Everybody knows that, but persuasion? That's not a thing, let alone a Nomord thing, let alone something a human could take and learn."

Nillan laughed.

"Puny, tiny little girl. Do they teach no history or legends in the Cleft? The Nomor—the beasts once had powers that we do not see in modern times. They probably lost them because these creatures were abusing humanity and the world just took the magic back for justice."

Allabva wasn't sure she saw the logic in his argument, but she was already tired of arguing with him. She hoped that he had as little idea as she used to have of the true nature of the Nomord, both female and male. She held her peace and did her best to avoid being yanked by the cord that Halmon held. She reminded herself again, that at least this time she knew that Hronomon would be following along unseen, ready to bust her out if needed.

When Allabva and all five Disaffected were reunited with the wagon, they hitched the horses back up, loaded Allabva in the wagon, and turned around and headed north. Allabva was once again gagged and Nillan knelt over her while they passed through the town, discretely threatening her with violence if she so much as moved and revealed her presence.

She lay still. There was little chance that anybody would see her among the men's supplies in the wagon under the now full darkness of night. If she wanted to make it through this ordeal safely, she was going to have to pick her battles and, just as before, how to identify the correct moment to make a break for it again.

The group passed through Palf Glen and left the town behind them as they traveled north toward the Roula Docks and the Tallens Road. They continued softly into the night as Allabva wondered why they were traveling at night, beyond simply leaving some space between them and the town behind them. They must have deduced that she would have been asleep during her time at Noteh's practice, and found some way to rest themselves as well. The thought that she may have disturbed their sleep schedule was encouraging, because it meant that she could affect them to some degree in order to frustrate their plans.

Hronomon had said he thought he may have influenced the group of men to lower their guard the last time she was in captivity. Maybe he was still on the job, and that was why they did not take her knife or flute, even though they now knew she carried these items. Or perhaps the three of them thought the knife was still missing. Either way, she would have kept her mouth shut about them even if she weren't gagged.

Since she couldn't do anything about it, Allabva resigned herself to her ride along in the wagon, even taking the opportunity to sleep again. If she had to face the dangers of being among hundreds of Disaffected in their encampment, at least she didn't have to do so red-eyed.

She woke up in the night when the wagon stopped, off the road in usual fashion, and the men set up camp with their watch as before. She guessed they had already passed the docks and begun to follow the Tallens Road, heading east. At this point they did check her for her knife. Nillan took it from her personally, and after a suspicious glance at Qurast, tucked it behind his own belt for safekeeping.

While their sleep schedule was evidently altered, the men appeared unfazed by it and traveled the same as they had before. They struck camp and resumed forward motion in mid-morning, having taken a sluggish start to the day. Nillan said there was no need to wait longer for them to rest since they could take turns sleeping in the wagon, so they departed, regardless.

Allabva tried to avoid meeting Nolder's and Qurast's eyes. She hoped they didn't face any grief from Nillan over her escape. Maybe she shouldn't care so much to hope that they could avoid trouble; after all, they had chosen to align themselves with him and act as accomplices in the theft of the horses and wagon. Besides, they chose to resent the Nomord. Allabva couldn't conceive of thinking ill of the magnificent creatures, so maybe there was something wrong with anybody who did manage to think ill of them.

But...Qurast and Nolder had helped her escape. She had to give them credit for that. It seemed incongruous to her that they held a grudge against the Nomord but showed obvious signs of having good hearts. Maybe they were just temporarily confused and needed some help to be brought back around.

On the other hand, Hronomon had said he had tried to influence the group into letting her go. Was it really Qurast's and Nolder's actions that helped her escape, or were they under some kind of magical-powered mind control?

Come to think of it, Allabva should learn more about this ability to influence minds that Hronomon had mentioned. It didn't seem right if it was some form of control. No matter if they wanted things to grow and be happy, control didn't seem ethical, and in Allabva's mind, the end did not always justify the means. She would have to ask him more about this when she got a chance.

For now, she waited. There wasn't really anything she could do, bound and gagged as she was. They didn't untie her and let her walk behind or alongside the wagon this time, leaving her helpless the entire time instead. They rode on, driving the horses at a quicker pace than before. Perhaps now they were drawing closer to the encampment if they decided they could tire their horses out like this.

CHAPTER 23

CATCH AND RELEASE

Allabva's ankle itched while she lay immobile in the wagon bed. It had been itching since walking out Noteh's door, but as the morning wore on, it grew nearly intolerable. Noteh had said to reapply the ointment in the morning. She might as well try.

"Mmffmm," Allabva said to the Nillan, raising her eyebrows to convey her intent to make a request. He didn't seem to be in as sour a mood at the moment.

"What?" he barked.

"Mmmmm. FFmmmmhhrrm."

"Tunny, ungag her. We'll probably put it back in after just a moment, though," he grinned.

Tunbloth was in the bed of the wagon, which was a deviation from the previous pattern of having Tunbloth and Halmon drive in the morning. Instead, Qurast sat with Halmon on the driver's bench.

Tunbloth untied the gag but stayed kneeling next to Allabva, ready to shut her up again at a moment's notice.

"Speak, little girl," Nillan invited, mocking. "Let us know how evil we are for wanting to bring freedom of thought to the people."

Allabva shook off the taunt and opened her mouth calmly. "You were right, I did see a doctor. She gave me a salve, and it's time to reapply it. May I do so?"

"Of course, little girl. Go right ahead," Nillan said.

Tunbloth moved to untie her bonds so that she could replace the ointment, but Nillan waved him off with a smirk. Allabva wanted to roll her eyes, but held her tongue.

"I said, go ahead, little girl. Put some fresh ointment on your poor little foot." Nillan waited for Allabva to protest or insult him, looking for an excuse to retaliate and stuff the gag back into her mouth.

Instead, Allabva breathed deeply, then said with all the calm she could muster, "Will you please untie me so that I can take care of my medical needs? I promise not to run off, and I request to be tied up again when I'm done."

Nillan's fun was ruined. "Alright, useless little girl. I'll give you this round." He nodded to Tunbloth, who then unbound her hands and feet.

Allabva sat up and took off her boots and then her socks, unwrapping the dressing on her right foot. Then she stalled, as she needed to make another request of the men. "May I have my bag for a moment, please?"

Tunbloth tossed it to her without a word, scornfully chewing on some bit of dried meat.

Allabva wordlessly opened the bag and extracted the minute jar containing the extra dose of Doctor Noteh's salve, opened it, and dipped her fingers to obtain the goop inside. She spread it thick around her injured ankle, and then thinly on the sore spots of skin on both her feet. Tunbloth watched with too much interest, but interest alone didn't hurt and there wasn't much she could do about it at the moment without making everything worse. She still held her tongue.

When she finished applying the salve, she closed the jar, put it back in her bag, and removed fresh socks from the bag. Unable to be sure her old socks would be undisturbed if left out to air, she stuffed them in the bag and handed the bag back to Tunbloth. Then she pulled on her left sock and was ready to apply a new dressing to her right ankle, but realized that she did not have a fresh bandage. Figuring that the old bandage still had a fresh end, she started wrapping her ankle and brace with the end that Doctor Noteh finished with the afternoon before. Pulling on her right sock, Allabva finished by putting both boots back on.

"I hereby request to be rebound and gagged, and will not cause any trouble."

Perhaps she overdid it with the noble meekness. A little.

The men tied her up again and the wagon rolled on, wearing through the day as everyone tired of the vibrations and as the horses tired of pulling.

Allabva wondered if the Nomord held any sympathy special to horses when they got overworked. For that matter, she wondered if they felt sympathy in general. Maybe she would find out someday.

As the day progressed, the mountain loomed closer, staying ahead and to their right as they traveled east by northeast. Allabva wondered how she was supposed to get to the top of that mountain when she was lying in the bed of a wagon below the foothills.

She also wondered what she would eat next. She had left the Notehs' kitchen without a single morsel, either offered or requested. At the time, she had hoped to find something later, not wanting to impose excessively on the doctor's kindness. She didn't expect to be caught again. Now her hunger returned, she had no food, and was unable even to search or ask for any without relying on the mercies of her captors, who had proven determined to hold her against her will.

After taking the opportunity to nap in the middle of the day, in the afternoon Allabva was pulled from her thoughts by a change in the talking coming from the front of the wagon. Tunbloth and Nolder, who had been speculating on the driver's bench concerning the organizational hierarchy of the Disaffected encampment where they would arrive in a few hours, now shifted from the idle jabber they had been entertaining, to more excited tones.

"There's one of the dirty white animals now!" Tunbloth alerted.

"It looks mighty suspicious, if you ask me," Nolder said. "Why is it standing right in the middle of the road like that?"

Nillan, Qurast, and Halmon all turned their heads and focused on the Nomord ahead of the wagon. Allabva wished she could see, but her peering from the wagon bed couldn't reveal the sight to her. She had a suspicion she knew who it was, though. She wriggled and leaned up against the side of the wagon, and saw Hronomon standing stately in plain view.

"You dumb horses are never there, never help when you could," Tunbloth yelled. "Where's my wife? Moron beast!"

Qurast wore a face of grief and pain, but said nothing, a single tear forming in one eye. Biting his cheek, he reached behind Allabva's neck and tugged once at the knot holding her gag in place, then he placed himself at the far side of the wagon before jumping out. Allabva struggled with the gag, moving her head back and forth to pull the knot loose. Then she pushed with her tongue and spat out the fabric, trying to lick the dry taste out of her mouth.

"Blighted Nomo-Nomo!" Nillan shot at the Nomord. "Get off the road!" He fished out Allabva's knife, unsheathed, and threw it, shouting, "Heal yourself after I cut you!"

The knife sailed through the air, turning end over end toward its mark. It appeared it may even strike Hronomon if he didn't move, which he showed no sign of doing. It was an expert throw over not a paltry distance, the blade turning toward Hronomon's neck a final time as it neared him. At the last moment and without flinching, he ducked his head down and to the side, using his single horn to deflect the blade, which bounced and skidded to the side of the road. He raised his head again and stared at the party in the wagon, once again unmoving.

Allabva was stunned at his intensity, and most of the Disaffected men were silent after the display. Not all, though.

Nillan had his head cocked, looking at Hronomon, thinking. Now he reeled on Allabva.

"Is this *him*? Is this the brute Halmon heard you talking about that first night?" he said, spittle flying. "This one is acting more alert than any other unicorn I've seen."

He had confirmed the connection they had suspected the whole time. Allabva looked back at him silently.

"You think we're scared?" Nillan said, rounding back on the Nomord. "You think you're smart because you can block a throw? Vile *unicorn*," he spat.

He jumped down from the wagon, then turned and reached in, grabbing Allabva's staff. With it he stepped out in front of the horses, approaching Hronomon while brandishing the branch.

"Run away while you still have a chance, beast!" Nillan taunted. "Your kind's time is almost up. We are going to take your power and actually do good with it. Just wait! But right now, get out of our way or we'll make you."

Nillan swung the staff hard at Hronomon's face, but the Nomord deftly dodged. Nillan took another swing, this time at his knees. Again Hronomon dodged, stepping out of the way. He said nothing, enduring the treatment as though a toddler were hitting him with soft fists.

"You think you're so tough. Let me hit you!" Nillan swung again and again as Hronomon side-stepped, ducked, or bounced out of reach. After several more tries, the Nomord kicked the man with a forehoof. Allabva could see that it was more of a shove, insistent but trying to avoid injuring the instigator. Nillan fell to the ground, releasing the staff to catch himself. He rose again, red-faced and furious.

"We'll get you! We're joining the Enlightened and we will build armies, forge weapons. We will overcome your kind."

"I do not doubt your sincerity," Hronomon spoke at last, "though you do not know the fullness of what you say. Sacalai will enslave you even if you do not see that you are enslaved. Her work began millennia ago; you are merely pawns in it."

"I'm nobody's pawn, you manipulative fiend," Nillan rejected. "I follow my own path."

"Yes, you make your own choices. Your will to choose is still not diminished, but it will be if you continue."

"Get out of my way," Nillan growled in hatred.

"I have terms," Hronomon offered.

"Terms," Nillan scorned. "Terms from an animal."

"I will move, and bother you no more. But you must meet my terms."

"And if I don't?"

"I can push you again."

"You mean kick!"

"If you insist. I can do it again, regardless of its name." Hronomon moved a single step toward Nillan.

"No! Never. No accords with a *unicorn*," Nillan said, but he backed up, nevertheless.

"What do you want, deceiver, abandoner?" Nolder called from his seat at the front of the wagon.

"Shut up, old man," Nillan reproached. "Daddy's talking."

"What are your terms, animal?" Nolder repeated.

Hronomon stepped around Nillan to speak directly with Nolder.

"I will not be ignored!" Nillan screamed.

He picked up Allabva's staff and wound up to club Hronomon's hindquarters.

The Nomord raised one leg and gave Nillan a soft kick again, effortlessly shoving him back and to the ground again.

"Give me nothing," Hronomon said, "but release the girl. Return to her that which you found her with, and let her out, unharmed."

Nolder squinted at him with a hard stare.

"Just what kind of Nomord are you?"

"Never you mind. The young woman will be released now, please."

"He's a male Nomo-Nomo," Nillan puzzled.

"No such thing," Halmon said.

"The girl." Hronomon raised his hind leg again, keeping Nillan from rejoining his crew on the wagon.

"I don't know what you're up to, but I'll find a way to stop you," Nolder said. "Sorry, Nil." He turned his face to the rear. "Qur—Alright."

He saw that Qurast had gotten out of the wagon.

"Halmon. Untie her."

"You think you're calling the shots now?" Halmon challenged.

"I think we're getting past this ugly beast safely and arriving in the camp tonight," Nolder answered. "Now untie her."

Halmon turned to loose Allabva's bonds and found her ungagged. "How—"

He looked back over his shoulder, where he saw Hronomon's hoof hovering in front of Nillan. "Never mind. I always knew there was something fishy about you. Don't let me catch you again, if you're smart. Next time, it will cost you more than your coin purse." He untied her bonds and gestured for her to get out of the wagon.

Allabva stalled, looking at Hronomon and then back at Halmon. "My bag, please."

"My pleasure." Halmon grabbed the bad and threw it hard toward Hronomon. "Go fetch."

Allabva breathed out her exasperation and climbed down from the wagon, unclasping her cloak due to the warmth of the afternoon, but leaving it hanging around her shoulders.

Hronomon turned his head to give a one-eyed look at Nillan. "Drop the staff. Don't throw it."

Nillan shoved the staff away from himself, letting it fall to the ground.

The Nomord continued commanding the situation. "Allabva, your bag looks rather light. Do you have much food left?"

Allabva shook her head. "None; I finished it yesterday morning."

"Give her food." Hronomon directed the men.

"You're not stealing our food!" Nillan said.

"Then consider it recompense for you kidnapping her. Twice. Either way, you committed an offense against her, and she happens to need food. Give her some food, and we'll call it even. That is, if that's all right with you?" he asked Allabva, who nodded.

"Provide her some rations, non-spoiled," Hronomon insisted. "Two meals' worth, to make up for her dinner and breakfast that you did not feed her in your custody."

"What do you know about our custody?" Halmon challenged.

Hronomon looked at Nillan and twitched his hind leg, which was hovering in front of the man. The disaffected leader returned Hronomon's gaze with hate, then turned his eyes to Halmon.

"Two meals' worth of rations. Give them to her."

Halmon looked equally displeased at the situation as Nillan did, but produced the food, handing it to Nolder to give to Allabva, as if he might dirty himself by handing it to her directly. Allabva took the food, holding it in her arms and moving toward her bag.

Hronomon spoke again to the men. "I'm afraid we can't let you arrive at the Disaffected encampment so quickly as you might do unhindered. Unhitch your horses."

Nillan was far from being on board for this. He folded his arms across his chest in defiance.

"Not a chance. Those are our property, fair and square. You might think you're an intelligent beast just because you can talk, but these can't even do that. They're ours, and you're not going to steal them from us."

"I'm not trying to steal them from you," Hronomon drawled, patience wearing thin. "I—"

"They're already stolen," Allabva said.

"Thank you, Allabva" Hronomon said. "Please leave this to me."

He looked again at the men.

"I'm not trying to steal them from you, no matter how ill-gotten they are. I'm only trying to cause you a minor delay. Unhitch the horses."

"I already said no," Nillan refused.

"Would you like to feel my hoof again?" Hronomon asked.

Then he turned toward the man and lowered his head.

"Or do you prefer to try the horn this time?"

Nillan said nothing and glowered in rage. Nolder found Qurast's eyes with his and gestured with his head for the younger man to comply with the Nomord's demands. Qurast moved to unhitch one while Tunbloth begrudgingly descended, pushed by Nolder, and unhitched the other.

Hronomon spoke again without breaking eye contact with Nillan.

"Now, lead them a few paces from the wagon."

The two men who had just unhitched the horses led them forward.

"Return to the wagon, all of you."

Hronomon stared at Nillan with both eyes and waited for him to move. When the man didn't move, Hronomon lurched a hair's width, attempting to intimidate him. Nillan moved then, and the whole party climbed aboard.

"Stay there and do not move," Hronomon gave the men a final instruction, then turned his gaze to Allabva. "Allabva, I am sorry to have to ask this of you. I know you have a kind heart and will not wish to do this, but our success depends upon us leaving this place safely. For that, these men must be delayed."

Allabva had reached Hronomon's side and was collecting the bag that had been launched and the staff that had been thrown down, putting the food inside the bag.

"What do I have to do?"

"Take your staff and strike the horses as hard as you can on their hindquarters."

"You're not scattering my horses!" Nillan protested again, standing to get out of the wagon.

"The horn, then?" Hronomon said, turning toward the man and leveling his horn at him.

Nillan sat back down.

"Please proceed, Allabva," Hronomon said.

Allabva furrowed her brow in anticipation of performing the unsavory act. Then, taking her stick by the narrow end and standing well to the side, wary of flying hooves, she swung it at the hindquarters of first one horse and then the other, prompting them to bolt a short way. One of them left the trail on the north side and wandered into the brush. Tunbloth bolted to his feet and jumped down from the wagon, only to be met face to face with Hronomon, who moved to block his path. Tunbloth thought better of acting at the moment and climbed back up.

Allabva walked over to her knife where it lay after Hronomon had deflected it, picking it up and holding it. "Please toss me the sheath," she said to Nillan.

"Gently, directly to her," Hronomon precluded a maverick throw off the road.

Nillan pulled out the sheath, then trying his luck just a little, threw it as hard as he could, beyond Allabva but still on the road. Hronomon let the infraction slide.

"Allabva," the Nomord addressed her. "Go collect your sheath, then continue walking forward. Do nothing else but walk forward. I will catch up with you soon."

Allabva took a deep breath and let it out slowly. Then she turned and walked away from the wagon, leaving Hronomon staring it down by himself. He had come and helped her physically in front of other humans. She supposed that this might mean he would not leave her again, having exposed himself to eyes that could report to Sacalai. Allabva wasn't sure if she should be comforted by the fact that he wouldn't leave again, or worried by the reasons why. Just in case, she picked up the pace, limping ahead rapidly as she leaned on her staff.

"Don't worry, little girl." Nillan's voice haunted her from behind. She did not stop or look back. "I will get mine. You think you're getting away with this, but I'd watch my back if I were you. Your *friend* is lucky to have caught us with no significant weapons. We'll make it to the encampment, all right. Then we'll come find you and it will be more than only five of us, try more like fifty."

So go on, little girl. Go ahead and feel safe right now. But don't worry. We'll catch up. Now we know your secret, we know you're fully in league with the beasts. We're going to make some changes in this world, and you're on the wrong side of things. Do you hear me? You're on the wrong side of things, you wretched witch! You will come to your end, alongside those filthy *unicorns!*"

Part V: Tallen Mountain

Chapter 24

Freedom

Allabva passed on ahead and out of sight of the wagon and Hronomon, trying not to pant for breath from the confrontation she felt, even though she had not looked at the bitter man during his farewell speech. Some time after she had rounded a curve and the wagon and men were no longer visible, Allabva opened her bag, removed the bundled food that Nolder had handed her, and began to eat.

They had provided her a couple of apples, some nuts, a vegetable she did not recognize, a few pieces of dried fish, and a bit of bread. She dug into the fish first. She wasn't the biggest lover of fish but right now she was hungry enough to enjoy anything, so she started with the thing she might not enjoy later.

She marched on, appreciating the fact that she now had an uninhibited view of the trees and the grass surrounding the road, as well as the mountain looming to her south. She took joy, although modest, at seeing birds flit about and pass over the trail.

With the warmth of the afternoon now added to the exercise provided by walking, Allabva removed her cloak entirely, then draped it over her left shoulder. She held it in place with her left hand, using her right hand to lean on the walking stick and avoid putting weight on her bad ankle. With her midday nap added onto her time asleep at Noteh's house and in the wagon overnight, she felt much better than she had before arriving in Palf Glen. However, she could certainly stand to rest more and eat a proper meal. For now, she kept walking.

Presently, Hronomon came galloping up the road behind her. Alarmed at what might have him at a full gallop, Allabva turned around to face him and prepared herself to run whenever he said where to go. But as he approached her, he slowed down to a trot and then a canter. As he came on line with her, he slowed to a walk.

"We must turn toward the mountain and head up now. There is a hiking trail coming up soon on our right that we will take to begin our ascent. I have given us enough of a lead so that we should have a head start up the mountain before anybody knows where we have gone."

Allabva spoke what had been on her mind on and off over the last couple of hours. "Will there be somewhere we can get some food?"

"I'm sorry, but not at this time. I know that your kind can survive up to a few weeks without food, although it decreases your capability when you do. You will have to go without right now. Follow me."

Hronomon turned left, heading north, away from the mountain, and stepped off the road and into the brush. Allabva wasn't sure what he was planning by heading the opposite direction he had just said they needed to go, but he had just saved her from the brigands like he said he would when it became necessary. Evidently he had some kind of plan, so she followed.

Hronomon kept talking.

"We are laying a false trail by crossing the road back and forth several times and doubling back. We have just enough of a head start so that we can properly lose ourselves so your pursuers cannot follow. Keep up, now."

Why did everybody keep saying that?

Hronomon lifted his hooves and stepped more quickly, forcing Allabva to hurry as well. As indicated, they looped and wound across the road, winding farther away than Allabva would expect that they might do, to the point that she wondered if the five Disaffected might catch up and see them in the act of trying to lay a false trail. But Hronomon did eventually slow to a walk again. Allabva felt lost by now, not quite sure even of which side of the road they were on.

"Now we climb," Hronomon said. "I will go slower now, but you must keep up. Remember that the fate of the world, of your mother and brother, hangs in the balance. Those men, especially the one I had to kick, will likely push ahead to their encampment. I do not know how determined the Disaffected are in general, but I imagine some of them will want to follow us. The influence of Sacalai is proven to be leaking out by actions of men such as that."

Hronomon set a much more sustainable pace, but it was still faster than Allabva had set several days before when they set out from the Cleft. It was also generally uphill as the smaller trail they now found themselves on snaked around and up and down through the foothills.

"Hronomon, I have some questions for you," Allabva breathed. She wondered where to start.

Hronomon turned his head to show her that he was listening.

"You said the Gha-Nomord can influence minds. Do you practice mind control? Is that how you got them to let me go the first time? Is that—" Another implication just hit her. "Did you use that to make me come on this journey? To make my mother let me come?"

Hronomon did not seem concerned or hurried by her questions. Once Allabva had finished asking and was waiting for an answer, Hronomon calmly replied.

"No, The Gha-Nomord cannot control minds. We only have influence. Yes, I exerted influence upon those men. No, I did not exert it on you or your mother."

"How can I be sure? How can I know my decisions are my own?"

"Your decisions are always your own. As I said, the Gha-Nomord cannot control minds. We can influence, like a convincing friend. We can try to sway you, but in the end, you decide. I cannot force your mind to make any decision."

Allabva had no way to be certain of that, but it seemed to make sense. She moved to her next question.

"If you exercised influence on their minds, why didn't those men let me go right from the start? Or, if they make their own decisions even when influenced, why did they disagree with each other?" Another idea hit her. "And why did you tell Nillan he was a pawn, if he is truly choosing for himself?"

"Because they have their own minds and their own wills and opinions. I can influence, I can push one way or another, but those who don't want to move my way won't do so. Nillan and his ilk willingly choose Sacalai's way. The more they do, they form habits of thought which they may not suspect or anticipate."

"But that much? Two of them actually helped me escape the first time, and one of those two ungagged me earlier than he had to the second time. But then that other one opposed you so much that he tried to attack you twice and you had to use bodily force against him. Should there be so much disparity between them?"

"Normally, I would not think so. They banded together in the first place for a reason. But I believe that as Sacalai extends her influence, especially right now to prevent us from reaching the Shrongelin, she will work hard to bend souls toward her will. Those who desire to listen to her will display characteristics of her personality, which we saw Nillan do. Those who truly want what is best will be easier to entreat and ready to listen to me or other Gha-Nomord. I think this afternoon we may have seen both things happening at once."

"If Sacalai is locked away in her prison but can influence these people here... Well, is she far away? If she can influence people this far away, then can you influence people just as far away as well?"

"No, only nearby. Sacalai is much more powerful than a lone Nomord." *Lone. Oh, right,* Allabva thought. "Where are all the other Gha-Nomord? Why are you the first one I've ever seen? The Ta-Nomord wander about throughout the world."

"You will see soon enough. The nature of the Construct requires our attention. We mutually support each other and must keep ourselves apart from mankind. As the shield becomes brittle, all the Gha-Nomord will need to gather the Ta-Nomord together so that we can forge the shield fresh again."

Allabva chewed on Hronomon's responses as the afternoon turned into evening and evening turned into night. Because Allabva had slept the previous night and then again during the day, she had sufficient energy to stay awake without feeling a great need to sleep for several hours after dark. Whenever she did yawn and wish that Hronomon would decide to stop, he seemed to speed up.

Eventually, the sky began to brighten and Allabva realized that they had continued their climb all night long.

Initially, the added light helped her shake off the sleepiness that had begun to slow her down. With this wakefulness, hunger returned and she opened her bag to retrieve food one last time. She made her way through her nourishment as slowly as she could bear, finishing it off by eating the second apple last, core and all. With this, she washed it down with water and began to feel the warmth of the sun on her shoulders.

"That's enough for now. I need to sleep if we're supposed to keep going all the way to the top. Let me just hunker down here for a couple of hours." Allabva took the liberty of taking a seat a few steps off the trail.

Hronomon said nothing, but peered down the mountainside to view the foothills and plains stretched out to the north and west, and the Roula Seas occupying a fair portion of the horizon in the distance. Receiving no objection from Hronomon, Allabva slid down to sit in front of the rock, tucked her knees to her chest, wrapped herself in her cloak with her head on her knees, and fell asleep with her bag and staff beside her.

Chapter 25

Pursued

After spending all night glancing backward and down-hill to see the torchlight snake slowly advancing closer, Allabva saw light appearing in the sky behind the mountain. Although most of her directional travel was still toward the south, the mountain consumed the whole of the view to the south and the east. Hunger bit at her gut as she continued on her feet into the morning after a fatiguing night constantly on the move. She had eaten two scant meals, courtesy of Nillan's crew at the insistence of Hronomon, since the beginning of the day under Doctor Noteh's charge, which was now three days ago.

Blessedly, one thing she didn't lack was water. As Nolder had told her, the Fonglan Gulf lay on the other side of this mountain, and the Inner Sea was not a great distance to the south, as far as weather patterns were concerned. While the mountaintop was capped in snow, clouds often gathered to obscure the upper reaches of the mountain and drop their water on its slopes. Consequently, she frequently came across the streams and was able to fill and refill her waterskin along the way. Despite having all the water she could drink, Allabva still had a dry throat, with her struggling in the cool air and the amount of sweating she was doing.

"We will lose sight of that group soon," Hronomon advised. The snake of torches had gotten closer throughout the night. "Not because they will stop following, but because they will put out their torches and will no longer stand out in the daylight."

Just what Allabva needed, a pursuing threat going phantom on her.

As the sun showed itself over the mountaintop, Allabva heard the first howls from dogs still quite distant behind her carried up the mountainside on an uphill wind.

"They must all be on horseback to be closing in this fast," Hronomon observed.

"I don't care how they're catching up so quickly," Allabva gasped. "I just want them to stop following us."

"I believe I know just how to accomplish that." Hronomon sounded hopeful, not confident.

"Let me guess—it involves continuing to press forward as fast as I can."

"Right you are. The one real thing we have in our favor is some terrain that will be more difficult for them than for us. Their horses are only a small advantage over your pace on this long distance, especially because of the unevenness of the terrain. Our hours are numbered before they catch up to us. Keep moving. We have to make it to the riven scree at the Slant."

Allabva wasn't fully convinced.

"How can their horses only be a small advantage? There's no way I can match the speed of a horse."

"True, you can't match the top speed of a horse. But you two-legs do a fair pace, and we equines can't maintain our top speed for long. Young as you are and in decent health, you have been doing well over long distance."

Allabva gritted her teeth against the pain in her ankle and the impending return of the emptiness in her gut. Then she sped up.

The morning passed as Allabva pushed herself as hard as she could to maintain her lead in front of the Disaffected. In the early afternoon Allabva and Hronomon came to a point in the trail where the mostly passable surface gave way to boulders mounting upwards.

The boulders made the trail more demanding, but it was still well within the realm of feasibility for both girl and Nomord. Hronomon half hopped and scrambled over the boulders while Allabva set one foot on the next boulder, leaned forward, and then pulled her other leg up behind her.

As she leaned forward and rocked her shoulders from side to side in her progression onward and upward, Delgan's flute fell out of the front of her blouse.

Delgan's flute! She had nearly forgotten its presence, unable to enjoy its sweet song during so many days in Nillan's captivity. While she placed one foot and one hand on the next boulder to continue her ascent, she grabbed the flute firmly in the other hand and spoke softly, "Beware the wolves!"

As music started, Hronomon looked at Allabva and the flute with surprise.

Oh, Allabva thought, *I guess he hadn't seen it play itself before.*

Hronomon stayed silent, reappraising Allabva and probably wondering where the flute came from, then turned forward again.

Allabva did not have the breath even to try to sing along with the flute, but she listened to its silvery tones and thought of Mother, Mellier, Brelin, everybody else back home, and particularly of Delgan. She mouthed the lyrics silently, restarting the flute's automated music several times in order to recite all the verses and iterations of the chorus.

> In the cool shade of the mount,
> My love came to call in the morning, (to me)
> And I knew not when he'd return,
> So I held him forever that day.

> Take me there, through the ash and pine,
> Take me there, to the desert or sea,
> Wherever you go, do not leave me here,
> I will not be parted from thee.

> O'er the deepest, bluest sea,
> My love went to sail in the morning, set free,
> And I stayed all alone in the shade,
> Wishing I could share his embrace.

> Take me there, through the ash and pine,
> Take me there, to the desert or sea,
> Wherever you go, do not leave me here,
> I will not be parted from thee.

> In the darkest, fiercest war,
> My love was affrighted to leave me, (weeping)
> And I feared he might cease to be,
> And could never come back home to me.

> Take me there, through the ash and pine,
> Take me there, to the desert or sea,
> Wherever you go, do not leave me here,
> I will not be parted from thee.
>
>
> In the cool shade of the mount,
> My love came to call in the morning, (to me)
> I had known not if he'd return,
> So I held him forever that day.
>
>
> In the cool shade of the mount,
> My love came to call in the morning, (to me)
> And I knew not when he'd return,
> So I held him forever that day.

Allabva didn't know if she would make it back to the Cleft, but she mentally thanked Fiewren for teaching her the words to the song as she wiped a tear from her eye.

Climbing over the last boulder in the present series, she looked ahead and found Hronomon staring her in the face.

"Do you need the music now?"

Allabva was a little taken aback by the suddenness of the question, but answered without hesitation as she continued walking again.

"It's really helping me. I've never been so far from my family before, or my home. I've been on the run for over a week and I feel like I'm starting to forget why it is I'm putting up with the hunger and the fatigue."

"You forgot why?"

"Not intellectually, but emotionally. I need to remember what it feels like to have something I care about to fight for."

"Does it do the job?"

"I think so. It makes me want to keep pushing on, rather than merely withstand the suffering."

Hronomon seemed to think about this for a moment.

"That is good. You should not lose your mind or heart in this fight. You will make it to the top of this mountain and your current hunger and fatigue will not last forever, but you will continue to be challenged until Sacalai's prison is remade. She will attempt to tear your mind and heart away from your home, and to tear you from yourself. Remember who you are. It will increase your chances of success in the end."

"Why do you ask if I need the music now? Did it bother you?" Allabva asked.

"I am weighing its value for our task. It could distract you. Or it could cover the noise of those following us, making us easier to catch unawares. But I suppose it is fine."

The trail started to have more and steeper inclined stretches, and began to zig-zag as it ascended. This blocked Allabva's view of the pursuing Disaffected, hiding them from sight as the landscape jutted out from the mountainside. The surrounding landscape was also now covered with frequent patches of forest tempered by occasional sections of bald rock or grassy meadow.

While Allabva had seen many types of trees on the plains and foothills below, the forest now alternated mostly between pine and aspen. She listened to the flute play its tune several more times throughout the afternoon and tried to lose herself in the beauty of the waving evergreens and the quaking aspens, mentally running from the stress and fatigue she currently endured.

Chapter 26
Riven Scree

Allabva felt an ominous feeling late in the afternoon as a wind picked up and the temperature began to drop. She had her cloak opened because of the warmth of the afternoon, but now she closed it and drew it tight around herself. She wondered if this might be weather manipulation by Hronomon or by Sacalai, or if it were natural. She wanted to ask him, but chose instead to continue to gasp for sufficient breath to keep moving.

A light fog began to form around them.

Allabva's feeling about the afternoon sank further as their pursuers caught up. The pair, human and Nomord, were in the pocket between two juttings-out, or fingers of mountain rock, beginning to near the finger ahead of them, when the pursuing party rounded the finger behind them and brought shouts of excitement from the pursuing Disaffected.

Allabva shouted in fright, "They've caught us!"

Hronomon answered, calmer at first but with urgency in his voice that rose as he spoke, "No, they haven't. We've made it, we're almost to the scree. Run, Allabva, now run!"

Allabva started running, ceasing to use her walking stick, and letting her bag bounce against her while she did. Normally the bag bouncing would have bothered her, but now she ran in terror, set only on the idea that the Disaffected not take her again. She sprinted forward, ignoring the pain in her ankle as she progressively made it worse again. Hronomon kept pace with her, holding his position behind her on the narrow trail.

As she ran, the trail seemed to stretch out in front of her, growing longer before she reached the point of the finger of the mountain. She reached it eventually, rounding the curve and staring nearly a league across until the next finger, nearly out of sight in the fog. In the intervening space where the trail followed the form of the mountain receding closer to the mountain's heart, she saw the scree.

Far above her, the mountain's slope surrendered to open air and a sheer rock face descended from the heights. The bald face of the cliff ended in a slope of loose rock. The scree sloped away from the cliff face at a dangerous angle, but the trail cut across the scree, giving no option but to pick their way and their footing carefully through the patch of treacherous loose stone. True to the descriptor Hronomon had used, *riven scree*, the rocky field was divided in two by a slope that was too steep for rock falling down from the cliff to settle on it, which afforded safer passage through the middle between the two halves of the loose field of rock.

Allabva's heart sank as she looked at the stark view. It was too far, and she was sure she wouldn't make it before the scrambling men and horses behind her caught up. Feeling defeated, she gritted her teeth and ran on.

"That's it, Allabva! Keep going! We're going to make it," Hronomon encouraged behind her.

"How can you say that we've made it? They've caught us already! We'll never make it to the other side of those rocks."

"No, young one. Those rocks are our salvation. Just keep going, and I will pull us through."

Allabva did what she was told, trying to maintain her sprint for the several hundred paces it would take her to arrive at the first of the loose rocks. As she ran, she quickly warmed up again, opening her cloak to disperse heat. She thought it may still be getting colder, and the fog was certainly growing more dense. Despite being closer to it, she could no longer see the far side of this canyon, nor the top of the cliff face. She could feel the humidity as she breathed heavily in and out.

Her pursuers were evidently also motivated by their proximity. Allabva had sped up, and Hronomon as well, but the clamor behind them grew louder and closer. They were close enough now that as Allabva and Hronomon rounded the finger to come in view of the scree, they never lost line of sight. Breath ragged, Allabva arrived at the rocks and stalled for a moment. Testing her footing on the first few, she found them poised and ready to slip. "We'll never make it across!"

"Just slow down," Hronomon instructed. "We can't run across this, but we can cross it, nevertheless. Hold your balance slowly, and watch your footing carefully."

Allabva held her arms out wide and bent her knees, stepping carefully and using her feet to find larger stones that would not move when she put her weight on them. Hronomon followed behind her, choosing his way with equal caution. While Hronomon's size was a disadvantage on this sloped field, along with his rigid hooves that would not grip a surface, the fact that he had four of them made it manageable. Allabva felt fortunate right now that she had picked up her staff the week before, and now she picked her way through the danger zone on three points of contact.

After Allabva and Hronomon had started across the scree, the Disaffected closed with them much more rapidly. The din from behind grew quickly and some of their words came through clearly. One voice in particular stood out as it spoke not only to its fellows, but also directly to Allabva.

"We'll get you, you stupid little girl! We're close now!"

Allabva felt a chill in her cheeks that would have gone deeper if her heart were not currently thumping so hard in her ears. Nillan was following. His determination to bring her suffering shocked her. If all decisions were one's own despite the influence of Sacalai, then this man was eating from her hand willfully.

Allabva began to nearly hop from stone to stone, her feet nimbly flying over the loose rocks. As she approached the rift dividing the scree field, her bad ankle gave out and she tumbled forward, falling to her hands and rolling and sliding downhill several paces. She screamed in fright and Hronomon lunged to grab her cloak with his teeth, but she was already beyond his reach.

She came to rest with several new cuts and scrapes, and then found that she was able to move laterally on all fours on the slant to arrive at the rift. Now finding solid purchase, she climbed upward, grabbing her discarded staff again.

She came back to the trail, and Hronomon pushed her onward. "Keep going. I will follow you soon."

"What?" Allabva was startled by the implications of what Hronomon said. "What are you doing now? You can't fight them on these rocks. You'll all fall to your deaths. They're getting slick in this fog. This fog..." She looked at Hronomon and considered again the source of the humidity, a realization lighting up her face. Then she furrowed her brow. A little fog wouldn't stop the Disaffected any more than it was stopping her.

"I'm not stopping to fight them," he said. "Keep going. Try to get across this next portion of the stone field as quickly as possible, but make sure your footing is good. Go!"

With that, he turned uphill, leaving the trail and climbing strenuously up the rift toward the top of the scree.

Allabva pressed on across the second portion of loose rock, picking her way with staff and feet, grateful that it was not nearly as wide as the first portion. She looked back at the men and horses following them across the loose stones, nearly a third of the way to the rift. Then she looked up at Hronomon again to see what he was going to do. She could see Nillan's gaze now, and he followed her eyes up to the climbing Nomord. As she felt a wave of relief, he assumed a horrified expression.

The Nomord had reached the top of the slant and positioned himself against the cliff wall. He climbed on crevices that Allabva couldn't see because of her distance, then, rearing up, he placed his front hooves against a large rock that had split itself from the cliff face, teetering over the northern scree where the men were now crossing. It stood vertically, threatening to turn and fall. Hronomon had arrived to help it.

Allabva heard cries of "Go back!" rise from the men as they struggled to turn their horses around on the narrow strip of trail they had. Allabva realized that as the large rock fell, it could have an impact on her side of the rift as well. While the large rock shook the ground a little where she stood on the southern scree, it shook many more rocks loose and sent them tumbling and sliding. This would shake the mountain enough that it may loosen the rocks where she stood.

She began to skip across the rocks faster as she went. Now that she had seen how they moved against each other, she could skip from rock to rock, allowing some of them to slip and fall away under her weight just as she shifted away from them. As she skipped, she aimed to place her feet on the rocks' edges so they would bite the soles of her boots for grip, Allabva being aware of them growing more slippery in the ever-thickening fog.

Allabva heard the mountain groan as Hronomon shifted the rock he was pushing. It fell away from the wall like a bridge lowering across a castle moat, then fell twice Allabva's height before hitting the northern scree with an immense crash. Hronomon fell after it, having lost the counterbalance he needed to stay in his elevated spot against the wall. Even as Allabva shouted, fearing for her friend, Hronomon caught himself, landing expertly on the rock he had felled. Then he jumped immediately away from it to land at the top of the rift as the rock slid out from under him.

As Allabva had supposed, the immense boulder began a chain reaction on the northern scree, and the whole face began to shift and slide in front of her eyes. She could now no longer see nor hear the party of Disaffected or their horses, as the fog had condensed to a point that the far side of the scree was beyond her vision. She wasn't yet so callous as to hope for their deaths, instead wishing that they would make it back to solid ground and would give up the chase.

Thinking of solid ground, Allabva turned in her direction of travel again and now sprinted across the loose rocks, taking advantage of the trail she could still see before it was wholly consumed.

The rockslide on the northern scree rumbled and screamed, deafening her and drowning out all thoughts except that of arriving at the far side. The rocks beneath her moved even before she stepped on them, the avalanche of stone becoming contagious and infecting the southern scree that she now crossed. She threw all caution to the wind, running and jumping, heedless of her painful foot.

Finally, Allabva threw herself on the dirt beyond the shifting stone, gasping from relief. Unable to hear herself sob, she shrieked the terror out.

Chapter 27

Beyond the Fog

T hen she thought of Hronomon. There was no way for him to cross now, with the field of rocks continuing to flow downhill. Her cries changed from those of relief to those of loss. She was alive, but the cursed Disaffected had won against her Nomord escort.

What would she do now? How could she make it the rest of the way up the mountain alone? Hronomon was dead.

But then she saw a shadowy white form in the mist in the corner of her eye. She lifted her tear-streaked face and looked up the slope of the scree, trying to peer through the dense fog. The phantasm was blurry, but it was moving fast and gracefully.

Hronomon came bounding down, slanting across the river of stone. He made a final leap away from the rocks, but his last step was poorly placed. He landed on the trail with unsure footing, falling to his belly and rolling, almost crashing into Allabva.

Hronomon rose shakily to his feet. Allabva jumped up from where she knelt and threw her arms around the Nomord's neck. He shifted uncertainly, but stayed where he was. She slowly drew back and wanted to tell him how relieved she was, but the rocks behind him still made any verbal communication inaudible.

Instead, the two of them advanced, side by side on the narrow path, both limping now, hawkishly watching their way along the trail through the dense mist. When they had placed enough distance behind them to be able to talk to each other, Hronomon addressed Allabva with reverence.

"Why were you crying? You had made it across, and you are all that is needed to bond with the Shrongelin. If you make it to the summit, then my primary mission is fulfilled, and the Shrongelin can perform his duty. Another Gha-Nomord will step forward to be Hronomon if I die, then become the new Shrongelin when the time comes. The cycle continues." He limped stoically forward, not turning his head toward Allabva while he spoke.

"Do you not know?" Allabva asked in disbelief. "Have you lost yourself so much in your mission? You matter too, Hronomon."

"Of course. The Construct matters, and I play my role in that. All I have, all I am, I give to the Construct. I stand between the innocent and ruin."

Allabva sniffled, eyes red with tears. "No, you Nomo-Nomo," she laughed. "*You* matter. Your life has intrinsic value, apart from any service you can render to the Construct, even if you have nobody to care about you. But I care about you, and I'm glad you're still alive, even though I don't know your proper name. You still have one, right?"

Hronomon was silent for several moments. He looked down at the trail ahead of him, then sideways at Allabva, then forward again in slow succession. He blinked sluggishly several times, then spoke again at last.

"Thank you. Thank you for reminding me what I am truly fighting for. Thank you for caring about me. I had given myself over so entirely to fighting for the Construct and restoring the shield again, that I did not realize how much of myself I was forgetting. I am glad that you are still alive as well, not only so that you can serve the Construct, but because it means that one more good person is still in this world."

Allabva laughed, overwhelmed by such thanks coming from an immortal, magical being. "I think you're still a little too given over to the Construct."

"No. It is impossible to be too dedicated to saving the world."

"Not at all," Allabva argued. "The way I see it, you do everything you can, you dedicate all your efforts wherever you can apply them. But some part of those efforts has to go to maintaining yourself. Part of you needs to remember that you count as an individual. Construct or no Construct, you count as my friend. Can you see that?"

He looked at her sharply at the mention of the word "friend."

"I must admit that I do not fully understand. You've barely known me a week and you call me a friend. We are simply working together with the same goal."

"Of course you're a friend," Allabva answered. "We're doing more than cooperating with each other; we fight for each other—I admit that count is a bit one-sided—we talk, and discuss the moral philosophy of our service to the Construct. We believe in and respect each other even if we disagree."

She looked at him and gave him a smile, then continued.

"You are peaceful company, steady and calming. I would pass time with you voluntarily. No world crisis necessary, and not just for the novelty of carrying a conversation with one of the Nomord. I care about you for who you are. I just wish that I knew your proper name. Are you allowed to tell me?"

Hronomon chewed on what Allabva had said, then lowered his head.

"I cannot tell you my name. I do not remember it."

"How can you forget your own name?" Allabva asked, amazed.

"I told you that being Hronomon comes with forgetfulness. Rather, becoming Hronomon causes one to forget. Just as I said that I give myself too completely to the Construct, this goes to the extent that I forgot who I was as an individual. I still do not recall."

"Will it ever come back?"

Allabva held one hand to her staff as she walked, but now the other hand came to her mouth in concern, her head stooped in weariness.

"Some things must. The Shrongelin must form a bond with a Companion. How to do that has been remembered by each one of them. But I do not know for sure if I will ever remember my own name, or what my favorite game was when I was a foal."

Allabva's head whipped erect, eyes wide at Hronomon. "The Nomord have games? I mean, I guess that's not surprising since the Ta-Nomord always seem so lighthearted, but I never really thought about it. You have multiple games, distinct pastimes that you shared with playmates."

"I—"

Allabva cut him off, eyes wide with realization. "Oh, my goodness. You were a foal once. The Nomord are born and grow. I've never seen a little Nomord, nor an old one. I always thought you were simply immortal, just... always around."

This time Hronomon laughed. He *laughed*. Maybe Allabva was getting to him.

"You're partly right," he admitted. "Yes. We are immortal. As long as we don't get smashed on sharp rocks, we live as long as we like. When we feel that we have experienced sufficient of what life has to offer, we can give up the ghost and make room for more Nomord in the world."

"So you don't grow old, but why have I never seen a foal?" Allabva inquired.

Hronomon harrumphed. "Needs of the Construct. The shield separates us, do you recall?"

"Oh," Allabva said, deflated. "That's right, the Ta-Nomord can't even see you. Stupid Sacalai," she spat.

Hronomon laughed again, but this time it was...haunted. Mirthless.

"I'm afraid I can assure you that Sacalai is certifiably not stupid. She possesses an extremely keen intellect and a diabolical knack for catching others off guard. If you go up against her, you must never let your guard down. She holds no compunctions against killing, whether human, Nomord, or other."

Allabva cocked her head as she identified a missing item of knowledge. "Is Sacalai Nomord?"

Hronomon shook his head in confusion, the equine version of a shrug. "I do not believe so."

"How can you not know? She wields magic."

"Nobody knows the fullness of her true nature," Hronomon informed Allabva.

"Well, I know that you forget things as Hronomon. But why doesn't anybody else know? Can't you go and talk to other Gha-Nomord and ask them? Weren't they there before the Construct as well?"

"There have been no new Nomord born since the institution of the Construct, so yes, we were all there. But in order to separate her from the world to keep the world safe, we had to seal up some things that would remain in our memories otherwise. Our understanding of her, just as her knowledge of this mountain used for the Shrongelin's bonding, is masked from our minds as an unintended consequence of the Construct. The secrets of her true nature abide with her, and nobody will know until the shield becomes sufficiently pervious. Besides, she doesn't make sense according to what we do know. We call Sacalai 'her,' do we not? And yet she can manipulate the weather from halfway across the world, and influence minds no matter where they happen to be. These are Gha-Nomord powers, not female abilities, and their scale far exceeds any of us. If she is Nomord, she is not like the rest of us."

Allabva was dumbstruck, haunted by the knowledge Hronomon had just imparted. Unsure how to respond or react to this unsettling information, Allabva barely managed to utter, "Step one, I summit this mountain and form the bond."

Hronomon nodded, a human expression, and the two walked on in silence. The fog was beginning to lift, but evening was giving way to night at the same time.

Hunger gripped Allabva's stomach as her head was weighed down with fatigue. Grasping Delgan's flute, she said the only thing she could think of that could help.

"Beware the wolves."

Chapter 28

Sharp Sticks

Allabva and Hronomon strode through the darkness of night, the sky now clear so they could see their way. Allabva had gotten so used to limping that she ceased even to notice that she was doing it. Hronomon still appeared somewhat awkward with his limp, his injury only several hours old. This high on the mountain, it was too cold for crickets; there were no insect sounds to be heard. Allabva did hear the whistling of the wind, the shaking of the aspens, her and Hronomon's footfalls on the path, and her own ragged breath.

Hunger gripped her body, made her feel weak, and as her body tried to conserve energy until its next meal, it chilled her fingers, toes, and nose. She wore gloves to keep the cold off. They helped a little, but with her fatigue, she could not be bothered to change her socks even though she knew fresh, dry socks would warm her better.

The night carried something majestic and unsettling at the same time. At this height she could look west and north and see great expanses, but it also meant that as she walked, half of the world around her felt like it fell away unnaturally, disappearing in the darkness below.

"Why do we have to meet him on a mountaintop?" Allabva asked her escort.

"It is the place designated in the Construct," Hronomon answered. "It is distant from the daily dealings of the world, normally unbothered by man or beast."

"Animals don't come here?"

"They do come here, but our destination is at the summit, too cold for the trees, far too cold for grass. There's no food. Animals have no need to visit the summit, so they don't go often."

"Oh. Can you make it warmer for us while we're here?"

There was a long silence before he answered.

"No. I am currently exhausted. I exerted myself greatly to bring the mist at the Slant, to make it as thick as it was, and to time it just right so that we could make it through, but the Disaffected could not see well enough to pass, and so that the stone would be wet and more likely to slip. I don't think you are aware of this, but it rained on the Slant, beginning just as we left. The weather is not easy to manipulate so precisely. That precision took a great deal out of me."

"Maybe I should play some music again to cheer us up."

"That would be nice, Allabva, but I do not think it prudent right now. It is possible that we could underestimate the Disaffected mob. Somebody could have made it across. I would hate to tell them with music how close they could be to catching up."

Hronomon stopped talking for a moment to cough.

"Actually, I've changed my mind. Whoever follows us is going to have to follow this trail. It's not a question of finding us, only a matter of pacing. You can if you want."

Allabva pulled out Delgan's flute, tucking her staff and her gloves under her arm so she could play the instrument with both hands. Wanting some variety and having listened to "In the Cool Shade of the Mount" several times recently, she tried the mood for "Five in the Morning, Five at Night."

After playing through it the normal way, she decided to make it match the current setting better and slowed it down significantly. Then, already bored with the simple tune, she started playing "In the Cool Shade of the Mount" by hand.

She made it through one verse and chorus, but on the second verse, Hronomon interrupted. "Can you play anything else?"

"No. This was given—lent to me only last week, and I never played it before. I haven't had time to learn anything else yet."

"I think you were walking faster just now when you weren't playing it, anyway. Perhaps silence is better tonight."

Allabva tucked the flute back into her blouse and pulled her gloves back on.

"I think so, too. I need my walking stick to make up for my ankle."

The pair walked on and Allabva now noticed more significantly the sound of her walking stick tap-tapping on the ground. She thought back to the last time she was so conscious of the sound her walking stick made. It wasn't a bad sound, but it made her think back to when, running in the night, she had been tripped by a rope across the road. She saw no connection between that night and this one, but it made her realize how much more one paid attention to the sounds when it was dark out.

She barely had time to register a new sound before her thoughts were invaded by things happening rapidly around her. It was a twang and a whistle that sounded remarkably like...

Allabva's mind was slow, struggling against too little sleep, but she snapped to alertness, anyway. Another twang and whistle sounded, and Hronomon screamed in pain.

He shouted, "Run, Allabva!"

Looking around to gather information and understand what was happening, Allabva saw that Hronomon's left hindquarter had an arrow sticking out of it. Another arrow whizzed past her, passing by on the outboard side, next to open air leading down off the mountain.

She jumped into motion forward along the trail, calling back to Hronomon, "Come on! Get out of range!"

Hronomon was doing the exact opposite. He turned around and charged to the rear, loosing an equine scream twice as loud as Allabva thought him capable of. As he ran back, two archers leapt into motion to save themselves from the Nomord's fury. They both left the trail, each going in the opposite direction from the other. The one on the downhill side leaped down, nearly falling as he haphazardly descended three times his height down the slope.

Seeing this, Hronomon turned around again and ran toward Allabva. "Get out of range. Run, do not walk. If they are to approach us, they will have to do so in a manner that will call our attention. Do not give them any shots."

Allabva ran forward, needing to use her staff on the uneven trail. Hronomon trotted behind her on the narrow path, now with an even more uneven gait. Allabva slowed down sooner than she had before, allowing her fatigue to show.

"We can't keep this up forever," she told Hronomon. "I can't, regardless of whether or not you can."

"It's not forever. It's only to the top of the mountain." Somehow his eyes held a smile.

"Is that a joke at a time like this?"

"Only half of one. What I said is true."

"I have to say, I don't understand Nomord humor," Allabva shook her head at him. "Anyway, I can't keep this up to the top of the mountain. My ankle is bad, I have no food... We have to stop them so they don't follow us anymore."

"Of course. I've been watching for an opportunity. We just need the right terrain feature. This could be a candidate up ahead."

Hronomon nodded ahead of them at a large boulder next to the path, pointing with his horn.

The boulder was taller than Hronomon was, and looked to be broad enough that it would hide both of them if they set themselves immediately on the other side of it. As they approached it, they saw that it did not offer a proper leeward side that would give them a place to hide from the archers. They continued on their way at a jogging pace, Hronomon keeping an eye out behind them and reporting occasionally that he saw the archers still following.

Eventually, they came to another large boulder while the archers were out of sight, which offered a leeward side with ground even enough for them to hide themselves and allow the archers to approach. They hid behind it, Hronomon waiting next to the trail and Allabva waiting behind him. As they waited for their pursuers to catch up, Allabva sat down and emptied her waterskin down her throat, catching her breath as well.

Hronomon took the opportunity to take a mouthful of aspen leaves from a tree they stood next to, then stood still. Allabva waited in suspense and watched Hronomon's ears twitch and turn this way and that. After a few minutes, his ears stood at attention, pointing toward the trail they had just come up.

Even though Allabva knew what the Nomord was listening for, she couldn't hear anything but the wind and her own breath. Without warning, Hronomon reared up on hind legs, his front hooves pawing the air while he moved forward and neighed menacingly. The two archers were there, successfully caught by surprise while they stalked their quadrupedal prey. Now they found themselves assaulted by their prey, arrows nocked but not held at the ready.

Hronomon caught one of the archers in the chest, a young man whom he kicked backward. The Disaffected lost hold of his bow and fell off the trail, tumbling several paces down the slope below. He grabbed at a tree trunk, but it slipped from his grasp and he landed backward against another tree, hitting his head.

In the moment when Hronomon kicked the first man, the second had raised his bow to the ready, pulled the bowstring taut, and released his arrow at the Nomord at point-blank range. The arrow having lost no momentum before it hit his target, Hronomon was fortunate that the man's hurried aim was poor. The arrow hit him in the side of the chest, underneath his torso at a glancing angle, passing through the surface flesh and exiting out his left flank.

Hronomon whinnied a shout back at the man, coming down on all fours immediately in front of him, head lowered to bring his horn into the fight. The Disaffected flinched at this but didn't give up.

"Get back, freak!" he shouted, holding his bow up to guard himself.

Hronomon didn't speak back to him, but leaned down, pushing on the bow hard. It broke with a great *crack* while pushing the man to the ground.

Allabva rushed forward and collected the first Disaffected's bow, then the arrow that had passed through the Nomord's wound. She awkwardly nocked the arrow and pointed it at the second man, seated on the trail, then back at the first man, who had been momentarily dazed but was standing up and searching for a way to help his companion.

"I would not if I were you," Allabva warned the dazed Disaffected, flagging him with the bloody arrow.

He stared back intensely, then responded by pulling two arrows from his belt-mounted quiver and holding them like daggers in his fists. "Let's do this, then." He set one foot forward to begin climbing back to the trail.

"I would not, either. You two should just go on your way," Hronomon added his warning. He raised one hoof toward the downed man, half-heartedly trying to place it on his chest.

The man scurried backward to escape, sneering. "You think you can rule humanity? You're just a selfish monster."

Hronomon tried again with his other front hoof. "I have no intentions of ruling. I only want to protect."

"Then protect yourself!"

The downed man pulled a knife from his belt and swung the blade in Hronomon's face. The Nomord pulled his head back quickly, avoiding the knife, then came back down and deftly placed a hoof on the man's leg, pinning it in place. The man shouted in pain, then attacked the hoofed leg with his knife. Hronomon raised the hoof and kicked the man in the chest, then leaned forward to push the Disaffected's torso down and pin him on his back against the ground. The man came to rest at an odd angle, his quiver wedged between his back and the ground

The younger man, still ascending from his landing spot, threw an arrow ineffectively at Hronomon, then grabbed another from his quiver.

"Don't," Allabva said to him. "I'll loose this arrow."

The grounded man groaned in pain, knife forgotten, falling from his hand.

The younger man might be attractive if his face weren't contorted with spite right now. Allabva ached over the senseless waste of his life because of misplaced hatred. It was such a shame. He probably wouldn't have any trouble finding a wife and starting a family if he weren't driven by anger. Instead he was wasting his youth on a lie.

"Fine, unicorn's slave. Have it your way."

He threw the two arrows in his hands to the ground at his feet, then started climbing uphill toward the trail where he had come from.

"Drop the rest of them," Hronomon demanded.

The younger Disaffected ground his teeth angrily, red-faced, as he undid the belt holding his quiver in place and threw it to the ground.

"Are you happy now? How am I supposed to hunt for food?"

He made a rude gesture and turned, dismissing himself to walk away.

Hronomon turned his face downward at the other man.

"Disarm yourself, and you may go as well."

The man glared up angrily, evidently considering whether there may be some other way out of this.

"Please decide quickly. We don't have all night," Hronomon said.

The man still did not respond, so Hronomon leaned forward gently to place a little more weight on the man's chest.

The man grunted and squinted, turning red in the face, then he opened his mouth.

"Alright," he groaned.

Hronomon removed his hoof from the man's chest and stepped back. The man brought himself up to his elbows and then his hands in a sitting position, then scooted backward away from Hronomon. Suddenly he jumped up, turning around to make a break for it. Hronomon lunged forward, grabbed the man's quiver in his teeth, and yanked backward.

The man was pulled off balance and fell to the ground again, his quiver now coming off his shoulder.

Hronomon continued to pull, walking backward as he did. He walked back several paces while the Disaffected attempted to hold on to the quiver and dislodge it from the Nomord's teeth. Hronomon did not let go, instead pulling upward and shaking, causing the man to be caught not only by his hands holding on to the quiver's strap, but also by his chin. The Nomord continued pulling in this manner until the man started choking and he unhooked his own chin from the strap, letting the quiver go.

The Disaffected man stood and turned to face Hronomon, regarding him with bitter contempt.

"I always knew you beasts were up to no good, and this treatment illustrates exactly what you always wanted to do, anyway."

"I know not what you mean that I always wanted to do. I have no desire to treat people with violence."

Hronomon spoke plainly and calmly to the man. The man did not return the favor.

He scowled. "Your kind always hated people. You try to fool us by healing people when it doesn't matter, then leave us alone when we need help from somebody like you."

Allabva watched Hronomon and wondered how he could stay so calm. She had to weigh in.

"Sir, this Nomord has treated you with as much respect as you allow him to. You came seeking to kill him. You intentionally wounded him, and yet he has responded only by asking you to go your way in peace."

"You call that peace? He knocked me down and put his hoof on my chest. Then he yanked me by the strap of my quiver, nearly breaking my neck!"

"He asked you to disarm yourself and you refused. Just leave us be and you will have no issues from us." The man was testing her patience, but Allabva was determined to would remain as calm as Hronomon.

"My friend was right. You're just a unicorn's slave, your mind infected by their deceit. I wouldn't expect somebody with such a weak mind to be redeemable. I would sooner die than let one of these in my grasp continue living." The man turned to walk, but stopped where he had been knocked to the ground the first time and grabbed his knife. He turned and whipped it at Hronomon in a blur.

Hronomon butted the knife out of the air with his horn like he had with Nillan's on the road. "If you are so determined..." Hronomon let the implications of what the man had last said hover for a moment, then he charged at the man with his horn held toward the man's chest.

The man ducked and rolled with a shout.

"No! That's not what I meant. You're not in my grasp. I was only trying to do what I could while I was close." He shouted his excuses rapidly, trying to tell Hronomon that he somehow wasn't serious.

Hronomon let the man dodge out of the way and circled about to come back and stand next to Allabva.

"Then go, and try to consider the fact that I am letting you go when I have no compelling reason to do so, as evidence that what I desire is peace. Allabva," Hronomon turned his head to face her. "Please gather all the arrows and the dagger. If they are too heavy for you, we can sling the quiver around my neck, but we cannot leave them for this man to pick them up."

Allabva moved to collect the weapons, taking the younger man's quiver and fastening it around her own waist, and placing the elder man's quiver draped around the Nomord's neck. She tucked the knife into a pocket that her new quiver had on the outside. Hronomon stared at the man, fixing him with his gaze.

Once Allabva had the weapons collected from the ground, Hronomon turned around to continue forward on the trail and motioned for Allabva to join him. The Disaffected man stood there dumbly. When Hronomon saw that the man wasn't moving to go, he did another about face and started walking purposefully toward the man.

"Go home and leave us be. I will not let you dodge my horn this time."

The man threw a thousand more daggers with his eyes, then turned and regressed down the trail, traveling home in the darkness.

Hronomon and Allabva continued on their way. Allabva was momentarily relieved of the pain in her ankle by the rush and pounding of blood in her chest after the encounter with the archers, but she knew that Hronomon was now attempting to hide a slightly more pronounced limp as he experienced the pain of his new wound.

"Why wouldn't that second man give up his weapons and go, even though it was obvious you had him beat?" Allabva asked Hronomon.

"Reminds you of Nillan, doesn't he?" Hronomon responded. "Some people are inflexible."

"You mean obstinate, right?"

"Partly so. This man and Nillan are certainly obstinate, aren't they? But I mean that they are set in their ideas and they refuse to allow that to be adjusted. When confronted with a compelling argument against their position, they still do not bend to align themselves with reason. They find it threatening to adjust their perceptions."

"But why?"

"I do not know. If I did, then perhaps I could get them to open up and make friends out of them. It is their choices that block this, not my preferences." His tone was sad, not angry.

They walked several paces with neither one saying anything.

"Hronomon?"

"Yes?"

"Do you think more of the Disaffected will catch up with us?"

"I guess time will tell. Not on horseback," he added. "That rock slide should have left the terrain too loose for any horse to cross in the near future."

"Are there other trails up this mountain?"

"Yes, but they don't come near this path until nearly at the summit. Also, this is the fastest way up, so if anybody else is coming up, they would have had to start earlier than we did if they wanted any hope of intercepting us. I think if any people catch up to us again, it will be from behind like the archers did."

"It probably won't be hard for anyone to catch up with us," Allabva panted. "I'm going pretty slow with no food or sleep. How do you keep up your energy?"

"My body is different from yours," The Nomord answered. "But I am wearing down as well."

"So somebody could catch up to us?"

"Of course. It's always a possibility."

"I guess we had better hurry."

Allabva tried to walk faster, but she was too weary to notice any difference in the outcome of her effort. As they ascended, she was reminded that it was still springtime. The night seemed to get colder as it went on, and in the hours before the first morning light they encountered the first patch of snow, hiding in a shady patch where the sun did not melt it. Allabva appreciated the sight of the snow, even though it marked the more savage frigidity of the mountain heights. To her, it represented purity existing in the midst of scarcity. Although scarcity and purity were not opposites, the symbol of purity gave her hope to carry on through the adversity.

Chapter 29

Fog of War

Allabva and Hronomon crested a rise and finally stared into the sun that had been giving them light for the past three and a half hours, Allabva now carrying both quivers. The mountain looming above them had blocked their direct sight of the sun even while it had been illuminating the trail for some time. Blinking in the stark light, Allabva had to close her eyes and shade her vision with her hand to continue to see where she was going. She felt weaker every hour, losing the sentiment that she got from the first snow she saw up close. Now it lay all around them and what she found herself thinking about was that drinking water would be harder to find, with most of it still frozen on the ground.

"Do you think we can hold on to a reasonable expectation of hope, still?" She asked Hronomon.

"Of course. We have to." His voice sounded strained.

"But is it reasonable? Do you think our success is inevitable?"

Hronomon blinked several times. "Not necessarily," he admitted. "There is always..." his speech slowed. "... the possibility of failure."

Allabva frowned at the Nomord, wondering about his change of tone. He had always seemed so determined previously. "But I suppose we just have to hold on to the possibility of success?"

"Yes, the possibility." The vanishment of his determination was concerning to Allabva. She wondered if a mood could be as infectious as she felt his was at this moment.

"Do you think I should drop these arrows and this bow now? Their weight slows me down."

"Might as well. Or maybe not. You might need to use them. Do you know how?"

Was that ambivalence? That didn't seem to be a regular feature of Hronomon's personality.

"I know the basics. You know where I grew up; it's not a large city. Everybody got some practice with a bow, in some field or another."

"Did you ever use one? Did you ever hunt?" This was starting to sound like small talk, something else that didn't seem typical for the hard-charging Nomord.

"No," Allabva answered. "I just did some target practice."

"Why don't you do some of that now?" He drawled. "Might as well." The tone of his last remark seemed maybe to cross the line into slightly pessimistic.

Allabva decided to do target practice as they walked. She figured the worst it could do would be to waste an arrow, losing it if her shot went bad, but on the other hand, it could break the monotony of the fatigue in her legs and the numbness in her mind. She wedged her staff between her bag and shoulder quiver, then removed an arrow from her waist quiver and nocked it. Taking aim on a point of the trail ahead of her, she loosed the arrow. It bounced off the ground and came to rest a few paces further ahead.

When she caught up to the arrow she had shot, she picked it up, nocked it again, took aim, and let it fly a second time. By the time she caught up to this one and picked it up again, she decided she was too tired to go on without using the staff as a walking stick. She stowed the arrow and the bow, which had a mounting clip on her shoulder quiver, resuming the tap-tap of her staff on the ground.

The weight of her mission slowly settled on Allabva's mind as a dark pall while she walked.

"What's the use? Sure, maybe I can make it to the top of this big rock, and maybe I bond with the Shrongelin. But then what?"

Hronomon considered her somberly. "Then your fight begins."

"That's what I'm talking about," Allabva barked. "What's the point? In the last week I fled my home in the dark of night, froze, wore out the soles of my feet, got robbed, abducted, tied up, sprained my ankle, got abducted again, and nearly constantly wondered where my next meal will come from. I'm out of food, I'm freezing again even though at the same time I'm in danger of sunburn, I haven't eaten in two days, and on top of that, if I could stop time, you know what I would do first? I wouldn't bother to fix any of that because I would sleep! If this isn't the fight already, what's the point of moving on to the next punishment? I'll just throw myself from the next cliff we pass and get it over with."

Anger contorted her face.

"You're not making bad arguments," Hronomon admitted.

Allabva gaped at him, shocked. "What is with you? You struck me as unshakable, but now you're agreeing with my despair. I'm feeling without hope and all you can say is that I'm right? You're supposed to egg me on, aren't you? I have to meet with the big old Shrongelin, it was decided when I left the Cleft with you, wasn't it? What about now?"

Hronomon's ears lay flat against his head and he showed his teeth. "Do not speak to me in that manner. You are a member of the human race, a short-lived creature who cannot fathom what I have seen, what I have done, what I have suffered on your behalf—"

Hronomon stopped his tirade cold, freezing in place on the trail as well. "Binterox!" He looked rapidly one way and another as if to locate something.

Allabva stopped as well, sullenly puzzling over Hronomon's behavior. "What was that word?" she asked suspiciously.

"It's a Binterox," he repeated.

"What's that supposed to mean?" Allabva eyed him warily.

"Our desperation and anger are not our own."

"Well, I'd say it's Sacalai's fault, but my feelings are pretty real." Her eyes had begun getting glossy with moisture before Hronomon stopped.

"Your experience is real; your emotions are fabricated and are not your own. Nor are mine."

"Will you tell me what you mean?"

"A Binterox is...an impossibility." His eyes were wide and his nostrils flared, inhaling more air to deal with a perceived threat.

"But what is it?"

"It is a thief, a perverter, a murderer. And...impossible." He breathed in and out rapidly, turning his head to catch some phantom scent.

Allabva's patience was thin and she scorned Hronomon's enigmatic behavior. "I'm afraid that doesn't tell me anything, you blabbering horse."

"Sorry." He appeared sincere. "A Binterox possesses stolen power that has only belonged to the Nomord since the last dragon died."

"Dragon? Are you trying to mess with my head now?" Allabva rolled her eyes.

"Allabva," Hronomon said her name sternly, "listen to me now. We are both irritated; it is the Binterox's work. I am trying to stay calm and believe me, it is not easy. Are you with me?"

"Yes..."

Hronomon took a deep breath. "There are lost things. Some are tragedies, like the dragons. Some are good to be gone and should never return."

"Like the Binterox?"

"Like the Binterox."

"So...what exactly is it?"

Hronomon resumed walking forward, toward the summit. Allabva fell in step.

"A Binterox is an abomination. Somebody who has come to possess an ability of the Nomord. One has evidently joined the Disaffected pursuit, and has come close enough to influence us."

"How does one come to possess the Nomord's power?" Allabva asked, a suspicion arising.

"One has to kill a Nomord."

"Was...is Sacalai a Binterox?"

"If so, she was the most powerful we ever encountered. All others were either killed or stripped of power when the Construct was instituted and she was imprisoned."

"Why didn't you do that to her?"

"She was too strong. She stole more magic, and more types of magic than anyone else had. If it were not such a sinister practice, her proliferation may have had her labeled a prodigy."

"What makes it such a sinister practice to steal Nomord magic?"

"It is how it is done. Every Nomord and every other magical creature is born with its magic inherent in its being. The magic is part of its mind, body, self. To steal that part of one's being requires a termination of the whole. A Binterox, therefore, is necessarily a murderer."

Allabva's step quickened, wanting to put more space between her and this creature that followed.

"What makes it impossible for there to be one here?"

"We destroyed any knowledge of how to accomplish the feat of becoming a Bintarox. It was lost to the world with Sacalai. The chances of anybody else figuring out how to do it independently are extremely low, and Sacalai's prison is not yet ruptured."

"So the Binterox had to kill a Nomord?"

"Yes, but we are not so easily killed."

"I can imagine; I've seen you in action."

True to his singular focus on their mission, Hronomon ignored the comment.

"The Ta-Nomord are common in the lands where men roam, but they are protected by the Construct. While Sacalai's prison remains intact, it should be impossible to commit violence against them. The Gha-Nomord keep ourselves apart, as is necessary to sustain the Construct. Until the Shrongelin and I came forth to find you and begin a cycle of renewing the Construct, we were all but unfindable to men. I do not know how this Binterox first found a Gha-Nomord, then managed to kill him."

"If the Binterox is using Nomord magic, then he cannot control us, right?"

"That is correct, but he can strongly influence our minds, our emotions. I still feel hopeless, by the way. But in the face of this hopelessness, I choose the path of determination."

Allabva took small comfort in the fact that the approaching enemy could not force her actions. If he had dug up ancient cryptic knowledge and on top of that, slain a Nomord (she assumed it was a he because of the strength it must have taken to kill one of the Nomord), Allabva didn't want to let him come any closer than he already was. She gritted her teeth against her feelings of despair. Maybe it was pointless to resist, insanity to press on, but it was what *she* wanted to do.

"We have to let the Binterox catch up to us," Hronomon said suddenly.

Allabva was alarmed.

"What?" she said, "Shouldn't we speed up so we can get out of range or something?"

"He is already catching up to us, and we have much ground to cover before we reach the summit. He is probably also not alone. He can't come with a large escort because the scree would not be passable by horses yet, so this means he is with a small party. We will hide ourselves and wait for them to catch up."

"What are we supposed to do when they reach us?"

Hronomon didn't answer, clopping along the trail sadly and looking for the ideal spot to set up an ambush.

"Hronomon, what are we supposed to do when they catch up?"

"We have to kill them."

"Does that somehow steal the power back?" Allabva wondered aloud.

"No, it was lost when the Nomord was killed. It is purely to rescue us. They are trying to catch up to us so they can kill us, but if we can let them catch up to us on our terms, then we still have a shot of making it up this mountain alive."

"Is there no other way?"

"I don't see one. You don't have to do anything. In fact, it may be helpful if you are visible ahead and I jump out from the side. You just distract them, and I'll do all the work."

Allabva considered what Hronomon meant, saying nothing for several paces.

"I appreciate you trying to protect me, both physically and emotionally. Several days ago, I was uneasy with telling a white lie, while you suggested that any means to achieve our goal was justified. But I think you and I see things the same way on today's problem. There's..."

Allabva continued walking, but held her breath for several seconds, feeling the weight of the discussion.

She continued in a low voice, almost a whisper.

"There's a difference between murder and killing, isn't there? But that doesn't make it easy, does it? To do what has to be done, I mean."

"No, it doesn't make it easy at all."

Hronomon's voice fell flat on the dirt and stone beneath their feet.

"Yes, there is a difference between murder and killing. I would say the difference is intent, or purpose. We are planning self-defense. We would gladly leave them alone if they would leave us alone."

Allabva's voice cracked as she spoke. "You're my friend, you know that. You have value just for being you. My mother taught me that everybody has value, even the darkest criminal."

"Your mother is wise."

"I always believed what she said, and I still do. This... This Binterox has value, too. It is a great sadness to have to plan what we are planning."

Hronomon regarded her in a new light. "I'm struggling to feel what I think I should feel, but even with the Binterox's influence, I have to say that I am impressed. If that is truly how you see things, then the kindness in your heart will make the Shrongelin's bond a very strong one. If we get free of the foul creature following us and make it to the top, I predict good things in our fight against Sacalai. Nevertheless, you are right. It is sad that this Binterox's life should be wasted, but it is not we who are wasting it. He chose to use his time and energy to make the world a worse place. When we remove him from it, the world will be better for it."

Allabva coughed, continuing to struggle with their pace, hunger, and fatigue.

"But it's always possible he could choose to turn around, right? We will remove that possibility if we kill him."

"Yes, it's possible, but so extremely unlikely, and we can only act with the information available to us. Besides, we are not acting as jury and executioner. We are acting in defense of ourselves and everyone else who would be a victim of this Binterox's influence."

Allabva looked at the Nomord with eyes reddening once again, weighed down by everything placed in her way on this journey.

"Very well," she heaved out. "I suppose the Binterox's companions are in the same boat. So how do I do my part? How do I end a life?" She stared at Hronomon through empty eyes, consigned to have to perform a distasteful action.

Chapter 30

Binterox

Allabva looked down the trail from her hidden vantage point. She saw a man appear around a bend in the trail, revealing himself among the aspens as he walked forward, scanning both sides of the trail with his eyes. He had a bow in one hand, his other hand holding an arrow nocked on the relaxed bowstring.

Allabva looked to Hronomon to verify whether he had seen the man.

"I see him," Hronomon confirmed. "I don't expect him to be the Binterox, but the next man following him."

"I don't see anybody else."

"He's there. He's just not in view yet. I can smell that there's more than one. This first man is acting as a bodyguard. We'll have to stay silent as they approach. Let him pass so the Binterox comes straight in front of me, then shoot him when I jump."

Allabva nodded to signify her understanding. She was getting to feel very tired of having this four-legged creature give her orders. Hopefully, once she got to the top of this mountain she could be rid of him and his demands that pulled her clear across from the Cleft and up this mountain on this crazy climb to meet the Shrongelin.

Allabva blinked and shook her head. The Binterox was close and more difficult to resist. She chose to direct her suspicions toward the man she could see and the expected party behind him. She had the bow in her hand and an arrow nocked, but she didn't bother flagging the man with her arrow, planning to wait until he was past her hiding point before she trained her aim on him. Otherwise, he might see her movement as she tracked him with the tip of the arrow.

A woman came into view. The newcomer walked confidently, flowing robes the color of the sky parting to reveal dark red boots striding forward. Her face showed features of a land Allabva hadn't seen before. Perhaps she was from the Glosen tribes? She bore an expression of concentration between her flowing black hair. As she strode along the path behind the archer in front of her, she did not look from side to side as he did. Rather, she kept herself simply walking ahead and moving her hands in reverse circles in front of her, then clenching and opening her fists, and going back to the circles again. It wasn't a precision movement, but one of distraction as she focused on something else.

Allabva looked at Hronomon to gauge his reaction. If this was the Binterox, then Allabva was surprised. Hronomon was biting the air and shaking his mane, eyes wide. Whether it was shock or concentration to resist the Binterox's influence was unclear, but it was obvious that the Nomord was starting to lose his calm. Allabva let her weapon rest on the ground and raised her open hands at him and softly lowered them several times in a calming gesture that she hoped would work.

Allabva rested between two rocks that reached to her elbows when she stood straight, but as the man and the woman drew nearer, Allabva crouched to hide herself, using the aspens to mask her face. Hronomon was on the other side of the trail opposite Allabva, poised on a rock that overlooked the trail from above the height of a man. He leaned back and crouched as the archer came forward so that he would stay hidden from view, and stayed there, motionless, while the man passed between Allabva and himself.

As Allabva was about to turn to position her bow toward the man's back and once again nock her arrow which she had set down, a second man came into view around the bend, carrying a crossbow with a bolt already set and wearing a sheathed sword at his belt. Hronomon had said he expected the Binterox to come with a few others as an escort so Allabva should not have been surprised, but she had forgotten when she saw the single archer followed by a woman. Allabva supposed the woman to be the Binterox, walking some distance behind the archer. In the same moment that she assumed the archer in front must be the entire escort, a second man came into view bringing up the rear.

She looked at Hronomon with wild eyes, hoping to find some sort of guidance that he could convey silently. He inclined his head to his right, pointing with his gaze and his horn toward the second man. Allabva gave him a signal with her thumb saying she was watching him, then awkwardly nodded instead, wondering if a Nomord would understand the thumb gesture since he was fingerless himself.

Apparently he had, because he directed his attention with his ears at the woman coming up the trail, whom he now could not see because of the rock he was hiding on top of. If Hronomon jumped down to the supposed Binterox, he would immediately alert both men to his and Allabva's presence. The archer would have to turn around, but the crossbowman would be ready to take a shot immediately.

Allabva nocked her arrow, pointed in the direction of the crossbowman, took aim, and tracked him as he walked. Without losing her lock on the crossbowman, she looked over to her right to see Hronomon preparing to pounce on the Binterox coming up the trail. Allabva assumed that the woman was the Binterox because she appeared to be protected by the other two people, but perhaps she was wrong. Perhaps they needed to wait longer for the real Binterox to show up.

But Hronomon was getting ready to jump from his perch on the large rock. Allabva sighted back in on the crossbowman and waited for the moment when Hronomon would jump, for in that moment she would loose her arrow at the man.

A shriek arose from the trail, taking Allabva by surprise. By the looks of it, it shocked Hronomon as well. He startled, convulsing momentarily, but stayed where he was on the rock.

"They are here!" The woman shouted. "The seeker unicorn and the Companion are here on top of us!"

While Allabva's alarm skyrocketed due to the sudden shout and the knowledge that they'd been discovered, she felt suddenly ten times more capable and a hundred times less angry at the world. It seemed the Binterox had ceased her attack for the moment.

After being startled, Hronomon didn't hesitate a moment. He leapt down from the rock and landed right in front of the woman. She fell back, splaying her hands and trying to catch herself. The poise with which she had marched up the trail just a moment before was gone, her carefully arranged hair flying this way and that.

"Go, Allabva!" Hronomon shouted at the top of his lungs.

Allabva saw the crossbowman look up and down the trail. She spared a peek at the bowman up the trail behind her, who also appeared to be looking for her. Allabva sighted back in on the crossbowman and pulled her bowstring taut, then let her arrow fly. Her novice at the technique showed as her arrow flew off to the left. The crossbow man saw the shaft fly by and whipped his head in Allabva's direction. As he did so, he shouted, "The Companion is in the trees on the south side!" He raised his crossbow, trying to find Allabva with his eyes.

Hronomon charged forward at the Binterox.

Time seemed to slow while Allabva nocked another arrow. The crossbowman, not seeing Allabva but realizing that his charge had come under danger, released a carefully aimed bolt at Hronomon.

Hronomon dodged the bolt at the same time that he closed with the woman, ramming into her and running her over with a few sickening thuds. From the moment when Hronomon had jumped down from the rock, the Binterox already hadn't stood a chance.

The crossbowman rapidly loaded another bolt and raised his weapon at Hronomon while Allabva also pulled her bowstring. They loosed in the same moment, the crossbow bolt burying itself in Hronomon's right shoulder while Allabva's arrow also found a target this time, falling low and hitting the man's outer left thigh.

The man shouted and dropped to the ground, then rolled off the trail to hide among the aspens, out of sight for the moment.

Hronomon, active in the effort of removing all future possibility that the Binterox could cause them or anyone else any harm, disregarded the new wound in his shoulder. He finished stamping and digging at the woman's corpse with his horn, glanced up to confirm that the crossbowman was stalled, then looked up the trail to find the bowman.

Allabva looked up the trail as well. The bowman now stood at the north side of the trail, hiding behind a tree, peeking out to take aim at Hronomon, who hugged the north side of the trail to make himself a more difficult target. Allabva might have wondered if the bowman forgot that she was on the south side, because he was in plain view to her. She turned to orient herself toward the east to get a better fix on the bowman, drawing another arrow from her belt quiver and hooking the back end onto the bowstring with one hand. She looked up and saw him attempting to lean out just enough from behind his tree that he would be able to take a shot at Hronomon without letting the Nomord see it beforehand.

She sighted in, breath ragged from the intensity of the moment, and let her arrow fly when the man had his chest facing her. The shot flew over his left shoulder and bounced off a rock behind him, disappearing in the woods. He flinched, followed the direction the arrow came from, and looked straight at Allabva with murder in his eyes. He had retained his arrow and now directed it toward her, loosing it at the same time that she ducked. It skidded across the rocks she had taken cover behind, passing directly over her head. His aim was true, but she was too fast. This time.

"The bowman knows my location!" Allabva shouted to Hronomon.

He responded with heavy hoofbeats dashing up the trail.

No. That hadn't been her intent. She yanked another arrow out and lifted her face just high enough to see over the rock. She ducked again as another arrow skidded overhead.

Guessing that she had a couple of seconds to work with, she stood tall and aimed at the man. He was faster than she thought, and the next thing she knew was a sudden headache as the man's next arrow deflected off her hood, tearing the fabric of her hood and piercing her scalp just above the forehead. It caught there, transferring its momentum to knocking her head back, but not piercing deeply into her skin or skull.

Allabva saw Hronomon now arriving at the man's tree and she tried to watch to know the outcome of their encounter, but the arrow was stuck to her head and threatening to hinder her movement. She reached up and tried to pull it free, but it held. Allabva caught sight of the crossbowman again, now creeping forward a few paces into the woods on the north side of the road, but she couldn't do anything about him, either, with the arrow shaft flopping on her head. She gritted her teeth and *pulled* the arrow with both hands, successfully ripping it free and inviting a flow of blood from her hair, down over her forehead. She could have vomited at the pain if she had had anything in her stomach to evacuate.

Dazed, Allabva was vaguely aware of Hronomon permanently taking down the bowman. After a few seconds of recovery, she was able to focus her eyes again. She looked up, and all was still but for the quaking of the aspens in the wind.

Taking stock of the area, she saw the woman's corpse on the trail, now joined several paces ahead by the bowman's body fallen at the edge of the trees. Hronomon stood over the fallen archer and raised his head to sniff the air. Assuming that the crossbowman would now be stalking toward Hronomon, she watched for any sign of movement that would betray his location.

Allabva nocked another arrow. Spying a gap bordered by a thicket of trees and thorny berry bushes on the other side of the trail, she realized that the crossbowman would likely have to pass through the gap to the other side of the bushes in order to get a good shot at Hronomon. She lay her aim in that gap and waited for the man to pass through it.

As Allabva waited with her bow at the ready and arrow pulled halfway back, she caught the telltale signs of movement as the man crept through the trees. As he approached the gap, Allabva expected him to be wary and look carefully before crossing it, but he appeared to be unaware that there was a gap exposing him. Perhaps the angle where she was made it obvious to her, but it did not show up where the man was standing.

He was so oblivious of the gap that he actually stopped in the middle of it and held the position while looking ahead to see if there may be some way to attack the Nomord without getting close or showing himself.

Allabva hesitated. *What am I doing?* Then, remembering her discussion with Hronomon before, she replied back to herself: *Simply what is necessary.*

She pulled the arrow all the way back. Then, considering how her previous shots had gone, she waited just another moment to make sure her aim and technique were good. She was about to take the shot when the man moved.

He stepped forward to pass through the brambles but stopped suddenly. Allabva saw him regard the bowman's corpse on the ground, chewing his tongue and frowning angrily. He glanced down at his wounded leg and winced, evidently weighing the potential consequences and the already-realized injury against the prospect of doing harm to a Nomord.

Allabva started to ask herself if the crossbowman was giving up, but then he spat and scowled hate into the woods around him. He checked his crossbow to ensure the bolt was set and cocked, then raised it again to the ready.

No, a voice inside Allabva told her. *He hates the Nomord more than he loves himself. He will not stop. We cannot continue our way, either up or down this mountain, if he is capable of following.*

With a steely coldness in her veins, she rechecked her aim and released the bowstring.

The man heard the twang of Allabva's bow and jerked, twisting and jumping to the side. Despite the rapidity of his reaction, her arrow still caught him in the arm. While the man attempted to recover sure footing after having been caught off guard, Hronomon rushed forward. He dodged around trees to reach the point where the man had stirred, and without hesitation he stabbed the man in the chest with his horn.

As Hronomon pulled back, the crossbowman glanced down at the sight of his new wound, but instead of blood rushing forth, a crystal formed, protruding from his chest. It cast forth from that site, an expanding growth of crystal roiling across his body until within seconds, he was completely enshrouded. Then the angled crystal shards receded into him so that he looked like a man made of cut glass, but still wore his outfit made of cloth and leather, holding a crossbow in one hand. Finally, the glass shattered and disappeared, leaving the man of flesh and skin once again in its place. No sooner had he reappeared in the flesh, than he collapsed to the ground and lay still.

Allabva was shocked. Blinking, she slowly recovered from the specter of the dead crossbowman, and climbed out from between the two rocks she had sheltered herself behind. She positioned herself on the trail once again and looked over at the bowman's and the Binterox's bodies, which had never turned to crystal as the crossbowman had. Shaking her head and trying to process it, Allabva was overcome once again with fatigue and hunger. Unsure what to do and clueless what to think about what she had just observed, she did the only thing she knew how to do at the moment: she turned herself uphill, and began to walk once more.

Hronomon had stood over the crossbowman's body for a minute, but now turned and joined Allabva, clopping along behind her.

Allabva walked in silence, apart from the tapping of her staff on the trail. After a time, she had to know.

"Hronomon, why did that man turn to glass? The other man and woman didn't do that."

"He was judging himself."

He said nothing more, as if that were explanation enough.

"I don't understand," Allabva said flatly.

Hronomon blew air through his lips.

"I keep forgetting that your short lifespan means there's so much you don't know. When my horn comes in contact with a mortal, I can force intense introspection. The man was confronted by his own unwillingness to reason, and his own bloodthirstiness stared back. He had nothing positive to resonate with, and the negative resonance killed him."

"That doesn't make sense," Allabva replied. "I touched your horn and nothing happened to me."

"That's not quite true. If I recall, you said 'what is this, an interview?'"

"Oh."

Allabva assumed Hronomon wasn't trying to be unkind with the factual correction.

"So why didn't I die?"

"Because you bear no malice. Your heart is in the right place. What you felt is what I saw. You felt me peering into you. Our contact caused an emotional introspection that resonated and reverberated back out to me. For you it was a positive experience, but for him it was death. For him, the outcome was his own fault and his own doing."

"I see."

Allabva wasn't totally sure that she understood it, but at least it was consistent with what she could remember. She trudged on, glad that she hadn't had to kill a sentient being. She had been ready, had been committed to following through, had even attempted to, but was spared of having that weigh on her conscience, justified or not, by chance and her own lack of expertise with a bow. If her mission continued further as it had, she would need to be prepared to take a life regardless of her reticence for the task.

She climbed slowly upward throughout the rest of that day, eating nothing, drinking nothing, knowing not whether she would have the strength to fight if they encountered any more dangers.

Seeking to bolster her spirits, Allabva took Delgan's flute out and held it in her hand.

"Beware the wolves," she breathed.

She needed this comfort to make it to the top.

CHAPTER 31

BEWARE THE WOLVES

Allabva Roalke of the Valley of the Five Moons plodded onward and upward in the earliest pre-dawn light, following Hronomon up the mountain. Her feet seemed to slow with each step, sweat glistening, then running down her face with the effort in rebellion against the snow on the ground beneath her feet. The trail was hard to see through the snow, but the moon allowed her to see well enough.

Hronomon, bearer of responsibility second only to the Shrongelin, with his keen intellect and mission to bring Allabva to him, turned his head back to one side to consider Allabva as her steps faltered from exhaustion. The single horn springing lively from his forehead, somehow suggesting motion and flowing energy despite its fixed position, glowed softly in the early morning light, somehow making its presence unmissable despite the perfect whiteness of his coat and the background of snow. The sight of the glowing protuberance drew the attention, and Allabva barely noticed the red of the blood coloring his flanks.

"Come, Allabva," he spoke, his somber voice painting a sonorous soundscape above the gentle clop of his hooves striking stone as they pierced the snowy layer. "I cannot carry you up this slope, and we must arrive by dawn. The Shron-gelin awaits us there."

Allabva breathed heavily, nodding acknowledgement to the Nomord's words. She coughed before replying.

"I haven't...slept—" her voice came in heaves. "—in two ...days."

Hronomon waited for her to catch up.

"I know. I am sorry. But you *must* stand atop the Summit Above the Aspens at the moment the sun breaks across the hills to the east. The world depends on your success, and you have little time remaining. We must climb."

Allabva looked up the slope ahead, trying to quantify the distance in how much time it would take to climb. It may take too long.

"We...can come back after?"

Her companion cocked his head to one side to think for a moment.

"Yes. It will slow you down afterwards, but I believe you can come back this way if necessary."

Without hesitation, Allabva dropped her bag on the trail, not caring how it fell. It didn't matter. She slogged on, walking slightly faster now, still leaning on her staff for support as she went.

An explosion of sound rent the air overhead. Allabva stumbled, falling to the ground as she looked up to see nearly red lightning snake through the sky, twitching and humming as it cast red sparks of fire. The tear in the sky seemed to drone louder and last longer than it had when she'd seen it back home. Was this a portent of something to come in the near future, or was it just another intermediate sign of the prison crumbling?

Allabva swallowed, looked forward again, and climbed back to her feet. She moved her feet faster now, impelled by an extra dose of fear. She climbed. Tired as she was, she had to keep climbing.

As she continued to gaze up the path beyond Hronomon, her fear grew. He saw the wolves at the same time she did, as the pack came over the next rise a few hundred spans ahead. The pack ran toward them, already heading their way before they came into view.

The Nomord's flanks tensed and quivered, preparing for another fight.

"Keep walking, Allabva," he bellowed. "That is the only thing that matters. I will keep them off you. You keep walking!"

She knew he was right, and what could she do against a pack of wolves anyway? She still had to steel herself to comply. Without giving a reply, she dedicated all her energy to continuing her steps.

The wolves seemed to accelerate into the last few seconds of their dash. A lone wolf would never attack one of the Nomord. Five or ten would keep their distance. But this pack was upwards of twenty wolves, seemingly driven by an external force, teeth bared and eyes intent.

As the wolves closed in on them, Allabva thought ruefully on the futility of everything she had gone through with Hronomon if it were to end here, a short distance away from her scheduled fateful meeting with the Shrongelin himself.

Beware the wolves, she thought to herself, feeling the small flute on its chain under her shirt.

She trudged on, hoping that Hronomon could keep them at bay.

"I haven't eaten... in three and a half days," she coughed.

Allabva kept walking, feeling the weakness in her thighs as they worked to lift her legs one at a time. She managed to lift them just high enough to drag her toe across the top of the snow to avoid having to drag through it laboriously.

The wolves set upon Hronomon with a great, raucous sound of growling and chaotic barking. He rose on his hind legs to greet them, his front hooves seeking faces and ribs. As he dropped to all fours again, he lowered his face to bring his horn into the fray.

At the same instant his hind legs shot out to his rear. The wolves expected this but didn't expect him to twist the way he did as he bucked, so he found targets anyway. His dance was quite different from that of a colt resisting its training to carry a rider for the first time. Hronomon, the Forerunner, was much more intentional and far more precise with his blows, not to mention he had an additional weapon on his forehead.

Allabva watched Hronomon fight the wolves, detached, turning her head to the side to see it through the still prevalent darkness as she continued hiking upward. She knew she should be awed by what she was watching, yet she found herself focusing on her steps. She must keep stepping forward. That was all there was for her.

Hronomon continued battling furiously. He slashed a wolf with his front hoof, smashing its jaws shut. He kicked another one through the air and Allabva watched it land fifteen paces away. It did not get up. A few wolves managed to land scratches on Hronomon's flank, chest, and hindquarters.

Beware the wolves.

Who would have thought that Delgan had given her such an appropriate gift?

Loan, Allabva mentally corrected herself. *I have to return home and give it back to him.*

Hronomon fought valiantly. Three more wolves went down, but his brilliant white coat was now slashed with red in more places than it should be.

Allabva held her hand to her cloak, feeling for the flute she had hidden under her shirt. She couldn't feel it with her hand, her glove and the piercing cold deadening the sensation in her fingers. She did feel it against her upper sternum, the small, hollow metal rod cool against her skin. She pulled on the chain it hung on, extracting the flute from her shirt.

"Beware the wolves."

Allabva could hear music, an evocative yet haunting tune. She knew the words to the song, and whispered to herself, trying not to hear the barks and yelps of the wolves or the fierce whinnies of her friend. Their job was to fight. Allabva's job was to walk. To trudge onward, upward.

Allabva heard a few more thuds, then a change in the commotion. Looking toward Hronomon again, she didn't register another three wolves lying still on the ground. What she did see was that some members of the pack had broken away from the fight with the Nomord. They were rushing at the easier target instead, the human girl.

Allabva's eyes burst wide open with fright. Fighting wasn't her job, not yet. Her job was walking.

The wolves approached, but as they neared, they appeared to slow down as if confused. They seemed...less intent to do her harm. Was this the flute's doing? Were they driven by Sacalai, and the music weakened that connection?

Hronomon untangled himself from his struggle, making a break for the wolves who were coming toward Allabva. Only one of the Nomord could have run so fast. He caught up to the wolves, catching one, then another in its flank with his horn and shoving them to the side.

The remaining wolves abandoned the hunt for Allabva and turned to face the ferocious Nomord to avoid being run through. As the party that had just been pursuing Allabva turned, the party that Hronomon had broken away from caught up. The reduced pack circled the Nomord, snarling and waiting for him to give them an opening.

The wolves appeared to have a weaker resolve when they neared Allabva, but then another crack raced through the sky.

Two in one day, minutes apart, Allabava thought. *That must mean something bad.*

She concentrated on the music and on putting one foot in front of the other. She tried to utter the lyrics to keep herself peaceful in mind, only a few breathy sounds escaping her lips.

The wolves, now as fierce as ever, snapped at Hronomon's fetlocks, then avoided his answering kicks. Others jumped in while he was busy, momentarily sinking teeth into his flanks. They had to work to avoid his horn, but they were still turning his coat redder.

Tears sprang from Allabva's eyes. She wished she could help, but was powerless to repel the wolves. She walked. That was her mission, and the world depended on it. She must meet the Shrongelin. Allabva continued walking, the tears streaming down her cheeks and freezing as they dropped to her coat.

A large wolf jumped in toward the Nomord and closed its jaws around his throat. His skin was too tough to tear but the wolf held on, disregarding his bucking up and down. Another snapped its teeth shut lower on his neck, then another jumped on his back.

Hronomon was finally overpowered, and he fell, releasing a deafening whinny. The pack swarmed in, but the white beast, now coated in red, did not give up the fight. He continued struggling even though he had lost his footing.

Allabva walked. She could hardly see the trail in front of her. What little the snow had left revealed, her tears earnestly attempted to blur from view. But she walked.

The wolves continued inflicting their wrath on the fearless Nomord. His struggling slowed. As his intensity finally waned, the pack turned to their true target, Allabva Roalke of the Cleft, the Companion of the Shrongelin. She heard them charging toward her...

Allabva used all her energy to keep walking.

Hronomon was downed, overwhelmed by the wolves that swarmed him.

Allabva kept walking. It was all that she could do. She could barely see the trail through the snow and her tears of fright and sadness, but she placed one foot in front of the other.

Then she again heard the thundering of hooves at a full gallop. The pack of wolves seemed to hear them, too. The barking gave way to growling and the wolves did not reach her.

Allabva blinked her tears away to look back. Hronomon was still down, surrounded by the pack. Yet the ground trembled under another galloping beast.

Allabva only saw a black blur as something passed her by and crashed into the waiting wolves with their teeth bared. The equine shadow took out two wolves on his first run at them, one with his horn and another with a hoof. He turned on a pin and immediately attacked again.

The Nightshade Unicorn, terror of legends, truly existed. He was here, on the mountain where Allabva was.

And he was terrifying. Shrongelin be blessed that this beast had chosen to attack the wolves instead of Allabva.

The Nightshade faced the wolf pack with shocking intensity, impaling and crushing the canids as the opportunity provided. He moved with such ferocity that the pack never stood a chance, his hooves striking and horn raking in a flurry that made Hronomon look slow.

After he had quickly slain seven of their number, the remainder backed off, knowing they had no hope of overpowering him. He stood, snorting steam out his nostrils while he breathed rapidly.

But they didn't leave immediately. They stood there, staring hungrily at the Nightshade, then at Allabva.

The nightmare beast stomped one hoof, warning the wolves of what would happen if they took a step toward her. His warning was met with growling, but none lifted a paw to run Allabva's direction. He reared up, preparing to charge them again if they should fail to yield.

A single wolf turned its attention to Allabva, then expectantly back to the Nightshade.

The midnight-coated Nomord spoke in a great voice. "You've lost this, Sacalai. I am coming for you."

Wait, Allabva thought.

One of the wolves opened its mouth, coughed twice, then replied, speaking in a voice that was not accustomed to speech.

"No, weak horseling. I am coming for you. It doesn't matter if you win this war. I know the bonding place for the Construct. Imprison me again if you will. I will remember this time. At the next cycle I will be waiting here for your successor."

"He can create the bond elsewhere."

"It won't be as strong. And my next prison will be easier to break out of. Even if it's not, the cycle continues, the Construct will eventually be depleted of candidates against me, and I will ultimately be free. Speaking of candidates, it looks like I've killed your Forerunner. Does your Construct compensate for that? Will you have a successor?"

What? The Forerunner as the Nightshade's successor?

The pieces fell together. A Gha-Nomord fighting against not just wolves, but against Sacalai, here on this mountaintop. Allabva's brain was racked with surprise.

So the Nightshade Unicorn is...

The sound that emanated from the Nightshade's, from the Shrongelin's throat, made Allabva realize that she had never heard a horse nor a Nomord growl before. He lunged forward toward the wolf who had spoken.

"Release these creatures!"

The wolves jumped back as the Shrongelin lurched forward, then the rest of the pack that still survived turned and disappeared down the mountain slope.

After watching them go, the Shrongelin stepped over to Hronomon and lowered his head to examine his compatriot. Hronomon was breathing, but raggedly. After muttering something to Hronomon, the Shrongelin raised his head and stepped away.

"Allabva Roalke of the Cleft," the Shrongelin addressed her. "Come. we have little time."

Allabva had ceased walking when the Nightshade made his appearance. It seemed to her that if he had come here, then she no longer needed to climb to the top to meet him. But he walked past her in the direction he had galloped from.

"But you're already here," she countered. "We have now met up. And Hronomon…"

"Indeed." The Shrongelin acknowledged. "He is gravely injured, but we have a mission. First we must form the bond, then we will come back here and see if there is anything we can do. If we do not go to the summit now, the world falls. Sacalai's followers will regroup, and we will not last until the next break of dawn."

Allabva simply nodded, lacking strength for anything more. Then she started walking again. Her feet were less heavy now that she had achieved half of her goal of meeting the Shrongelin, but her heart was weighted down at the gravity of Hronomon's injuries. She sped her pace a little, understanding the urgency to complete the task at hand.

So, she walked. She climbed up to the crest she saw ahead in the eerie silence, and was dismayed to see another crest further still. Upon the third crest stood the Shrongelin, waiting for her, a dark stain in the sky now gaining significant light.

At long last, Allabva stood beside the Shrongelin atop the Summit Above the Aspens, feeling completely bereft of energy and mirth.

"Allabva," he said, "you come willingly and selflessly, and under your own power?"

"Yes," she spoke thinly, heaving for breath.

"Did you receive any magical assistance which bolstered or served in place of your own physical strength to come here?"

"No."

"Good. We are to share a bond. Through this bond I will share power with you, and you will magnify it back to me. Will you bear the burden of strength with honor? Will you do so with respect to me and all those who are innocent of malice?"

"Yes, of course."

"Will you use it to lighten loads and to protect?" he challenged. "Will you serve the Construct and consider it your life's work to ensure that the world is protected from Sacalai and her influence?"

"Yes. I will do whatever it takes."

She shivered. At the summit, a steady wind blew at her, keeping freezing winds constantly flowing through her cloak.

"Very well. Now we wait a moment."

Allabva looked at the great beast quizzically, but he only looked east. She took the opportunity to look him over. His horn was flattened, forming a shape like a cutlass blade with what looked like its cutting edge forward. His eyes were fearsome, sharp, intelligent beneath his tangled mane. His black fur, with many pock marks and warts, covered a body that was full of muscle. His hooves were cracked and splintered. But looking back up, she knew this grizzled creature only appeared hateful. He was the Shrongelin; Allabva could feel it.

They remained for a brief period, silently facing toward the east. Then the sun broke brilliantly over the horizon. The Nomord took his signal and addressed the new Companion.

"Allabva Roalke of the Cleft, here, at the meeting place of earth and sky, at the advent of light within the season of new growth, we forge a bond, after the fashion which any Gha-Nomord can forge, but with more focus and with more specific purpose. This bond is forged in the Construct to overcome the evil of Sacalai. So let it be done."

He finished speaking and leaned forward, bringing his head down to touch Allabva's forehead with the tip of his horn.

Allabva gasped in shock, falling down on the rock laid bare of snow by the wind. Sent into her mind, for several moments she didn't feel the cold of the wind or the warmth of the sunlight. Instead, she felt... Pain. Sadness. Hate. Not her hate, but from an enemy, directed incessantly at her over the last four thousand years. It was impossible to escape, impossible to overcome.

Was this what the Shrongelin felt? Did Hronomon feel a portion of this? That would explain Hronomon's grave attitude. Is this why the Shrongelin now appeared as he did? Did it turn him into the Nightshade? It was unbearable. Grotesque.

Then the agony faded and gave way to a succession of her own trials. She was mentally sent back along her journey since leaving the Cleft, experiencing it all again in an instant. She went back further, feeling every emotional discomfort in her life. Then that, too, faded.

It was replaced by a sensation of oppression against her very being. She gasped for air, blind and deaf to the world around her. Heaving with effort to stay alive, she persisted in her desire to remain. But not for her own sake. She desired to live for others. To serve. To make a difference in at least one life, somewhere. The more people she could help, the better.

She would resist the pain. For her mother and Mellier. For Delgan, for Brelin. For Banduchy and Fiewren and their children. For anybody else who wanted to live beautifully.

With that thought, breathing came easier again. Coming back to herself, she began to note the sensations around her. Warmth. Cold. Her weight on the stone. She opened her eyes.

Then, without a hint of shaking, and noticing but not subject to the biting cold, she stood back up. The pain was gone from her feet, her ankle. Her scalp where the arrow had struck. Sleep had fled from her eyes, and though she felt that she could eat, she wasn't suffering for want of food or drink at the moment.

She felt *strong*.

"Shrongelin? How is—" she stopped herself.

Something needed her attention. It was terribly urgent. What was it?

"Hronomon!"

Allabva sprinted back down the path, closing quickly with the Forerunner's position. Was it really such a short distance from here to the summit? It had seemed so long just a few minutes before.

The Nomord lay still in the snow. He had stopped breathing.

"Hronomon, are you well?" Allabva asked feebly, fighting against realization.

Fighting against helplessness.

She dropped to both knees and cradled his head, setting his cheek on her lap.

"How can we help you?"

He didn't respond.

The Shrongelin approach down the trail...laughing?

Allabva was offended.

"How can you be happy right now?" she shouted at the Nightshade.

The Shrongelin spoke happily.

"We have won a great victory today. It was not *the* victory, but we have conquered true."

Allabva stared at the Guardian, shocked at this disregard for his Forerunner. She looked back down at Hronomon.

"I—I don't..."

"You reached me. We attained the bond, and Sacalai's forces will find it much more difficult to stop us now. We have rebuffed her for a time, knocked her back…"

The glory in his eyes faded, and he seemed to realize what was happening at his feet.

Allabva looked up through bleary eyes, lip quivering. "Nightshade…Shrongelin, please help him!"

The Shrongelin was at a loss.

"I—" he stammered. "—I cannot. It is beyond me."

"How can it be?" she blurted. "I feel all this strength. My wounds are healed. You did that up there!"

Allabva shouted, pointing up the mountain slope.

"You healed me up there. Do it now, here!" she gestured to Hronomon.

"No—" the Shrongelin began. "—No."

"What do you mean 'no?!'"

The Shrongelin bowed his head in sadness.

"I am no healer. I am Gha-Nomord. As the Guardian, my bond with you was forged as part of the Construct, which was created in cooperation between the Gha-Nomord and Ta-Nomord."

Allabva bent over Hronomon's head, rubbing his neck with one hand and crying over his face.

The Shrongelin continued softly.

"There is Ta-Nomord power in the Construct, expressed here during the forming and the setting of our bond. That is what healed you. Without Ta-Nomord here, there is no more healing. I have no means to help Hronomon. To help… Eretuquein."

He paused to breathe deeply.

"That was his name. Eretuquein was always one of the great Nomord. He gave himself to his mission. It is an awful evil that…"

He trailed off while Allabva wept.

Then, "We must do the same, Companion. We must take this mission to the ends of the earth if necessary. A new Forerunner will step into his place. There is much to protect. Come. Your arrival and the forging of the bond made me forget the attacks and my pain for a brief moment, for which I am grateful."

He breathed in resolve.

"Come," he repeated with his deep voice. "We have armies to assemble."

Physically, Allabva felt like she could jump down the mountain in one bound. Emotionally, she was powerless. Her friend was gone.

"Just give me half an hour!" she wailed, echoing her mother's request to Hronomon a week and a half prior, and sobbing over his inert form.

The Shrongelin stood over her silently and waited.

Finally, several minutes later, with wet cheeks and red eyes, Allabva lifted her head, knowing she had to pick herself up. Hrono—Eretuquein the Forerunner had fulfilled his crucial mission and brought the Shrongelin his Companion. She would honor that by fulfilling her mission. She looked up to the Nightshade Unicorn, the Shrongelin, and stood with clenched fists, determination flowing through her veins.

"What do I have to do now?"

THE END

EPILOGUE: THE STORM TURNS

T ylonus set his foot at the mouth of the cave and waited for Vlon and Rhaslemonor to catch up while he gazed into its dark depths. With no natural illumination inside, and the cold night surrounding him outside, the lantern he carried didn't give enough light for him to see much.

After their arrival at Mascaldinig, the isle of the Night-shade Unicorn, the isle where all the Gha-Nomord remained gathered to sustain the shield containing Sacalai, he had spent time, along with Vlon and Pontil, learning at the feet of their horned hosts. They learned the history of the Construct, the scale of the threat of Sacalai, and the Nomord had invited mutual sharing of information concerning more recent events, as well as discussion of impending future events.

On that first day on the island, after Tylonus had overcome his immediate shock of coming face-to-face with the legend-spoken harbinger of calamity, he had stopped screaming and bolted. Of course, the frightful and somber Nomord easily chased him down. The wizened beast had spoken calmly, shown himself to be a rational creature that had no desire to harm Tylonus. The Nightshade, the chief of the Gha-Nomord, had invited Tylonus to listen. To see other Nomord.

Tylonus had carefully maintained his distance, cautiously following a good hundred paces behind the stallion, not believing his words. Then Hronomon had come. Hronomon bore the spotless, gleaming appearance of the many Ta-Nomord Tylonus had seen in his life, wore that semblance that emanated goodwill. Hronomon had come forward, Tylonus holding his ground, and spoken to him. Approached slowly. Touched Tylonus. And then Hronomon had vouched to his fellow Nomord on Tylonus's behalf.

In that moment Tylonus was taken aback—this *Nightmare* Unicorn had to be assured that *Tylonus* had good intentions? Hronomon had then vouched to Tylonus on the Shrongelin's behalf. *This* was the *Shrongelin*? The Shrongelin wasn't human, fine. But he and the Nightshade were one and the same? Legends had collided in Tylonus's mind.

But Hronomon's gift as the Forerunner figured in here. Just has Hronomon had *seen* the heart of Tylonus, Tylonus had seen Hronomon's. Mutual moral trust was possible. It took more time for them to entrust Tylonus with all the lore he had to learn, but the time had come.

He had lived among the Nomord since that day. Pontil and Vlon as well. Lived among them, sat in council with them. Planned with them. Had visited Sacalai's prison with them.

That was a harrowing experience. A magic contained her, held her in place, and shadowed her. Cast illusions. Whether it was her or the prison itself producing the ever-changing imagery, not even the Shrongelin himself knew. But the shadowed image they saw did not hold shape. It shifted, sometimes humanoid, sometimes on four legs, sometimes winged.

The Construct was a great piece of magic, they had explained to him. It held her prison, was the framework upon which it was built. The prison periodically failed after a time, but the Construct remained. The architect had been the wisest among the Nomord, the Ta-Nomord known as the first Mhosorem. Mhosorem had poured all her magic into the Construct, acting as its focal point while it was cast. While all the Nomord had lent a hand—or hoof—to its formation, Mhosorem had been rendered mortal, a husk in their eyes. She lived out her days to a natural death, but that did not change the fact that she had given her life to forming it.

The first Mhosorem having lost her power, another took her place, similar to the cycle of the Shrongelin. But unlike the Shrongelin, the Mhosorem held an inactive role in the cycle itself. As such, the second Mhosorem was still alive, but living in a daze as all the Ta-Nomord did between calamities. No, the Gha-Nomord hadn't seen her since the beginning, but the cycle didn't give them much time to socialize with their female counterparts before the prison was re-sealed, the Ta-Nomord voluntarily lost conscious thought once more, and the all the Gha-Nomord were called back to Mascaldinig to maintain the shield again.

So the Construct still held mysteries, some intentional, others not. While the place of bonding for the Shrongelin's Companion was set and pre-determined, the knowledge of it was masked from Sacalai's mind. Along with this orchestrated forgetfulness, the Nomord had also forgotten the manner of Sacalai's being while she was locked away. Nobody knew who or what she really was behind that menacing magical might. Her image never held. What was constant in the chamber holding her, was a feeling of dread and hate. It permeated one's being. It made a visitor want to flee.

Despite some things remaining hidden, Tylonus and the two sailors had learned from the Gha-Nomord, and had enlightened them in return. They shared information of the nations around the world. The Nomord showed greater trust to Tylonus and Vlon than they did to Pontil, and had asked some questions when he was absent. Vlon and Tylonus had told what they knew of governments and armies. Who was aligned to whom, which lands had a well-regulated militia, or ranks full of rag-tag recruits. While neither of them had a military background, they had drawn maps from memory and discussed how to issue a rallying cry around the world.

They had stayed on the island. It was rare for humans to land on the island; a minor piece of the Construct maintained stormy waters to keep visitors away until the time came again for the Nomord to leave it. Never before had a human arrived at such an opportune time to be able to help them gain an upper hand.

Significant time had passed since their arrival, and they lived on the natural fruits of the land. Some unfamiliar animals lived here, but he had learned not to be alarmed by them, even if their behavior was odd at times. The Nomord blamed the strength of the Construct's magic for this, and the same for the twisted plants he saw.

Tylonus wanted to go home, but he now knew the importance of their mission. He had to stay in order to have the best bet at protecting his family from the disaster that would come. Hronomon and the Shrongelin had hopes now, that with this information they could get a leg up on the storm. They had always had to hold the shield as long as possible; once they forayed out into the world, the shield would be slightly weakened by their distance. They never had this advance intelligence before.

Additionally, they had asked Tylonus for guidance on where to seek a suitable Companion for the Shrongelin. They had come to him in confidence, with not even Vlon present.

They needed somebody trustworthy, unselfish, undaunted, and persistent. Tylonus deliberated internally, ultimately recommending a search in a place he had visited, a people with a reputation for being safe, welcoming, and honest. He felt sure they would find a Companion there.

Again, they had seemed somewhat encouraged. They fought to seal Sacalai up again, the Shrongelin with his dour attitude hoping not to destroy Sacalai, but to re-imprison her promptly enough to avoid calamity this time, and allow humanity to strengthen itself. They hoped that if humanity were strong enough, they might unite enough power so that a successor Shrongelin and Companion might one day permanently vanquish the threat at last. They supposed they could finally gain an advantage with his help.

But then, two days after the Hronomon and the Shrongelin had left the island, calling upon winter storm after winter storm until they could walk from Mascaldinig in the Islewilds, to the Rimewaste north of Malnonny, the first crack appeared in the night sky.

Tylonus had been shaken. A thundering crash had woken him in the wee hours, making him sit bolt upright in his makeshift bed in the hut he and the sailors had built to share. Pontil had shouted something about dark doom and hidden under the covers. But Tylonus and Vlon, looking around, saw a light outside.

A great rift cut through the clouds, bordered by red sparks and showing the stars in between. It hummed, twitching, widening and narrowing for half a minute, before collapsing and vanishing, leaving the clouds twisting and writhing in the sky where the crack had vanished.

After the sky had cracked, Tylonus had run to learn from the Nomord what it meant. The prison was decaying. Tylonus thought he could almost feel the menace that the Nomord held here, on this very island.

He and Vlon had a particular Gha-Nomord named Rhaslemonor appointed as their mentor, who had bonded them and Pontil. They needed to learn how to use the bond, how to fight, so they could instruct other humans. This, along with the information they had brought from outside, would hopefully give the Nomord and their allies-to-be an edge in this cycle's fight against Sacalai.

So they trained. They practiced. They wrote down anything they learned that they thought could be helpful to others. They didn't have much paper, only a few letters they'd had on them and the backs of the trade documents Tylonus had grabbed during the sinking of the *Armadillo*. So they prioritized. When the time came to leave this isle, they would distribute the information, pass it on to others to speed up their learning.

That night of the first omen in the sky, Tylonus had begged Rhaslemonor to agree that the prison cracking meant it was time to set out in force.

Rhaslemonor had disagreed; this was a normal part of the cycle, even if it did come a little fast after the Shrongelin's and Hronomon's departure. They needed to stick to the plan and prepare as much as they could until it was time for the Gha-Nomord to move.

A few months later the sky had cracked again, this time during the few short hours of daylight the island received in mid spring. Again, Rhaslemonor assured him that it was part of the cycle. Tylonus had begrudgingly continued with their preparations. Then the third rift shattered the sky only a week and half later, waking Tylonus up again in the dead of night, then a fourth one only a few minutes later.

Tylonus hadn't been swayed this time. He drew it out from Rhaslemonor that the events were unusually close together, then insisted that they visit Sacalai's prison again.

Here he stood, an hour and a half after the final crack in the sky, at the threshold of a cut down into the earth where the magic of the Construct had hidden the enemy from the sight of day. Vlon caught up to Tylonus, incredibly telling jokes to the Nomord.

"How can you joke at a time like this?" Tylonus asked him.

"Well, Ty, I do what I can. Haven't you any sense of humor?" The sailor smiled at him in the light of the lantern.

"Of course I do. You know I have children." Tylonus kept himself focused on the trail down into the cave.

"Do you mean you actually told jokes, once upon a time?"

"As I said, I have children back home."

"If they made you happy enough to have a sense of humor, then why did you leave them?" Vlon prodded.

"You already know that, too," Tylonus replied.

"Heh. You earn a coin on the farm, you earn a coin on the sea, what's the difference? Stay with what makes you happy, I always say."

Vlon entered the cave and Tylonus resumed walking, Rhaslemonor following behind the two men.

"Hey, Rhas?" Tylonus said, glancing back at the Nomord.

Rhaslemonor said nothing but looked at Tylonus expectantly.

"Did the Shrongelin ever tell jokes? Or Hronomon?"

"Of course. The Shrongelin used to be a bit of a prankster, even. But they both carry a great weight now, more than the rest of us, so they spare little attention to mirth."

Tylonus looked to Vlon. "You hear that? I'm carrying a great weight, too. I rest my case."

Vlon shook his head, disappointed at the somber tack of conversation Tylonus chose to take. "You're only carrying the lantern. That's not such a great weight. Maybe because it's light!"

Rhaslemonor tossed his head appreciatively at the pun, but Tylonus grimaced at the low attempt to ease his mood. He didn't respond, preferring instead to walk in silence down into the depths beneath the island. Tylonus told himself that Vlon didn't understand; he had no family to protect. Tylonus had to do everything he could to prevent, to prepare, to defend against the storm. Sacalai couldn't...

A light grew ahead of them as they approached the chamber where Sacalai had been contained for time unknown—the Nomord had declined to tell Tylonus how many Construct cycles they had already passed. How many Shrongelins had been rendered powerless and died of old age. The light flickered, blue, red, green, yellow, and continued as it brightened.

Finally, they entered the great chamber, a cavern seventy paces across, the shape of a round loaf of bread as its ceiling sloped up toward the center. There was no exit but for the tunnel that the three of them had just descended, opening its maw into the cavern. The rock walls and ceiling appeared to be volcanic rock, but looked as if uncut, simply having cooled in this shape with the large bubble to house the lone inmate.

In the center of the cavern sat a ball of light large enough to hold two horses, one in front of the other, and equal in dimension in every direction. The bottom of the ball was sunken into the floor, so Tylonus supposed the occupant could be standing on flat ground, level with him standing outside it.

Rhaslemonor and Vlon entered the cavern behind Tylonus, expecting to see the same thing as before. But this time was different.

"Rhas, what is that? What does this mean?" Tylonus said quietly. He thought he had seen drawings of this animal, but did not know why it should be here.

Thankfully, Vlon uttered no nonsense at this moment.

Instead of a shadowy image, shifting between humanoid and quadruped, winged, or anything else, a solid form could be clearly seen through the twisting and flashing illumination. Rather than morphing, it held firm, showing the form of a great, hairy, four-legged beast, three grown human arm spans from nose to tail.

Supported by thick legs and feet, its shaggy flanks rallied up from rump to shoulders, then its neck sloped down to a large head that hung low. Its pointy ears faced Tylonus while dark eyes contemplated him and his companions with contempt. It brandished its face as a weapon, wielding two menacing horns, one upon the forehead as long as a hand span, and a sick, curved horn more than twice as long as the first, perched on its nose.

Rhaslemonor replied, unsure of himself, dryly reciting an apparent fact. "That is a woolly rhino, native to the northern Glosen tribal lands. I...I do not..."

The rhino spoke slowly in a deep, rumbling voice.

"It means I win decisively at last, Nomord. This is end of your Construct. This will be the last time we play. Tell the Nightshade his trick with my wolves was not enough. He won the battle; I will win the war. I am coming for him and his insignificant Companion."

Pronunciation Guide

While many of the uncommon names appearing in this book will be easy for the reader pronounce, I'm aware that I've included several difficult names. Therefore, I have provided this pronunciation guide for characters and places.

Those names which are made up of common English words are omitted, while the names unique to the world of the Nightshade Unicorn, no matter how simple, have been included. If the reader encounters any names in the book which are missing from this Pronunciation Guide, I would appreciate being advised so they can be included in the future.

Please note that the tick mark (`) precedes the the accentuated syllable.

Ex.:

Apple: `App-uhl

Characters

Characters are listed in alphabetical order by first or only name given in the book.

Aulbwin Tonalstga: 'Ahl-bwin Ton-'alst-ga
Allabva Roalke: Uh-'lab-vuh 'Rowlk
Alvern Swiskopfel: 'Al-vern Swiss-'cop-ful
Amarkal: 'A-mar-kal
Ambinos: 'Am-bin-ose
Banduchy: 'Band-oo-key
Binterox: 'Bin-ter-ox
Brelin: 'Brel-in
Brolfith Noteh: 'Brol-fith 'No-teh
Churloe Tunnigan: 'Chur-low 'Tun-again
Clonnel: 'Clon-uhl
Delgan Dlorovin: 'Del-gun 'Dlore-oh-vin
Eretuquein: 'Air-too-cane
Faethlen Roalke: 'Fayth-len 'Rowlk
Fiewren: 'Fee-ren
Gha-Nomord: 'Gah-Num-ord
Halmon: 'Hal-men
Hronomon: 'Hroh-nuh-mohn
Jonder: 'John-der
Mellier: 'Mel-ee-er
Mhosorem: 'Mow-zoe-rem
Navvaron: Na-'var-en
Nillan Protfund: 'Nill-un 'Prot-fund
Nolder Lawgrin: 'Nol-der 'Law-grin
Nomord: Num-'ord
Ntoffel: N-'tah-ful
Pontil: 'Pon-tul
Qurast: 'Cure-ast
Rauling: 'Raw-ling
Rhaslemonor: 'Rahz-lem-on-or
Rubiro: Roo-'beer-oh
Sacalai: Suh-'caw-lie

Shrongelin: Shrong-ga-lin
Ta-Nomord: `Ta-Num-ord
Thonalu: `Tho-na-lew (Uses the 'th' from "with.")
Tunbloth: `Tun-bloth
Tunralger Faetlan: Tun-`ral-gher `Fayt-len (Uses 'g' from "gun.")
Tylonus: Tie-`low-nis
Ultlan: `Ult-lan
Umblan: `Um-blan
Vlon: `Vlon
Yalnan: `Yal-nan ("Yal" rhymes with "pal.")
Yalrou Tonalstga: `Yahl-roo Ton-`alst-ga
Zlana Noteh: `Zlah-nuh `No-teh

PLACES

Due to the story in this book taking place almost completely within the bounds of Eslarna, some place names appear only on the map, not in the story. However, you can expect these and more locations to appear in future books.

Alervayn: `Al-er-vane ("Al" rhymes with "pal.")
Amonfweer: `Ay-min-fweer
Apthane: `App-thane (Uses 'th' from "with.")
Arn: `Arn
Arnlia: `Arn-lee-uh
Bolsnard: `Bowlz-nard
Colnarn: `Coal-narn
Colnuinard: `Coal-new-in-ard
Cylgiana: `Sill-gee-ana (Uses 'g' from "age.")
Darlte: `Darl-teh

Dullsworthen: `Dulls-worth-en

Eslarna: Es-`lar-na

Fonglan: `Fong-len

Glosen: `Glow-zen

Holbonin: Hole-`bone-in

Littonwelt: `Litton-welt

Malmar: `Mal-mar

Malnonny: Mal-`non-ee

Mascaldinig: Mass-`cal-din-ig

Nolnarn: `Nol-narn

Roula: `Roo-la

Novulm: `No-vulm

Nylorna: Nye-`lor-nuh

Palf: `Palf

Parfall: `Par-fall

Roula: `Roo-la

Tallen: `Tal-in

Tallens: `Tal-ins

Tallensworth: `Tal-ins-worth

Islewilds: `Aisle-wilds

Rimewaste: `Rime-waste

Turilnia: `Too-`ril-nia

Weslan: `Wess-lan

Ylonga: Y-`lon-ga

T.S. Pedramon grew up and went to school as a musician, taught music, then joined the US Marine Corps and served as a Marine Musician on the clarinet. After two tours he graduated from Officer Candidate School and served as a Cyberspace Warfare Officer. He settled into full-time story writing upon leaving Active Duty service. He is fluent in English, Spanish, and Dad jokes. He resides on the US East Coast with his family, a parakeet named William Cutie, and a black one-eyed cat named Skippy.

Pedramon has enjoyed reading *Animorphs*, *Dragonriders of Pern*, *Wheel of Time*, *Fablehaven*, *Lord of the Rings*, *Born to Run*, clarinet sheet music, *Bird Talk Magazine*, the *Holy Bible*, the *Book of Mormon*, and much more.

You can connect with him at:

www.pedramon.com